DARK BRIDWELL

BY

VARDIS FISHER

Author of 'Toilers of the Hills'

ORIGINALLY PUBLISHED BY
HOUGHTON MIFFLIN COMPANY
BOSTON AND NEW YORK
The Riverside Press Cambridge
1931

CONTENTS

DARK BRIDWELL

. .

PROLOGUE

DARK BRIDWELL

..

PROLOGUE

THE great tableland of rolling hills, known as Antelope, Idaho, is bounded on the east and north by the South Fork of Snake River. After leaving its source, some beautiful Wyoming lakes, the stream flows quietly through the Jackson Hole country; but in spring and summer it gathers, creek by creek, the white wintry acres of the Teton peaks, and becomes broad and deep before it passes Jackson City and plunges into the mountains flanking the east and south. Among the scalped altitudes between Jackson and Bear River, it has long ago sunk an enormous gorge, upon parts of which the sun never shines; from whence it emerges to take Bear River into its current, to flow across the length of Grand Valley, and to vanish into sunless foam between two mountain walls; to emerge again and pass quietly over the twelve miles of Swan Valley, and then to find its deep and dark boundary of the Antelope Hills.

Between Swan Valley, once a haven of swans, and the broad rich valley lying from the Antelope Hills to Oregon, is a distance of twenty miles. It is perhaps chiefly from this distance of turns, of sharp angles and elbows and curves, that the river got its name.

The entire Antelope benchland was once its bed. But little by little, through countless centuries of toil, the river has narrowed its shores and cut downward, until to-day it lies four hundred feet below those hills, where it moved in a wide lake, and left its gravel to be buried by wind and dust. In sinking its channel, it has eaten away the flesh of earth and left curious skeletons of rock. It has left tablelands of stone, long since bedded again with soil, some of which now lie in long shelves, two hundred feet above its passage, and some of which are small bottomlands only a little above its present level. Of these latter, there are a dozen principal ones between the two valleys. The largest, named Conant but pronounced Coonard by every one here, contains an area of several square miles. The others are smaller, combining altogether not more than five hundred acres of tillable soil. The largest of these was homesteaded nearly thirty years ago by Joe Hunter, and is to-day known as Hunter Bottom, or as Black Canyon, because it looks upon a deep and dark canyon lying in the east. Straight across the river from it is a smaller one, of not more than forty acres; it is now known as the Bridwell Place. It was here that Charley Bridwell and his family lived for twenty-one years.

To this river bottom there came in 1889 a man named Silas Bane and his wife Miranda. They followed an old game trail up the north bank of the river, Silas walking in front and leading a horse upon which Miranda sat, and Miranda leading a burro freighted with a camp outfit and food. On the next morning, the woman crawled out of a small tepee and looked around her. This is what she saw.

Against her back, as she faced the south, was a group of mountain peaks varying in height, the tallest rising to more than two thousand feet. At her left was a deep black canyon, lying in the mountains and the sky. Upon the east stood an enormous block of mountain, sculptured in gray and green, and topped with crags that looked like fortresses of stone. Out of the southeast, Snake River came straight toward her. Two hundred yards from her feet, it broke upon innumerable tons of rock: mammoth gray piles, scrags and boulders and ledges: and recoiled upon itself in an appalling fury of boiling mud and clouds of spray, of black shoulders of water rearing and crumbling and falling down like avalanches of shattered glass. Gathering its thunderous masses, the river turned westward, tumbling its muddy acres of wave and foam, flinging itself like a great arm into the southwest; plunging again with senseless violence against the naked whipped rocks on the other side, and then pouring through a narrow gorge of gray wet stone.

Directly across the river, she saw a bottomland of two hundred acres, a wilderness of cottonwoods and willows and wild grass in the wettest part, of chokeberry and aspen and buckbrush where the earth sloped upward. The southern wall of this bottom was a precipice of black rock, running east and west. Beyond it, four hundred feet above the river, lay the Antelope benchland, gray and desolate, where nothing lived save cattle and the coyote and the gray wolf. Upon her right were other mountains, split in two by the river's passage to the valley and the sea.

She was down in a hole. Except when she turned to the black canyon at her left, she could see no more than a mile of earth, no matter where she looked. The bottom upon which she stood was a parched slope of tableland that lay from the mountains behind her to the river before, as if the mountain's base had slid to the water's edge. At her left was a half-acre table, low by the river, covered with an almost impenetrable thicket of chokeberry and willow, cactus and thistle and briar. The larger slope itself was also covered with thistles and starved weeds, and with a low wiry bush that looked lifeless.

This place was Miranda Bane's home for seven years.

Silas built a one-room cabin of cottonwood logs. He freighted a handplow in and broke several acres of sod. He built a harrow with wooden teeth, he scattered alfalfa seed upon the land. Out of the canyon at the left came a full swift stream of mountain water; and after shaping a ditch along the top of his farm, Silas diverted a part of the stream into his ditch and strove to irrigate his new home. And he did, after months of labor, and in time he had several acres of lucerne, a garden, and the beginning of an orchard. He trapped bear and mountain lions, wolves and wildcats, otter and beaver and mink, all of which lived abundantly around him; and in winter-time he killed elk and deer, which foraged down from the cold mountains to pillage his haystack. He was happy, too, in the way of those hardy men who love the outposts of human life; and if he saw no face in a twelvemonth but that of his wife, he cared little.

But the childless Miranda cared. During the long winters, buried under impassable snows, she saw nothing but the bleeding pelts which Silas spiked to the walls of their house and the enormous loneliness of this world. During the summer, she saw only the black canyon, alive with wild beasts; the hungry searching of a mighty river; and the barren Rattlesnake Trail which led westward past Rattlesnake Point. This latter was a craggy tower of rock, thrust out of the mountain and set upon the river's edge. Its trail, made in former times by elk and deer, was her only way of escape; and even so, it was a dangerous way, because snakes lay there behind every stone, and horses fought back from making the passage.

Rattlesnakes were also numerous over the bottom-land, and upon the small brush-glutted table where Silas had built his hay-corral and his barn. Not infrequently, during her seven years, Miranda found snakes within her own house; and her ears, in time, became alert chiefly to one sound: that of the rattler ready to strike. This sound haunted her most, but there were others, too, which made nightmare of her sleep. Down from the canyon came coyotes, sometimes in herds of forty or more, to smell the stabled beasts and to make the night loud with their dismal wailing. Less often she heard the deeper bay of a wolf, or the shrill roar of a lion. And sometimes in midwinter, after a period of intolerable cold, Silas would discover that an elk had been slain and eaten almost at his stable door.

And so Miranda Bane, driven almost mad by years of solitude or of hideous yowling, and by a hungry death that lived on all sides, persuaded Silas at last to move to a spot where rattlesnakes would not coil under her very doorstep, and where the winters would be less bitter and white. Of a cottonwood tree he built a raft and rode the river to the valley below. For seventeen dollars and an old nag, he sold his right to the land, and his lean improvements, to Charley Bridwell; and on a July morning, Silas and his wife loaded their burro with pelts and household things and turned westward over Rattlesnake Trail, leaving behind them a stunted orchard, a few acres of hay, and a broken handplow.

In July of the next year, Charley took possession of this bottomland and called it home. He brought with him his young wife Lela, whom he had married when she was only fifteen, and their daughter and two sons. For twenty-one years they lived on this spot which had driven the Banes from it in defeat. They lived without neighbors, save the Hunters who came four years later, and almost without friends; and they lived in such curious fashion that they excited the wonder and talk of people in three counties.

Charley himself became a legend. As a matter of fact, the stories multiplied until the man was lost among them, and none knew precisely what manner of person he was. Wherever his name was known, it was said that Charley Bridwell had the world beat as a drunkard; that he was a thief who took what he wanted if he could get his hands on it; that he was a brute who flogged his sons until blood ran down their backs; that he was a bold hunter, a dead-shot, and the most fearless man who ever came down from a tree to slay a grizzly. It was also said of him, and with not a little joy by some, that he was the laziest man who ever drew the breath of life; that he loved his wife with the kind of pure and romantic love beyond understanding; and that he was a philosopher who had read all books and had built a home for his mind among the wisdoms of the world. And it was also believed, by most of those who knew him, that this man, whose grinning cruelty made blood turn cold, whose devilish pranks frightened folk out of their wits, was the jolliest fun-maker and the tenderest of heart of all men to be found anywhere.

Lela Bridwell also became a legendary person, especially in her later years; and so did her two youngest sons. They were all strange — save possibly one girl — and mysterious and inscrutable. To the people of the Antelope benchland, after it was homesteaded, and to the people of the valley lying westward, they came to be known as 'those strange Bridwells.' For a score of years, the father and mother lived an isolated life on what is now called the Bridwell Place. They were mountain-walled, with never more than a rattle-snake trail leading to their doorstep; and for twenty years, Lela never went more than five miles beyond her home yard. Few understood them, but nearly everybody loved them. People watched them from afar, spun legends about them, and found them more baffling in each year. Those strange Bridwells...

This is their story.

Book I
CHARLEY

Book I
CHARLEY

I

CHARLEY BRIDWELL — it is said his name was Francis, but that he detested it and took the name of Charley when he was still a youth — was six feet tall, florid, and fat. His hair was reddish and thin, his forehead broad and full, his face very large and round. He always wore tobacco-juiced, copperish mustaches that hung raggedly over his mouth.

His eyes were his most striking feature. They were of pale green color and full of laughter, but they were also two small cunning windows that opened on his soul. Both his cruelty and his gentleness, his hatreds and his whimsical indolence, were in his eyes; and in consequence, they invited to friendship, even while they repelled by the flickers in them of shrewd knowledge and crafty design. When Charley looked at his wife, his eyes became tender and mellow, and there was no hint in them of the darkened dead years across which he had taken his shiftless way; but when he looked at anything for which he had contempt, his eyes gleamed with venomous spite, and had the cold lidless appearance of the eyes of a lizard.

His body had the large shapelessness of a bear. His shoulders and waist and hips were all round and full, so that he gave the impression of being boneless. His neck was short and deep and wore a roll of fat. His feet, which were his physical pride, were comfortable in a number seven shoe; but his hands were huge and strong, and strangely incongruous with the rest of him.

He chewed tobacco constantly, and no man ever watched him enjoy the stuff without wishing to chew also; because Charley did not let his quid soak, in the manner of most men, but tongued it greedily from jowl to jowl, chewing it as if it were gum, spitting its dark juice and smacking his lips. When he drew his plug forth, he would stare at it with great friendliness, bite into it with eager hunger, and then roll the quid about in his mouth, as if to taste its full flavor with all the power he had. And if any one were watching him, he would smell of the fragrant plug, slap it against his thigh, and then roar with jolly laughter.

His clothes hung to him as if prepared at any moment to let go. He usually wore a blue denim shirt and a great pair of baggy trousers, of corduroy or moleskin. Never, unless forced to it, did he wear overalls, which he regarded as a symbol of slavery. He was a grotesque figure, this man of more than two hundred pounds, standing in his roomy trousers upon his absurdly small feet.

Where Charley came from, nobody knew. It was generally supposed that he had been a kind of vagabond, slouching from place to place, taking when he could, and with unmatchable gusto, all the good sensuous things of life. He ate food with the same ravenous zest with which he chewed tobacco, and he slept prodigiously, buried under a cannonade of snores.

Now and then, at very rare intervals, he had done manual labor for other men; but never in his life had he done a full day's work for himself, and it was his intention never to do so. Many years after he came to the Bridwell Place, when the Antelope Hills had been turned into dry-farms, men would come to him in harvest time and implore him to lend a hand. Usually he would not. He would rock with silent mirth and stare at the bench-farmer with shrewd eyes. He would say scathing things of people who spent all their years turning furrows and filling them up.

'If you work all the time,' he would ask, 'when the hell do you intend to live? Won't you never learn it ain't any fun to slave your guts out?'

'I know it,' his neighbor would say, a little abashed by such reasoning. 'But if I don't work I guess I'd starve.'

'Nonsense,' Charley would retort, biting deep into his plug and looking at the man with philosophic eyes. 'I don't work. I set around like a knot on a log. And there you plug away, tryun to grow wheat without rain, gettun your damn ears full of dust. The old God Almighty never meant us to work. He don't work. I amagine he just sets on His throne and don't wiggle His little finger in a coon's age.'

'Mebbe you're right, Charley, damned if I'n say. But if I didn't tear into it, the old missus would knock my skull off. I'n see your point, but I got to take aholt of things and plug along.'

'And when you're old, then what'll you do? You'll raise Ned with all that-there dust, and in the end you'll

be all humped over, and mebbe you'll have enough to
buy you a good coffin and that's all. Your joints will
pop when you set down. You'll get all full of aches and
pains and shivers and then you'll roll over on your
belly and die. What's the sense in all that?'

'I don't know, Charley, but I guess I got to plug
along. The whole world, it just plugs along.'

'That's what's wrong with the damn world,'
Charley said. And from such remarks as these grew
the legend that Charley Bridwell was a philosopher of
uncommon skill.

Nevertheless, he would go once in a while, and he
would work perhaps one day — surely never more
than two — with an effortless ease that became the
subject of talk. Furthermore, he would turn his labor
into fun, laughing and spitting his juice and mocking
those who toiled with their hands — as if the way to
heaven lay along furrows and over wheatfields! —
until his distracted employer would agonize between
toil and philosophy, and almost decide to sell his
plows and his pitchforks. But all of this is ahead of
the story.

If people never learned where Charley came from,
they knew even less why he bestowed himself finally
upon that isolated barren bottomland where he spent
the best part of his years. He was a queer duck, they
said, and they could say no more. Perhaps he was a
little bit out of his wits. Just the same, he was a jolly
and likable old stinker, as well as the laziest man that
ever meditated on nonsense. He would eat another's
fatted steer; and if no steer was to be had, he would

shoot a bear and live for days on nothing but its flesh. 'But he seems to be happy,' people would say. 'My God, I guess he's about the happiest person I ever seen.'

And if they knew little of Charley, except the dubious knowledge of patient surmise, they knew much less of Charley's wife. Those who saw her, when she first came to the place, declared she was the loveliest woman they had ever known. She was tall and slender and quiet, with a great mass of brown hair that fell in long ringlets below her waist, with eyes as blue as the sky's blue after a rain. Her voice was low and sweet, her movements were rich with dignity and grace. But more than this, curious people never learned, not in all the years of her life.

If Charley had chosen to speak, he could have told them but little more. He could have told that she was an orphan and homeless when he discovered her in the raw and whiskey-soaked town of Pocatello; that she had made him lead a sober life during his courtship. But why she loved him, even until that bitter and tragic day in 1917, when she came to the end of her hope and her strength, nobody knew, and Charley least of all.

Still, in spite of his drunkenness, in spite of his periodic and unpitying devilries, Charley was a lovable man. His fund of nonsense was endless; his heart was deep and generous; and though he had little to give, he was always willing to give what he had; and in bitterest weather, over the most treacherous of dark trails, he would carry help and cheer to a sick person,

or work tirelessly to give a decent burial to one who
had died. Even those loved him whose fattened steers
he ambushed and ate. Even Joe Hunter loved him,
who gave to him year after year of food and farm
machinery, and more than human patience. Jed
Thornberg loved him, gaunt, silent, morose Jed, whom
Charley once knocked down and kicked in his teeth,
and for whom he named his second son.

But there were two people who hated Charley with
an intense and implacable hatred. One of these was
that son named for the man whose teeth Charley had
kicked out. This hatred sprang from a scene of ex-
quisite tenderness; it fed upon sullen and lonely years,
upon bold and desperate experience; until it shaped
itself into a threat of murder, until it split wide open
an evening in midwinter, when the snow lay six feet
deep, and the river was an inky blackness under its
shed of ice. The other person who hated him was a
sheepherder named Adolph Buck. And these two
hatreds, their reasons and their consequences, must
form a large part of this tale.

In the mind of every one, Charley's reason for coming to the Bridwell Place remained a dark riddle.
People conjectured over and under the truth, and were
forever baffled. Had he fled from crime? Did there
lie, in the man's inscrutable heart, a bitter contempt
for human beings? Or was he so downright lazy that
he wanted to find a spot where none could see his
shame? Why was he without ambition and a wish to
hoard against his old age, and a love for the various

and eager life of pool-halls and carnivals and city streets? None knew; and as years passed and curiosity waned, he was dismissed into the category of strange and likable and unimportant things.

The answer, perhaps, is to be found in his homely philosophy. He detested work, not because he was lazy, but because he believed that work was senseless. People rose with the sun, he often said, and rushed through the day to find the sunset; whereupon they ate and slept and rose again. Instead of sitting to mark the passing of hours, they mounted time as if it were a saddle-horse and rode it in pursuit of rainbows. They wrestled with labor, disputed with the hours, and then were dumped into a hole and lost under a ton of sod. Almost before they knew it, even while they were counting their profits and loss, they opened a door and looked into a waiting grave.

There was Joe Hunter, for instance, who became, in 1901, Charley's neighbor across the river. Joe gave his flesh and bone to the grubbing-out of all manner of tangled brush that covered his land. He worked from five in the morning until ten at night, seldom missing either a Sunday or a holiday. He slaved endlessly, until his body was bent and his hands gnarled, and his mind twisted like the dollar sign; and what would he ever get from his labor, save a little pile of money and a larger patch of lucerne? As a matter of fact, Joe worked in such a blind and stubborn way that time passed him where he bent over his grubbing-hoe or his plow handles, and the seasons snowed him under with age. He would stand up at last and find himself an old man. He was, for Charley Bridwell, a symbol of the stupidity and folly of life.

Charley was content, indeed, to be lessoned by the cow and the horse, and by all the other uncivilized things of sky and earth. He observed that beasts ate and lay down and dreamed their dreams. When food was abundant, they fattened their ribs against a time when food would be scarce; and when food was scarce, they took what they could find and gave their worries to the winds. They lived a full life, and their years lay long behind them. When they looked back, they saw, not hours that overflowed with toil, but meditative whiles bedded in clover, afternoons built of shadow and quiet. They had seen the body of time, leisurely and calm, high and round and philosophic like the sky. They had seen hours laid end to end between sunrise and sunset, each with its measure of happiness and thought. But for those besieged by effort, for those, like Joe Hunter, who were forever chasing events into their graves, time was a swift pilgrimage to a tombstone.

'I don't know,' these people would say, 'where the day has gone to. I've been busy, God knows, but I don't seem to get anything done.'

When remembering such people, Charley thought of the river before him. It was an absurd stream. It was blind. It sought its bed, its ancient worn path, with the swift-moving belly of its waves, indifferent to everything above or around it. He had once known, on the other hand, a broad calm river as lazy as afternoon shadows. As if weary with going, it seemed to lie upon its back in the sun and to care little whether it ever found the sea. It tasted the full meaning of its banks and bottom, of its journey; it ran out into side channels, explored the country roundabout, and returned.

'That,' Charley reflected, 'is the way life should be.'

What he detested, really, was civilized life. He was annoyed and distressed by the hurrying throngs of city streets. 'Where,' he would ask himself, 'are all these damn people going to? And why are they in such a hurry about it?' He hated trains, that rushed across country belching their smoke, laying the miles under their spinning wheels. When the automobile came, he hated it, and always preferred to float down the river on a log, or to ride a lazy nag that walked ten miles in four hours. Why, he wanted to know, was there so much infernal speed in the world? If people had wings, they would chase the sun around the earth; they would fly to the moon; they would be like overgrown insects, always darting hither and yon until they wore their wings out; and at last, they would sit on a limb somewhere, waiting for their end.

'I'm sick of all this damn racket and hubbub,' Charley declared one day, in July of 1897, while sitting in a Pocatello saloon with a bottle of whiskey before him. He looked across the table at Ben Haggerty, with whom he had ridden the blinds from Texas to Idaho.

'Uh-huh,' declared Ben, nodding his drunken head. 'Well, whush you plan to do about it?'

'I've bought me a farm, up in a hole on Snake River. I'll live there. Until I die I'll live there.'

'Uh-huh,' said Ben, showing yellow teeth in a grin. 'But what about the misshus?'

For several moments Charley was silent.

'I'll take care of her,' he said.

He took care of her in a way that was peculiarly his own. He had been thirty-two when he married Lela, a shy, unhappy child, growing to womanhood among men who stared at her with lewd eyes. For Charley Bridwell, who had known only the harlots of mining-camps and road-gangs, Lela was a symbol of all that was good and pure. He became her slave, and he remained her slave until he died. But because he was afraid she would leave him, afraid she would tire of his lazy or drunken hours, he set his cunning mind to the task of making her his own. With shrewd and deft patience, he insinuated into her thoughts the conviction that the world would hate her if she ever left him. He suggested, adroitly and little by little, that she was a social outcast when he found her, and that people already looked upon her with suspicion. He said that if she left him, people would think she had always been a whore at heart, and that she married him to escape whoredom, and then regretted her choice. And so simple was she, so untaught in the ways of life, that she came to believe her journey lay inexorably with his. She came to regard him, indeed, as a kind of knight who had rescued her from inevitable sin.

When Charley declared, therefore, that they must

leave Pocatello and find a home elsewhere, and when he pictured for her the alluring peace and seclusion of their river farm, she went eagerly and without question. Her confidence in him was complete, and her love for him, even until the last, was passionate and deep. And if years taught her hate, it was less of him than of things which she did not understand; and even in the hour when she rose and denounced him, her memory brightly enshrined this man who, from the beginning to the end, was devoted and tender.

'Up there,' he said, 'we'll have the nicest little home ever was. Not a neighbor in sight. Not a human being in miles.' He kissed her young throat, he looked into her childlike blue eyes, candid and unwavering. 'We'll be happy,' he declared, 'happy as a knot on a log.' His voice trembled and his big awkward hands trembled. With a horny palm he caressed her long soft curls. Then he turned away, unable to endure the emotion within him. He drew forth his plug and tore from it a ragged quid.

'Look at this God damn town,' he said, staring from a window at a tangle of railroad yards. 'Who wants to live in a ugly hellhole like this? But wait till you see Burns Canyon, right at your kitchen door.' He stood by the window, looking at the blackened world outside, remembering the wild beauty of his new home.

'There's wild flowers and birds,' he said. 'Do you like such things?'

'Yes,' she said, 'I love flowers and birds.'

'Then you'll be happy as a wart on a toad.'

He remained by the window, staring at dirty walls

and smudged roofs. And he was reflecting that upon the Snake River bottom, to which there led only a rattlesnake trail, no men would look at her with greedy eyes, or offer to her more than he could offer. If any did, there would be the Winchester rifle above the door.

II

AND so, on July 14, 1897, Charley took his family to Lorenzo, a one-store settlement, and equipped himself for his journey into the southeast. His entire worldly possessions were two old nags, given to him by Sam Jarrup, a wealthy cattleman; a worn-out saddle, for which he traded an Indian blanket; his rifle and a pistol; a roll of bedding and a bundle of food. He rode ahead upon one nag, with his five-year-old daughter Beth sitting before him, with his two sons, Thiel and Jed, clinging behind. Upon the other horse Lela rode the saddle, with the rifle slung under one wing, with food and bedding piled behind her. Under a sweltering sun the caravan moved slowly through Butler's Island, crossed the ferry at Heise Hot Springs, and halted for the night in a cottonwood grove by the river.

The remaining distance of fifteen miles lay over an old game trail. From the first foothills the trail climbed a mountain, then pitched downward into a canyon, and thereupon for many miles was under the shadow of the river's gorge. Ten miles beyond Heise they came upon the Tompkins place, a tiny farm cleared out of a cottonwood bottom; and here they stopped to lunch and to talk with Jim Tompkins and his wife.

Jim had lived here for thirteen years, a strange recluse who trapped and cultivated his garden and ignored the world. He was a huge man with an enormous thicket of beard. His wife was a fat and silent woman, into whose face and ways had entered the loneliness of the mountains around her. They had several queer, unclean children who almost never saw any human beings but themselves; and they came forth to stare at Charley and his family as if they were creatures from another world.

Jim had a keg of wine which he drew out of wild gooseberries; and of this he offered generous measures to every one, including his youngest child, a girl of three. He smoked a corncob pipe and grunted, while his eyes, bushed with long tangled hair, peered with undisguised pleasure at Charley's wife.

'So you're off to Burns,' he said, and tamped tobacco into his pipe with a huge root of a thumb. 'It's a damn rattlesnake bottom.'

Charley laughed and drank his gooseberry wine.

'Rattlesnakes don't bother me. I sleep with them anunder my pillow.'

'I'n amagine,' said Jim, and the bushwork of his beard fell back into a smile. 'Well, there's plenty trappun. The wolves is as thick as the rattlers. Only nobody don't pay nothun for wolves.'

He looked again at Lela, perhaps wondering what she thought of wolves and snakes. He glanced at her smooth white hands, and then looked at his wife where she sat, morose and shapeless.

'Mebbe you need some more traps,' he said. 'I'n borrow you some for a while.'

'Fine!' said Charley, and slapped his knee. 'That's a good drink you make.'

It was Charley's sly way, when a loan or a gift was imminent, to speak of other matters. He would fall into jolly banter, talk of irrelevant things, and introduce as a kind of afterthought the subject upon which his heart was set. He turned to Jim's eldest child, a rugged gaping lad of twelve.

'I'll tell you,' he said to the boy, 'what I'll do. I'll make my halter-ropes out of rattlesnakes. I'll use a rattlesnake for a quirt. And if my kids won't be good, I'll blister their hinders with a live snake. How's that suit you?'

The lad gaped with protest. He looked at his father and snickered.

'And as for wolves and bears and lions,' Charley went on, still addressing the astonished youth, 'I'll carry them little beasts around in my pockets. I'll eat a whole bear for my breakfast, teeth and backbone and toenails. How's that, now?'

'I guess you won't,' said the boy, again looking at his father.

'You think I won't?' said Charley, pretending to be vexed. 'I'll walk a grizzly bear on his front legs, see, like this, just make a wheelbarrow out of him. And as for wolves, hickory Josephat! I'll hang them up in trees by their tails. Come up tomorrow, and you'll see wolves hangun all over my place by their tails.'

'Oh, yes, I'll bet!'

'How much will you bet? Come, pull out your money. How much do you want to bet?'

'I ain't got no money,' said the lad, abashed.

'Now as for traps,' said Charley, 'I could use a few.'

'Jack,' said his father, 'run out and get a bunch a traps. Skin along, now.'

Jack hesitated. He stared with doubt and wonder at Charley, still deliberating the picture of wolves hanging by their tails. He then vanished and returned, dragging by their chains a dozen traps. Among them was a bear-trap, with two great iron jaws full of teeth; two smaller traps, also with teeth, for wolves and wildcats; and others still smaller, for muskrat and mink. Charley strapped all these to the cargo behind Lela's saddle and then turned to Jack.

'If you see any strangers roamun around,' he said, 'send them up to my place. You and me, let's scare the daylights out of a million greenhorns.'

'Sure,' said Jack. He stretched his mouth into a broad, malicious grin. 'I know a feller to bring up. He's a sheepherder.'

'All right, Jack, you bring him up. We'll scare cats and dogs out of him.'

'We sure will,' said Jack, drawing his grin to his ears.

Charley helped Lela to her saddle. He then led his own nag to a mound of earth, set his children upon her sharp back, and threw his leg over between Thiel and Beth.

'Come and see us sometime,' said Mrs. Tompkins, speaking to Lela. Lela gave her a bright nod.

'You come and see us,' said Charley. 'We'll be right to home. There ain't many places to go up our way.'

The older Tompkins children giggled. They liked this fat, jolly man who beamed at life and promised to hang wolves up by their tails. The caravan moved off; and when Lela looked back, before dropping over a hill and out of sight, she saw the entire family staring after her.

The trail now lay in the shadow of a sheer wall of stone that rose two hundred feet above the river. They crossed a furious stream that fell out of a canyon upon their left; and Charley pointed to an old cabin in the canyon mouth, in which, he said, lived Henry Bord the trapper. Henry had lived in that dirt-roofed shack for twenty years. He was a queer one: tall, gaunt, silent, and a woman-hater. 'His wife,' said Charley, 'run off with his brother Jim, and he never seen her apern strings again.' Ten miles up the river, in the mouth of Hewarchable, he had another cabin; and in winter-time, he made regular trips between his two homes, setting his traps and gathering his prey.

When looking around her now, Lela saw only great mountain shoulders upon her left, laid wide open, here and there, by canyons built down to the river's edge; the swift and turbulent river upon her right, banked with ledges of rock; and ahead of her she saw only the winding gorge, and the mountains set upon the east. Her eyes were alert for snakes and wolves, but she saw none. She saw none until the trail fell downward over a landslide of stone. Then Charley stopped and pointed to a coiled gray mass behind a rock. The reptile lifted its head, shook its rattles, and thrust forth its tongue. Charley aimed his pistol and fired. The snake fell back in a writhing heap, with its head blown off.

Assured by his deadly aim, Lela stared at the world with happier eyes. She had heard that he was an expert marksman; she had heard him called Deadshot Charley, in the Pocatello town. She looked at his round bearlike shoulders, as he rode ahead of her, and felt that she had placed herself in superbly efficient hands. Her feeling grew, a few minutes later, when he stopped again. Dismounting, he got the rifle, laid it across the rump of the forward nag, and fired. Then Lela saw a flock of geese rise, flapping great wings and honking; and by the river upon an acre of pebbles, she saw one turn round and round, with its wings outspread, and then lie still. Charley went down through the brush and got it. It was a large gray thing with blood and water on its lovely feathers. With a withe he bound it to the traps. Then he climbed upon his horse and rode forward, now whistling a gay tune.

The trail led for a mile close to the river-bank and through heavy timber: cottonwood and maple and cedar and pine. Charley began to sing, and Lela listened to the words of his song.

> My true-love, she's a blue-eyed dandy,
> Ding dong doodle all the day!
> A kiss from her is as sweet as candy,
> Ho a ding dong doodle all the day!

Lela reflected that the farther he got into the mountains and away from people, the happier he seemed to become. She had never heard him sing before. She had never heard the song which he was singing now.

My true-love, she lives by the river,
  A ding dong doodle all the day!
A hop skip and jump and I'll be with her,
  Ho a ding dong doodle all the day!

He looked back and asked, 'How are you there? All right?'

'I guess so,' said Lela, looking around at her cargo.

'We'll soon be there. Another hop and a skip.'

She thought he must be very strong, because he was now carrying Jed in his arms. She looked at Thiel, sitting with his short legs spread across the mare's back, his hands clutching his father's shirt. Then she listened again to the loud rich baritone of Charley's song.

My true-love is a blue-eyed daisy,
  A ding dong doodle all the day!
If she ever leaves me, I'll go crazy,
  Ho a ding dong doodle all the day!

Lela considered the meaning of these lines. She had never thought of leaving him. She was sure, in this hour, that she never would.

My true-love is a sunshine daisy,
  A ding dong doodle all the day!
I won't let her work and I'm too lazy,
  Ho a ding dong doodle all the day!

They passed through a small open space and Lela looked at the river. It came boiling around a wide curve and plunged against the bank near her. A great cottonwood tree had fallen out over the waters, with its roots still clutching the bank; and the waters roared through the lower branches and filled the trunk with constant shuddering. Then the trail left the timber and climbed over a small rocky tableland, covered with sagebrush six feet tall. Upon reaching the crest of this tableland, Lela saw before her a black tower of stone. It resembled a huge face and throat, thrust out of the mountain and set upon the river's brink. This bluff, Charley told her, was Rattlesnake Point, and just beyond it lay their home. All over this point were snakes as thick as the hair on a burro. There were snakes on their farm, too, he said; but they were lazy creatures that seldom struck unless stepped on. Now and then they bit a careless beast, and the beast crawled off and became frightfully sick, or perhaps died. He had once seen a rattler strike a sheep. It had got its fangs caught in the wool, whereupon the sheep rushed off madly, dragging the astonished reptile after it like a halter-rope.

At the Point he stopped, and when Lela rode up to him, he nodded at a clump of sage and told her to listen. She heard a dry sharp rattle.

'He's in there,' said Charley. 'I don't see him, but he's there as big as life.' After a moment he added: 'I guess he's just shakun his tail to scare a skunk.'

'Is there a lot of skunks here?' asked Lela.

'More skunks than trees,' he said. 'They go about in droves, like a herd of sheep.'

'I can smell a skunk,' she said.

He laughed, set Jed upon his other arm, and drew forth his plug. He bit off a huge quid, tongued it, and smacked his lips and said:

'Skunks don't smell bad till you kick um. Then they smell like the whole world.'

Lela looked forty feet below her, where the river was dashing itself violently upon piles of naked wet rock. Charley began to whistle and rode on again. Before her now, Lela saw the river coming around a curve in the southeast, dividing itself into three channels, each a mighty stream, and then joining the entire force of its waters to hurl against Rattlesnake Point. In the east stood the gigantic architecture of a mountain range, vanishing into pale blue distance. Along the river at her right was a tangled growth of hawbush and willow and chokeberry. The chokeberry was loaded with white and pink blossoms; and so the fringe of brush, a half-mile in length, was a lovely and fragrant whiteness, full of the green of willow and hawbush. She filled her lungs with the odors, and with the wet smell of the river, and with the pine and maple and cedar smell that rode out of Burns Canyon upon a wind.

They went across the tableland and drew up at the cabin which Silas had built. Charley lifted Jed and Beth, threw one leg over, and slid to the ground. He set Thiel on the earth and then turned to Lela.

'This,' he said, with a sweeping gesture at the mountains and sky, 'is our home.' He helped Lela down from the saddle. He looked at his daughter and sons. 'How you like it?' he asked. Beth sighed like an old woman and looked around her. The boys stood with their sober eyes interrogating their mother.

Leaving the nags drooping, and the children blinking in the sun, Charley and his wife entered the one-room house. Its single door opened upon the east, its single window looked upon the south. Its ceiling was of pine poles and earth, its floor was of rough lumber mixed with unbarked slabs, all of which Silas had gathered from fragments of rafts, stranded upon the river islands. Its only table was a rude thing made of pine legs and a rough lumber top, and it was spiked to the west wall. A small iron stove stood in one corner. The rest of the furnishings consisted of four boxes for chairs, each nailed to wooden legs within the corners; a slab cupboard of three shelves, also spiked to the wall; and some smaller equipment, including an iron bake-oven, a few pots and dishes, and a sadiron. Against the north wall stood two thirty-gallon oak barrels.

Charley looked with happy eyes at all these things. He sat on the box-chairs and found that they were strong. He held pots up to the light to see if they had holes in their bottoms. He peered into the stove.

'Everything is jim-dandy,' he said. 'How do you like it?'

Lela smiled, remembering their ugly Pocatello room, thinking of the awful beauty of the world outside.

'But where,' she asked, 'is our bed?'

'Oh, our bed,' said Charley. 'Well, our bedding is on that old filly out there. And as for a bed, I'll fix it up. You watch and see how I fix it up. I'll make you a bed as soft as cat-fur.'

At this moment Beth came to the doorway and said

that Jed had disappeared. The parents ran outside. They looked around, but Jed was nowhere in sight. Thiel, the older son, was standing by the nag, patiently waiting. Lela rushed about, a little frantic, and called to her lost son.

'Now don't get upset,' Charley admonished. 'Just a minute now. I'll have him by his heels in a jiffy.'

He dropped upon his hands and knees and followed Jed's trail. He barked, in an absurd way, like a dog, and he smelled of the earth; he fell back on his haunches and howled like a coyote, and again went forward, hopping like a great beast. He went through a patch of wheat grass, down a slope toward Burns Creek, and then over a pile of cobblestones where Silas had done some placer mining. And when he found Jed, he was amazed, because that three-year-old youngster lay on his belly at the mouth of a fresh hole in the earth, and he was looking eye to eye with a badger that snapped its teeth. He was striking at the badger with a stick. Charley grasped the child by his heels and carried him back, head downward. He took his pistol, then, and strode over to the hole, waiting there until the badger appeared; whereupon he shot the beast and dragged it forth. And this daring pilgrimage, undertaken at the age of three, was only a foretaste of that reckless devilment to which Jed Bridwell devoted his early years.

A little while later, after Charley had unpacked and turned the horses free, he built a fire in the stove and told Lela they would have the goose for supper. Roasted wild goose, he said, banked over with mushrooms; and his mouth watered. He went to a wet patch of earth near the river and gathered a panful of mushrooms. Then, while Lela gave her time to the making of supper, he went a short way up Burns to some low-spreading firs and stripped their softer branches. He returned, carrying a huge armful, and upon hands and knees he spread them against the north wall. With a hatchet he chopped off the thicker or dryer parts; he patted the mass, feeling for sharp twigs and knots; and when satisfied, he spread blankets upon the boughs and lay down.

It was an excellent bed, he declared: as soft as feathers, as soft as the down on a duck. They would all sleep like logs. Their bed would have a sweet clean smell. Every time they turned over, its fragrance would fill their breath and the house, and they would sink into sleep that was like death. He sniffed the air. The room was full of the odor of fir boughs and of roasting goose. Outside, a burning red sun was scalding the mountains with gold. Charley carried more twigs into the house and made a bed for his sons. And then, while the goose cooked, while Lela stared from the window at the most glorious sunset she had ever seen, Charley got out his fishing tackle and said he would catch their breakfast.

He went down where the cold crystal water of Burns Creek dashed into the boiling mud of the river, cut a willow for a rod, and attached a line. He baited the hook with a piece of goose gizzard and set his pole, with his line far out where the two waters met. The end of the pole he thrust into earth and then banked it

around with stones. He sat under a flowering chokeberry, chewed tobacco with philosophic content, and
waited. When he saw the line run taut, he walked over
and led a two-pound trout to the shore. He set his
pole again. But instead of sitting down now, he
walked about, looking for signs of fresh game. Upon a
leaf-bedded trail, among a bunch of aspens, his keen
eyes saw the track of a deer. The beast had gone
mountainward into Burns. He also saw the fresh
tracks of wolves and wildcats, and one which he took
to be that of a mountain lion. He caught three more
trout, gathered a great armful of chokeberry blossoms,
and returned to the house.

The sun had gone down, but upon mountain peaks
in the east it threw a golden light. The western sky
was full of orange flame. The golden light rose from
the peaks, became a warm pool in the eastern blue, and
dusk like films of smoke lay upon the wild beauty of
this world. Above the Antelope Hills, he saw a veil of
wind.

In the house Lela had found an oil lamp, trimmed
its wick, and set it burning feebly upon the table.
Charley went over to her and drew her into his armful
of chokeberry blossoms. Then, upon the box-chairs,
they all sat around the table, with a brown fragrant
goose before them, flanked with piles of black greasy
mushrooms. There was no bread, nothing but mushrooms and wild flesh. Charley carved with his pocket
knife. He gave a luscious dripping leg to Lela, and
took the other to his own tin plate. To Beth and Thiel,
he gave slabs of breast, and to Jed he gave an entire

wing. Jed took it in his eager hands, looked up at his father for a moment with unfathomable dark eyes, and then buried his teeth into the meat.

With gusto and a smacking of lips, Charley stoked himself with heaps of mushrooms and goose. Then he sat back, waiting until his wife and children had eaten as much as they could; whereupon he devoured everything that was left. He stripped flesh from bones, nibbled at the intricate joints of wings, and with a finger he wiped grease from the plate and sucked it into his mouth. After helping Lela wash and dry the dishes, he sat with her on the doorstep, and together they looked into the beauty of a darkening and uncivilized world. Against her she held the armful of blossoms.

Upon the cottonwood walls behind them, the fire made witchery of shadow and light.

III

AND in this simple fashion they lived. For twenty-one years, their bed was pine boughs, piled upon the floor. When the boughs withered and became hard, Charley would use them for firewood, and for the bed he would gather fresh armfuls. Often their diet was entirely one of meat. They brought only a few pounds of flour with them, and this Lela used to make gravies and meat sauces, or tiny biscuits for the children. In this year, and in most of the years that followed, they also had preserves and jellies made of wild fruits: chokeberries and currants, gooseberries and grapes. In late August of this summer, Charley climbed far into the mountains and brought back a pail of thimbleberries, and a pail of dark red huckleberries, most delicious of all wild fruits.

And also in this summer he did a little work. His plan was to cover his thirty-odd acres with alfalfa and clover, to get a small herd of sheep and a cow or two, and to do nothing thereafter except harvest his hay and dream his dreams. And so, during the deep yellow days of August, he gave short whiles to the irrigation ditch which Silas had built. With an old shovel and an axe, he scooped out the earth where the banks had caved in, and he cut the brush away. Sweat ran down his full cheeks and dripped from the ragged ends of his mustache; it soaked his shirt until his shirt was dark and drenched. But he never labored more than two hours in one day.

And all the while, when at work or when idle, he watched Lela with shrewd eyes. He searched her for signs of discontent, of longing for another country or another way of life. Day by day, too, he gently insinuated his philosophy into her emotions and thoughts. He drugged her mind, laid her ambitions beyond reach; and for many years he thought her strange quiet was happiness. The world, he declared, of which she knew very little, was incredibly sinful and vile. Most of the men were lustful hoodlums and knaves, most of the women were harlots and hellcats. Life lay spread out under the sky in a lewd carnival of antics and sprees, of skylarking and bastardy and brawls. Good deeds were as rare as pumpkins on pine trees....

And Charley more than half-believed all this, because he had spent his years among miners and lumberjacks, where whiskey ran like water down throats, where women sold their youth and flesh. Memories of these years, gorged with sensual things, coiled like snakes in his mind and looked out of his green eyes. And Lela believed it also, for she had known only rough men whose ways were as coarse as their hands, and women in whom desire was a handful of silver. But she did not like to have him speak of his old life or of the world he had left. For the most part he turned these into jest, but now and then his eyes darkened, and a bitter cruelty paralyzed his mouth.

'That world,' he would say, pointing westward, as if he were pointing to hell itself. 'It's a rotten world, fallun over itself to get nowhere.'

And then he would speak of the world to which

they had come. It was clean and good, it was full of sweet and ancient peace; and he loved even rattlesnakes when he remembered the miners of northern Idaho. He loved twilights full of birds and no human sound. He loved the mornings, spilling their golden laziness over the earth.

But though Lela believed, in a simple childlike way, that she had been transported to the loveliest place anywhere, she was sometimes strangely shaken when she looked at the river, washing downward over its path, and at the wild tree-bedded bluffs and peaks around her. She would look at her children and wonder what their education would be. She would look at her home and wonder if she would never have more than boxes for chairs, more than pine boughs for a bed. And upon her, even during these first weeks, there would fall a melancholy, a deep and nameless unhappiness, that was to grow with the years, that was to sleep in her heart and await its tremendous hour. Because under her earnestness, deeper than the birdlike joy which she often felt, there was a dark heritage of adolescent doubt and pain. There were memories of childhood years, half-crazed and altogether lonely, when she had been an orphan, dragged from place to place, cuffed and abused. And there was in her, too, a lively ambition, a wish to toil and build, and hoard savings against her old age. But all this in her Charley never understood. In her blue eyes, he saw an infrequent madness, and it troubled him. It made his love for her unreasoning, a desperate greedy devotion, and it made of his jealousy in later years an inner storm of delirium. It stampeded his thoughts, churned his emotions into whey, and left him white and helpless with his own wrath.

But though the look in her eyes baffled him, he did perceive, time and again, that Lela was anchored to an unhappy fixed thought, and that when she smiled at his nonsense, she did not know that she smiled. He would try then to amuse her in another way, to make her forget whatever it was that she remembered. He ransacked his resourceful mind, and even took chances against death.

One morning, after returning from the ditch and surprising her in a quiet mood, he stared at her for many moments. He said she needed a change. They would climb the mountain and roll rocks down. Had she ever seen what rocks could do?

'It's a sight to make whiskers sprout on your chin. On the mountain up there, God piled a whole landslide. He hoped some one would have sense enough to roll them down.... God was a great old joker, and that's something people ain't never understood yet.'

He approached her with ponderous timidity. He wanted to kiss her, but she did not seem to like to be kissed by his bushy mouth. Not on her own lovely mouth, anyway. He touched her arm and trembled. And then, turning quickly aside, he asked:

'Well, shall we go?'

He saddled one of the nags, placed Beth and Thiel behind the saddle, and helped Lela to the seat. He carried Jed in his arms. They climbed the great mountain that stood north of their cabin and went westward along its back. They came to a large pile of boulders, varying in weight from a hundred pounds to several tons. These all lay on the mountain's spine, some half-sunk in the earth, others whipped clear by storm and wind. Charley stood the children around him and then took Lela in his arms, holding her close for a little while. He next tied the horse to a sagebrush and turned to the rocks.

They all sat down, using some stone slabs as a backrest, and looked over a wide panorama of mountains and hills. From the east the earth rose in gigantic peak after peak, the more distant ones still streaked with snow. In the southeast lay the deep winding gorge of the river, its more visible walls black with shadow. To the south they looked across Hunter Bottom, at the long broad shelf above it, at the entire acreage of the Antelope Hills, at the blue mountains beyond. In the west they could see the twisting walled journey of the river, and far away, the pale purple haze of Snake River Valley. A thousand feet below them was their house, the rugged slope of their farm, and the river. Now cleaned of its muddy snow-waters, it was as bright as scoured tin. Sunlight trembled on its surface and spilled a shimmering radiance in the tiny valleys of its waves.

Charley breathed heavily with content and sunned himself. This vast amphitheater, it seemed to him, was full of timeless laziness and centuries of peace. It was a huge bowl of sunshine and solitude, inviting to drowsy indolence and murmurous afternoon hours. The drooping quiet horse stood near the cabin and looked no more alive than did the trees around it, Down there, too, snakes and lizards were drunk with sunlight and the hushed noontime of earth; and squirrels slept like dead things in their holes. Even the sun was a lazy thing, burning in a haze of mellow slumber. Only the river moved.

And the river, Charley reflected, was where no river should ever be. Its silly frenzy, the impetuous nonsense of its blustering journey, belonged to another part of the world. In its place there should be a blue lake, deep and still; a calm mirror of water that would hold the sky and the white cotton piles of its bedding. The river annoyed him. It came violently around a curve, as if it were going somewhere and knew where it was going; as if it had work to do between its source and its graveyard of the sea. But it had nothing to do that was worth doing. It would wash banks away, build new channels and leave its old ones dry, tear trees out and hurl them in tangled masses upon gravel bars; and in time it would again seek its old channels and bury the new ones under rock and sand. Over and over, forever changing and forever the same; forever turning the new into the old and the old into the new; forever roaring among its extravagant blunders, tameless and furious and futile. It was an absurd thing. It was the stormiest idiot among all the headstrong fools of life. Men were like it. They built and tore down and built again. And then they died.

But those mountains, he reflected next, were different. They were great hulks of philosophy and peace. Instead of rushing around and shaking the earth, they sat on their heels and let time move over them with good things. From the passing years they took loveliness and set out their gardens of trees; they drew seasons down to them and drank their poetry; and they took on a wise and ancient look.... But the river, on the other hand, choked itself in spring-time with mud and its floating cargo of death; and in winter-time it choked itself with ice, smothered itself under its frozen craggy roofs, and often completely dammed its passage and had to burst its banks. Yes, he decided, it was very much like men: men did the same thing. Their emotions froze up. They built barriers against themselves and ran pell-mell over their banks. And in spring-time they became hysterically busy, turning their furrows and sowing; running around like ants and storing a lot of stuff they would never use; rolling events over and over, as tumblebugs rolled balls of manure, and leaving them to rot in the sun....

He folded his arms over his round belly and shut his eyes. It was good to sit here and soak himself full of sunshine; to feel his blood warm with delicious and ancient laziness; to sense his kinship with the effortless sky. It was good to reflect that he had nothing to do. It was good, unspeakably good.... Then he remembered why he had come here, and he looked at Lela's face. She was staring with darkened eyes at the river where it severed the western mountains. Her face was intent and lonely; her mouth quivered a little with an unspoken wish or a haunting thought.

'I feel happy as sunshine,' he said. His voice was casual, but he was shrewdly watching her.

'Yes,' said Lela.

He supposed he should be gay, should make her smile and forget; but he was so full of golden peace that it was a great effort to speak. He wondered why she liked to have everything dramatized. Movement and sound filled her with delight; silence frightened her. But she would learn, and in time she would be as lovely and lazy as an apple tree in bloom. Nevertheless, until then he must do what he could.

He stood up with a groan that scattered his sunshine and looked at the rocks. He chose one that rested precariously upon a pile, put his hands under its upper edge, and said:

'Now watch. Ten jumps and you won't never see this rock again. You'd better give it a long good-bye look.'

Lela arose, her lips parted, her eyes shining with excitement. Charley stared at her, marveling at the change in her face. Then he lifted until his face was a furious red, until a roll of muscle ringed his neck; and little by little he turned the huge stone over and sent it downward. It ran like a wheel for a few yards and then leapt into the air; it leapt again and again, increasing each time the arc of its flight; and like a hideous gray beast, it sprang with incredible speed into its last leap, shot out over a long rainbow curve, and struck the river with such a thundering crash that Lela felt the mountain tremble. Charley looked at her face and marveled again: it was like the face of a child on Christmas Eve. He looked around for other boulders, wondering what in the descent of that stone could fill her with such breathless awe. He sent many more down, choosing each time a larger one, and watching, not the mad plunge of rock, but the face of his wife. Becoming both fascinated and troubled by something in her eyes, around her mouth, in the way she clenched her hands, he worked until he dripped sweat, until his breath scalded his lungs.

And at last he found an enormous boulder, balanced upon a fulcrum of smaller ones. Falling to his knees, he dug the earth away from the fulcrum, undermining it little by little; and then there was a crunching of stone, the great boulder rocked for a moment, toppled and plunged. Its flight was something that Lela never forgot.

In the brush along the river there were a few cottonwood trees. The other stones had missed these in their flight, or had sailed over their tops. But the huge one did not. At the beginning of its journey, it slid instead of turning over, and drew after it a small landslide of rock and earth. Then it gathered speed and wheeled. In its first leap it looked like a house. It leapt again and again, and when it struck ground, the mountain shuddered; and at last, having gone mad and blind with speed, it rose like an elephant, and took its horrible way over that long rainbow curve. Lela clutched her throat and held her breath; and while she stared, with her blue eyes bulging, the huge stone-beast went down over its curve and struck a large cottonwood midway between its base and top. It demolished the tree clear to its roots; and without a pause it plunged into the river, and a tower of water boiled upward and fell like shattered trunks of ice.

She screamed and covered her face with her hands. Charley ran to her, thinking she had been bitten by a snake. He took her hands from her face and looked at her, and he made an animal-like cry for what he saw. Precisely what he saw he never could have told. It was the quivering of her mouth, the crazed haggard darkness that looked out of her mind.

'Lela!' he cried. 'Are you hurt?'

She threw herself into his arms and clung to him; she wept and shook. He held her and strove to understand. When he looked helplessly around him, he saw only his three children, interrogating him with mute eyes. He saw that Jed was scowling. Without speaking, for he could think of nothing to say, he held his wife to him and kissed her cheeks with his ragged mouth. He looked at the imperturbable peace of the mountains, and then down at the river, rolling its valleyed waters to the sea; and he felt dimly that in this treacherous gleaming stream lay the secret of her outburst. In an event that happened on the following Sunday, he blundered very close to the truth.

During the intervening while, he strove, by means of song and nonsense, to keep her cheerful and happy. On Sunday morning he scrubbed the floor, looking much like a bear as he crawled around on hands and knees; and he scoured the walls. Lela chased spiders from the ceiling and destroyed their webs. When their work was done, the cabin smelled clean and wet.

'Now let's go in our orchard,' said Charley, 'and pick some fruit.'

He took his rifle from above the door, explaining that they might come upon a bear among the currant bushes.

'If we do,' he said, 'you climb a tree. Just throw the kids up in the limbs and start climbun.'

'Oh, yes,' said Lela. 'Just amagine me climbun a tree.'

'You got a-learn how,' said Charley, squinting along the barrel of his gun. 'I'll learn you to shoot, too. If you'n shoot straight and climb trees, you'll be safe as a skunk in a badger hole.'

'Do skunks go down badger holes?'

He held the gun to the light and looked through its barrel. Skunks, he said, went headfirst into badger holes; and when the badgers came in, the skunks emptied their foul arsenals of poison, whereupon the badgers fled stinking over the world, digging everywhere in an effort to lose their smell. It was a grand sight, indeed, to see a badger going yapping and blinded because he found a stranger on his doorstep.

And there were porcupines, he said, observing that she was interested, and drawing upon his lore of wild animal life. These cunning beasts routed the skunks. They would lie in the curve of a trail, pretending to be asleep; and when the unwary skunk came upon them, they would strike with their tail, one swift sudden blow, and the skunk would scuttle off, with a roach of quills from his rump to his eyes.

'How long is the quills?' asked Lela.

'A foot or two,' he said, grinning at his words. 'If you see a skunk runnun hellety loot, with something stickun out of him like a young forest, you'll know he bumped headon in a porky. He'll make a loud noise like a steam whistle.'

Lela stared at him, not knowing whether he spoke truth or falsehood. But she liked the way in which he dramatized his legends of unfamiliar things. He invested all beasts with a strangely human emotion, bringing into one kingdom of comedy and grief all the life of earth, from ants to mountain lions.

With two pails, and with the children trailing behind, they went to the river-bank where currants and wild gooseberries grew. The berries were black things full of dark red light; the currants were a lemon yellow, and good to taste. After filling their pails, they followed a wooded path down the bank, and near the junction of Burns and the river they sat under a haw-bush. Then Charley thought of something to do.

'Did you know,' he asked, 'that I'm the best swimmer in Idaho?' He boasted a little of his prowess against whirlpool and wave. He could swim this river on his back, he declared, with Lela sitting astride his belly; and though she did not believe him now, the time came when she did. Would she like to have him show her some fancy stuff?

They sat looking at the convulsion of waters, breaking the backs of waves over great wet stones, and spuming high into the air; swirling in tumultuous ravening greed, sucking downward in spinning bowls of foam, and rising in small gray hills to hurl a torn wet waste upon the shore. The gleaming stones vanished when a hill of water fell over them; appeared again when the water broke and scattered, their gray backs reminding Lela of sunken beasts. The spray was whipped upward and hurled in bright beads at her feet. Showers of flung beads caught the sunlight and were momentarily full of rainbows; and then fell like handfuls of small stones.

And as Charley watched, there came upon him that strange and deep emotion that always took him by the throat when he saw life wrenched into blind violence. It was a lust to kill, as if through murder he would have to seek his way to peace. It was a black power that gripped him and made him do brutal or reckless deeds. He had little strength against it; and if he did not abuse man or beast, drawing from savagery an aftermath of calm, he had to give himself to some fierce experience. In former times, he had often found his peace through drunkenness.

He stood up, telling Lela to sit here, and not to move for any reason under the sun; and he went up the river a hundred yards where a tower of rock lay upon the bank. He began to chuckle as soon as he was out of sight. Then he stood upon this rock, in clear view of her, and shouted; and though she could not hear him she saw him, after a few moments, and wondered what he intended to do. She watched him intently, and the children watched also.

He flung his arms up and down. He sat on his heels and stood up and sat down, as though unlimbering his legs. And then, without removing even his shoes, he threw his arms skyward and plunged headfirst into the river.

Lela sprang to her feet with a cry. She stared with all her sight, but she could see nothing, save the furious waters. Charley's head emerged at last; he waved to her, and again disappeared. She cried again and was breathless, because he was coming inevitably into the raging inferno at her feet. She waited, hardly breathing at all, and with a terrible pain in her heart. Her ears were full of the river's madness, and her eyes saw only the waters, boiling in their whirlpools of life and death. Time passed, and it seemed to her that she waited for hours. Look as she might, she could see no sign of him. She stared down the river, but for two hundred yards there was nothing but foam and spray. She stared up the river, wondering if he would swim upstream. Then she stared before her, at the gray wet stones that vanished and appeared; and a horrible certainty paralyzed her. He was dead.... He was dead. She strove to understand this thought, to realize how this thing had happened. He had jumped into the river, he had tried to swim to her; he had got his head bashed on a rock, and now he was dead. They had come out to gather berries, only a little while ago, and she had listened to his talk; and now he was gone. Somewhere down the stream, he was now floating like a tree. She wanted to run down the bank, but she could not move. He was dead....

'He is dead,' she murmured, over and over. But the words were meaningless, for she could see no sign of his death. If her vision were sharp enough, she could see blood out there, little currents of red like strings, a thin veil of red upon the waves. She stared, trying to see blood. She looked at the water that came shoreward, trying to see blood. She looked at the chains of water, tossed skyward in loops, trying to see red in their falling beads.... And then, little by little, the whole river seemed to become red, to become a crater of boiling blood. Blood stemmed from its whirlpools, was spouted into long crimson ropes, was borne away in scarlet mist. Her breath was a sucking sound in her throat. She tried to move, but could not; and then she seemed to be moving, spinning round and round, and the water seemed to be very still, as if frozen in its patterns. She swayed dizzily, and she murmured over and over, 'He is dead.... He is dead....'

How long she stood there, she never knew, but it seemed ages. She felt at last something clutching her skirts; and when she looked down, she saw Beth pointing at the river. Lela raised her eyes, the waters again were frantic with life, and the illusion of her own movement vanished.

'Look!' Beth cried. 'See Daddy out there!'

Lela looked and saw. She saw a face grinning at her above one of the gray stones; but even while she stared, a mountain of water rose and broke, and the face disappeared. She waited. The water rolled back into valleys and the face reappeared, still grinning in a devilish way. It was triumphant. It was less the face of a man than of a river demon. She doubted that she saw it at all.

'Do you see him?' she asked of Beth.

'See him grin!' cried Beth. 'See him grin!'

'Do you see him?' she asked her sons. They nodded assent without taking their eyes from the vision.

Another wall of water rose and swept over the rock. Again the face emerged, still grinning, with hair hanging over it like strings. She could see nothing but the face. It seemed to be growing like fungus to the stone. She could not see hands or arms: she could see only the face growing out of the rock. Another hill of water deluged the masklike grin; and when Lela looked again, the face was gone. The boulder appeared, but the face was gone. She screamed and fell fainting to the earth.

When she came to and sat up in deathly sickness, she saw Charley emerge like a strange beast from the river and come toward her. Her blurred sight saw only the water pumping out of his shoes, water falling in streams from his clothes, water running away from him like frightened snakes. She saw blood on his face and her vision darkened....

Then she was sitting up again, and there was something cool on her face. She heard a sound of voices under the water's roar. The world cleared, little by little, and she looked upon a flood of sunshine.

'How are you?' asked Charley. 'Did I scare you half to death?' His voice was low, tender.

'I guess so,' she said, and shuddered. Her tongue was dry and hot. Charley brought water, using his hat for a pail, and Lela drank. He bathed her face. She put forth a hand to touch him, to be sure that he was there. Then she saw blood trickling from a wound in his forehead.

'You're hurt,' she said.

'No,' Charley declared. 'Just got a little bump. You feel all right now?'

'Yes, I feel all right now.'

'I bumped on a rock. For a minute I thought I was a goner. Sure you feel all right?'

'Yes, I'm all right now.'

'Well, I'll move out in the sun and dry off.'

'Not now. Wait just a minute.'

'All right,' he said, and drew forth a water-soaked plug. He bit off a juicy quid and sighed. Lela sat with one hand to her brow, thinking, trying to understand. Again she reached out and touched him.

'I'm here all right,' he said, and laughed. 'But I'm wet as the bottom of a well.' He looked at the river and added: 'When my kids is a little bigger, I'll throw them out there and learn them to swim. Just throw them in and walk away.'

'Oh, I guess!' said Lela. She thought he was jesting. She lived to learn that he was often most in earnest when his tone was most casual.

'Well,' he said, 'let's go out and sun ourselves.'

They stood up. Before turning away, Lela looked at the river. She saw water spread over the stone, behind which Charley had lain, and then draw back in curling hunger. And suddenly she screamed, a wild cry of madness and fear. Charley turned quickly and she fell shuddering into his wet arms.

IV

CHARLEY came close to the truth, but he missed it. After considering the matter, trying to fathom the cause of her cry, he knew only that the frenzy of the river and the flight of the stones excited her in a strange way. Perhaps it was because they took on an aspect of life. The dramatizing of dead things stirred her deeply, brought her out of calm and made her eager for work, left her unhappy and restless for many days. But the reasons were dark to him.

One evening he told tales of hunting, elaborating small events into great spectacles of danger and daring. From fierce monsters of the forest, he escaped time and again by the skin of his teeth. He climbed trees (in his narrative) and sat all night in a limb's crotch; he descended, with the coming of daylight, and fought hand-to-hand in deadly combat. On another time, he prowled at midnight through a dark country of wild-cats, and saw their yellow eyes in the gloom; and on still another, he ran through a desolate fire-swept region, and leapt over a fallen tree into a nest of wolves. The bitch was lying on her side, suckling her young; and she sprang upon him, all snarls and fangs, and he choked her with his naked hands....

These legends of his past, half-true and half-false, he told to her, all the while watching her face. He saw her face become tortured with suspense, her hands tremble in her lap. He heard her breath choke. But most of all, he saw her eyes darken with fear, and with something deeper than fear; until she cried like a child and shook all night in his arms.

Her emotion, it seemed to him, was more than that of fright. He sometimes doubted that it was fright at all. It was a kind of hunger, a starved feeding upon wild moments. She wanted him to raven her peace, to shake her with the violence of desperate things, even while she begged him to stop. She hungered, in an inexplicable way, for a dangerous and busy life; she hated the serene and uneventful days which he loved.

Charley perceived all this, however obscurely, and wondered what sort of person he had wedded. He had always thought of her as an innocent and simple child, a lovely girl made for a quiet and lovely place; and he was appalled by what he saw in her mouth, by the shadows that rose to her eyes.

And so, in spite of her crazed joy that followed upon the heels of what he said and did, he devoted himself less and less to narratives of wild drama and to his own ingenious exploits. He had come here to seek a quiet life. He fell more and more into indolence and silence. Sitting on the doorstep, in mellow afternoon hours, he would chew tobacco and look with sleepy eyes at the ageless things around him. He ate hugely from piles of fried trout, fat roasted goose and duck, pheasant and rabbit and grouse. He snored through profound and dreamless sleep.

One morning a stray deer came up the river and stood two hundred yards away, looking with astonishment at what it saw. Charley quickly seized his rifle and broke the animal's neck. He quartered the beast, put it into burlap sacks, and stored it in cool shadows above the waters of Burns Creek. And he stuffed himself with fried and roasted venison until he grunted like a fattened hog and waddled like a duck.

When autumn approached, and the maples in Burns were a sheet of flame, he made his few and simple entrenchments against the coming winter. Upon his nags, he took his family to the Tompkins place, and then went alone to the valley to provision himself. He had no money, not even a penny; but he promised the Lorenzo merchant that he would fill his store with pelts a few months hence, and was permitted to buy on credit. He chose first a large supply of ammunition and tobacco, fifteen one-pound plugs of the latter. Then he bought salt and pepper, sugar and coffee, and fifty pounds of flour; a pair of shoes and a cheap coat for Lela, some mittens and gumshoes for himself.

'I guess that's all I need,' he said, and looked around him. 'But mebbe I'd better think a little.'

'Canned goods?' suggested the tall rugged keeper. 'Some perserves and beans and corn. How about some bacon?... Well, I guess you got plenty socks and underwear.'

'Oh, some thread. Good God, needles and thread. And throw in some buttons, mixed sizes.'

'Traps?' said the merchant. 'How about them?... Well, I guess you got plenty traps. Some coyote scent? How about a good skinnun knife?... Well, I guess you got a skinnun knife. How about some lard?'

'Oh, my God!' cried Charley. 'Fish-hooks. About two dozen.'

'About a cap, now. Say, you don't need some good snowshoes? Well, I guess you got snowshoes. Would you be needun some coal oil?'

'Holy hell, yes. Two gallons.'

'And extra chimbleys? Wicks? A lamp, mebbe. No? — you got a lamp. Well, your wife need a wash-tub? A skillet or two. How about some washun soap?'

'Let me think,' said Charley, staring at everything in the store.

'All right.'

They looked at each other. They looked around them, each thinking of Charley's needs.

'No,' said Charley, 'I guess that's all. That's plenty to last till spring.... Hell, though, I need more salt. A hundred pounds salt. And listen, Dave.'

'Yes?' said Dave, listening.

'A quart whiskey, Dave. That'll make the bill moren you said. But I'll line your old store with furs. I'll run a whole raft a furs down the river.'

'All right,' said Dave, dragging forth a bottle.

'Open her up, Dave. I ain't had a drink in two months.'

Dave opened the bottle and Charley poured it down him as if it were water. He wiped his mouth and said:

'Make it two bottles, Dave. I'll run a raft a furs down here as big as a freight train.... Dave, could you make it four? With that stuff in me, I'll come home ever night with my pockets full a wildcats. And the beaver up there is as thick as your beard. And the mink run around like squirrels. Dave, could you make it six?'

'No,' said Dave, 'I'n make it five,' and he set four more bottles upon the counter.

Charley spent the night drunk, brawling in a saloon; cursing the earth and its gold-grubbing people; or boasting mightily of his new home. He lost his calm, his lazy, slouching friendliness, and swore at every face in sight. He drank glass after glass of whiskey and rum, promising to pay for them with beaver pelts a mile high, and still kept his feet, for in his day he had been an unconquerable drinker. He ground an exhausted quid under his heel and made the saloon ring with his oaths. When a tall lewd cowboy badgered him, demanding to know what he had done with 'that-there purty female you took up in them hills,' Charley strode over and knocked the man down. Then other men closed in and pitched him sprawling into darkness.

He found a warm quiet spot and tried to sleep. But he did not sleep. He lay for hours, thinking of Lela. When daylight came, he turned to his provisions, after arousing Dave from slumber, and freighted his nags; and then, feeling chastened by the raw morning air, he set out into the southeast. The mare behind him staggered under her load. Once she fell, and Charley thought she had broken her neck; but when he kicked her ribs and twisted her tail, she recovered her legs. He stared at her for a few moments, reflecting that he would use her to bait his traps. Then he mounted and rode onward, singing to keep himself awake, wondering if Lela would be glad to see him again. From time to time he dug into his cargo for a bottle. Once he stopped for a little while and napped by the roadside.

Upon reaching the Tompkins place, he borrowed another horse for Lela and Beth.

'Come up and see us,' he said to Jim. 'My God, come up and have a real feed.'

'Well, mebbe,' said Jim, staring at Lela's legs, now bared to the knees as she sat astride the horse. 'But 'twill be a hard winter. I see signs.'

'Bear signs?' asked Charley, and the women laughed. Jack, the twelve-year-old lad, fought to get the joke; and when he got it, after a few moments, he let off a violent roar.

'Oh-ahh!' he cried, sucking his breath in and turning purple with joy.

'Or deer signs?' said Charley, grinning at the choking lad who bent double.

'"Twill be a hard winter,' said Jim calmly. 'The squirrels holed early this-here year.'

'What do they hold to?' asked Charley, winking at Jack.

Jack composed his face and considered the matter. Seeing nothing funny in Charley's last question, he sighed and looked hopeful.

'You notice the leaves is fallun early,' said Jim. He gathered a handful of aspen leaves, glancing at Lela's legs as he bent over.

'Is that right, now?' asked Charley, again winking at Jack, who was looking at him with the simple expectancy of a dog. 'Well, everything has to fall. Eve fell, and now the leaves has to fall.'

This jest also was too much for Jack's untutored mind. He swallowed hard and again looked hopeful. To his father he said encouragingly:

'What other signs you know?'

'You notice how the cricks dried up sooner?' Jim asked, ignoring his son. 'Even some cricks what never did dry up before.'

'Oh, the cricks,' said Charley; and as soon as he spoke, Jack began to grin in anticipation. 'Well, what about the crickets?'

This jest was not over Jack's head. He was breathless for a moment, as if tasting the full flavor of it; and then he split with mirth and fell together like a broken stem.

'Whoopee God!' he cried, drunk with delight. Then he sobered his face, giving to it a preposterous gravity, and asked of his father: 'Well, what about the crickets?'

'Shut up, you simple fool!' cried his father. This rebuke, given before company, disconcerted Jack a little. He looked at Charley, his eyes imploring guidance and insight.

'The crickets,' said Charley, 'is all that's left of the cricks.'

'Is that right, Pop?' asked Jack, affecting a grotesque innocence.

'I said shut up!' roared his father. 'Get your simple hinder in the house.'

'Well, come up and see us,' said Lela to Mrs. Tompkins.

'Well, mebbe,' she said, in her heavy, lifeless voice. 'But he won't go nowheres.'

'Come without him,' said Charley. 'There ain't no bears in the trail.' Jack snickered. 'Come before the snow flies.'

'Well, mebbe,' said Mrs. Tompkins, standing with her younger brood clinging to her dress.

'Just turn the river around and make it run backwards,' said Charley. 'Then you'n float up on a raft.'

Jack snickered again and put a hand over his mouth. He stood there shaking, with his hand over his mouth, with his eyes worshiping Charley.

'Well, get up,' said Charley, kicking his nag's ribs. 'I'll send this filly back. Or mebbe I'll use her for coyote bait.' After going a little way, he looked around and said to Jack: 'Don't forget to send that greenhorn up. I want a-see how fast he'n climb a tree.'

'I will!' Jack shouted. 'I'll fetch him myself!'

'Well, good-bye,' said Lela.

'Good-bye.'

'Good-bye.'

V

HAVING foraged to the valley and got all he could for nothing more than a promise, Charley further entrenched himself against bitter weather. He restored fallen chinks to the cabin, and plastered mud between the logs. He threw a ton of earth upon the roof. His two old nags he kept here, telling Lela that they could prowl around as long as they could stand, and that he would then use them to bait his traps. When she asked what he would use to harvest hay, he grinned at the Antelope Hills. In summer-time, he said, those hills were lousy with horses. He would run a couple down and use them.

He next considered the matter of food. He would scald himself with effort, he supposed, in hunting wild beasts down and dragging them home. But the thing had to be done. Then he could idle through the long winter, barricaded against storm and cold. Then he could roast himself by a hot stove, letting the snows drift overhead, and the winds whip the darkness into glacial typhoons.

And so in October, he would take his rifle, a hatchet, and a hunting-knife, and ride away up Burns. Many times he returned, bringing only some pine-hens which he knocked out of trees with stones; and to fend off starvation, he would have to go out at dusk to catch trout, or he would crawl upon his belly across pebbles and sand until he came within range of ducks and geese.

But one morning he rode farther up Burns and came upon an abundance of fresh sign. He chose the tracks of three elk and followed them, his keen eyes never losing their trail over bedded leaves or across acres of stone. Then he tied his horse to a cedar, took the windward side, and went on afoot. Rising over the crest of a canyon's back, he saw them below him, quietly feeding: three large fat bulls. His first shot broke the neck of one, his second shot dropped another, but it got its feet and ran again, with one thigh dragging. His third shot broke its back. The other bull vanished among trees, and for a few moments Charley saw only the majestic spread of its antlers. He brought his horse to the scene; and then, without skinning them, he gutted the two he had slain, putting their hearts and livers into a sack; and with his hatchet he split them wide open, chopping through their spines, and cut off their heads. The two halves of one he roped on the nag, and then walked the three miles back to the house, whistling merrily all the while. He carried the bloody slabs into the house and threw them upon the floor. After cutting out a large roast of tenderloin, he told Lela to have a huge supper waiting, and went back after the other beast. But the other bull, when he found it, was only a red skeleton and a pile of torn guts. Wolves had made their feast and gone.

On a subsequent journey, he ran into an adventure that almost cost him his life. Down a mountain-side, through a dense growth of pine and fir, he had been following the trail of two deer. When he emerged into a small grassy clearing, he saw before him, not more than fifty yards away, an enormous grizzly bear.

He could have doubled back and avoided an encounter; because he knew that grizzlies, though they made way for nothing at all, never attacked a human being until molested. But Charley did not retreat. He saw that this huge male was fat; he decided to slay it and take the more tender parts home. Still, he knew that a 30-30 Winchester was a feeble weapon with which to attack such a foe. While he debated the matter, the beast looked at him, without anger, almost without interest. Charley resolved to take a chance. He looked around and saw that a slender fir stood thirty feet behind. He marked its precise spot. He looked over the ground between him and the tree, to be sure no fallen timber was there. He thrust his hatchet, handle first, into a trouser pocket, so that he could draw it quickly. And all the while the bear looked at him, waiting to see what he would do.

Dropping, next, to one knee, Charley took steady aim. He drew the rifle bead upon the animal's side, just back of the left shoulder blade. He fired, and saw the hair part as the bullet entered. Then events happened with appalling suddenness. When he threw the rifle lever, the cartridge jammed and stuck. The bear swung in its tracks and came toward him. It came in great rolling leaps, with its red jaws open. Charley turned and dashed for the tree. At the base of the tree he dropped his gun; the hatchet fell from his pocket. Behind him he heard the crashing of brush and felt the

beast's breath; and when he was ten feet up, climbing
with all his might, ripping his clothes from him and
gouging his flesh on knots, he was nearly shaken down
as the bear rose on its hind legs and grasped the trunk.
The bear hugged the trunk and shook the tree, and it
began to roar with rage and pain. Charley looked
down into its savage red mouth, and then climbed
higher, until he sat in the crotch made by a limb. But
even so, he knew that his position was a dangerous one.
The tree was smaller than he had supposed; it shook
in the beast's clutch. It might be torn from its roots
and flung down.

It was at this point that Charley's cool and resourceful mind thought of a plan. Around the tree and over
the clearing the grass was rank and dry. He clung to
the swaying tree and dug into his pockets for matches;
he broke some dry twigs and scuffed them between his
hands; and after setting the twigs afire, and schooling
the blaze until it was eager, he dropped the flaming
mass. The grass awoke, the flame mounted on a wind
and spread; and with a thundering roar of fury and
fright, the beast turned with its hair smoking and disappeared into the woods. Charley slid down the tree,
recovered his rifle, now blackened a little, and took the
windward side of the flames. The fire now, driven by
a canyon wind, was an orange lake among the upper
trees.

He did not follow the bear into the downward forest.
He skirted the timber, instead, and ran below to see if
the beast had emerged. It had not. It was still within
six or seven acres of forest. Finding the windward

side, Charley made a large torch and then ran along the border of the woods, igniting the grass. He next climbed the mountain, went upon the blackened area where the fire had first been, and waited for the bear to come out. After deliberating, he climbed a pine that spread into a fork twenty feet from the earth. The smoke of his second fire filled the woods. He could see flame run up the dead trees, and the glow of red valleys under the green.

Then the bear came lumbering out, frantic with terror, and headed straight toward him. His first shot, placed in its throat, made it stumble, but again it came on, seeing nothing, wild and blind. His second shot parted the hair on its shoulder. His third bored through the beast's ribs and found its heart. And even then, it ran for a dozen yards and shook the earth with its roars.

Charley came down from his perch and chuckled. With a fresh quid in his cheek, and his gun within reach, he got his hatchet and set to work. This was the largest grizzly he had ever seen. He skinned it carefully, severing the head at the first joint, leaving the skull and face attached to the hide. The green pelt was so heavy that he staggered under its weight. He chose some of the tenderest parts of flesh — the heart and liver, the tenderloin, chunks of shoulder and ham — and loaded these and the pelt upon his nag.

Two hours later, he carried the bloody dripping meat into the house, and later salted it down in one of the barrels. The enormous hide he took in also, and for hours he worked over it, massaging it with his hands as

it dried, until it was soft enough to be used. He gouged
the eyes out and left only the large black sockets. He
cut the tongue out, dug from the throat into the skull,
scooped the brain out and put it into a glass jar. He
then put the pelt under the bed for a mattress, with
the head visible upon the floor, with the sockets staring
at the west wall.

Again and again, during the latter part of October,
he searched the mountains for food. Coming upon a
brown bear with two cubs, he slew the cubs and salted
them away. On his last day out, he got two black-
tailed deer, and decided that his winter's store was
complete. The two thirty-gallon barrels stood outside,
against the north wall. They were full of salted or
smoked flesh stripped from the bones. In one was the
flesh of the grizzly and the two cubs; in the other was
the flesh of the elk and one of the deer. The other deer
hung in a burlap sack from a cedar above Burns Creek.

'We're all set,' he declared, thinking happily of the
two barrels. 'We're rich as kings. Let the winds blow
and the winter come. Let the trees bust open with
cold. We're snug as two bugs in a rug.' He chuckled
for a few moments and added: 'When spring comes,
fat'll hang around our bellies like waddles.'

'You mean like wattles,' said Lela.

'Like wattles,' he said, looking at her. 'Little
woman, ain't I the good old pervider? Don't I do
good for a man's got no money?'

'You done very well,' she said. 'But we'll all smell
wild, eatun so much wild meat.'

'We'll all get wild. We'll throw our clothes away

and grow hair. After I eat some more that-there
grizzly, I'll growl in my sleep.'

'You do now,' said Lela. 'You sound like a bear now.
And you look like a bear.'

'All right, little woman, I feel like a bear. I'll take
off my clothes and then I'll be a bare bear.'

'That ain't so funny,' said Lela.

He shook with jolly laughter and went to the door
to spit. Then he fell upon hands and knees and pretended he was a bear. He chased Beth around the
room, growling at her, showing his teeth. She fled to
the stove and grasped an iron lid-lifter.

'I'll bust your head!' she cried, frightened by his
roaring.

He growled and snarled; he sniffed, and reached toward her with a huge paw. Beth dropped the iron and
ran around him and out of the house. He followed her,
still upon hands and knees; and from the doorway,
Lela saw him pursue her across the yard and into
brush by the river.

One of the things of which Charley was proudest was
his imitation of the sounds of wild beasts. He could
honk like geese or quack like mallards. He could
almost exactly reproduce the dismal wail or the snapping bark of coyotes; the deeper and more savage baying of wolves; or the strange whistle of a bull elk. And
he could so precisely imitate the growls of bears that,
in later years, he so frightened unsuspecting men that
they climbed trees and shook with terror. In later
years, too, he would cross the river to borrow machinery or food, and so terrify the Hunter lads, by sneaking

upon them through brush and letting off his savage roars, that they would flee screaming to their mother and sob for hours. All such pranks filled him with unspeakable happiness.

And to-night, after darkness fell and he had gone to the creek to hang the deer flesh, he decided to terrify his wife and babes. He was ashamed of his thought, but his impulse was irresistible. And so he sat behind a bush and began to bay like a wolf. Now and then, thinking of the growing panic within, he would stop to chuckle. He would lie back and laugh until he shook like jelly. Then he would multiply his sounds: the desperate snarling wrath of wolves, the shrill bleak hunger of coyotes, the madness of infuriated bears. The mountains around him rang and echoed, the air was heavy with untamed cries. He crept toward the house, still pouring forth his lonely wails and agonized yowling and wild roars. But again, overcome by thoughts of his wide-eyed sons, trembling by their mother's knee, he choked with snickers and guffaws. He laughed until tears ran down his fat cheeks. And again he crept forward, and under the window he broke into piercing hisses and snarls. He rose and peered inside. In the middle of the room stood Lela, with the rifle in her hands. Jed was standing near, clutching the hatchet.

Charley broke into loud uncontrollable laughter and went in. He lay on the floor and roared and wept. He laughed until he was exhausted; and even then he shook with silent joy.

And all the while, Lela sat on a box-chair, with the

gun across her lap, watching him. This deep vein of cruelty in him, this lusting after visions of terror, which in later years leapt into strange and diabolic deeds, was something that she could not understand. It became the darkest riddle of her life. On this night she forgave him. She perceived that his cruelty was somehow related to his clowning; and she liked his antics. But in later years...

In years to come, when she was to see the brute in him fully awakened; when she was to watch the bitter hatred between him and Jed; when she was to see his eyes burn green, like the eyes of a wildcat, even while he laughed... even while he laughed.... But tonight she smiled, as she stared at him lying there, shaking with his dark and infernal joy.

VI

AFTER gathering wood, and stacking it end-up behind the house, Charley's work was done. The nights, in early December, were bitter gray cold; and then the snow came. It came out of the west, at first like a great somber sheet, and then like a moving blurred wall of light and dark. The sun vanished, and daylight was taken into the enormous dusk. Trees became streaks of murk; the river was a faintly luminous darkness; the mountains stood like towers of shadow in the gloom. The higher peaks gathered their wintry loneliness and disappeared.

For many days the sky was full of storm, and the snow fell. It came down in a soundless deluge; and from the window, Lela watched its swirling constellations, falling to their cool white bed. Twilight was a soft darkening of earth, and dawn was no more than a wide dim opening of gray light. Bushes along the river-bank took their mantle and hid in silence. Under their branches, topped with white, snowbirds were exiled to their winter homes.

Charley liked the deep windless storm, and the warm dark hermitage of his house. He would not care, he said, if they were snowed under so completely that only the stovepipe emerged. Indeed, he would like to be. A wall of white, then, would be banked against their window; and they could open the door and see nothing but another wall. They would be covered over, buried under a clean depth of peace, and they could eat their food and soak their lazy bones by the fire.

He liked the cool silence, the hushed industry of the hours. Three times in every day he sat before a variety of meats — fried venison or trout, boiled hunks of elk shoulder, huge smoking roasts of bear — and stuffed himself until he groaned. Then he would bite off a quid, stretch belly downward upon the floor, and squirt his juice through a crack. And as Lela stared at him, smacking over his food or his quid, she wondered if there could be found, anywhere in the world, another human being so full of peace.

When he was not eating, or resting his fat body, he gave his time to odd and irrepressible clowning, now making faces until Beth and Thiel howled with glee, now imitating the sound of mice and squirrels and songbirds, or now affecting to be so grief-stricken that Beth implored him to stop. With looped strings he caught mice that ventured into the house, put them into empty jars, and fed them from day to day. Sometimes with mittened hands he would take them out, tie an elk bone to their tails, and roar with joy when the tiny beasts labored across the floor, dragging the bones and shrieking. He clipped their whiskers, and from one he shaved the hair, stropping his razor again and again before the task was done. Lela thought this shaved mouse was the most hideous thing she had ever seen.

After contriving a pitfall, he captured two large pack-rats, tied their tails together, and set them free.

They pulled against each other, clawing and screeching; they turned and fought until one was dead, the other smutched with blood; and then, without severing their tails, he tossed them out upon the snow.

When he did these more cruel things, Jed always stood by, watching intently with grave and darkened eyes. For hours at a time, he would sit and watch the imprisoned mice. He would shake them in the bottles, roll the bottles over the floor. When nobody was looking his way, he would thrust a hot stove iron into a bottle and sear the terrified creatures until their hides smoked. Or he would sit in a corner, staring speculatively at his father, thinking his own small dark thoughts.

The sky cleared, after two weeks of steady snowfall, and to a pine tree, a hundred yards from the house, Charley shoveled a path. The tree had low heavy branches that spread far out, and under these limbs was a cold bare seclusion which the Bridwells used for an outhouse. Declaring that a cold snap was imminent, Charley next cut two slender curved firs and made a pair of skis, patiently hewing with an axe and then shaping and planing with his hunting-knife.

During the following weeks, Lela and the children would often stand in the front yard, from which he had scooped the snow, and watch his antics. He would climb the mountain, when the snow was soft and buried him to his crotch, and later when it had a thick crust that supported his weight, and attempt to ride down upon his skis. Halfway down his skis would nose-dive, and Charley would plunge headlong and roll end over end, throwing up white clouds. Lela would hear his laughter and his jolly oaths. She would see him pick himself up, coated with snow, and climb again; again poise and start downward, only to sail swiftly for a little way, and then dive and roll like a barrel.

Later, after the crust had formed, he climbed with the aid of an axe, striking the blade ahead of him and drawing himself upward. And in two unforgettable flights, in which his skis were controlled, he sped down that high steep mountain at appalling speed, and out over the slope of the farm almost to the river, bearing all the while the axe in one hand. Usually, though, his skis spread and dumped him, and down the frozen mountain he would roll like a boulder, and so swiftly that Lela held her breath. Then he would enter the house, with a ravenous appetite, stoke himself with juicy slabs of meat, and spread his hands before a red-hot stove.

His nags, meanwhile, had been foraging in snow belly deep, eating leaves and bark, or pawing the snow away to get at withered grass, and daily becoming thinner until they were only hide and bone. Charley drove them one morning into brush by the river and shot them both. With an axe he split one carcass open, spread the ribbed slabs apart, and set his bear trap within. Around the other body he set traps, covering them with branches and snow; and along the river, he laid traps for otter and mink. His setting of traps led to two dramatic events. The first of these did much to fill Lela with dread. Out of the second grew one of the most persistent legends concerning Charley Bridwell.

Going one morning to the slain nags, he found in the traps a coyote and a huge gray wolf. He shot the coyote, and was on the point of shooting the wolf when it occurred to him that perhaps Lela would like to see this fierce beast. Setting his gun by a tree, he went back to the house.

'I been down to the traps,' he said, warming his hands at the stove. 'I got a greedy-gut down there. Would you like to see him?'

'What,' asked Lela, 'is a greedy-gut?'

'A wolf. But it's the biggest son-of-a-bitch I ever seen. He's quite a picture.'

'What's he doing now?'

'Just workun his rage up. Just wonderun if he's come to the end of his rope.'

'He can't get out, can he?'

'Can a man get out of a grave when he's buried alive?' asked Charley, winking at Beth. 'He's as good as buried. He knows it, too.'

'All right,' said Lela, 'I'd like to take a look.'

Charley carried her to the traps, with her legs around his waist, her arms around his throat. He kicked snow away and set her upon a frozen spot of earth. Then Lela looked at the wolf.

She had never seen anything as savage and enraged as this trapped beast. Its gaunt back was arched and its fur stood on end. Its wild eyes, glowing with hatred, burned and darkened. But it was the animal's mouth that made her shrink. Its lips were drawn back from dripping teeth, and these teeth made a steady clicking sound. The teeth were long and white, a great mouthful of savage snapping bone. Trembling with fear and fury, shaking as if it had been beaten, the wolf with its pale untamed eyes, eyes agleam with a kind of venomous ghastly sickness, looked from one to the other, and never paused in the metallic clicking of its teeth. Lela stepped back into the snow and turned away.

'Would you like him for a pet?' asked Charley, calmly watching her.

'Shoot it!' she cried. 'Charley, don't let it suffer any more!' She felt deathly sick; she retched and tried to vomit. When she saw Charley reach for the gun, she put hands to her ears. She heard a shot. When she looked around, a few moments later, the wolf was a heap of quivering fur. Then she saw Jed. He had followed them, climbing in and out of Charley's snow-tracks; and he was now peering over a white bank, his sober dark eyes staring at the slain beast.

Out of the other event, which happened a week later, grew the story that Charley Bridwell was a dangerous fool who would shoot a man at the drop of a hat.

'He'll shoot you down in cold blood,' a valley cattleman often declared. 'When he's jolly, he's all right. He's a good chap when you don't rub him the wrong way. But if you rub him the wrong way, if you get him in one of them damn tantrums, don't waste no time makun your tracks. If he calls you a liar, just grin and bear it. But if you want your head blowed off, call him a liar, too.'

But other people said: 'Charley's all right. He never did shoot a man. Mebbe he did take a pot shot at Bill Biggers, but Bill is a damn liar and nobody can't believe him. Anyway, what was old Bill snoopun around for? Christ a-mighty, he's always snoopun around somewheres...'

And so this story, like many others relating to Charley, was corrupted from mouth to mouth, until none believed it who knew Charley well. Nevertheless, it had a small basis in fact.

He went to his river traps one evening and learned that some one had taken an animal from one trap, and had found and sprung all the others. As was his custom, he said nothing of the matter to his wife. He was sure that Henry Bord, the silent old codger down the river, was not guilty. The theft had been committed by a stranger. Charley grinned and laid his plans.

Baiting his traps again, and waiting until he had caught an otter, he left the animal in the trap and hid. The time was a little before daylight, but everything was clearly visible in the pale white light of the snow. From the river-bank, south of Rattlesnake Point, he saw a man put out in a boat. He saw the man reach the near bank, chain his boat to a willow, and come up the river along the shelf of ice. He could see the man's gun, a gleaming knife in his belt, and the clouds of his breath. And at last he saw the man approach the trap, pause to look around him and listen, and then thrust his knife into the otter's throat. Then Charley left his hiding-place and went toward him.

The sound of his feet on the frozen snow reached the

man's ears, and the man swung around. He was a large black-bearded person with small cold eyes.

'Hello,' said Charley, and he grinned. It was an evil grin. The man did not speak. He looked hard at Charley and waited. 'I guess,' Charley went on, 'your memory is a little bad. Have you forgot you never set that-there trap?' Still the man did not speak, but there was a change in his cold eyes. 'Well, did you forget?' Charley asked softly.

The man was as motionless as stone. His eyes looked frozen. Charley's grin spread, and he chuckled; his chuckle was a threat. Without looking away from those small intent eyes, he bit into his plug. He tongued tobacco from cheek to cheek and spoke again.

'Fellers like you, they sometimes get shot. Now I once knowed a man forgot what traps he set, and he got his head blowed off. He was found stiff as a poker, with enough lead in him to sink a ship.'

Suddenly the man came to life. He started to raise his gun.

'Don't do that,' said Charley, grasping his arm. 'This is no place to have a shootun match. Put your gun down.' The man lowered his gun. His eyes were still intent, frozen. 'You see them brush,' Charley said. 'Well, now, you go down to that end, I'll go up to the other end. Then we'll come together.' He spit on the gray ice. 'Is that all right? If it ain't, don't come this far up the river next time.'

He turned away and walked up the shelf of ice. The man stared after him.

'Take good care yourself,' Charley said. 'Don't get

a catridge stuck in your gun. And when you see me peekun around a bush, just blaze away.'

The man turned westward. He had not spoken a word. Charley went up the shelf of ice that lay over the river. He looked back, now and then, and saw that the man was walking rapidly. He saw him turn to the right and vanish into the brush. Then Charley entered the snow-tangled growth and went westward, moving as swiftly as he could through the deep snow that sank under him, and stopping when he thought the man might be within two hundred yards. His method now became cunning and sly. When he went forward, he crawled on his belly in the snow, with his arms and the gun across the back of his neck and with his head down, so that an unexpected shot would most likely hit him in the shoulder. He moved forward each time behind a group of bushes that were thick and snow-filled. He would then softly thrust his gun barrel through the clump of snow and brush and peer through the hole which he had made. But he did not look for the man. He knew that this black-bearded giant would come, if he came at all, in the quiet way of a wild beast. What Charley looked for, when he peered through the hole, was a barely perceptible darkening, or a greater intensity of light, either of which would indicate the stealthy movement of the man behind an impenetrable shelter.

Now and then, Charley would laugh silently, because threat of danger always filled him with joy; or he would sprawl alertly behind a clump, softly chewing his tobacco and meditating. After a long scrutiny, if he saw no light-change among the bushes and trees ahead, he would again move forward, going flat upon his belly and choosing a path in which his low movement would cause no visible difference in the gloom above him. In this fashion, now crawling forward, now staring through a hole, he covered half the distance between the starting-points; and he was beginning to think that the man had fled when he suddenly became rigid. He was low on the earth and almost buried in snow, staring through a small dark tunnel, made by a long snow-weighted branch, when his keen eyes saw, not more than fifty yards ahead, a scarcely visible darkening. This darkening filled a small open space behind a dense pile of brush and snow. He could not see this space, but he knew by the contour of the brush that it was there. He watched without breathing and saw changes just above and beyond the bushpile which told him that something was moving behind that shelter. He knew then that the bearded fellow was keeping his rendezvous with death. He liked the man's courage. Instead of hatred, he now felt only admiration and sympathy.

Drawing his gun so slowly that his arms hardly moved, he inserted it gently into the tunnel under the limb; he lowered his head, little by little, until his cheek was against the stock; and then, without moving even a finger, he waited. He would wait until the man became impatient and betrayed himself.

He waited a long while. His enemy, apparently, was determined to advance no farther, and was also waiting. Charley grinned into the tunnel where the cold barrel gleamed. His hands were red and frozen, but he did not think of his hands. He could feel his body freezing in the snow, melting the snow and sinking, and then growing cold. His feet seemed to have been cut off. But he did not move. He sent his breath out slowly so that it would make no cloud. And he kept his eyes fixed upon that clump of brush. After a few minutes, he could no longer see changes in the light above, and he supposed that the man was also lying upon his belly, motionless in the snow.

Perhaps half an hour passed before anything happened. Then Charley saw a faint darkness, and a little later he saw something slowly moving at the right of the snow-bank. He closed his eyes and opened them to sharpen his vision. But there could be no doubt about it: he was staring at about eight inches of rifle stock. He could see only this. The man, he now knew, had got upon his knees. The man had grown tired of his bitter vigil and was preparing to advance or retreat. Even at this moment, while he knelt there deliberating, his finger was on the trigger, his cold eyes were searching the bushes and trees ahead.

Very slowly, Charley moved his front sight two inches to the left. He trained the bead upon those eight inches of brown wood. For several moments he stared along the barrel, aiming at that smooth stock. Then he fired.

The events that followed astonished him. He still lay on his belly, ready to fire again if he must. But there was no need to fire again. He heard a roar, more like that of a wild beast than of a man, and a shattering of brush. He heard the man plunging westward, smiting the limbs in his path, falling over buried trees. The sound of retreat was furious and blind. It grew fainter and fainter, and then there was silence.

Charley rose to his feet, stiff and frozen, and took a long breath. He dug his red hands into snow and spread snow over his face. He beat his body and kicked a tree with his feet. Then he went forward to the pile of brush. His steel-jacketed ball had completely shattered the gun stock and it lay here in splinters. In his flight, the man had lost his cap, which now hung from a limb. Putting the cap on, and going out upon the shelf of ice, Charley saw the man unchain his boat and push into the river. Aiming six inches above the boat prow, Charley fired again. He imagined he hit the boat, or very close to it, for the man redoubled his efforts and soon vanished down the stream.

He got the dead otter and went home. For a long while he sat in the house and chuckled, exploding into a roar from time to time, and slapping his thigh. When Lela asked what he was laughing at, he said it was memory of a coyote that made him rock and split. It was such a coyote as she had never seen.

'It must a-been awful funny,' she said, smiling to see his jolly red face.

'It was. It was the damndest funniest coyote I ever seen.'

For days thereafter he laughed whenever he remembered. While sitting at the table, he would suddenly think of the bearded fellow, of what the man's feelings had been when he saw his gun knocked into splinters; and he would go outside, choking on his food until his eyes bulged; spitting elk meat upon the snow and then roaring until he wept. And sometimes, when lying in bed, he would begin to chuckle, and his chuckle would grow into a great bellowing joy....

But Lela never learned the truth. She imagined he must have seen a very strange beast. She laughed with him and said:

'It sure must a-been an awful funny thing.'

Until at last, when Charley began to shake, his family laughed with him. All but Jed. Jed did not even grin.

VII

Snow fell again, until it lay more than three feet deep on the Bridwell place. Upon the mountains in the east, Charley declared, only the tallest trees would be sticking out; and even on the peaks to the north, it would bury an elephant.

When the sky cleared, there came the bitterest cold Lela had ever known. It struck into the house, when she opened the door, filling the room with sudden glacial rigor. When she went outside, the gray air made her quake; a raw canyon wind stung her cheeks, drew her mouth into a helpless pucker, and was like fire in her ears. Fleeing into the house, she would stand by a red stove, her flesh twitching in the warmth, her mind remembering the paralyzed whiteness of the outside world.

The barrels of meat were still by the north wall, with slabs of wood over their tops. When Charley brought a chunk of flesh inside, it was frozen almost as hard as stone, and he had to chop it with an axe. When he chopped, the flesh fell in chips like wood, and the smooth wall of it gleamed with frost, and was like ice to the hands. With his hunting-knife, he sliced shavings off, and these broke in two like dry bark.

The cold bit into green aspens until they were as hard as rock. When Charley tried to cut one of them down, his axe rebounded from the blow, leaving only a frozen scar on the trunk. The green limbs of bushes were as stiff as iron bolts. The leaves in the privy-shelter, under the pine, crumbled under Lela's shoes, brittle as flaked cereal. And the snow everywhere became so rigid in its deepening crust that it was like a white tableland of stone.

Of all visible outside things, only the river moved; but little by little, the petrifying chill sank into its icy waters, and at last there was no sign of movement in it anywhere. Below Rattlesnake Point, the cold white banks laid their shelf farther, day by day, into the current, until the two banks met and congealed. Then the floating ice of the stream built the grotesque towers and crags of its gorge; and from the window, Lela watched the awful beauty of its change. The flowing slush struck the ragged, tumbled bridge of ice and became a part of the bridge; and this steady building went on, until the white roof disappeared around the curve in the southeast, and there was no sign of moving water. The river would freeze over, Charley said, for miles and miles, perhaps clear to the Wyoming source. It would curl downward out of the mountains like a great white snake.

Hour after hour, Lela would sit by the window, looking out. Never before in her life had there been such a vision of wild and pitiless beauty. The mountains did not seem to be mountains at all, save where there rested an unburied area of timber; and even this timber seemed to be only a shadow or a black hole. Stupendous mounds of whiteness surrounded her; great dazzling illuminations that were blinding; huge pillows of glittering frozen silence. In Hunter Bottom

the trees and brush were ragged acres of shadow, or
only dark streaks against a white wall. The river was a
winding back of ice, thrown up into pinnacles and
crags and blocks.

Overhead at twilight, she would see flying ducks,
sometimes so many that the sky was darkened, wing-
ing their way to the unfrozen springs of the marsh
meadows. The wild geese had gone south. Once
Charley crossed the river, going over the bridge of ice,
and shot three lovely drakes. Now and then, also, he
went out into the bitter gray dawn, and caught trout
through a hole which he chopped in an eddy. But for
the most part, he did not stir from the house, except to
bring water from Burns or to chop wood.

He hated the cold white desert of winter months.
The house was his heaven, with its red stove; and he
would sit by the fire or lie upon the bed, drawing the
melting heat into his flesh and singing his songs. He
took a child's joy in keeping frost off the inside of the
panes. When he saw it forming, chilling the room's
moisture into the lovely glazed language of winter, he
would devote himself to the stove until its entire top
was a sheet of red.

In the stable which Silas had built, Charley had
stored his whiskey, wrapped thickly with gunny-
sacking and two ragged horse blankets. Each morning,
after going to the pine tree, he would enter the stable
and take a small drink; whereupon he would chew
tobacco and kinnikinnick bark to kill the odor on his
breath. He was happy, and he asked for nothing more
than he had.

Lela was happy, too, in this one-room haven which was the only spot of warmth and life in the frozen loneliness around her. She sat by the window, awed and a little troubled by the changeless estranged world; but the solitary untenanted desert of white, the great mountainous calm, fed something within her, and taught her old and unhappy memories the peace of sleep. In winters that were to come, her sunken ambitions were to be awakened and led to a tragic hour; but not in this winter, or in the next three or four. She found joy in her cooking, and she prepared meat in more ways than Charley had ever heard of; with the flour she made biscuits for the children, spreading them with fat and jam; and in every day she gave them a little of the wild fruit which she had canned — Charley never ate anything but gravies and meat. Or she watched her husband's clowning and listened to his songs.

He had a good voice. Sitting by the fire, hunched forward, he would sing for hours, stopping now and then to spit into the stove. His songs were chiefly those of cowboys, and of the rough events of pioneering life. His favorite was the 'Lone Star Trail,' and he sang or whistled this much of his time.

> I'll drive them heifers to the top of the hill,
> And I'll kiss that girl, by God, I will;
>   Come a ki yi yippi yi yay yi yay,
>   Come a yi ki yippi yi yay!
>
> My hand on the horn and my rump in the saddle,
> I'm the darunest fool that ever punched cattle;
>   Come a ki yi yippi yi yay yi yay,
>   Come a ki yi yippi yi yay!

Oh, a stray in the herd and the boss said kill it,
So I hit it in the rump with a redhot skillet;
  Come a ki yi yippi yi yay yi yay,
  Come a yi ki yippi yi yay!

Oh, I slapped the boss with my old slouch hat,
And I said, you son-of-a-bitch, take that,
  Come a ki yi yippi yi yay yi yay,
  Come a ki yi yippi yi yay!

Or sometimes he would sing:

The hinges, they're of leather, and the windows gunnysack,
  While the dirt roof ain't much good against the rain;
And I hear the slinkun coyote where he leads his hungry pack
  Round my little old log cabin on the plain.

Because their kerosene was low, they would often
sit for long hours after dark, with no light save that of
the stove and of the gleaming world outside. Charley
would sing then, while they all sat around the fire:

Oh, my hat in my hand and a heifer by the tail,
I'm on my way on the lone star trail....

Or they would listen to the coyotes, which came down
from the frozen solitudes and often wailed all night.
When they came too close, lured by the smell of meat
and warmth, Charley would go to the door, with Lela
and the children around him, and look out. They
could see the slinking starved beasts, not more than a
hundred yards away, sitting like shadows upon the
whiteness, or trotting back and forth with their noses
pointed at the house. Sometimes he would shoot one,
and the others would devour it, fighting among themselves, snarling and yapping.

After going to bed, Lela would lie awake and listen to the shrill wintry wailing of coyotes and wolves. Everything around her seemed to be mountain-wild. Under her was the bear pelt and a half-dozen skins of otter and mink and the hide of the timber wolf: all used as a mattress for one large bed during the bitter weather. She could smell these, the strong wild smell of hide and fur; she could put her hand out and feel the thick hair. She could hear the fierce hunger-song of the living, she could smell the strong scent of the dead. And though she trembled a little, when unexpectedly touching fur, or when hearing a sudden forlorn and fawning wail, she liked the drama of this life and she was unafraid. She would lie on Charley's arm, thinking of the deep calm power of his way; she would remember the gun above the door.

He would kiss the long brown curls of her hair and pat her reassuringly; and if the animals barked and howled too long or too savagely, he would begin to sing, and the wild sounds outside would melt and flow into strange music, as if the white mountains spoke. The sounds would bring to her a sleepy quiet, and she would look at the legs and arms of shadow, dancing on the walls; at the glowing friendly stove; at the wan ghostliness of the window. With her toes, she would pat her children, asleep at the bed's foot. Then Charley would sleep, too, and his snoring and the life of the fire and the dismal hunger outside would run into one sound, all meaningless and remote at last, and she would slip into dreams. When she awoke, her mind would be a blur of midnight memory; and when she looked out upon the world, she would see no sign of living thing — nothing but a dark stain on the hillside snow where a beast had been slain and eaten.

In three different times the wolves came down at midnight, a pack of more than twenty tall gaunt beasts; and the deep wild baying of these frightened her a little. Their sound was so wild and menacing, so full of deep-lunged power, or so like imploring of gray starved loneliness, that she shuddered in Charley's arms. She looked at the window, thinking they might shatter the glass and leap in; but Charley soothed her fear and laughed softly at her words. If they were to jump inside, he said, he would stick a hot poker down their throats. He would set their tails afire.

Nevertheless, he crawled out, after a while, drew on his trousers and shoes, and grasped his gun. He went outside. Not far ahead, the wolves trotted back and forth, looking at him. They seemed to be very tall, and of nothing but hide and bones. He chose one which he thought might be the ringleader and sent a bullet into its heart. It plunged twice and lay still. The pack looked for a moment at the fallen one, and then pounced upon it, tearing with fangs and claws. Charley shot two more and returned to bed, reflecting that he could not afford ammunition for coyotes and wolves.

All night, during the coldest weather, he kept the fire going, leaving his bed time and again to fill the stove with wood.

In this winter, and in many winters that came after,

Lela saw no one but her family and Henry Bord. But Henry never entered the house. He was a woman-hater, Charley said, and he rarely spoke, even to men. On one day he would go up the river, on the next he would return, making the journey between his two cabins and gathering his prey. From the window Lela could see him, tall and rawboned, unshaven and unclean.

'He stinks,' Charley would say. 'I don't think he ever bathes. He smells like a cow stable.'

His words left Lela thinking of Charley's personal cleanliness. He bathed often, even in winter-time. When the snow was soft he had gone into the brush, stripped off his clothes, and washed himself in the snow. After the cold came, he cut a hole in the crust and called the place his bathtub. Naked, he would dig down to the softer snow and scrub himself, coming up red and glowing and full of vigor. He carried water to the house for Lela and the children, heating it in a small tub; but now and then, in milder weather, he had taken his sons out with him and thrown them naked into snowdrifts.

'It's good for their hides,' he said. 'The Indians is the cleanest people I know. They never bathe in hot water. In the dead of winter, they jump into a river full a mush ice.'

Charley also kept himself shaved, though he never trimmed his ragged mustache; and he always laundered their underclothes and spread them to dry. He left only the cooking for Lela, and sometimes he helped with that.

These few tasks filled only a small part of the winter days. He had intended to gather pelts for the Lorenzo merchant, but his traps had been buried in the second snowstorm. And the few skins which he had he decided not to sell. He said he would make them into clothes. And so he tanned them, after a process learned from Indians, and with the aid of the bear's brain which he had saved for this purpose: and then he would sit in the afternoons, with needle and waxed thread, sewing the soft fur into warm things. He made a cap for himself and one for Lela, both round and tight-fitting, and low enough to cover their ears. He made small and misshapen fur jackets for the children, sewing on them buttons clipped from Silas Bane's old overalls. He tried to make fur mittens, but the intricate shaping of fingers was too much for him. Then he tanned the elk hide, after first removing the hair, and made for Lela a buckskin coat. When all his needlework was done, he looked with pride at his craftsmanship and gave himself again to laziness.

His sons, fitted out in their new things, and with their feet and legs wrapped in gunnysacking, would go out and roll in the snow; and Lela would go, too, in her buckskin jacket and fur cap, and with Charley's gumshoes on her feet. Charley would hear them playing outside, and he would chuckle and grin, and chew his tobacco by the fire. This, he believed, was the only sensible way of life. Let the fools in the valley sit around and plan their April sowing, gather their posts and build their hencoops, and hope that God in another year would be kind. God was always kind to

those who took His earth for what it was made for.
He frowned at those, Charley imagined, who gutted it
with plows and filled it with dust; dreamed of huge
estates and herds of beef, and an eventual home in a
sunnier clime; and made their fools' prayers for special
kindness.

Life, as nearly as he could tell, was a blind and remorseless game, like a handful of dice or a round of
faro, with an invisible sphinx dealing the result. The
sky was a blue emptiness, good to look at and to
breathe, but as deaf as an elk's antlers; and heaven
was a pious whimwham. He could see this much, and
he cared to see no more. It was good to have a wife
whom he loved, a refuge where he could drowse his
emotions, and a warm place to sleep. It was good to
sit idly by, drawing life and laziness out of time, feeling
the sensuous passing of hours.

He chuckled and thought of his hungry stomach.
Supper stood ahead, with its chunks of rich juicy elk,
battened with strips of brown liver and dripping
morsels of fat. He went to the stable for an appetizer,
drew forth a cold bottle, and let an ounce of whiskey
run down his throat. He wiped his mouth, stroked the
bottle and stared at it, and then turned away to chew
bitter aspen bark.

Little by little, the desperate weather softened, and
the chill drew away to cold altitudes. The feeble
yellow sun burned golden again, and they awoke one
morning to find the world yellow with warmth. From
the valley came a melting wind, and under the chem-

istry of heat the world became dripping and wet. The river barked and snapped as its rigid iciness turned into gray water; its crags crumbled and broke, large cracks fell open, and the long back growled and sank. The lower end of the gorge split asunder into icebergs, and these floated away; and hour by hour, before Lela's eyes, she saw great chunks burst open and turn valleyward; until at last the river was a long winding caravan of ice-boulders, eating at banks which diminished as these, too, added to the white cargo of the stream.

The snow on the mountains became heavy with wetness. Lela was awakened one night by a thunderous roar. It sounded like the falling of a mountain, but Charley said it was only a snowslide, somewhere near. On the next morning she saw what had happened. From a tall steep bluff, built like a shoulder on the east side of Burns, the entire body of snow had crashed downward, uprooting trees and leaving a hillside of aspens in a flattened tangle. The avalanche now lay in the creek-bed, its countless tons piled so high that even the cottonwoods were buried. Burns Creek, meanwhile, had become a frenzied torrent; and through this ponderous mass of snow it cut a channel and rushed out from a ragged white cavern.

Other torrents came down from other mountains, and from the mountain behind the house. Dark streams, choked with mud and stones, came down furious and unquelled, wreaking new trails, gutting the slope of their farm, and undermining boulders that took to flight and found the river. Near the house was a great pit in the earth, dug there by Silas in his search for gold; and into this pit a stream plunged, and the hole became a thing of black water, boiling upward, and spreading a blanket of water over its south bank. The snows found Charley's irrigation ditch, melted its banks, tore holes in its lower side.

But it was the river that became the most magnificent spectacle of the untamed. Day by day its dark body grew, adding to its depth and breadth; spreading over islands until trees and bushes stood in its gray waters; and steadily increasing the impetuous violence of its rush to the sea. It swung out of the southeast in a muddy ravaging volume, shot round a curve to the mouth of Burns, and fell upon itself there in a mighty churning of whirlpools and undertows. Its waves swept up from their valleys, rose in a muddy wall, and broke and fell in heavy tons. Huge rims of water swung around and around, making great curved bowls whose sides seemed to be smooth flowing rock. Water stood up in sudden small mountains, lashing out with enormous manes, hurling a thousand pounds into ropes that fell like showers of cobblestones. It rose in a broad wet breast, moving out of its depth in a great rhythm; and upon the shore, this breast would fall in a wide flat sound, and then break into innumerable frantic torrents sucking backward.

Upon the river they saw strange cargo, gathered from the islands and banks. Huge piles of brush would bear down into Burns junction, and not even a stick would be visible on the way out. Green cottonwoods were flung end over end, now rearing midway in the stream, as if growing there for a moment; and then crashing down and out of sight. Lela saw such trees, a foot in diameter at their base, carried into the appalling frenzy of the junction, and sucked under and broken in two as if they were twigs. She saw trees drawn down, with all their branches intact; and when she saw the trunks again, they were naked, with every limb torn away.

She was frightened by this river, drunk with its fury and power. In night-time she heard its booming language; it beat upon her thoughts and terrified her dreams. Its moving body of thunder filled these lowlands, from mountain wall to mountain wall. She wondered if she would not rise some morning, look into the southeast, and see there a high breast of water, coming down to bury her and everything that lived below the peaks. Within her grew the feeling that she lived below the earth's surface, in a vast subterranean passage open to the sky and air. When she looked up, she could see only her prison walls and the sun. But in another and deeper way, she loved this melodrama of spring.

But Charley hated it. He hated the river's senseless going to an unknown and futile end; the loud tongue of its monologue; its grotesque buffoonery; its crazed barnstorming on its way to the sea. And its stage-struck gestures, its steady infernal booming, awakened a cruel hunger that had stood unused in his being. He stepped out of long indolence, feeling the great surging of life, yet despising it. How, he wondered, could a man rest in peace, when Nature dramatized even the melting of snows?

VIII

In late April, Charley went out and got an elk, and for a while he was happy and well-fed. When the warm lazy days of summer came, he had to stir himself again in search of food. He caught fish, he killed some wild geese, but in spite of his efforts, their fare was a lean one. He spaded a small area and planted a garden. He borrowed a few potatoes from Joe Hunter and planted these also. And then, while wondering what he would eat during the next two months, he had an opportunity laid in his lap.

Jack Tompkins came up the river and said that a man had been drowned near Dry Canyon. Charley grunted and yawned, because many people were drowned in Snake River, and drowning was hardly news. But this man, Jack declared, was not an ordinary fellow. He was a rich fool who rolled in money, who owned mines and banks and railroads, and enough land to fill a dozen counties. A reward of four hundred dollars was offered.

'How'd he drown himself?' asked Charley. 'What was the silly poop tryun to do?'

'Fishun!' said Jack, quivering with excitement. 'My Pop, he says you're the best river-man in the world. He says you could find that-there body in a jiffy. Fishun, that's what. He waded out in hip boots. He got too deep, and the water just run in his boots, and he couldn't move. My Pop says ——'

'Up by Dry Canyon, you said. Well, Jack, mebbe your idea ain't so bad. Four hundred dollars, huh, Jack?'

'Four hundred!' gasped Jack, to whom this sum was inconceivable wealth. 'My Pop, he says you're the best river-man hereabouts. You'n find that-there body, he says.'

'How long ago, Jack?'

'Two weeks. Two weeks last Monday.'

'Last Monday,' said Charley, whose Mondays had lost themselves. 'What's to-day?'

'Wednesday,' said Jack, staring at him hopefully. 'You'n find the body in just a jiffy. Four hundred dollars, think!'

'How you know there's a reward?'

'I know well enough. A sheepherder told us. I seen the sign says so. Lots a people is huntun for it now. But my Pop, he says you're the only man born could find it. He told me to come and tell you. He said you should ought to hurry ——'

'Well,' said Charley, looking at the river, 'mebbe I will. How about to borrow your horse, Jack?'

'Sure,' said Jack. He looked at the horse and considered. 'And mebbe if you found it, why, mebbe ——'

'You're right, Jack. If I find it, you get five dollars.'

'Five dollars!' cried Jack, who had been hoping for one.

And so Charley wrapped some fried trout in a towel, tied the towel like a belt around his waist, with the lump of fish on his back, got his rifle, and mounted the horse and rode away. Dry Canyon was five miles up the river, and the way was difficult. The horse upon which Charley sat was a starved scarecrow, old and tender-footed; he wheezed and staggered under his burden. The path was an elk trail; and when it climbed too sharply, Charley would slide off and lead the horse; whereupon, gaining the crest, he would mount again and ride on, singing his songs and wondering what he would do with four hundred dollars. That he would find the corpse he hardly doubted. The other hunters were probably valley fools, who scurried like rabbits from bush to bush, or ran pell-mell over the islands. They would not know that the body would be entombed in brush and mud and perhaps invisible.

The time was noon when he reached Dry Canyon. After turning the horse free, he found some driftwood and set about making a raft. He chose three small dry logs, carried them to the water, and bound them together with grapevine withes. Mounting the raft then, with his gun in one hand and a club in the other, he pushed out into the current. He ignored the extreme banks, because drowned things rarely lodged there; but he stopped and explored every island, going upon the leeward side of driftwood piles and of willows, once submerged in the flood waters, but now banked around with sand. But he did not search these piles, as most body-hunters did. He knew that if he did not smell the corpse, he would never find it.

After walking back and forth over an island, sniffing the air, catching the odors of every breeze, he would push again into the river and anchor at the next. He smelt mud and dry timbers and sand, the fragrance of young leaves and of green willow, of clean warm beaches and of stagnant pools. At dusk he came unexpectedly upon a flock of wild geese, and through an acre of brush he stole up and shot the head off the largest one. He took the goose to his raft and ate his meal of fried trout. Then he drifted to the next island, walked twice across its length, and went to the next. He floated downward between gloomy mountains, with black waters under him, a moonless sky overhead. At midnight he reached the island that lay south from his home.

While he was trudging wearily across it, chewing tobacco and keeping a philosophic mind, he got a sudden whiff of something foul. Turning, with his nose pointed into the wind, he sniffed like a dog, but for several moments smelt nothing more. Then he moved about, east and west, into the breeze and away from it; and again, out of air that was fragrant and clean, he picked a brief rottenness. He walked against the wind, and around and around; but for half an hour the source of the stink eluded him. And at last, when he was wondering if he had imagined the smell, the air became heavy with stench and filled his breath with mephitic waves. He walked again into the breeze, his throat full of rank odor, resembling that of mixed skunk and stinkbush.

In a pile of driftwood and sand he discovered the corpse. The moon had risen now, and he could see quite clearly. The dead man was entirely buried in old mud, save his head and one hand and one foot. Upon his foot and leg he still had the rubber boot. His face and hand were gleaming fleshless bone. The eye-sockets were empty, and what remained of the hair was playing in the wind. Charley knelt to look at the teeth, and saw that one was capped with gold. He noted other identifying marks, looked around him for a few moments, and then went home, riding his raft to the home bank. He crept into bed, and the night buried him in dreamless sleep.

On the next morning Jack appeared from nowhere, having slept in a blanket under a bush.

'You find him?' asked Jack, again quivering with excitement.

Charley gave the lad a droll wink.

'Yes,' he said, 'I find him.'

'Where?' asked Jack.

'Don't be curious, son. Just hop on your scarecrow and hit the grit.' He walked over and laid a hand on Jack's trembling shoulder. 'If you hurry, I'll make it ten dollars. But you got a-kick up the dust.'

Jack lost no time in kicking up the dust. Without eating breakfast, he brought his horse to the dooryard and mounted, with a heavy cudgel in his hand.

'Tell them,' said Charley, 'not to come without the greenbacks. We won't fool around with no wind-jammers, huh, Jack?'

'Not for Christ sake!' declared Jack, scowling at the western sky.

'Remember, we don't want no check. We want the money right in our fists. Ain't that right, Jack?'

'By God, yes,' said Jack.

'All right. Now skin out like a streak.'

Jack stroked with the club and the horse groaned and stiffened.

'Kick him in his poop,' said Jack, smiting right and left.

Charley entered the house and returned with a rawhide quirt. He threw it and Jack caught it deftly from the air. Then he laid it in cruel bitter blows upon shoulders and flanks, neck and ears. He urged the beast into a gallop. When Charley saw him rounding the Point, Jack was still slashing right and left with his whip.

'He'll probably kill him,' said Charley, turning to Lela, who had been watching them. 'He'll ride him until his tongue hangs so far down he'll step on it.' He chuckled and turned toward the river.

'Where'd you find him?' asked Lela.

'Right out there.' He pointed to the island.

It was a strange world, Lela reflected. For two weeks a dead man had been lying there, only a few hundred yards away, rotting in wind and sun, with vultures eating his eyes out. She remembered now having seen these ragged ugly creatures, flying from the cottonwood banks to the island; and she had seen hawks, flying round and round the sky.

The time was midnight when Jack returned, bringing with him two men. He galloped up over the farm with loud whoops, to let Charley know that he was coming; and Charley groaned and crawled out of bed. He dressed and went outside, after ignoring the imperious raps on the door. He saw before him two tall well-dressed men, two fat horses with gleaming saddles, and a third horse that carried a pack-saddle, large panniers, and a roll of canvas. One of the men stepped forward and spoke.

'Where's the body?' he asked. His tone was crisp and a little arrogant. Resenting this arrogance, Charley bit into his plug and grinned.

'Where's the money?' he said.

'We got the money all right. But you don't get a cent till we see the body.'

'No?' said Charley. He stepped forward and looked in the man's eyes. They were gray insolent eyes, and Charley hated them. He hated the contempt which these men felt for him and his simple way of life.

'You talk about money,' cried the spokesman scornfully, 'when George Humbert lies dead! Did you ever hear of George Humbert?'

'Never did,' said Charley quietly. 'But he's nothun but a rotten carcass now. I seen him yesterday, but he didn't impress me much.... Well, if you want a-know where he is, fork over the greenbacks.'

The spokesman turned away to consult with the other man. Jack stood by Charley, swallowing hard now and then, looking up with troubled eyes. The spokesman came back.

'Do you mean,' he demanded, 'that you won't show us the body till we give you the money?'

'Near as I remember, that's what I mean.' Charley grinned at the angry flushed face.

The man stepped forward, his anger deepening.

'Life don't mean a thing to you, then, but gold! You hunt dead bodies for gold! Is that your game?'

Charley's eyes gleamed wickedly, but he held his temper in. He looked steadily at the man's enraged face.

'Did you offer a reward for this carcass, or didn't you?'

'We did.'

'How much?'

'Four hundred dollars.'

'All right. Dig up the four hundred.'

'You admit, then,' said the man bitingly, 'that you hunt bodies for gold?'

'What do you hunt them for? Fun?'

'You admit you're just a kind of vulture. Is that it?'

This was too much for Charley's good-humor. He hated bickering and cross-purposes; and he was sleepy. He stepped close to the man and poked his clean flannel shirt with a menacing finger.

'You've went far enough,' he said, and his grin made the man recoil. 'Another yeep like that and some one'll be offerun a reward for you. Now, down to business. If you want a-know where that damn rotten carcass is, fork over the money. If you don't want a-do that, go find the body yourself.'

The two men consulted again.

'But,' said the spokesman at last, 'how do we know the body you found is the body we want?'

'Did it have gum boots on?'

'Yes.'

'All right. Did it have a gold tooth?'

'Yes.'

'Was it a little ball-headed and with some gray hair on the temples?'

'Yes,' said the man, turning to look at his silent partner.

'And was the shirt made a blue corduroy?'

'Yes, that's right.'

'Very well, then. Shuffle out the greenbacks.'

After another brief conference, the man drew a roll from his pocket and handed it to Charley.

'Just give me time to count this,' said Charley. He told Jack to strike matches, and Jack struck matches while Charley counted the notes. 'Correct,' he said, stuffing the money into a pocket. 'See them willows out on that bar? That big patch, then the smaller patch. Your carcass is buried in the mud just west them small willows.'

'But how'll we get over there?' the spokesman asked.

'Swim.'

The men looked at him incredulously.

'But we can't swim,' said one. 'Not and carry a body, anyway.'

'Build a raft,' Charley said.

'Listen here, you should deliver the body to us. What do you think that four hundred dollars is for?'

'Findun it, man, findun it. Do you think I'd fool around with a body falls apart like a dead cat? That's your job.'

'Just the same, you should help us get it.'

Charley considered. He thought of an easy and simple vengeance.

'All right,' he said.

He entered the house and hid the money under the bear pelt. He kissed Lela and told her he would not be long. Under his left armpit, and beneath his shirt, he hung his six-shooter from a strap around his neck.

'Let's go,' he said, and the three of them walked to the river, with Jack trailing behind. To his old raft, which he had dragged upon the bank, he bound another cottonwood log. Then he took Jack aside and told him to remain on the shore. 'That raft,' he said, gurgling with malicious joy, 'will probably sink and drown them damn fools.'

With the aid of the men, he pushed the raft out and they all stood upon it. It sank eighteen inches below the water's surface. Watching the men, Charley saw that the silent one was shaking with fright.

'I won't ride this!' he cried, his mind full of George Humbert's fate. He sprang to the bank and kicked water from his shoes.

'We'll build a bigger raft,' said the other.

Charley demurred, saying that this raft would float an elephant; but the men got another log and bound it to the floating four. When they all stood upon the larger raft, it bore their weight without sinking more than an inch or two. Even so, it was a dangerous craft in such a stream.

'I won't go,' said the man. His teeth chattered. 'How much will you charge to fetch the body over here?'

'More,' said Charley, 'than you could pack in gold dust.'

'I'll go,' said the other man. He went to the pack-horse and got a large bag of stout heavy canvas. Charley gave him a long club for a paddle, and took another for himself. They then pushed into the stream. The swift current caught the raft and swung it around, threatening, for a moment, to pitch it end over end.

'Hang on,' said Charley, grinning at the man's white face. Charley knelt on the raft and plied furiously with his oar, and the stranger marveled at his strength and skill. After crossing the running part, they struck an eddy that swirled around and around. It was in this eddy that Charley yielded to his impulse. He still burned under the contempt and insults of these men; and besides this, a dark and sinister part of him found devilish joy in humiliating the timid, in watching their bones shake, in hearing their gurgling yells of terror and their mad shouts for help. And so, pretending to be busy stroking with his oar, he moved suddenly to an extreme edge of the raft and then sprang back; and the man was pitched into the eddy.

He went under with a scream that was choked off by the water, and came up clawing and bellowing. 'Help!' he roared, and the mountains rang with the echo. He sank again, his voice gurgling and hissing; and again he rose, pawing with blind and frantic zeal. 'Help!' he wailed, his voice becoming more feeble and waterlogged. Charley maneuvered the raft close to him and thrust an oar out to violent hands.

'Grab it,' he said, 'and hang on.'

Panic-stricken, the man seized the oar and was dragged toward the raft. Charley stood on one edge, while the man drew himself up over the other, drenched and wild-eyed. Without a word, Charley then rowed to the bank, and the man leapt off to sand that sucked him down, knee-deep. Again he roared for help, thinking now that he had fallen into quicksands. Charley anchored the raft and lay upon cobblestones. He shook with uncontrollable laughter, yet he made no audible sound; and the man dug himself out and came over, his lower legs soaked with mud, water running from his hair and clothes. Still without speaking, Charley took the canvas bag and went up the island, with the man coming after. His teeth chattered, and now and then he coughed or moaned. Charley led him to the pile of brush and pointed to the ghastly corpse in the mud.

'My notion,' he said, 'is for you to take your clothes off and dig him out. Then bathe yourself and we'll be gone.'

The man stared at him with interrogating eyes; he looked at the fleshless face and shuddered; he pinched his nostrils together and turned away.

'Hurry up,' said Charley. 'It's soon daylight.'

The man meekly obeyed, removing all his clothes first, and then pawing at the mud. He used his hands as shovels to scoop the mud away, now and then going to the windward side for fresh air. When the corpse lay stark and clear in moonlight, the man took the canvas bag and little by little wormed the soft mass into it, after first drawing the boots off and throwing them away. These boots were strapped to the body's waist; and to unfasten them, the man had to reach under the body, with his cheek almost against the dead flesh. When the task was finished, the man found water and scrubbed himself and put on his clothes.

Charley, meanwhile, had calmly sat on the windward side, chewing tobacco and watching the labor. Each one next grasped two corners of the bag, and they carried the body to the raft. Then the man looked at the river, his eyes darkening with fear. And when, after pushing the raft out until it floated, Charley looked at the man, he saw that the fellow was weeping, shaking with great sobs; and Charley felt a strange deep compassion, his power for sympathy lying in him, side by side, with his lust for cruel things. He believed, furthermore, that this man was no coward, because a coward could never have faced the gruesome moonlit work which this man had done. He tapped his shoulder and spoke. The trip back, he said, would be simple enough; the dead body would help to balance the raft. The man looked up and his eyes were wet.

'I'm a coward,' he said. 'But I can't swim.'

'That's all right,' said Charley. 'Just hang on the center. There ain't no danger at all.'

The man looked around him and then stepped upon the raft. He knelt by the dead body and clutched the withes round the middle logs. Charley pushed the raft across the eddy, stroking powerfully, and struck the swirling current. In spite of his strength and skill, he had difficulty getting the craft out of the swift waters; and it was carried rapidly downstream and brought to bank at Rattlesnake Point. Jack and the other man had gone westward and waited here. Charley helped carry the body to the saddle and to bind it in the panniers. Then the stranger faced him and held out his hand.

'You might like to know,' he said, 'that this is my father. Well, I'm glad I met you. Good-bye.'

In the dusk of morning, Charley watched the caravan go westward over Rattlesnake Trail and disappear. He and Jack returned to the house, and he gave Jack ten dollars. Jack's eyes were full of unspeakable joy. He fingered his money and whispered:

'I hope some more rich fellers gets drownded. Don't you?'

'Shame on you, Jack,' Charley said.

During his years here, many people were drowned and washed up within a few miles of his place. But all of them, save one, were poor people, and no reward was offered for their recovery. Nevertheless, Charley found many of them, hunting for the fun of the search, or because of his sympathy for those who grieved. His reputation grew as a body-finder, and during his last years on the Bridwell place, people would come and implore his aid, and with jolly zest he would search day and night until the corpse was found.

'Old Charley Bridwell,' folk would say, 'could find a drownded rat. Just you throw a rat in at Coonard, and Charley, he'll find it in twenty-four hours.'

'A rat! Why, my God, he don't need nothun big as a rat. Just you throw a bedbug in the ocean and Charley can find it.'

'Sure, I guess you're right.'

IX

WITH three hundred and ninety dollars in his fist, Charley felt oppressively rich. He wanted to spend it at once.

'I think, though,' said Lela, who had secret notions of her own, 'that you should give me some of it.'

'Sure thing,' said Charley, looking at his wad of greenbacks. In a moment of generosity, which he forever regretted, he gave to Lela half of the money; and she buried it in a glass jar, and she kept it buried for many years.

'I think to hit the grit,' said Charley, 'and spend mine right away.' And he did.

With a rope and his six-shooter, he went to the river one morning, with Lela and the children. He kissed her good-bye, telling her not to be lonesome during his absence, which would not be long. Then he tied the rope around his waist; and without removing his clothes he swam the river on his back, holding the gun above the water with one hand, and stroking with his other. From the opposite bank he waved to her and vanished into brush.

Crossing meadowlands, he climbed the mountain and stood upon the Antelope Hills. Everywhere were herds of cattle and horses, feeding upon the deep grass and fattening against the winter months. Breaking dry twigs into small pieces and putting these in his hat, Charley approached a large mare, shaking his hat to decoy the beast into thinking that he had oats. The mare regarded him with doubt; but his words were gentle, and the dry sound in his hat seemed genuine. And so he got his rope around her neck before her eager nose discovered his treachery. Then he looked at her, wondering if she had ever been ridden. There were no saddle scars on her back; but a tuft of gray hair on her neck showed that she had known a collar. He looped the rope over her nose, stroked her smooth hide, meanwhile studying the language of her eyes, and then sprang upon her. She stiffened into utter rigidity. He patted her shoulder and spoke to her, and very gently he prodded her with his heels. But she did not move. He jumped off and studied her eyes again. Deciding that she was more lazy than wild, he again mounted, and struck her a sharp blow with the knotted end of the rope. She stiffened and shuddered, and turned her head to look at him. Then she snorted with fear and rage, and bounded forward in great churning leaps; and Charley was hurled over her head and sent spinning into a growth of sage. The mare ran off, blowing madly, with the rope dragging after her.

'Well, well,' said Charley, sitting up and rubbing his burning cheeks. He looked at blood on his hands. Then he lay on his back and laughed loudly into the sky. After a few minutes he sat up and took a quid of tobacco; but again mirth seized him, his quid was blown out in a violent guffaw, and he fell back convulsed.

An hour later he walked over the hills, shaking twigs in his hat, trying to approach another beast. He found a huge bony horse, too tired or too lazy to run. Upon its back he rode to the valley, guiding the animal by kicking at its jaws. Darkness was falling when he entered Lorenzo and drew up at the solitary store.

He bought first a halter and a pack-saddle and two large panniers. Upon this saddle he loaded a great cargo. He loaded upon it two hundred pounds of flour, a hundred pounds of salt and sugar and lard, and a hundred pounds of canned goods. In addition to these he had thirty pounds of lucerne seed, fifty pounds of ammunition and tobacco and whiskey, a shovel and two pitchforks and a pile of clothes; a single-barreled shotgun and a gunnysack full of smaller things; so that the weight all told was more than five hundred pounds. And even so, he had money left, after paying for all these and for what he had bought in the previous year. There remained, as a matter of fact, sixty-seven dollars and thirty cents; and Charley didn't know what to do with this. He looked around for something costly and of little weight, but he saw nothing that he could use.

Whereupon, with midnight approaching, he took his journey into the southeast, walking before and leading the horse. He carried with him a quart of whiskey, and from time to time he would stop and drink; wipe his mouth and sigh, and go forth again into the night. Trekking homeward over thirty miles, along almost impassable roads or dim trails, half-drunk and dog-tired, he consoled himself with the thought that his future was safe against labor and journey for at least a twelvemonth. In a gray dawn he halted to rest, and gathered for the horse some lucerne, growing by the wayside. Then he drank again and went on.

The time was mid-afternoon when he reached the Tompkins place. He stumbled wearily into the yard and sank exhausted by the door. When Jim appeared, Charley handed to him the half-empty bottle of whiskey, and Jim's stony face softened as he drank. Jack drew near, hopeful but polite.

'Give him a shot,' said Charley.

Blinking like a sucking calf, Jack poured whiskey down his thirsty throat until his father snatched the bottle away.

'Lead this old bastard up to my place,' said Charley, addressing himself to Jack. 'Take the whiskey along to cure your rattlesnake bites.'

Jack eagerly grasped the bottle, picked up the halter rope, and set forth. Charley staggered into the shade of a cottonwood and fell into profound sleep.

Dusk was upon him when he went to the house.

'Have a good nap?' asked Jim.

'Just dandy,' said Charley. 'Fill my belly and I'll hit the trail.'

Mrs. Tompkins rose from a gloomy corner and set before him a tin plate, a knife and a fork, and a pot of boiled meat. Charley ate the entire hind quarters of a woodchuck. Its flavor, especially of the tawny fat, was even more rank and wild than that of bear meat, but Charley devoured it with great gusto, reflecting meanwhile that Jim's larder was more poverty-ridden than his own. A man had to be down on his heels to stomach woodchuck.

'I could get you some reddishes,' said Mrs. Tompkins, 'and make you some tea. We ain't a bit a bread.'

'No, thanks,' said Charley. 'This is fine.'

'I understan you found the body all right,' said Jim, quietly smoking his corncob pipe.

'Yep,' said Charley. 'It wasn't no trick. You could smell it from here to London.'

'I guess it was pity damn rotten,' said Jim.

'Rotten as a old ewe full a maggots,' Charley said.

'What you want a-talk about that for?' asked Mrs. Tompkins of her husband. 'You want a-make him sick at his stomick?'

'Never mind,' said Jim, removing his pipe to scowl at his wife. 'You couldn't make old Charley sick at his stomick. Huh, Charley?'

'God, no,' said Charley. 'I could set on the damn fool and eat mince pie.'

'I don't see how you could,' said Mrs. Tompkins calmly. 'I couldn't. I'd throw up my whole insides.'

'How'd he get drownded so easy?' asked Jim.

'Just waded out in gum boots. Got his boots full and was a plumb goner.'

'Must a-been a hell of a greenhorn,' said Jim. 'One a these-here rich greenhorns, wasn't he?'

'Green as a pine tree,' said Charley, stripping flesh from a thigh bone.

'And rich, you say?' asked Mrs. Tompkins, her voice hoarse with resentment.

'Rich as a gold mine.'

'And a plumb damn fool,' said Jim. 'I guess all rich men is plumb damn fools.'

Charley wiped his mustache on his sleeve and stood up.

'Well,' he said, 'now to hit the high lonesome. Why don't you folks never come and see us?'

'We will,' said Jim. 'We're just too gol-damn busy.'

'Yes, you're awful busy,' said his wife.

'We'll be up your way,' said Jim. 'I got a little patch a hay to put in. Then we'll visit some.'

'You see a man wants work, send him up.'

'Sure, I'll send him up.'

Charley jested for a few moments with the children, who had stood around him watching him eat. Then he went into the yard and looked eastward.

'Well,' he said, 'come up when you can.'

'All right. And you come down.'

'But don't wait for us. Come any old time. You got horses and we have to foot it.'

'All right. But you come down.'

'I'll see. Well, good-bye.'

'Good-bye, Charley.'

'Good-bye.'

Charley took the trail at a brisk pace. He supposed that Jack had long ago reached the house and unloaded the cargo. But Jack had done nothing of the kind. A mile up the trail, Charley came upon that enterprising youth, drunk and muttering and unable to stand. The weary beast had lain down in the trail and stretched his aching limbs.

'What the Christ!' Charley roared, thinking of Lela, still waiting for him. He stooped and shook the lad, who lay sprawled on his back. By him was the empty whiskey bottle. 'Get up!' cried Charley. But Jack did not get up. He stared with unfocused eyes and gibbered.

'Gog eggy moarg?' he asked, as if his tongue were made of soaked cowhide.

'What?' asked Charley.

'Yoog gog eggy moarg?'

Charley looked around him. Then he went to the river and returned with his hat full of water. He dashed this into Jack's patiently drunken face. The youth did not even gasp.

'Stob thag!' he said.

Charley picked him up and carried him to the river; he ducked him completely, and Jack came up, spitting water and cursing.

'Wake up!' roared Charley, again shaking him.

'I seg stob it!' cried Jack.

Charley grasped him by his trousers and one shoulder and plunged him in again and again.

'Now stand up,' he said.

Jack swayed on his legs. There was no meaning in his eyes. Leaving him there, Charley went back to the prone beast. He kicked the horse's ribs, but the horse would make no effort to rise. While sweating and cursing, trying to get the animal on its legs, he heard a sudden splash. Leaping down through the brush, he found Jack gurgling in the eddy and ploughing with his arms. Charley pulled him out and shook him.

'I seg stob it!' Jack bellowed. 'Cag you leeb me aloag?'

Charley led the drenched lad back to the trail. He

set him against a stone, and again strove to get the horse up. Upon hands and knees, he wormed his shoulders under the cargo, and with a knife blade he gouged the beast's flank. The horse spread its front legs and groaned. It strove to rise and fell back and strove again to rise; and little by little, Charley got under the pack and lifted with his great strength. Jack, meanwhile, was pulling at the beast's tail. 'Twist it,' said Charley, and again he prodded with the blade. The horse made a tremendous effort and got his legs.

'Think you'n get home all right?' asked Charley.

'I doag know,' said Jack, rubbing at his eyes.

'Just follow the trail,' said Charley. He drew forth a dollar and pressed it into Jack's hand. This, more than the water, seemed to sober the lad. He shivered in his wet clothes. 'And don't forget to fetch a greenhorn up.'

'Uh huh,' said Jack, staring at the coin.

Charley picked up the halter rope and followed the trail. At midnight he arrived at his own door. Leaving the weary beast under its load, he ran in to find Lela. He took her in his arms, murmuring soft words, kissing her long hair.

'You get awful lonesome?' he asked.

'A little,' she said.

'Come and see what I got,' said Charley, and he led her into the moonlight. She saw the horse, braced patiently upon his weary legs, supporting a huge pile of things; and while she watched, Charley untied ropes and carried the stuff into the house. He then lit the lamp, and by its feeble yellow flame, he showed Lela the many things he had bought for her: clothes and cooking utensils, and even brush and paints, which she had once expressed a wish for. Her hands trembled as she lifted one thing and another; she sat on his lap and kissed his ragged mouth.

X

A WEEK later, Charley played upon an unsuspecting youth one of those pranks which delighted his soul. In itself, it was a harmless piece of devilment; but it had far-reaching results in three lives. It directed one life toward a tragic romance, and two lives toward hatred and revenge.

Remembering Charley's wish for a greenhorn, as well as his need of a hired man, Jack Tompkins found both of these in Adolph Buck, a youth of eighteen who was a sheepherder. Adolph was a rugged fellow, with scowling brows, deep-set treacherous eyes, and humorless lips that hardly moved when he talked. Under his swagger and boasting he was a coward. 'He's got a yeller streak in him,' Jim Tompkins said, 'as wide as a mule trail.'

One morning Jack rounded the Point and came galloping toward the house, flogging his beast's ears with his hat. He was trembling with anticipation of fun, and bursting with things to be told.

'He's comun!' he shouted at Charley. 'Get set, a greenhorn's comun! He wants a job, but you'n play a trick on him first. Hurry, by God, he's just back there a mile or so!'

'Who is he?' asked Charley, grinning at Jack's eager malice.

'Adolph Buck. Hurry, and we'n play a trick on him. He'll hove in sight any minute now.'

'Is he walkun up?'

'Yes, a-walkun and a-cussun his luck. Pop says he's a coward, so let's fix him good and proper.... Well, what'll we do?'

'Let me think,' said Charley.

'Think fast,' said Jack, looking anxiously down the river. 'Let's scare his daylights out. Let's scare him till he blows his lungs out. We can, sure we can!'

'All right, Jack. Tie your filly up and take that lariat off of your saddle.'

Jack sprang to earth and Charley went inside. He came out with the grizzly pelt. Together they went into the heavy brush by the stable. Two trails led to the stable: one down Burns Creek and one from the house, the latter running through a tangle of choke-berry and hawbush. In a dense narrow part of this trail, Charley spread the lariat in a wide loop, disguising it with grass and twigs; and the other end he tied to a tree.

'When he comes,' said Charley, 'tell him I'm out to the stable. Get him to come down the other trail.'

'All right,' said Jack, his eyes shining.

Upon hands and knees Charley wrapped the huge pelt around him and crawled into undergrowth.

'I'm ready!' he called. 'Go back to the house and wait. Don't touch the rope.'

Hysterical with giggles, Jack went up the north path and then to the house. Two hundred yards into the west, he saw Adolph coming. He clapped hands to his mouth to choke his mirth. In the doorway Lela stood, watching him.

'What's my man up to now?' she asked, frowning at the brush where the stable was hidden.

'Just you wait!' said Jack, agonized by glee. 'Hush!' he whispered. 'Here he comes. Now don't you let off a yeep.'

Adolph came up, swinging his arms and scowling at everything in sight.

'Thought you was pretty damn smart to run off!' he said to Jack. 'Why didn't you let me ride part-way?'

'I forgot,' said Jack, trying to compose his tortured face. 'Charley's down there by the stable. Here, I'll show you the way.'

'To hell with you, son. I'n find my way all right.'

'Here, now!' Jack protested, when Adolph started upon the wrong path. 'That's full rattlesnakes. I'll show you a better way.'

Adolph stopped and looked doubtful.

'I ain't afraid rattlesnakes,' he said.

'You'll get bit in two,' Jack assured him earnestly. 'Charley, he's got bit a dozen times that way. Here, this is the right road down.' He went eastward and pointed to the trail leading out of Burns. Adolph turned and looked at him, suspiciously, but with a tremendous effort, Jack made his face inscrutable.

'All right,' said Adolph, and took the north trail.

As soon as Adolph had vanished, Jack fell to the earth and choked with smothered howls, clutching his mouth and writhing until tears blinded him. This would be the greatest event of his life! Adolph would come tearing out of that thicket with his hair standing up and his flesh on fire.

Charley, meanwhile, was peering out of the undergrowth and giggling like a child. When he heard feet on the path, he uttered a low growl. The feet stopped.

'Hey, Charley!' called a perturbed voice.

Charley was silent. The feet came again, slowly, and again the voice called. Waiting until Adolph had reached the stable, Charley crawled around through the brush and shut off the north trail. Then he shook with savage growls and snarls and deep roars. Adolph gave one desperate yell of terror; and finding his retreat cut off, and not knowing of the other path, he mounted the stable with the alacrity of a cat. Charley shook the brush near him and roared hideously.

'Help!' Adolph bellowed, standing on the stable and shaking with fright. 'Jack, fetch a gun! Charley, help!'

There was a brief silence. Walking to the edge of the roof, Adolph peered down, and he recoiled from what he saw. He saw a great furred shape that looked as large as a house. Then the furious growls came again, roars and hisses and heavy breath; and he saw the beast erect itself and shake the brush. Running to the other side of the roof, Adolph shouted for help, and looked wildly for a path out of the dense timbers; and he saw the trail which ran westward. He felt a beating in the stable, he heard growls that were becoming more savage and hungry. With another shout for aid, he sprang down and took to his heels on the westward path; and quite as Charley had planned, Adolph stepped into the loop, and at the rope's end he was jerked violently backward, and hurled clawing into a thicket of rose briars and thistles. Thinking the beast had overhauled him, he went mad with fear, and his insane cries rang from mountain to mountain. Charley multiplied his hissings and roars; but Adolph did not hear these. He shouted frantic yelps, headlong maddened agony, and he fought with blind power, still convinced that he was in the bear's clutch. He tore wildly at brush, shouting with all his might; sticks gouged his flesh, the dust of weed pods filled his eyes, and blood ran down his face and arms.

Charley then went quickly up the north trail, taking the pelt with him and hiding it in the house. He seized his gun, and, accompanied by Jack, who had laughed until he was white and exhausted, he ran down the other trail until he came to Adolph. Adolph was still fighting like a trapped wolf.

'What's the matter here?' asked Charley.

His loud words sobered Adolph a little. He listened for a moment and again roared for help.

'What you tryun to do!' Charley shouted.

Adolph sat up and looked around him, his face bloody and pale, his body trembling so that his teeth chattered. Then he saw the rope which had captured him; and with something indescribable in his eyes, a blend of shame and fear and rage, he loosened the rope, flung it from him, and strove to stand up. But he still shook so desperately that he sank to the earth and groaned.

'I seen a bear,' he said, almost in a whisper. 'I thought he had me.' He looked back at the stable and listened. 'Where is he?' he asked feebly, his breath wheezing between his teeth.

'He was there,' said Charley soberly. 'I heard him, too. But you scairt him so he's probably busted his brains out against a tree.' He listened. 'I don't hear him,' he said.

For several moments Adolph sat looking at the earth, still bewildered, ashamed; he touched the burning wounds on his face; he rubbed his eyes. Though reassured, he was still deeply frightened.

'Well, let's get another gun,' said Charley. 'You and me, we'll track him and shoot his ears off.'

He and Jack went over the trail, and Adolph followed close behind, shaking from head to feet. When they came upon the level where the house stood, Adolph turned and listened. And suddenly, in spite of all he could do, an uncontrollable fear seized him and he started to run. He went like an antelope westward, never looking back, never pausing save when he stumbled and rolled end over end. He gained Rattlesnake Point and disappeared.

Charley lay upon his back in the front yard and shook with laughter. He laughed until his face was wet with tears, until the sound in his throat was only a hoarse cawing. Imitating him, whom he regarded as the most ingenious soul alive, Jack also lay down and laughed until he wept. Lela stood in the door and watched them with unfriendly eyes. She never forgot the white bloody face of Adolph Buck, or the incredible speed with which he heeled it into the west. She never forgot the devilish joy in Charley's eyes.

She never forgot the terror and the wild flight; but most of all she remembered an event of the hour that followed. She was accustomed to brutal men, to the coarse and earthy ways of pioneers. She had seen passion strip men until they were savage and murderous. But she could not understand the strange mixture in Charley of tenderness and cruelty; his generous sympathy in one hour, his infernal pranks in the next. In a later year, she saw him as a giant of mercy when Joe Hunter and his family were all helpless with smallpox; but in later years, too, she saw him inflict upon human beings such punishment as she had never thought any man capable of.

It was a premonition of these things, and the bitterness of their paradox, that made her turn into the house now and lie upon the bed. She did not weep. She stared at the ceiling, and she felt sick and lost. Charley entered the house, a few minutes later, and knelt at her side. He kissed her hands, a little timidly, as if he questioned his right. He kissed her long curls and murmured endearments. This tall queenly woman was his goddess, his ideal, his anchor; without her, he knew that he would become a drunkard and ride life swiftly to its end. She was the only person he ever loved deeply, save possibly his oldest daughter; and his great love filled his years, became his religion and his church.

And even now, as he knelt there, it was a thing that shook him and made of him a simple child. The cruelty of his nature sank to sleep, and left only an infinite tenderness, a hunger, an emotion like prayer. But the emotion was inarticulate. He did not know how to express it, except by kissing her hands and her curls, by murmuring the old trite words of love, by humbling himself at her feet.

He knew, as he bowed here, that his prank had upset her, that she grieved over his desperate nonsense. But he realized, too, that he could never control the devil within him, or modify his ways, and that it would be folly to try. Two hungers reached out of him: one for the deep and simple moods of love, in which he would feel purged and glorified; and the other for rough experience, in which the distortions of his soul would feed upon another's pain. These two hungers, related in a strange way unperceived by him, were both rooted in his heart. He could have said he was sorry, but he was not sorry, and he was not a hypocrite. He could have promised never to jest again, but the promise would have been a lie, and he never lied to his wife. He gave voice to nothing that he did not mean. His whole life was a rather weird epic of sincerity, of following his impulses, of leading his emotions to those experiences for which they hungered.

And so, while kneeling here, he expressed no regret and made no promise. He tried only to bestow upon her the great tenderness which he felt. When Lela looked at him, she saw nothing in his eyes but warm and lovely things. She looked at the huge form of him, kneeling there; and he seemed to her to be only an overgrown boy, without knowledge of shame and with an insatiable zest for life. Something within him dramatized facts, converted the commonplace into a great spectacle; something within him was untamed and ancient, as if his emotions ran back to a time when all men were brutes, and love stood far ahead.

She turned to him, drawn inescapably into his warmth, his strength. She kissed his mouth and his clean-shaven cheeks, she drew his head to her breast. He fell upon his stomach and put his arms around her. He caressed her body and his face lay in the glory of her hair.

And while they were so, with Charley smelling her curls and feeling that the whole meaning of life was circumferenced by this hour, four-year-old Jed stood back and watched. His small face was dark with resentment. He went to the stove, got the iron lid-lifter, and moved quietly to his father; and with all his might he smote with the iron upon his father's back.

The blow, even in such young hands, was heavy and bruising. Charley roared with surprise and pain; and before he could turn over, Jed smote him again and again. Springing to his feet, Charley looked down at the child; and the child, his eyes dark with hatred, looked up at his father.

'You little beast!' Charley cried, staring at the small determined fist that clutched the iron. He sat on the floor and told Jed to come to him. Jed came, raising the iron as he did so; and he struck such a furious blow that he missed and fell. He recovered his feet, undaunted, eager, and struck again.

'My God!' said Charley, appalled. 'Do you want to kill your old man?'

'Yes,' said Jed, and attempted to strike again.

Then something within Charley snapped; a blind fury gripped him. He seized Jed, with his huge hands on the small throat, and shook the child. He rose to his feet, lifting Jed by his throat, and shook him so savagely that Jed's face turned purple and his eyes bulged. He set Jed down, and Jed fell over, his eyes glazed; and Charley glared at him. Lela remained on the bed, breathless, knowing that interference would be madness. Jed struggled on the floor and got his feet again. He was shaken but undaunted. He picked up the iron and advanced to strike.

'I'll kill you!' he cried, in a shrill voice of anguish and rage. He struck his father's knee and then looked up at his father's face. He smote again and again. He stood there, trembling, baffled. Charley knelt and grasped his son's shoulders, looking into his eyes. He stared for several moments, and he saw there more than he could ever have described. It was utter fearlessness, and a small but deadly hate.

Charley Bridwell faltered in his life only three times. This was the first. He pushed his son from him and left the house. He went to a tree and sat there for a long while.

XI

UP the river one morning came Jeff Briggs, a long lanky fellow, seeking work. Charley hired him at once. He sent him back to the Tompkins place to borrow a team and a set of harness. With an old hand plow, Jeff then turned the sod, pulverized it with a homemade harrow of logs and wooden spikes, and sowed the acres to lucerne. He then went to the valley and bought young fruit trees — apple and plum and pear — and some raspberry and currant and gooseberry shrubs, as well as many kinds of garden seed, and set all these into garden and orchard. To the labor Charley would now and then lend a hand, but for the most part he sat lazily by and gave orders. His only worry was concerned with Jeff's lewd stares at Lela.

At first, Jeff leered at her boldly, and scattered his honeyed words with a prodigal hand. But learning, little by little, that Charley frowned upon his lustful ogling, he became furtive and sly. He would wait until Charley went fishing, or vanished for another reason, and then he would go quickly to the house.

'God, you're a purty woman,' he would say, staring at Lela over a tin drinking-cup. 'For why'd you ever come up here?'

'I like it here,' Lela would say icily.

'Purty as a pitcher,' said Jeff, his hopeful ardor undiminished. 'I'd lope with a woman like you. If you'd say the word, we'd hit the drift.'

'You'd better go to work. If Charley comes in, he might fly in a temper.'

'To hell with Charley,' said Jeff. 'Say, will you look at them-there hands?' He spread his broad hairy hands for her approval. 'Do I look like I'd be runnun from a fat man? Say, I'm a ornery cuss when my Irish gets up.'

'You're paid to work, not to stand there and yammer,' said Lela, nettled by his allusion to Charley's plumpness. 'So run along.'

'Paid to work!' he cried. 'Well, say, and don't I work? Don't I do all the work around here?... God, though, you're some pitcher! I could lope with a woman like you.' He stared at her with fervent eyes.

'Go on to work. We don't want no trouble.'

'Trouble! Say, I'm a reglar tapeworm for trouble. I'm tougher than a hair halter. And when a woman like you's in the case ——'

Lela left him standing there, lustful-eyed and cunning, and went to the river.

Two days later, Jeff sat up in his hard bed under a pine tree, and watched the house. When he saw Charley leave with his fishing-pole, he drew on his trousers and his shoes and slunk around bushes to the house. He entered and surprised Lela upon her knees, putting the children to bed.

'I can't sleep,' he declared, ignoring the children. 'I just think a you all night. All last night I dreamt a you.'

With her back toward him, Lela said nothing. She tried not to listen.

'That's the God's truth,' said Jeff, advancing a step. 'Say, you'll drive me plumb loco. I can't sleep a lick. Your old man's got his crust to a-brung a pitcher like you up here.... Say, Lela ——'

'Don't call me Lela! And go on back to your bed.'

'I can't,' said Jeff, and something desperate was entering his voice. 'I can't sleep a lick. I just think a you all night. I — I — Lela ——'

'I said don't call me Lela!'

Jeff glanced swiftly at the door and toward the river. He swallowed, with his Adam's-apple running up and down, and advanced another step. His loose sensual mouth was twitching, his long hungry arms reached forward, tense and afraid. The children were watching him now. Jed sat up and looked intently in the gloom. Then Lela stood up and turned to face this desperate wooer. Jeff's arms dropped helplessly at his sides; he glanced around and licked his dry lips.

'I can't sleep,' he said feebly. 'I just lay and think if you was in my arms. I'll soon be plumb wall-eyed. Lela!'

'Get back to your bed!' cried Lela, frightened by the passion in his face, the starved glitter of his eyes.

'I can't,' Jeff protested. 'I'll go plumb bughouse. I just lay and think if you was in my arms. I try not to think. I try to sleep. But I can't. I love you, that's it. Lela, I love you!'

The last words were a whisper that rode out on his fierce hot breath. His eyes were greedy, searching; he swallowed again and again, the big lump running up and down his throat. For several moments they stood thus, looking at each other. Lela found him stupid and repulsive, but she was a little pleased, nevertheless, by his earnest avowal of love, and her emotions were strangely stirred. In Charley's face she had never seen such desperate craving.

'You'd better go,' she said, her voice becoming more gentle. 'If Charley finds you here ——'

'I ain't afraid Charley!' he breathed. His addled mind believed now that she loved him, that she was afraid of her husband. 'We'll run away,' he said, and again his long arms came to life, moving toward her, trembling. 'We'n run away now.'

'Get out!' cried Lela.

'Kiss me,' murmured Jeff, convinced beyond all doubt that she was terrorized by her husband. 'Then I'll go to bed. And to-morrow —— Oh, say you love me! Just whisper it, Lela!' He grasped her arm and drew her toward him. Lela recoiled, turning momentarily rigid, and then smote him a burning blow on his face. Jeff fell back, staggered by this turn of events. His eyes glowed with a mixture of lust and idiocy. He looked around, like an animal at bay, and Lela stepped back, her hands reaching for the six-shooter on the wall. Then Jeff approached, crouching a little, staring with drunken eyes at this lovely woman whose bower of hair had transformed him from a plodding animal, from a loveless wandering hobo, into a thing of uncontrollable desire.

He was still approaching, and Lela's shaking hand was reaching for the gun, when Charley's form darkened the doorway. His shrewd mind understood the

situation at once. Another man might have given way
to rage, and wreaked his fury upon the lank body of
this prowler; but not Charley Bridwell. He stood there
and chuckled. It was a mirthless chuckle, unhuman
and diabolic and ruthless. The sound of it unnerved
Jeff more than fury could have done; it filled his mind
with sinister meaning, made him quake with fear. He
withdrew to a wall, feeling blindly for a weapon, his
eyes never leaving Charley's face. Charley advanced,
still chuckling, and drew thirty dollars from his pocket.
He handed the money to Jeff.

'Skin out,' he said. 'Make tracks like you never
made tracks before.'

Without a word, Jeff slunk from the house and
vanished into the moonless west.

Annoyed and distressed by the way men ogled his
wife, Charley decided to finish the work himself. He
plowed irrigation ditches, and built small dikes and
levees upon the slope of his farm; and later, when the
delicate alfalfa shoots appeared, he spent many hours
watering them. He gave care to the old and new trees
of his orchard, pulverizing the soil at their roots, laying
small ditches between the rows; and he broke a plot of
sod for next summer's potato patch. Once this foundation of his future was laid, he knew his labor would be
small: tending his garden, harvesting his twenty acres
of hay, milking his cow. In a few years his sons would
be able to do this work, and he could sit in lazy happiness, now and then slaying a wild beast for food or
gathering a few pelts with which to buy clothes. He

could grow indolently ripe and full, letting the mad world spin toward its catastrophes, letting other men spend their years for broad estates. The seasons of his life would march in quiet cycles. His body would soak up sunshine, drowse through the warm months, and sheathe itself in fat against the cold. He would love his wife and cultivate a peaceful mind....

And so he did, in the following years, as well as he could. If certain events, ripened in darkness or shaped into irony by random jest, took on the black hue of the tragic, led to bitter and unforeseen ends, the fault was not wholly his own. They grew in part out of his cruelty, and even out of his love; but in part, too, they sprang from soil which he never touched. And at the end of his life, when looking back over his years, it seemed to him vulgarly ironic that some of his best intentions had borne the bitterest fruit, whereas none of his thefts, for instance, had given birth to an unhappy hour.

In a later time, when the mountainous country around him, north and east of the river, had been set aside as a federal reserve, and had come to be rich grazing land for cattle and sheep; and when, as a result of this, deer and elk and even bear had been driven to remote places, Charley preyed upon everything within reach. In every summer, until Lela reached her turning point, he ambushed fat wethers and steers and ate them, never bothering to efface brands or dewlaps or earmarks, or to hide the bones. It became commonly known that he used many things which were not his. He made no denials when questioned. His grin was a jolly and cunning admission; but nobody had him arrested, and nobody, save in two instances, seemed greatly to care.

In other matters, too, his transgressions neither haunted nor punished him. When his hay was crotch-deep, he borrowed the machinery wherewith to harvest it, including even pitchforks and hay-knives. From Joe Hunter he borrowed mowing-machine and hayrake, Jackson-fork and derrick cable and wagon, transporting all these with a small rowboat. On one return journey his boat turned over, and he lost nearly half of Joe's wagon in the river; and for days, Joe and his wife dredged the river before recovering their property. On another time he was taking a hayrake home, having between the shafts a nervous animal which he had caught on the Antelope benchland; and the horse became frightened and ran. Charley jumped off the rake seat and saw the terrified beast vanish up the river. When he found the rake, it was completely demolished against a cottonwood. The horse and harness he never saw again. And when Joe inquired about his rake, Charley told him it was a pile of ruins; and when Joe bought a new rake in the next season, Charley borrowed that one also. From Joe he also borrowed flour and sugar, tobacco and ammunition, oats and alfalfa seed, and even clothes; and of these he never repaid an item.

'Joe Hunter,' Charley would declare, 'can't say no. He tries to like hell, but he can't. He's a pretty good guy.'

Time and again, Joe resolved to say no. After

Charley lost the wagon, after he demolished the rake, Joe fell into a long and brooding rage. 'I won't loan him another thing long as I live!' he declared. And when Charley came again, full of sunshine and nonsense, Joe scowled and was silent; and Charley, whose knowledge of men was shrewd, talked for a long while of irrelevant matters. He talked until he saw that Joe's scowling interior was filling with light and good-will; and then, very gently, he insinuated his wish, withdrawing quickly if he saw Joe's brow darken, returning again when the brow had cleared. And he got what he went after. He always did. He was even too sly for Mrs. Hunter, a person with a more invincible will than Joe's, and with a clearer insight into Charley's ways. As a matter of fact, both Joe and his wife loved this lazy shameless man; his visits brought sunshine and laughter into the dark labor of their days. Everybody loved him, save Jed and Adolph Buck.

When Joe and his wife went into angry conference, each inveighing against their parasitic neighbor, they remembered that in times of trouble, in days and nights when sickness lay heavy upon them, it was Charley Bridwell who sprang to their aid. It was Charley who came and cut wood and did the chores, in one bitter dead winter; it was Charley who, upon snowshoes, took his long way into the valley for medicines; and it was Charley, more than any other in this part of earth, who seemed to have boundless sympathy and kindness, even though his heart was sometimes dark and cruel. And their conference of harsh words was softened, little by little, as they thought of his patient heroism; and their memory of him was a warm happiness in their lives.

And others who came to revile him remained to shake his hand. He brought from the Antelope benchland, in each summer, two horses with which to harvest his hay. In the year of 1906 a horse died on his hands, and word reached the owner that Charley had killed it. The owner came up Rattlesnake Trail and to Charley's door. He was a large man, with a stony weatherbeaten face and fearless gray eyes. He hallooed at the house, and when Charley came out, the stranger sat for a little while and looked at him. Then he said:

'I understand you killed one a my horses. Is it the truth or not?'

'How do you know it's yourn?' asked Charley, noting the six-shooter strapped to the man's waist.

'I'll know in a jiffy if I'n see it.'

'All right,' said Charley, 'we'll go have a look.'

He led the man down to the stable and pointed to a pile of hide and bones. The man dismounted and searched the hide. He found his brand on the left thigh. He then looked at the shrunken skull and found another identifying mark. Rising to his full height, he said:

'It's mine.'

'I thought it might be,' said Charley softly. 'Well, it ain't worth much to you now.'

The stranger looked at him in amazement.

'It's mine,' he said. 'I'd like to know what the hell ——'

'Ever notice this thistle in her neck?' interrupted

Charley. He stooped over the carcass. He pointed to a dry ulcerous scar. 'It was a sick nag. I done all I could to save her life. But I never knowed a horse to outlive a thistle.' He turned to Thiel, who stood by him. 'Take this gentleman's horse in and feed him. Then go tell your mother to make dinner for one extra.' He again addressed the stranger. 'You must a-misused this mare. Ever use a sweenied collar on her?'

'No,' said the man, forgetting that he was angry.

'Some one did,' said Charley, speaking as if the mare's death had grieved him. 'Some damn fool ruined her. You'n see how far this hole runs down.'

The man bent over. He stared at the hole which the ulcer had eaten into the beast's neck.

'Yes,' he said, 'I knowed she had a bad thistle.'

'The worst I ever seen,' said Charley. 'But you can't cure a thistle. You just as well try and cure a chicken with its head chopped off. When a horse gets a thistle, you just as well shoot him and snake him off in the brush....'

He talked on and on, quietly; shrewdly watching the man's face; and the man wondered why the mare had not died long ago.

'You must be a kind of vetenery,' he said.

'If anybody'n save a horse's life,' said Charley, 'I can. But there was no savun this bastard's life. She was a plumb goner. When I seen her out on the Antelope Hills, I thought I might save her. But soon as I got her over here and seen how she staggered, I knowed her life wasn't worth a tin hoot. I worked with the bastard night after night. But there wasn't no fight left in her....'

He went into the stable, where the other horse stood before a mangerful of green alfalfa; and the man followed him.

'When I got this-here horse,' said Charley, 'he was just a rack of bones. He's fat now and snorts when you touch him. He's as full of vim and grit as a man who lives on raw eggs.'

He talked of this horse until the stranger got the notion, implied but never stated in what Charley said, that this animal had been rescued from starvation. He began to think of Charley as a kind person who corralled old bony derelicts and fattened them, who gathered sick beasts and tried to save their lives; and it seemed altogether best that his ulcerous mare was dead.

Then Charley drew forth a bottle of whiskey from a hiding-place and the man took a deep drink, his eyes glowing with life as the alcohol found and warmed his stomach. He returned the bottle and wiped his mouth. Charley drank next, and then the man drank again. They went outside and looked at the pile of bones. The man again examined the hide and stared at his brand. He walked around and looked at the withered skull.

'She always was a God-damn no-account,' he said, now speaking resentfully. 'I never got a decent day's work out of the son-of-a-bitch.'

'When they get a thistle,' said Charley, 'you about as well knock them in the head. I'd as live try and save a sick turkey as a mare with a galded neck.'

'It's the truth,' said the man, and he kicked the skull. 'I should a-shot the bitch last summer. I knowed she was a goner.'

'She probably just stood around and et good hay. Them kind's always a dead loss.'

'I should a-blowed her brains out,' said the man, venting his resentment in another kick. 'That's what you should a-done, instead doctorun the bitch. You should a-used a axe on her.'

'But she wasn't mine,' said the cunning Charley. 'I thought I could cure her. I've cured a hell of a lot of them in my day. But I never bucked up against such a plumb goner as this one.'

'You should a-busted her with a axe.'

'But she wasn't mine, I thought mebbe the owner wanted to keep her.'

'Keep her, hell!' the man cried, again smiting the skull. 'I'm glad the son-of-a-bitch is dead.'

They went into the stable and drank again. Then they went to the house, and the stranger told Lela he was glad his old nag was a bunch of bones. She was a dead loss. If he had not kept around him a herd of worthless hacks, eating him out of house and home, he would be a wealthy man now. He always put these matters off, instead of grabbing an axe and doing what any sensible man would do.

He then sat at the table with Charley and his family, and he ate abundantly of green vegetables and fruit and mountain trout.

'After this,' he said to Charley, 'when you want some horses to use a little while, just go out and lasso some of mine. I got some good ones on them hills. Christ, a man'd think I don't have nothun but old sick mares!' He spoke as if he had treated Charley basely, as if he himself had given to this man a sick beast. And when he was ready to leave, he declared again that Charley should go out and choose the best of the lot. He'd rather have his horses well-cared-for, by a man who knew diseases and their cures, than to have them roaming the Antelope Hills, being stolen by Star Valley cowpunchers, or turning their heels up after eating larkspur. He spoke, indeed, as if it would be a favor to him were Charley to catch and work his animals.

'Come up and see us some time,' said Charley. 'Bring your wife and we'll snake out some fish.'

'By God, I will,' the man said. He looked around him with grateful eyes. Then he gave Charley a warm handshake and rode away into the west.

And in such fashion Charley lived, a jolly and contented parasite, who took what he wanted from other folk, and gave in return, not gold, but a sense of humanity and fellowship; who lifted burdens from shoulders, stripped rage away, and sent people from him with memories of kindness and of talk that was friendly and good. The mare, it is true, did not die of ulcer at all. She died one night, after coming in drenched from mowing, because she slipped away and foundered herself on the cold waters of Burns Creek. But there was no sense, Charley reflected, in making a man wretched over a dead event. The truth did not

lie in building the future upon old bones. It did not lie
in feuds and bitter memories, in a sense of defeat and
loss. It lay rather in the lurking sunlit vision, standing
in all the accidents of ill luck and chance. The mate-
rials of misfortune, when turned over and over in the
sun, offered a new certainty of faith, a shining width
of calm; but when pondered in darkness, when brooded
over in the gloomy recesses of a man's mind, they were
black with the elements of death. Such a small matter
as a foundered mare or a smashed hayrake could dwarf
a man's soul, send him down his years with a savage
and futile sense of wrongdoing, of an unfriendly earth
and a pitiless God; unless, indeed, the circumstance
were spread out in the warmth of good-fellowship, and
then withdrawn to the unimportant dead.

And so Charley took, perhaps, less than he paid for,
and gave more than gold could have given. He opened
doors upon paths that men had been blind to. An
atheist himself, he filled people, nevertheless, with that
religion which grows in a sense of kinship, and with
that prayer which is thankfulness for the power to give.
From Joe Hunter he took most, and Joe, himself
struggling in bitter poverty, often wished that Charley
would never again darken his sight. But in later years,
after Charley had been overwhelmed by a tragic hour,
after he had fled and left the Bridwell place desolate
and empty, Joe realized that something fine, a glory
and a faith, had passed from his life.

From cattlemen and sheepmen, Charley also took
much; but in two hours of lazy irrelevant talk, he
would give to these men what neither cattle nor sheep

could have purchased. He gave them a sense of the
deep rich fullness of life: the broad valleys of it,
gardened and quiet, and its great ancient mountains of peace. His talk opened their minds, until
their thoughts looked from clear windows; until their
thoughts reached out to new intimacies, became warm
and living things; until their hunger fed upon the
earth's abundance, and their starved memories fell
away. They would shake with laughter at his droll
jests; they would feel in him the vitality of a beating
heart; and they would sit down with him to meals, no
matter how simple, and eat as they had never eaten
before.

But while he loafed and dreamed down the years,
and became a legend in four counties, his wife retired
into silence, and his children ran wild. His infrequent
but violent cruelty, as well, perhaps, as his lazy ways,
became midwife and nurse to the desperate proud life
of his second son. Before he was fifteen, Jed Bridwell's
name made timid folk quake; and it made even the
bolder ones stop in their speech and look thoughtful
for a long while.

'Him!' women cried, and shuddered. 'Thank God,
I ain't got no son like him! I'd go crazy as a bedbug if
he was my son.'

'He's a little beast,' one would say. 'A wildcat,
that's what he is. I don't know why God ever lets
such unhuman people be born.'

'If he was mine ——'

'Oh, yes, if he was yourn! What would you do?
Well, what *could* you do?'

'I don't know. I'd straighten him up some ways. My Lord, you know what he done when my husbun was up there?'

'No, but I can guess. I got my ideas what a little beast like him would do.'

'And so handsome,' the other mourned. 'A finer-lookun lad I never did see.'

'Oh, sure, good looks. But angels ain't made out of good looks. He was borned with a devil in him.'

'Ten devils, I say. One devil couldn't never do all the things he's done...'

And so Jed's name, like his father's, became one to conjure with. His life became a saga of fearlessness and hate.

Book II
JED

BOOK II
JED
I

UPON that day when Jed was choked, after striking his father with the stove iron, something happened within him. His emotions darkened, and lived and grew in darkness. His father's face, convulsed by rage, hung like a picture in his memory; and from that hour, Jed felt for him a deadly hatred, and this hatred fed upon brutal events until it filled his life.

But even before that hour, Jed had been a sullen lad who never wept and rarely smiled. Together with the Bridwell lust for devilment, he inherited the deep brooding intensity of his mother; and these two made of him a strange child. When only a babe, he gave way to fury that appalled Lela, that made Charley call him a fiend in human skin. And it was perhaps because Charley recognized in his son much of his own violent emotion that he conceived for him a strong dislike. This dislike, which Jed felt more certainly as he grew older, encouraged and fostered the morbid side of him.

Everything around him, for that matter, invited him to solitude or to reckless deeds. The great mountains, the untamed headstrong river, the wild animal life and the lonely blockade of winter months — he felt the power of all these, and their ruthlessness, and their savage ways. He took the spirit of them into his soul. The people whom he met, besides his own kin, were coarse in speech and thought. Sly sheepherders became his tutor, feeding his hungry imagination, suggesting deeds that he had never done. The early events of his life, often the tasks which his father gave him to do, shaped his emotions into a pattern of pride and revenge.

And so he grew, schooled by savagery. Cruelty in his life was a meaningless word. Suffering and pain he was accustomed to from his first years. The agony of a tortured thing meant no more to him than the flow of the river or the cutting down of a tree; and he looked upon death as calmly as he looked upon life.

It was commonly declared, in talk about him, that he was not only incredibly brutal, but that he took devilish pleasure in watching grief or the prolonged suffering of a dying thing. This surmise was wholly false. He never tortured a creature for the joy of seeing it writhe. He never thought of the pain at all. The reason for his wild doings was a more subtle one, and never understood by those who condemned him. He was an artist, matching his wits against those of man and beast. When, by some cunning ingenuity, some skillful plan, he trapped a coyote or brought a live vulture to earth, humiliated a man whom he disliked or outraged a child for whom he had contempt, his joy was profound; but it was never joy in the cruelty itself. The pain was incidental. It was entirely beyond his concern, save as it was a visible measure of his triumph.

He became an artist in these matters because he
hated his father and wished to excel him. If his father
had not played pranks, if he had not tied elk bones to
the tails of mice, terrorized greenhorns and humiliated
insolent wayfarers, Jed would never have done so.
Devoted to his mother and jealous of his father, he
watched Charley's doings; and he saw unmistakably
that the man took most pride in his malignant jests.
Jed was consumed, therefore, by a wish to excel his
father's cunning ingenuities.

And he did.

His first major prank, undertaken when he was six,
almost cost him his life. A sheepherder, riding a mare
and leading a pack-mule, drew up one morning at the
Bridwell door. He went inside to talk with Charley,
and Jed walked around the beasts, wondering if he
could steal something or frighten them into the river.
When he walked behind the mule, at a safe distance,
the mule struck at him with a lean hind leg. Jed
looked at the mule and considered. It was his desire to
have the mule kick at him repeatedly.

Near by was the pit where Silas Bane had dug for
gold. Jed got a sharp stick and crawled down into this
pit. He then told Thiel to back the mule against the
bank so he could jab its heel. His brother led the beast
over to the hole; he turned him around. Whereupon,
lying belly downward under the bank, Jed reached over
with his stick and thrust it against the mule's heel. The
mule struck, his powerfully muscled leg passing over
Jed. Thiel bent over and roared, but Jed never laughed

when executing one of his plans. His face was grave and thoughtful. He pushed his stick up and jabbed the heel again and again; and each time the leg came out like a sudden gray streak above him. He liked the threat, the imminence of death. He jabbed again, and now the mule kept kicking, as if its leg were a wound-up mechanism. Then the beast became unmanageably restive and turned away.

'Back him around,' Jed ordered. 'I could see blood on his foot.'

Thiel struggled with the mule and swung him around. Jed thrust again at the sore heel, but the animal did not strike. Encouraged by this, Jed became bolder. He climbed head and shoulders above the bank. He was preparing for a more vigorous thrust when the mule turned its enraged eyes backward and saw him. It kicked swiftly, a clean powerful blow; and the hoof struck Jed squarely above the right eye and knocked him headfirst into the pit.

Thiel ran to the brink. Jed was sitting up, with blood washing down his face, over his clothes. The gaping wound spurted blood, and Jed put his hand over it, trying to stop the flow. He wiped blood from his left eye — his right eye was blinded — and looked up at his brother.

'Don't tell the old man,' he said, speaking calmly. 'I'll be all right in a minute.'

But Thiel was so horrified by the sight that he ran crying to the house. Then Jed heard the running of many feet. His father sprang down into the pit and seized him, and Jed fought to be free. He was humiliated by this accident. His plan had miscarried, and he was now being trundled like a babe.

'Let me go!' he yelled.

He fought like a wildcat, and Charley shook him until his teeth clicked. He was carried into the house. The sheepherder held him next, and upon the wound, Charley placed a large dripping quid of tobacco and bound it there with torn strips of a towel. Jed was then made to lie down. His face was white and sullen, but he was happy, because Lela sat by him and held his hands.

This wound left an ugly crooked scar that cut across the outer corner of his eyebrow. It added to the savage expression of his face, but also, in a strange way, it made him more handsome, especially after he had grown to manhood. Like a symbol of his dark and reckless years, it lay on his brow and gave an alluring charm to his scowl. And it also filled him with hatred of mules, upon one of whose tribe he later wreaked a horrible vengeance.

In the next summer, Charley's acres of lucerne drank the air and sunshine; the slender stalks thickened and pushed their roots downward; and he was lazily contemplating the green young life when a horde of thieves closed in. These were the woodchucks. They came from holes on the river's bank, down the northern mountain-side, and from their rocky retreats in Rattlesnake Point. Many of them migrated to the field and dug their homes there. And early in every morning, and in every twilight, they mowed the hay with their sharp teeth and devoured it. Day by day their areas grew larger, as if fire-swept; and Charley saw that something would have to be done.

'You lazy wallopers,' he said to his sons. 'Why don't you earn your board and keep? Skin out there and kill them greedy-guts.'

'How?' asked Thiel, looking at his brother.

'Set your traps and then bust them on the head.'

'But we ain't enough traps,' said Thiel.

'Go down to Jim's and borrow some. Big lubbers like you, standun there askun me how. Use your wits. Ain't you got any brains at all?'

'Brains!' cried Jed, scowling at his father. 'Sure we got brains. We got as many brains as you.'

'Oh, you think so, my fine lad? Then prove it.'

Jed lost no time trying to prove it. With Thiel he went to the Tompkins place and returned laden with traps; and in his valiant effort to save the hay, he found his first great opportunity to show his skill, to match his cunning against the cunning of wild things. He set traps at the mouth of holes and in runways; and every morning he would go out early, with a kingbolt in his hand, and smite the heads of the trapped creatures until he had crushed their skulls. Though a rugged lad, he was only seven; and sometimes he had to beat a long while upon the older and tougher beasts. Often they cried, but Jed gave no heed to their cries. He smote until the quivering carcass was still, and then he removed it and threw it into the brush by the river. Now and then they snapped and struck at him, and he liked those best which strove to fight. Opposition added zest to his murderous doings, gave the relish of combat, and made his victory sweeter.

Often he found other kinds of animals in his traps: porcupines and skunks and weasels, or now and then a pheasant or songbird or hawk, and infrequently a rattlesnake. No matter what he found, he dispatched it and set his traps again. Out of this summer's earnest labor came some amusing adventures.

He went out one morning to the river-bank, while Thiel took the north side of the field, and found in a trap the largest skunk he had ever seen. The skunk was held by one hind foot, and as soon as Jed appeared, it showed a desire to fight. Remembering a former encounter, he tried to approach the animal face to face, now running to the right or to the left when it turned its hinder toward him. Unsuccessful in this, he gathered rocks and stoned the creature; and when it lay sprawled as if lifeless, he came up with the kingbolt and delivered his mightiest blow on the skull. He struck again and again, but the eyes remained open, staring at him. He fell into a horrible rage because the eyes would not close. The air reeked with the beast's poison and scalded his eyes, was a ghastly odor in his breath, a heavy thick stench in his clothes and in all his being. But he fought on, desperately, bringing his iron down in vicious thudding blows on the head. He beat the body until the flesh was as soft as jelly; and again he smote the skull. He began to cry, but his tears were tears of fury because of the burning pain in his eyes, the rottenness in his breath. Rubbing his eyes with one hand, he struck wildly with the other.

'You son-of-a-bitch!' he screamed, stroking with all his might.

Then he searched about him and found a heavy stone. Wielding this with both hands, he brought it crushingly upon the carcass; lifted it above his head and again brought it down. He looked at the creature and saw that its eyes were glassy.

Instead of going home at once, he went to his other traps. In one of these he found an overgrown porcupine, splendidly regal in its mantle of quills, erected, gleaming. He walked around and around the creature, and it strove to keep its broad flat tail toward him. When Jed poked it with a long stick, the tail came down in a sudden heavy blow. He hardly knew how to dispatch this animal. He wanted to do the job alone; and for a little while he hurled stones at the bright dangerous back. The small black eyes looked at him like two cunning beads. He got a club and smote the head. But after several minutes, the creature seemed to be as full of life as ever, and Jed shouted to his brother for help. When Thiel came, Jed declared angrily:

'I can't beat him to death a-tall. He gets more alive all the time.'

'Good Jesus, you stink!' cried Thiel, sniffing the air.

Around their parents, the Bridwell lads never used obscene or profane language; but when alone, they used all the oaths they had ever heard, taking pride in their store of abusive terms.

'Good Jesus yourself!' cried Jed, standing sturdily

on his legs, considering this problem. 'I been battlun a skunk.'

'Did you kill him?' Jed shrugged his seven-year-old shoulders. 'A porkypine,' Thiel added, 'is tough as a hair halter. Mebbe we'd best let the old man kill it.'

'—— the old man!' cried Jed. 'We'n do it ourselves.'

He gave instructions; and with a forked stick, Thiel prodded the creature and maneuvered it upon its back. He held it there, with the prongs against its soft belly, and Jed knelt by its throat. Taking from his pocket the blade of a knife, he cut the animal's throat, thrusting the blade farther and farther into the wound and the warm blood until he found the jugular vein. He stood up, his hands wet with blood, and wiped the blood on his homemade trousers. The dying creature gurgled and blew a froth of blood from its nose. There must be a better way, Jed declared, to kill these beasts. It was nonsense to whale away at them for half an hour.

'Sure,' said Thiel, who was hardly more than an echo of his aggressive brother.

'We could poke these woodchucks' eyes out. They couldn't see to eat no lucerne if they was blind.'

'I guess not,' said Thiel doubtfully, repelled by such a savage notion.

'We could blind them and let them go.'

'The old man might not like that,' suggested Thiel.

'To hell with the old man.'

They went to the house, each reflecting upon the matter. When Jed entered the house, Charley let off a roar of astonishment.

'Get out!' he cried. 'Go wash yourself!'

Jed scowled at his father and then went to Burns Creek. Using mud for soap, he scrubbed his face and hands. He sniffed his clothes and seemed to smell nothing at all. He beat at his clothes, to send the air through them; he pulled them away from his body to let them ventilate. But when he entered the house again, his father met him with a bellow of rage.

'Vamoose!' he cried. 'Take them duds off and wash them.'

Lela found some other clothes: a torn shirt and some ragged patched trousers, and with these Jed went again to the creek. He put his foul clothes under water and piled stones on them. He lathered his sturdy body with mud; he filled his thick dark hair with mud and held his head under the water; and when he seemed to smell fresh and clean, he put on his ragged garments and went again to the house. But the odor of skunk clung, as if it had entered his body and breath; and for many days he carried it with him.

The Bridwells at this time had a dog, a lean starved mongrel left here by a sheepherder. One morning Jed took this dog with him when he went to tend his traps; and upon finding another porcupine captured, he encouraged the dog to attack. The dog needed much encouragement. For a few moments he barked in an earnestly dismal way, as if remembering his old experiences with quills; he lifted his face to the sky and wailed. When Jed said 'Sikkim!' and clapped his hands, the gaunt hound dived yelping into brush, as if on the scent of prey. He came back and looked at Jed with eloquent eyes, as if imploring him not to question his courage and to be reasonable in his whims. But Jed was unrelenting. He attacked the creature with a stick, and the dog meanwhile set up a forlorn howling, stopping now and then to see what success Jed was having.

'Sikkim!' cried Jed. 'You damn coward, sikkim!'

When Jed turned the porcupine sprawling on its back, the dog gave one desperate yelp and sprang to the combat. He tried to get his teeth in the soft un-quilled belly, but he was too eager and he fumbled. The flat gleaming tail smote his face and left upon it a roach of quills. Then the dog abandoned discretion and buried his dripping jaws into flesh. When the battle was done and the porcupine lay dead, with its belly ripped open from throat to rump, the dog turned away and began to whimper, his lust for slaughter gone, his lips and tongue and jaws bedded with quills.

Jed looked at him with contempt. He had contempt for anything, including himself, that got worsted in a fight. He went to the house with the dog, and when Charley saw it he shook with laughter. Then he scowled at his son and asked:

'What you been up to?'

'Nothun,' said Jed. 'It's the pooch is been up to things.'

Charley bound the dog's legs with stout cord. Then with a pair of pliers he set about extracting the quills. Blood ran from the creature's mouth, and the froth of madness was on his lips. When the operation was done, and the cord removed from his legs, the dog vanished westward and was never seen again on the Bridwell place.

II

With his brother's aid, Jed captured and killed most of the woodchucks. Some of the older ones were too sly for him. They evaded his traps, no matter how cunningly he set them; and in late afternoon they would forage in the hay, sitting up now and then to see if danger lurked. Jed was at the end of his wits. 'We need a gun,' he told Thiel. Then he thought of a plan.

He dug holes in the runways, which led to the mountain or the river's bank, and over these holes he placed a cover of slender branches, grass and old leaves, and a sheet of earth. The woodchucks were deceived and tumbled into the pitfalls, but they were also ingenious in a way he had not thought of. Finding themselves trapped, they dug into the earth and upward and escaped.

'Judas God!' Jed exclaimed, when he learned of this. He sat by one of his futile decoys and planned again. For several days he was sullen, having been outwitted and humiliated. His dreams were full of woodchucks that sat up and barked at him with insolent triumph, until he would wake and then lie sleepless, searching his mind for a plan. During the days he would go off alone and think until his head ached. His self-esteem demanded that he conquer these creatures, and pile their bones with the bones of their fellows. 'Let's ask the old man what to do,' Thiel said, but his brother scorned this suggestion. He said he would find a way or drown himself. He would find a way, or he would jump into the river and bash his head on a rock.

He again dug deathtraps, but he lined them now with flat stones, so that they were floored and walled with rock; and again he covered them artfully with brush and earth. Into these holes even the oldest and wisest fell, even the patriarchs of the tribe, and they remained there. Jed looked down at them and he was full of joy. He despised them and their dark terrified eyes. And there was no sense, he told Thiel, in killing them at all: they would throw earth in and bury them alive. But Thiel objected. His less ferocious nature recoiled from a thought of smothered agony and death.

'You're chicken-hearted,' Jed declared. 'You're like a girl. You should ought to wear a dress.'

'It ain't that,' Thiel lied. 'I want a-see how many bones we'll have. I want the old man to see.'

This notion appealed to Jed. He also wanted the old man to see. And so he crushed the captives and dragged them forth.

When most of the woodchucks had become a heap of bones, Jed looked around him for other worlds to conquer. He had outwitted and annihilated an entire tribe of thieves. His fierce ego had grown mightily in its exercise of skill. And against what, he wondered, could he now match himself?

He answered this question one late August morning while gathering his traps. In one of the stronger traps he found a rattlesnake. The steel jaws were clamped against the reptile's belly, squeezing it so tightly that hide met hide. It seemed to be almost severed. But it was still alive. It was still alert and dangerous.

Jed had never killed a snake. He had never studied one at close range. He now sat and looked at it for a long while. He stared at its flat ancient-looking face, at its pale cold eyes, at its black forked tongue that shot out at him again and again. He had in snakes, he realized, a more deadly enemy than woodchucks; a more powerful and cunning foe than those fat-bellied creatures that did no more than squeal when he struck them. And he was ashamed for having taken so much pride in the destruction of things that had no power to fight. Hereafter, if he trapped woodchucks, he would do so unwillingly, fully aware of the unequal struggle. Hereafter he would pit himself against foes worthy of him: snakes and porcupines and skunks and badgers and wildcats. And when he grew up, he would match himself against valley greenhorns and grizzlies and mountain lions. Such feeble warriors as woodchucks and weasels, and perhaps even skunks, he would leave to Thiel.

When he heard a rattle, he crawled around and looked at the tail. Affixed to this tail he saw the rattles, encased in something that looked like a withered pod; and with a gesture of contempt, he seized the rattles and tore them from the body. He looked then for blood, but there was none. He crawled back and stared again at the deadly face, wondering if there was any blood in a snake. With his blade he thrust into the flesh. There was no blood on the knife when he withdrew it; there was only a sort of sticky fluid. He hardly knew what to think of these creatures. He knew they were venomous, that one blow of their lethal fangs would cause violent death; that they lived on mice and rats, and even larger game, and swallowed their victims whole. But why they crawled on their bellies, why they were legless and prone, and why they never blinked their eyes, were curious matters that he did not understand. Nevertheless, he saw in these long gleaming butchers a worthy foe, an enemy equipped with death in its mouth, and he rejoiced in this opportunity to show his skill. He looked into the crafty eyes watching him and declared war on the entire kingdom of rattlesnakes.

He studied this snake for a long while, as if to read in its hideous face all the secret notions of its kind. He intended to kill it soon and examine its mouth; but now he was interested in the eyes, in those small lidless mirrors of the creature's soul. They fascinated him, they drew him nearer, in spite of his will. They were unwavering, strangely hypnotic, and they shone with malignant hatred. They were like liquid venom. His father said that snakes looked at birds until the birds were helpless; and Jed now felt that this was so. Now and again the tongue shot out at him, but save for this movement, the head and body were motionless as stone. There was a horrible fascination, too, in this tongue: it flickered like small black lightning. It came out of that stony mouth, wrought its speech of challenge, and vanished; and the eyes seemed to watch for the tongue's effect.

Jed began to feel drugged and heavy in his limbs. His eyes were so unblinking and attentive that they burned. He seemed to feel a change going on within him, as if wild tongues of the jungle were teaching their secrets and the ruthless ways of the jungle-heart; as if this bitter tongue were licking into his blood, leaving its poison there, and its desperate tamelessness. Though they were enemies, the spirit of this snake was his spirit; their two souls reached back anciently to the same dark source. Their ancestry was the same wilderness of desire. This was something which he vaguely felt, but did not understand. The emotion which filled this hour of looking, eye to eye, was one in which he felt kinship, even with reptiles. But he felt, too, an ageless enmity, as if for innumerable years he had been defending his life against such paralyzing eyes as these, such forked tongues. And when he stood up, at last, he was trembling with fury and with a lust for battle.

He got a flat stone and threw it under the snake as it rose to strike. With a boulder in his hands, he stood above the snake and waited until it sank upon the stone; and when he struck, the blow crushed the head and throat. When the thing was certainly dead, he sat by it and examined its mouth, being careful not to get its poison in open scratches on his hands. He looked at its fangs and its tongue and into its narrow throat; at its ugly smashed face and eyes. And having satisfied himself of the structure of all these, he took the snake out of the trap and laid it like a gray rope over a stone.

But it was not in this summer that he engaged his

enemies in death. The snakes all seemed to vanish while he was laying his plans; autumn came and bitter cold. Through the winter he carried his dream of conquest. Sitting by the fire, moody and silent, he visioned himself as a mighty warrior, piling dead reptiles mountain-high. He saw himself tying them end to end, and stretching the rope of their dead bodies from Rattlesnake Point to the mouth of Burns. He saw himself using them as quirts to flog a certain sheepherder whom he despised.

Sometimes he would go out, barefooted, into the white winter world, and look for something to conquer; but there was nothing at all. Those howling dervishes called coyotes and wolves excited him with their snarling rage; the midnight cry of a wildcat made his heart leap; but he had no weapons against these. He looked at his father's rifle, wishing he might take it and go forth, or that he might snare beasts in traps and club their heads off. Some day he would, but not now. He had to be a boy now and have his ears scrubbed. He had to busy himself now with such dull matters as wood-chopping and water-carrying, and with learning to read and write.

Of his dreams he spoke to no one. He regarded his brother as a coward who belonged in the house. He had already climbed taller trees, jumped off higher ledges, and offered a stiffer insolence to their father's wrath. He had dared everything suggested by Thiel and had gone him one better. No: Thiel had the courage of a groundhog and the ingenuity of a fool hen....

'What are you thinkun about?' his mother would ask, troubled by his long silences.

'Nothun,' Jed would say, aroused from his wolfish dreams.

'He's thinkun his girl,' said Beth, giggling.

Jed had once gone fishing with a Tompkins lass, a little pugnosed girl of four. He now looked scornfully at his sister.

'And you,' he said, 'I guess you're thinkun your feller.'

'Sure,' said Beth, remembering an hour when a sheepherder fondled her on his lap.

'You're a fool,' Jed declared, and returned to his dreams.

Charley Bridwell had strange notions of education. He wanted his children to be able to read and write; but above all, he wanted them to be able to spell any word in the English tongue. His idea of a well-educated person was one who could spell anything. Among other books he had got a red-backed speller, used in the upper grades; and before any of his children were nine, they could correctly spell any word in the book, even though they knew the meanings of very few. They pronounced these words, too, in Charley's own fashion; and they were encouraged to use them in speech. Before Jed was seven, he could spell paragon and regeneracy and contemplate, tuberculosis and dissonance and fundamental; but he had no idea of what they meant. It was Charley who tutored them in spelling; it was he who made them display their knowledge, much to the astonishment of visitors. This astonishment made him glow with pride.

Taking the red-backed speller, he would say:

'Well, let's see what you know. Thiel, spell de-nun-see-a-shun.... Correct. Now spell an-thro-pol-o-gee. ... That's right. Jed, spell fill-o-soph-i-cul.... That's it. Now spell mag-nif-i-sens.... Mebbe,' Charley would say, addressing a gaping visitor, 'you'd like to try and stick them. Don't try and be easy. Any damn word you'n think of.'

'Why,' the sheepherder would say, 'I don't know any words big as them. By God, they could spell any words I know, easy as fallun off a log. I ain't had much learnun.'

'Well, try one,' Charley would urge. 'If they can't spell it, I'll skin them alive.'

'Well... well, let me think. I can't seem to think a nothun hard. Well, I guess mebbe they'n spell such a word as lightnun. Now that's a word always stuck me.'

'Lightnun!' cried Beth scornfully, and she and Thiel spelled it in chorus.

'Good Lord!' said the shepherd, appalled.

'Try them again,' said Charley.

'All right. But, by Jesus, that's the biggest word I know. I never had much learnun, for a fact. But mebbe I'n think.... Can they spell — uh — larryat?'

'L-a-r-i-a-t,' said the children.

The shepherd mopped his brow.

'Was that right?' he asked of Charley. 'Is larryat spelled that way?'

'Try them again,' Charley urged. 'Sure, you'n stick them. And if you do I'll skin their pelts off.'

'Well,' said the visitor desperately, 'let me think hard.... There's another word always stuck me. It means handy-like.... Oh, yes, convenyunt, that's it. Can they spell it?'

Beth and Thiel spelled it in one voice.

'Well,' he said, 'I guess they'n spell about everything.' He looked at them with wondering eyes. 'And do they know the meanuns all them words?'

'Sure,' said Charley. 'Ask one.'

'Well, any them first words.'

Charley opened the book.

'Beth,' he said, 'what's the meanun of denunciation?' She pondered for a few moments.

'A big noise,' she said. 'A big noise like a thunderstorm.'

'Is that right?' Charley asked the herder.

'Good God,' he said, 'don't ask me. I never heared it before.'

'Thiel, what's the meanun of fundamental?'

'That,' said Beth, 'means — it means fun, just silly fun.'

The meanings which Beth and Thiel gave to words were suggested by their sound or by the separate sense of their parts. Such words as contemplate suggested nothing to them, and when asked to define one of this sort, they blurted the first meaning they could think of. And encouraged by their strange father, they sometimes used in talk words that were meaningless to them, save as they invested them in their own way; and after staring incredulously, people went home and told great tales of the Bridwell children. The stories grew until it was declared that Charley's family, even though it had never seen the inside of a schoolhouse, was as well educated as folk anywhere.

After being called a fool, Beth stared at her brother, thinking meanwhile of stupendous words. 'You're a significance,' she said. This abuse brought no response; and after deliberating again she added: 'You're a dissipate.'

Jed did not reply. He sat with his chin cupped in his hands, thinking of snakes and vultures. After murdering all the snakes, he planned to assault things of the air. If he could capture hawks and vultures, and perhaps an eagle, he would put his old man's small doings to shame....

'He's a fulcrum,' said Thiel.

'Sure he is,' said Beth. 'He's that and a random, too.'

Because any one, Jed was reflecting, could take a gun and shoot things. It was no feat at all to knock creatures over with powder and lead; to step out of the door and bang away; or even to catch them in traps. But to invade the air, in a way yet to be thought of, and bring to earth those creatures that flew with the sun would be a trick to make his old man gasp. He looked at his father, remembering the man's boasting and his pranks, and his hearty laughter whenever he thought of Jed's battle with the skunks, or his being kicked end over end by a mule. What, he asked himself, had his old man ever done that was worth talking about....

'Jed's thinkun his girl,' said Beth again, and she giggled. 'Jed's thinkun his girl, Jed's thinkun his girl.'

Jed rose and went over to her.

'Now you shut up!' he cried. 'I'll smack your jib.'

'Oh, you want a-fight, mebbe.'

Jed wanted to wrestle with her. He liked to struggle with his sister and feel his hands on her warm flesh. To do so was pleasurable, though he didn't know why. A sheepherder, grinning lewdly, had told him he should, and that he ought to do other matters that were dark in Jed's mind. 'Throw her down,' the herder had said. 'Look and see what a girl's like. I bet you don't know what a girl's like.' 'I sure do!' Jed had cried contemptuously. 'I seen her all over. I know.' 'Well, I'll tell you what you'n do,' and he had told Jed what he could do; but Jed had not understood very well. Still, he had liked to think of doing it. And he was thinking of the matter now, while staring at Beth in a way that troubled her.

'What you want?' she asked.

'I want you should shut your jib.'

'Well, I won't. Just want away, but I won't. See'—and she opened her mouth until he could see the darkness of her throat.

'Stop it!' he cried furiously, and struck her.

'Here!' said Charley, who was lying on the floor, spitting juice into a crack. 'What's the matter you kids?'

'She won't shut her mouth,' Jed declared.

'He wants I should shut my mouth,' said Beth.

'Leave her alone,' said Charley.

'Get your lessons,' said Lela, who was preparing supper.

Jed looked at his sister, baffled, eager. He seized her and began to struggle. She embraced his head, and he put his arms around her and fell to the floor. He lay on top of her, still struggling, and she kicked at him with her legs and still held his face against her breast.

'Stop your racket!' bellowed Charley. 'Jed, let her alone! Jed!'

Jed rose from her body and sat again by the fire. When he looked at Beth, she made a face at him and thumbed her nose. There was something in her eyes that thrilled him. Well, he could do nothing now. But when summer came, he would get her alone somewhere, and then God help her!

III

AFTER the snows melted, Jed, now a rugged lad of eight, went eagerly to work. He set traps for woodchucks because his father commanded him to do so; but he gave his enthusiasm to the extermination of rattlesnakes. Many of these he stoned to death. But after a while he tired of this method; it was not cunning enough. He desired, moreover, to take some of these creatures alive; to study them, to see how long they could live without food; to see in what manner they would die.

And so, out in the brush by the river, he built an enclosure of stones, setting the foundation in earth and plastering the walls with mud. His prison, when finished, was six feet square and its walls were four feet high. He next made a lariat of stout cord. Coming upon a snake, he would maneuver it until the creature lifted its head and throat; and then he would throw at it with his loop. In this fashion he captured several; but when he started to drag them, the smooth bodies slipped out of the loop and got away.

Failing in this method, he decided to become more daring. Gathering some perforated tin, which Silas Bane had used in sifting gold from gravel, together with wire and a pair of old scissors, he went alone to a wooded retreat and fashioned a suit of armor. He cut the tin into parts, and after shaping each part to his limbs or body, he laced them together with wire.

When completely dressed in his suit of mail, only his head and hands and feet were exposed. For his hands he took a pair of his father's tough buckskin gloves; for his head and feet he had no covering at all.

Taking his armor with him, he went along the river so that none could see, and emerged at the Point. Then he donned his suit and gloves and looked for a snake. When he approached one, it crawled off, sounding its evil warning and shooting with its tongue. Without hesitating, save only to look at his armor and see that it was all right, Jed ran forward; and when he came near, the snake stopped and reared. Jed paused for a moment, and the snake wavered before him, ready to strike. He advanced two quick steps, his gloved hands ready to seize. He heard a sudden sharp blow, the sound of fangs against tin; he saw the gray coiling creature, but he was unable to grasp it; and again he heard a strike. He sprang back, then, fearful of being bitten in his naked feet or throat. The snake was still there, rearing its deadly body, licking with its tongue. Jed sprang forward again, but the thing evaded him like a supple shadow, and struck repeatedly at his legs. Baffled, furious, Jed leapt back.

After considering, he went to the river and got a long willow forked at one end. He found another reptile and engaged it in battle. Instead of advancing now within close range, he attacked with the stick, striving to pin the creature between the prongs. And at last he did. Forcing the prongs against earth, with the gleaming body between them, he went forward, sliding the willow through one gloved hand. He approached from the tail-end, but the body coiled up and backward, ready to strike. Shaking the tin of his right arm until it came down over the glove's gauntlet, and grasping the willow with his left hand, with his right he quickly seized the throat and choked it. Holding the throat in his right hand, grasping the smooth cold body in his left, he carried the snake to his prison.

In this way he captured so many that the floor of his prison came to be a mass of coiled bodies and hideous alert heads. And in time, too, he threw his armor away, and used only the gloves and the forked stick. Into his captives he tossed, now and then, the disemboweled carcass of a woodchuck or dead ground squirrels. The other snakes for miles down the river he hunted and stoned. He preserved the rattles of each, hiding them under the naked roots of a pine; and before his labor was done, in this and in following years, he had enough rattles to fill a pail. He reduced Rattlesnake Point to a mere name; because in later years, nobody could find a reptile between Burns Creek and the Tompkins place.

Often he would sit on the stone wall, staring with pride into his venomous den. His breath would come slow and deep, and his eyes would darken, as he sensed fully their tamelessness and their power. He loved their jungle ferocity, and the lidless cunning hatred of their eyes.

And at last he was not content to watch them. He wanted to stroke their glittering bodies, to stare at close range into their evil eyes and mouth. He was even tempted to cover himself wholly with tin and to go down and sit among them, laughing at each futile hiss and blow; to conquer them until they would not strike at all, until they would lie there, defeated, undone. This desire, which seemed to him at first to be madness, grew in his heart until it became an obsession; lay like a coiled lust in his dreams; made him tremble until sweat stood on his brow. He felt that he had captured but had not conquered these creatures; that even though imprisoned they regarded him with contempt. He fought against the wish. He fought it for days, with sullen stubbornness. He strove to give his time and his thoughts to other matters. But in the end he yielded, feeling that he must go down into the den, even at the risk of his life; feeling that he must humiliate these proud things until they were abject and beaten.

For many days he made preparations, taking almost as much joy in these as in the thought of his daring adventure. With unfailing patience he made tin boots for his feet and legs; he doubled the thickness of his armor; and with Thiel standing by, aghast, he climbed over the wall and descended, kicking the bodies away so that he could stand on earth. To his astonishment, not a reptile struck. They coiled away from him, and some of them did not even thrust forth their tongues. He asked Thiel for a stick; and with this he prodded them, he struck at their faces. But they lay in a helpless mass, conquered, debased.

Jed climbed out and threw his armor away. He was satisfied. Peace filled his mind and pride looked out of his dark eyes. He had mastered rattlesnakes, and henceforth he would have no interest in them. He wondered what he could conquer next.

He conquered the river next, but this was a victory which he had thrust upon him.

When Thiel told Beth of Jed's descent into the pit, and when Beth reported the matter to her father, Charley cried out in rage. He had become more and more distressed and annoyed by his reckless son, of whose doings he had report time and again; and he resorted to a discipline peculiar to him. Calling his sons, he asked:

'Ain't you brats got a thing to do? Well, I'll give you something to do. Come along.'

He went toward a long deep eddy below Burns Creek, and the boys followed, without any notion of what lay ahead. Thiel said they were in for it. 'Judas God, he intends to beat us again!'

Jed shrugged. Twice in his life he had been brutally flogged by his father; but he suffered punishment without a whimper, quietly biding his time.

'You think?' whispered Thiel.

'I don't give a tin hoot,' Jed declared. 'My time'll come. My time'll come, and then I'll do him up good and proper.'

'But we ain't done nothun,' said Thiel, whose less rugged body withered under the rod.

'Shut up. What's a beatun anyhow!'

'But we ain't done nothun,' Thiel persisted, remembering the way Charley had looked at them.

'I know it. But we'll be big some day. Then we'll kill the bastard.'

'Let's run away,' said Thiel. He looked back over his shoulder and stopped.

Jed shrugged. 'Run away! I wouldn't run from anything. Come on.'

Charley went to the river and waited for them.

'Take off your rags,' he said. He was grinning.

'Why?' asked Jed.

'Don't why me. Move quick.'

Convinced now that they were to be flogged — because their father always stripped them before punishing — they began to undress. Thiel shivered. His hands fumbled at buttons, but Jed's hands were as steady as his father's. He was undressed first. He stood patiently and looked at the river, thinking of that distant hour in which he would strike his old man down.

'Hurry up,' said Charley, addressing Thiel.

'I am,' said Thiel, staring with blurred eyes at his shirt-front. When he could no longer hesitate, he threw his shirt off and waited, naked and trembling.

Then Charley pushed into the water a boat which he had found lodged on an island, and told them to get in. He followed them and rowed out where the water was dark and deep. He said it was time for them to learn to swim, and picking them up by leg and shoulder he pitched them in headfirst. He returned to the bank and watched. They fought the water, sinking completely and then rising; blowing water from their lungs and flailing with their arms. 'Stop splashun around!'

he shouted. 'Swim like you should!' Thiel sank again and rose, shouting for help. 'Keep your head,' his brother told him, now paddling like a dog. 'If you lose your head, you'll drown.'

'I am drownun!' gurgled Thiel, pawing with frantic arms. Ready to plunge in if necessary, Charley sat in the boat and chuckled. Jed had learned, by calm experimenting, that he could most easily keep afloat upon his back. He told Thiel to lie on his back. But Thiel was standing straight up, with his head rising and sinking, with his mouth spouting water and cries and with his arms wildly threshing. 'Do like me,' Jed told him, paddling gently and looking at the sky. 'Lay on your back.' But Thiel was unable to lie on his back. In dog-fashion he struggled desperately toward the shore, sinking time and again under his efforts, and fell on the bank, exhausted. Jed swam slowly on his back, stroking softly with his arms and moving his legs up and down. He remained afloat for several minutes, wondering why he had never done this before; and then he swam to the bank. He looked scornfully at his gasping brother, and gave his father one triumphant glance.

In the days that followed, the lads went often to the river and soon became expert swimmers. Within a week, Jed had swum the stream in its most dangerous passage, and thereafter he took to water like a seal. After learning to remain under for fully a minute, he would dive to the eddy's bottom and frighten the lazy suckers that slept there. He plunged into whirlpools and explored their depths; he floated like a cork over the mightiest waves; and he leapt headfirst in curved graceful flight from high banks and towers of stone. Thiel also became a skillful diver, but he never followed his brother in Jed's most reckless adventures.

One afternoon Jed suggested that they go over and scare the Hunter brats out of their wits. The older Hunter lad was seven and his brother was five. Thiel agreed. And so they swam the river in their clothes and went drenched to the Hunter door.

'We want your boys to go swimmun,' said Jed, speaking to Mrs. Hunter. She looked at Jed with distrust.

'They'n go watch you boys,' she said, 'but they mustn't go in the water.'

'All right. We'll swim and they'n watch.'

They returned to the river, with the shy and timid lads following. By a broad deep eddy they took off their clothes.

'Can't you kids swim?' asked Jed scornfully.

'No,' said the older lad, whose name was Vridar.

'All right. You'n watch us.'

Jed and Thiel plunged in, and for an hour the Hunter boys sat breathless, watching their feats. They saw the swimmers disappear, and during what seemed a long while they stared at water, but nothing emerged. Then, fifty yards away, they saw a leg pushed up, then two legs, but nothing more; or they saw only a rump, or a hand that wiggled its fingers. Near the shore they saw a slim white body, swimming far under, its legs kicking out like the legs of a frog, its eyes wide open.

'Heavens!' they cried, and sat spellbound.

Then Jed came to the bank.

'You want a-learn?' he asked.

'No,' said Vridar. 'Mother said not to go in the water.'

Jed looked at them with contempt.

'All right,' he said, 'watch now.'

He climbed a tall cottonwood that grew on the brink. On a horizontal limb thirty feet from earth, he walked out and poised. Then he fell like a white bird through the air and vanished. The boys stared until their eyes ached, and a minute later they saw a naked rump break the water's surface. They blushed at this shameless display of nakedness.... Jed and Thiel came to the bank and put on their clothes. Jed looked at the boys. Their eyes held the wonder of his skill and daring.

'Come over and visit us some time,' he said. 'I'll show you some other things. I'll show you my rattle-snake-pen.' He considered for a few moments and added: 'You got a sister?'

'Just a baby sister,' said Vridar.

'You ever see a girl naked?'

'N-no.'

'Well, come over and I'll show you one.'

With their clothes on, the Bridwell boys entered the river. They swam across the eddy and took the moving stream, and the Hunter lads saw them carried down and down, their two heads bobbing like driftwood; saw them draw steadily to the far shore, gain the bank and disappear. They looked at each other and sighed and turned home.

IV

IT was this promise, to show the Hunter lads a naked girl, that led a year later to the most horrible beating Jed ever got. In July, Mrs. Hunter came over to visit, rowing the boat herself and bringing the boys with her. While she talked with Lela, her sons went out with the Bridwell children. Jed showed them his pile of rattles, the old bones of woodchucks and skunks, and the snake-pen full of dry skins, for the snakes had all starved to death. He watched the boys' faces while he showed these things, or while he talked, and he was pleased by the awe and wonder of their eyes. In the presence of such cowards as these, he felt like a great conqueror; and he embroidered his tales of daring until the lads shivered and looked toward the house.

Accompanied also by Thiel and Beth, he marched from place to place like a showman, pointing to the skulls of his enemies. Then they all went to the garden, where they ate carrots and turnips; and thence to the orchard, where Jed encouraged the boys to eat of the hard bitter flesh of green apples and plums. Whereupon, wondering what he could do next to delight or amaze his visitors, he thought of the promise which he made a year ago.

'So you never seen a girl,' he said. 'Honest to God?'

The boys assured him, in the name of this dread power, that they never had.

'Well,' Jed declared, 'you'n see one now.'

He sprang at his sister and clutched her hair.

'Stop it!' Beth cried. 'You little beast, you!'

But Jed did not stop. He went about his work with deadly earnestness. With his arms around Beth, he wrestled with her; he flung her to the ground; but when he tried to pull her dress up, she smote his face and bit his arm. He fought desperately. In former times he had thrown Beth down and sat upon her, and he could do it again. Stepping back from her blows, he scowled while considering the best way to upset her. He dived at her legs, got his arms around them, and brought her violently to earth.

'Stop it!' Beth screamed. 'I'll kill you! I'll poke your damn eyes out!'

Jed burrowed his face in her clothes. He bit her flesh until she howled. He hugged her, with all his strength, and strove to pull her dress up. She begged him to stop. She promised to kill him if he did not stop. And Thiel stood by, not knowing whether to aid or not. He was afraid Beth might tell, and he trembled at his vision of Charley's wrath. The Hunter lads stood frightened by a tree, not knowing whether they were watching fun or murder. The two on the ground struggled savagely, rolling over and over and clawing; and when Beth was white and exhausted, she lay on her back, and Jed lifted her dress and pulled her bloomers down.

'Now you'n see,' he gasped, and the Hunter lads peered. Jed got his feet and looked at his sister. 'Well, you'n get up now,' he declared.

Unashamed but furious, Beth rose and went to the house, and the Hunter lads followed her.

'Now we're in for it,' said Thiel, staring after them.

'She won't tell,' Jed declared. 'If she does, I'll kill her.'

Beth did not tell. But the boys went shyly to their mother and whispered of what they had seen. Mrs. Hunter was outraged. She had taught her sons that nakedness is the most shameful thing in life. With her face scarlet, she rose to go, but Charley's shrewd eyes had been watching her, and he guessed the meaning of what she had been told.

Charley Bridwell was a strange man in more ways than one. He never spoke coarsely of women or of love, and he hated lewd jests. His clowning was often brutal, but never unclean. He wished, moreover, to have clean-minded children, and he always went blind with humiliation and rage when he learned of their nasty devilment.

Going outside now, he shouted for his sons, and they appeared promptly from the orchard and came toward him. He took them into brush by the river.

'What you been up to?' he asked, speaking to Thiel.

It was characteristic of Thiel, both now and in later years, that he never tried to save his own skin in those matters which were not of his doing. He looked at Jed and was silent.

'What you been up to?' Charley asked his younger son.

'Nothun much,' Jed declared. 'I was just foolun with Beth.'

'What for?'

Jed looked unflinchingly at his father's eyes. He shrugged.

'Why,' he said, 'I was showun her to them Hunter kids.'

'You mean you pulled her dress up?'

'Yes.'

'Get your shirts off.'

'It was just me,' Jed declared. 'Thiel, he didn't do nothun.'

'Don't back-talk. Get your shirts off.'

He went into brush and cut a chokeberry cudgel, two feet long and thicker than a man's thumb. Jed took his shirt off and stood waiting, naked to his waist. White and trembling, Thiel stood with his shirt on, looking round him with haunted eyes. When he saw the club, his lips began to quiver.

'Get that shirt off!' Charley roared.

With shaking hands, Thiel unbuttoned his shirt and slipped it off. Jed was looking at him with contempt.

'You'n go over behind the stable,' said Charley, 'and wait.'

'Thiel never done nothun,' Jed declared again. 'It was me.'

'Get along with you!'

Jed went over to the stable. As he stepped around the corner, he looked back. He saw Charley grasp Thiel and bend him over his knee. He thought of swimming the river and running away, but he would not run from punishment. His time would come. An hour would come, somewhere in the future, in which he would strike this monster dead. He listened and heard the dull bitter blows of the rod. He heard Thiel moaning.... Yes, his time would come, his hour of triumph. He would choke his father until the man's tongue fell out; he would flog him until his back was a jelly of flesh and blood....

When he heard his name called, he went without faltering. His first vision was of Thiel, staggering toward the house; his second was of Charley, kneeling with the club in his hand; his third was of Charley's eyes. Without a tremor, Jed bent over his father's leg, pressing his teeth together and closing his eyes, and the club came down in brutal burning blows. When the flogging was done, a part of the bark had been stripped from the green cudgel, and its white torn surface was stained with blood.

Jed stood up, his eyes sick and dark with pain, his will unbroken. He gave his father one glance, a look of unutterable loathing, and picked up his shirt and went slowly toward the house. Inside, he found the women lamenting over Thiel. Thiel lay on the floor. His back was ridged like a washboard, the welts lying from his neck to his rump as large as his little finger. These welts were purple with clotted blood under the hide, and from some open wounds the blood ran. Thiel groaned like one dying. Lela, her face as white as snow, knelt at his side, weeping with crazed gurgling sounds, and Mrs. Hunter also knelt on the floor, her face violent with hatred and shame. Jed sat on a chair, feeling dizzy in spite of himself, feeling a desperate nausea in his stomach, a trembling darkness behind his eyes.

When his mother saw him, she came over, but Jed
waved her off. He was all right, he said. When Lela
saw his back, she gave a low insane cry and sank to the
floor, with the world darkening. Jed knelt on the floor,
intending to comfort his mother; but a swift bitter sickness made him reel. He went to the wash-basin and
thrust his face into cold water. He laved his forehead;
but when he stood up again, dizziness swept him. He
fell to the floor and a horrible dark pain sucked at his
mind until all memory was gone.

When consciousness returned — he never knew how
long afterward — there was a cool feeling on his back.
He remembered then that he had fainted, and humiliation choked him. He sprang to his feet, and the cold
wet rags dropped from his back to the floor. 'I'm all
right,' he protested, when Mrs. Hunter came to him.
'Take care of Thiel. I don't need no help.'

Thiel, now lying face downward on the bed, was still
moaning. Wet towels covered his back. Waiting until
no one was watching him, save Beth, Jed took his shirt
and left the house. He went quickly to the brush by
the river and disappeared. Finding a cool quiet shelter,
he put his shirt on, to keep flies off his wounds, and lay
on his belly with his head on his arms. His mind was
busy with thoughts of vengeance. Projecting himself
into the years, into a time when he would be a strong
man, he shaped each cunning detail of that hour in
which he would avenge his outraged soul. He would
seize Charley by the throat and choke him until the
man's eyes bulged and his tongue stuck out; and then,
after cutting the toughest branch from a hawbush, he

would flog him until his back was a welter of broken flesh. He would fill his wounds with earth and briars; he would cover his back with salt. Or perhaps he would not flog him at all. He would tell him to stand up and fight like a man. He would say, 'You beat me when I was small. Now, you big coward, come on and fight!' And he would strike with hard fists until he had knocked the man's eyes out; until he had driven his teeth down his throat; until he had splintered his jaws as if they were jaws of glass.... Or he would give a knife to his father and take another to himself; and with these knives they would fight. He would rip the man's belly open, disembowel him as he would a woodchuck; he would stick the blade in his cruel heart and turn it around and around.... Or he would blow him sky-high with a stick of dynamite....

Jed lay here for a long while, his eyes agleam with his thoughts. He heard oars in the river and knew that Mrs. Hunter was going home. A little later, he heard feet and a voice softly calling him. It was Beth's voice. Believing that she had betrayed him, Jed sat up and planned to murder her. He looked around him for a club. He would knock her silly and throw her into the river.

'Here I am,' he said, speaking quietly so that she would not flee. She came into his shelter.

'What you out here for?' asked Beth.

'Whose business is it?' asked Jed, still searching for a club. This girl had told tales, and now she came to mock him. He set his teeth and shook with rage.

'Why don't you come to the house?' she said. 'Mamma wants you.'

On hands and knees he crawled around in the brush. He laid hold of a club and came toward her.

Beth saw his eyes and guessed their intent. 'Stop it!' she cried. 'I didn't tell on you.'

'You didn't!' he said, still coming toward her. She backed against a clump of bushes and stood there, trembling with fear. Jed stood up and faced her. 'Then who did?'

'Them Hunter kids, they told. Jed, put that club down.'

'Them Hunter kids,' he said, and, as this idea sank into his mind, his hands relaxed and the club dropped. He came close to Beth and looked at her searchingly. 'Don't you lie,' he said. 'You done it.'

'I didn't. Them Hunter kids, they told.'

'Which one?'

'I don't know. I guess the oldest one.'

'Is that the God's truth?'

'Yes, it's the God's truth. I ain't never told on you yet. I won't never tell on you.'

Jed sat down, his eyes full of a new vision.

'What's the old man up to?'

'I don't know. He ain't in the house. He went away.'

'Well, I plan to stay here. You tell mamma you couldn't find me.'

'Jed, please come to the house.'

'I said no! And don't you tell where I am.'

'I won't tell.' Beth came over and sat by him. 'I'll stay with you,' she said.

'No, you go on back. I'n stay alone. I don't want no damn wet rags on me. And don't you tell.'

'I won't tell.'

'Promise. Cross your heart and hope to die you won't.'

'All right. I cross my heart and hope to die I won't.'

When Beth was gone, Jed found a more secure refuge and planned to spend the night there. After darkness fell, he heard Lela calling his name, and he saw the yellow patch of lantern light which she carried. It went to the orchard and then westward and out of sight. He wanted to go to her, but she would take him to the house and he would have to face Charley. He did not know that Charley had gone to the valley on a raft, and that he would soon be spending himself in shame and drunkenness.... The light appeared, and came along the brush by the river. Again and again he heard his name. He thought his mother was weeping. The light went to the stable and into the woods east and vanished.

Jed lay face downward and tried to sleep, but pain scalded his back and his whole body ached. The shirt stuck to his back. He went to the river and lay in cold water to soak the shirt off. When it came off, he wrung water out of it and whipped it in a wind. Returning to his shelter, he bedded a small area with dry leaves and again strove to sleep. He would feel slumber upon him, its darkness and quiet, when a sudden pain would turn in his flesh like a knife, and he would sit up cursing. Looking through the bushes and across the river, he saw the dim acreage of the Hunter place and meditated on revenge. Hunched forward over his knees, stretching his flesh so that the burning pain would be less severe, he brooded and laid his plan. He sat here all night, thinking now of his father, now of the Hunter lad, and shaping vengeance for both. When morning came, he went to the house, shirtless and haggard, but undaunted.

It was two months later when he wreaked his first vengeance. Several times in August he and Thiel swam the river and hid in brush on the Hunter demesne, waiting for the boys to get a safe distance from the house. Jed saw them at play; carrying water from a spring; gathering wood close by; but never out of their mother's sight. He tried to lure them by imitating birds, by shaking the willows in which he hid, but his efforts frightened them. In September his hour arrived.

The older boy was on the extreme eastern end of the farm, a half-mile from the house, tramping in plowed earth behind a team and a harrow. For a little while, Jed looked south and west for signs of Joe or his wife. Then he and Thiel went forth.

When the lad saw them coming, he stopped. Jed faced him and stared with unpitying eyes.

'Well,' he asked, 'how's mamma's little tattletale to-day?'

Vridar did not speak. His eyes filled with dread, and he looked westward where the house lay out of sight.

'I amagine you know what I'm here for,' Jed went on. 'You just as well start bawlun and shoutun for your ma.'

'Leave me alone!' cried Vridar, shaking with fright.

'Yes, I'll leave you alone.' Jed drew a knife-blade from his pocket. 'We'll fix you all right,' he said. When he stepped forward, the lad became panic-stricken. Jed laid hands upon him and he screamed.

'Quit it!' he yelled, hitting out blindly with both hands.

'Throw him down,' Jed told his brother, 'while I sharpen my knife.'

Thiel seized Vridar and hurled him to the earth, and Vridar went mad with terror. He fought like a wild thing, but Thiel was two years older and much stronger, and he had no difficulty in pinning the lad to the ground.

'Get him ready,' Jed commanded, pretending meanwhile to whet the blade on a harrow tooth. 'We'll learn this tattletale a lesson. I guess mebbe I'll whack his tongue out, too.'

He bent over and scowled at the white frenzied face. Vridar was on his back between Thiel's legs, and Thiel had the boy's arms spread out with his knees upon them. The froth of madness slithered from the boy's mouth. Jed looked around him, to be sure nobody was drawing near, and then he knelt in the earth with the blade gleaming in his hand. Vridar saw the blade and gave one choked insane cry.

'You run and blab to your ma,' Jed told him. 'So I plan to fix you now, for good and all.' He waved his blade and then looked at the boy's face. It was such a horribly distorted face, so appallingly stricken with rage and fear, that he looked away for a moment and

considered. He had been bluffing in his threats. He
wondered if he had gone far enough. But when he
thought of his flogging, of his nights and days of pain,
he resolved to give this youngster an unforgettable
lesson.

'Get him ready,' he said to Thiel. 'No, you hold him
and I will.' He unbuttoned the lad's trousers and exposed him; he moved forward with the blade. But at
this moment Vridar gave such a weird gurgling scream
that Jed sprang to his feet. 'Let him up,' he said.
Thiel rose to his feet. The boy lay there in plowed
ground, panting, ghastly. When he strove to rise, he
trembled and fell back and screamed again.

'Stop that noise!' Jed roared. 'Judas God, you
ain't hurt, are you? Shut up, or I'll choke you!'

The boy struggled again, with his eyes shut, striking
blindly at the demons around him. Jed and Thiel
waited. Then the lad became calmer; he sat up,
shaking and white.

'Now, listen!' Jed cried. 'You damn little sneak, if
you ever tell on us again, I'll come over and fix you
sure as Christ. I'll cut your tongue out. I might even
dig your eyes out. You tattletale brat, don't forget it.'
He looked at Thiel. 'Well, let's poke his mouth full of
dirt,' he said.

He grasped the quivering lad and threw him down.
He stuffed earth into his mouth until the boy choked
and turned purple. When released, Vridar writhed on
the ground, coughing earth from his lungs, his eyes
bulging. Jed then thrust the blade into the horses, and
with a snort they plunged forward. They ran off

wildly, jerking the harrow after them, and vanished crashing into heavy acres of brush. Then Jed and Thiel ran eastward toward the river. Upon looking back, they saw Vridar lying on the earth as if dead.

V

BETWEEN the summer of his ninth year and the autumn of his thirteenth lay those deeds which carried Jed's name into distant places. At the end of these years there fell an experience that changed his way of life. But during this while, he missed no chance to conquer and humiliate those enemies, either man or beast, against which he had enlisted his skill. In most of his adventures, Thiel was a dependable henchman, but he did not have Jed's imagination, his fearlessness, or his relish for combat.

Jed divided the world sharply into the good and the bad. In defense of what seemed to him to be good, he was a bold knight, ready to risk his neck. For his mother or for Beth, both of whom he loved, he would have fought a den of wildcats. He liked flowers and birds. He liked certain trees, such as the maple and the fir; but the spiked hawbush drew his wrath. Thorns and briars and thistles, like rattlesnakes and skunks, seemed to him to be symbols of that power for evil which he saw in life. He liked Henry Bord the trapper, and sometimes went down to sit with him and to drink his gooseberry wine. But he disliked most of the sheepherders and cattlemen who came his way; they seemed to him to be treacherous and cowardly.

His likes and dislikes were often founded in casual things. Sitting down one time to rest, he put forth a hand and was stung by a cactus, and thereafter this thing belonged with the Devil. On the other hand, he once lay in the orchard, staring at a blue sky; and there came down to him the fragrance of an apple tree in bloom, and the glory of it brought tears to his eyes. An apple tree, like his own mother, was a symbol of the good.

And if he was unwavering in his loyalties, he was implacable in his hatreds. Once he decided that a thing was his enemy, he found no peace until he had destroyed it. At everything he met, whether animal or plant, he stared with sober eyes, searching its power for evil or for good. If he decided it was evil, he at once laid plans against it.

Among his foes in his tenth year were vultures and hawks, hornets and rams. He enlisted against hornets because one of them stung him on his mouth. He hunted their gray cones out and knocked them from limbs. One day, while riding a horse, he came upon a great gray home and smote it with a club. He had intended to gallop off, but the bees fell in a swarm, his horse turned rigid under their needles, and Jed was almost stung to death. For days his eyes were swollen almost shut and his face was a mass of poisoned lumps.

One afternoon, when he was upon Rattlesnake Point, experimenting with lizards, he saw a herd of sheep coming up the river, moving to the head of Burns. There were many thousand of them, and they covered like a gray blanket the entire slope of the mountain. When the vanguard came up, he stood among them as they passed. His impression of these creatures was not a happy one. He saw old witless ewes with foul tails, snorting mucus from their noses. They had recently been sheared, and they were now ugly gaunt beasts, with short wool that was yellowish from muck or that was black with dirt. Upon the right side of each was a brand, a great S a foot high; it was made of coal tar, and was black and greasy in the sun. The ungainly lambs seemed to be all legs and tail; their incessant bleating was a mixture of despair and idiocy. When the ewes stopped for a moment, the larger lambs would run to them, thrust their heads under flanks, and bunt so savagely that their mothers' rumps were knocked off the earth; whereupon the ewes would go forward again, their dull bleak stare fixed upon nothing, and the lambs would look stupidly around them and resume their bleating.

Jed decided that sheep were the silliest of all creatures. The stench of their bodies filled his nostrils, and behind them he saw that they had peppered the earth with their small hard dung. They trampled all the summer flowers underfoot. They moved steadily forward like an irresistible gray pestilence.

After the thousands had come and passed, he saw herders bringing a drove of rams. These were nobler beasts, he thought; they wore great coiled horns, and their noses and tails were clean. Their eyes carried more meaning and courage. He liked them. But while he was standing by a horse, talking with the rider, an event bowled him over and changed his opinion of rams. He remembered later that he should have been forewarned, because on the herder's face he had seen a sly grin. He heard a sound behind him, and before he could turn he was knocked spinning by a blow on his rump. After picking himself up, he saw a huge horned ram staring at him, enraged and ready for another assault. The ram came with its head down. Jed grasped the horns, but the furious rush knocked him down, and sharp feet gouged his flesh. He got up and seized a stone as large as his fist. He hurled this at the beast's head, but the ram came again, now aided by another, and again Jed was felled and trampled. Two herders then rode upon the creatures and drove them away. Jed heard their loud laughter as they went down the mountain and out of sight. He looked after them, humiliated, shaking with fury. Against the herder who had not warned him, and against the entire kingdom of sheep, which he now looked upon as Satan's own kind, he laid a vow of vengeance.

In this summer he was given a half-dozen foundlings by the owner of the herd. Two of these were rams. He gave the ewes to Beth; and for the rams he built a corral, to shield them from coyotes, and became their treacherous nurse. Teaching them to feed by letting them suck his thumb in a pan of milk, he then stoked them night and morning until their bellies stuck out like huge pods. After they became husky youngsters, he would go out to their pen and devote hours to them. He rubbed their tiny horns until they were furious; upon hands and knees he bunted with them, rubbing his hair into their eyes; and when they turned away, tired of futile effort, he yanked their tails and made them fight again. By the time they were half-grown, they would lower their heads when he came out and show an eagerness for combat.

In the following winter he converted one corner of the pen into a warm shelter. He chose for them the greenest of alfalfa leaves; he wrapped old horse blankets around them during bitter weather; and in every day he would enter their cold home and engage them in struggle. With delight he watched their horns grow into rugged coils; he saw their eyes take on a deeper and more relentless ferocity; and he saw their bodies fill with greed and strength. And by the following spring they were lusty brutes with savage eyes.

With Thiel's help he now took them out of the pen. To make them still more ferocious, the boys would grasp one by its horns, throw it to the ground, and roll it over and over, but never abuse it enough to daunt its courage. They rode them, kicking heels into their flanks; they twisted their tails and slapped their faces; pulled wool from their hides and thrust pepper into their mouths. And when the tutoring was done, these two rams were the most savage, shepherds declared, that had ever gone undocked. When they were loose, Beth and Lela never dared leave the house; and Charley himself, when going one morning for his appetizer, was caught unexpectedly and knocked end over end. But he did not mind. He saw in these bucks a great fund of sport; he liked the desperate way in which they attacked every human being in sight.

Out of Burns one afternoon rode the herder who had laughed at Jed. As soon as he dismounted and entered the house, Jed sought his brother and gave instructions.

Thiel was to lure the man out and down to the barn. He could tell him he knew where Charley kept his whiskey, or that he had a wolf in a trap — anything to get him outside. And so Thiel entered the house, grinning a little in spite of himself; and his father grinned, too, guessing what was in his son's mind.

Winking at Thiel, he said: 'Let's go down to the stable. I got something there mebbe you'll like.' And he winked at the man, suggesting by his wink that the matter was one not to be spoken of around women.

'Sure,' said the herder, a long lewd-faced chap. He glanced at Lela and then winked at Charley. Beth looked at her mother and grinned, knowing what was to come, but there was no joy in such pranks for Lela.

Charley left the house, followed by the herder and Thiel. Thiel then fell behind and slipped over to the pen, where Jed was waiting. As Charley and the herder passed, the former talking loudly and pointing south at nothing at all, to draw the man's eyes from the pen, the boys opened the gate, and the rams went forth at full speed. When Charley saw the gate open, he ran.

'What's the big hurry?' his guest called after him. 'Hey, there!' Hearing then a rush of feet behind him, the man swung around; and as he did so, the two rams struck. One caught him squarely in his groin; and as he fell, half-spinning, the other delivered its horns against his rump. The two blows not only felled him, but left him momentarily dazed. The bucks waited, ready to attack. When the herder roared and got his feet, he went down again under the deadly assault.

While Charley lured the bucks away, and then took the cursing herder to the barn for a drink, Jed gave his time to another matter. He had not yet avenged his humiliation on Rattlesnake Point.

'Let's fix his horse,' he said to Thiel, and together they went to the animal.

'How?' asked Thiel.

'Let me think. I want a-make him buck.'

'We'n put something anunder his tail,' Thiel suggested.

'No, we'll put something anunder the saddle.'

'What?' asked Thiel, looking toward the barn.

'Well, shut up. Let me think a minute.'

'Some barb wire, that'd do.'

'No, that wouldn't do.'

'Some pins, how's that? We could stick them in the blanket.'

Jed thought this idea was not bad, but he never used his brother's ideas. Running quickly upon the rocky mountain-side, he uprooted some prickly pears, and from the ditch bank he took the dry and needle-stemmed pods of thistles. Returning with bleeding fingers, he dropped the bellyband, lifted the saddle and blanket, and placed the spiked and needled plants on the horse's back. Then he gently lowered the blanket and saddle and fastened the cinch. With Thiel he jumped into the mine-hole and waited.

Peering over the rim, a while later, he saw Charley and the herder approaching from the southwest. To evade the bucks, which Jed had penned, they had gone down the river and thence to the orchard. Jed thought, the herder was staggering. He had probably filled himself with whiskey and would be in fine fettle to mount an outraged cayuse. Thiel was choking with uncontrollable glee.

'Shut up!' Jed whispered.

By the horse the two men stood for a little while. The herder waved his arms drunkenly and filled the air with loud words. He put a foot in a stirrup and again addressed the mountains with his arms. The horse looked around at him. Then the herder swung up and threw his leg over the saddle. For a moment nothing happened; but when the herder leaned down to speak, the horse stiffened as if from an electric shock. Its ears stood up and its eyes turned backward.

'Hain't up!' the man shouted, but the horse did not move. It braced its legs and turned rigid. 'What's a-matter this bustard?' the rider asked of the sky. 'Charley, hit him a jolt. Knock him on his old poop.'

'Just a minute,' said Charley, looking around him for a board. He suspected the rascality of his sons.

'The God dimn bustard!' the man roared, and reaching forward he cuffed sullen ears. 'Smash him, Charley! Lay the bustard flat!'

Charley found a stout slab of pine and laid it in a smacking blow on the beast's hip.

'Bust him again!' yelled the herder, furiously digging with his heels. 'Slough him across his poop!'

Charley smote again, and Thiel gurgled with unutterable joy. And still the animal stood rigid, as if he had grown out of earth and had no power to move. The herder dismounted, sputtering with amazement, and stared at the beast.

'He don't look sick!' he cried. 'What can ail the rack a bones?'

He walked twice around the horse, searching him for some visible sign of woe. Then he mounted again and dug savagely with his heels.

'If I had my spurs,' he bellowed, 'it's bum certain I'd move him! Charley, smash him again! Bust him over his tail!'

'Wait a minute,' said Charley.

He went to the mountain-side to get a prickly pear, and while he was gone, the herder yanked furiously at the horse's ears. He cuffed them, and the horse lowered its head, with ears laid back in a dark threat. Charley came with the pear and thrust it under the horse's tail. The tail came down, rigid and powerful, and pressed spikes into the animal's flesh. The beast snorted then; it lowered its head as a signal of danger; it plunged forward and gave the most fearful exhibition of bucking that Jed had ever seen. Rearing and mowing the air with its forelegs; pitching its hinder skyward until its head smote the ground; twisting and whirling savagely, reeling, churning, mad. The herder grasped the horn with both hands. He lost the stirrups, was pitched to the rear of the saddle and then forward; was almost ended up and sent headlong; came down clutching and fighting to hang on. And he probably would have hung on if the saddle had not turned and sent him spinning; whereupon the maddened beast went bucking over the lucerne, with the saddle under its belly, kicking and lashing until the cinch broke and it was free. The herder came staggering back, cursing with the full power of his lungs.

'In God's green earth!' he roared. 'What got in the lousy bustard? In the mighty name a Christ Jesus! He never done no such pranks before this!... The spavin-jinted, thistle-necked hurrycane! The misruble loud-poopun snort-eyed son-of-a-bitch! I never seen him do that, not in the ten year I owned him! The God all-hemlock! Never till this minute has that critter bucked!... I'll shoot him, Charley, where's your gun?'

Charley was lying on the earth, soaked through and through with laughter. He moaned and pawed the air, feasting gluttonously on this incident, shuttling with his fat frantic legs, howling and wheezing his ravenous joy. In the mine-hole Thiel was also squealing with happiness, but the face of Jed Bridwell was sober and intent. He had avenged another outrage. He was satisfied.

VI

JED was not always busy with devilment; and if he gave much time to avenging himself or to the destruction of his foes, it was largely because he had nothing else to do. In July of each summer now, Charley borrowed the Hunter mowing-machine and wagon and hayrake, and his sons harvested twenty acres of hay. Sometimes Charley would help, but more often he would lie in the shade, chewing tobacco and growing fat.

But Jed did not mind his father's laziness. Resolved to be different from his old man, he looked upon indolence with contempt and kept himself busy. He liked to ride a mower, to smell the rich succulent alfalfa, to load its fragrant piles upon a wagon and build them into a stack. He liked to gather fruit from the orchard, to weed among the earth-smells of the garden, or to gather wild berries for his mother's use. He gathered wood, too, and kept a great pile behind the stove; and sometimes he milked the cow. But all these matters filled only a small part of his life. And when not busy harvesting or doing things for his mother, he was driven by the rugged health of his mind and body to occupy himself elsewhere.

Upon all creatures that had humiliated him, save only his father and mules, he had wreaked a satisfying vengeance; and an opportunity to even his score with mules came in his twelfth year. He had learned earlier that on the tenth of August, Ham Blodgett, the camp-mover of the Spaulding herds, would come up the river with a caravan of supplies. Jed knew what this caravan would be like. Ham would ride ahead, and behind him would come a half-dozen mules, each roped to the tail of the one before, and each freighted with salt and food.

Taking Thiel into his confidence, Jed laid his plans. They would climb up the north mountain and send boulders down. They might knock Ham into the river, Thiel said; but Jed shrugged and declared he didn't give a lickety whoop about Ham Blodgett. It was Ham who had whispered to him, years ago, of what he might and should do with his sister. It was this lewd fellow who had told him of what Charley did to Lela, after the lights were out. It was Ham who had more airs than a studhorse....

And so, on the morning of the eleventh, Jed and Thiel climbed the mountain and set to work. Jed sent many boulders down, hoping to learn the size and shape of those which would most likely strike the trail. The smaller ones, weighing about fifty pounds, usually flew in a long arc over the path. The stones weighing a hundred pounds also took their last rebound from earth north of the trail, and sprang thence to the water. Their larger arcs were five or six. But boulders twice as large, Jed discovered, were less erratic in flight; they were likely to descend upon or near the trail, and then leap into their last majestic flight.

Accordingly, he chose the heavier stones, and with Thiel's aid he rolled many of them to the brink. He went then to an aspen grove lying north and got a long dry pole. He laid this pole on the brink, and against it he placed a row of boulders, all precariously poised so that when the pole was jerked away they would begin their downward journey. Whereupon, drenched with sweat, he lay down and waited.

'Like as not,' Thiel protested, 'we'll slew old Ham. I ain't sure we should do this.'

'If you're afraid, run on to the house.'

'I ain't. But I don't want a-kill no one.'

'It's bum certain we won't. Anyway, who'll know we done it?'

'The old man, he'll know.'

'You're afraid you'll get another beatun. You should ought to a-been a girl.'

'Oh, sow-belly! I guess you like them beatuns.'

'You ain't nothun to worry about. The old man is about shot his wad. He won't never lick us again.'

'No, like hell he won't.'

'If he does, we'll kill him.'

Thiel turned his pale blue eyes upon the west. His hands were trembling. He hoped Ham Blodgett would not come. He got up and walked around, still looking into the west.

Jed watched him, his eyes dark and derisive.

'Set down!' he said.

'I won't!' cried Thiel hotly. 'We'll be in a pickle for this. I just feel we'll kill him dead.'

'Go on to the house.'

'I won't. I ain't no quitter.'

'You act like one.'

'Well, you act like a damn fool. You act like you want your skin took off.'

Jed sat up and looked at his brother.

'Listen here. If the old man ever licks me again, I'll kill him.'

For several moments Thiel stared at the desperate language of Jed's eyes.

'How?' he asked, almost in a whisper.

'What's it matter how! There's ways to do it. I'n bust him with a kingbolt. I'n cut his old guts open with a knife.'

'My God,' said Thiel, 'you must have a string loose!'

'I've stood all I'll stand. If he beats me again, I'll knock him to hell and gone. I'll kill him like he was a rattlesnake.'

'Let's don't talk about it,' said Thiel.

'But you,' Jed went on, 'you'll just set around on your hind-end and let him whale you. When you're growed-up, I guess he'll still beat the tar out of you.'

'When I'm growed-up,' said Thiel, staring far away at blue mountains, 'I won't be here. But I don't want a-kill nobody.'

'Some things is good,' Jed declared, 'and some is bad. The bad things should ought a-be killed. Human or beast, it's all the same to me.'

'Well, I don't want a-talk about it.'

'No, you want a-get your old back blistered.'

Jed lay down and looked at the sky. His mood was savage, but the sky was a soft tender blue, and a hungry emotion took him by the throat. He wanted deeply something that he had never had. What was the world like, he wondered, beyond these mountains and against the sea. He would go there some day. He would say good-bye to all that he had known, to the loneliness and dead bones, to the fragrant loveliness of the orchard and to his mother's mouth; he would go far away and never come back. He would go out into the strange deep world, of which he knew little; and his hunger would find there the thing which his heart craved. Lovely women were there, sheepherders said, and palaces of joy and laughter and song. Not devilish laughter like his father's, not songs of cowpunchers and miners, not women like his mother whose face was a record of pain: no, but another language of life, another speech besides vengeance, another plan...

'There he comes!' cried Thiel.

Jed rose from his dream and saw the caravan rounding the Point. With one finger he traced the white furrow on his brow and looked down at the mules with sullen hatred. He hoped the stones would not demolish Ham, but he could not be bothered. He was intent on the mules, on those sinister long-eared beasts that struck and kicked, or shook the mountains with their infernal bray. Grasping one end of the pole, he said:

'When I jerk this, you lay down on your belly. Don't let him see you.'

And then he waited, while the caravan of beasts, one horse and seven mules, came slowly up the trail. He could hear Ham whistling. He thought of what Ham's consternation would be, and a grim pleasure was warm in his throat.

'You lay down now,' he said. 'I'n jerk this pole.'

Thiel lay behind a rock and peered down. He began to laugh, but his laugh was only a crazed giggle of joy and fear.

'I hope it busts them all to splinters,' Jed declared. 'See that-there big jackass in the middle. I hope he gets one flop in his guts.'

Jed waited again, impatiently. When the beasts were a few yards west of the danger zone, he jerked the pole, and fifteen huge boulders turned downward. The rider, still unaware of this descending avalanche, whistled loudly and turned to look at his cargo. Then he heard the first deadly plunge of stone and looked up. Without hesitating, he leapt from his horse and ran. Jed, meanwhile, face downward and hidden, was watching the gray flights, and wondering if all the stones would miss. Save two which got a bad start they were sailing neck and neck, smiting the earth with thirteen terrific blows, and then mounting into a longer arc. On their third mighty leap, they were not in a great circle like flying ducks: some of them had struck softer earth and been less violent in the rebound; but the half-dozen leaders shot forth, traversed their rainbow curve and came down. They all fell short of the caravan, rose tremendously again, and swept over the beasts and into the river. Behind them, flying in confusion, came the nine other stones, and one of these, as if shot with deadly aim from a cannon, struck a mule squarely on its side and hurled the astounded brute a hundred yards away.

The rider, meanwhile, had been heeling it to safety. He stopped and looked back, and when he saw the

mule lifted and hurled into death, he ran again, and
never paused until he reached the house. Jed had
stood up to watch the man go, and behind him stood
Thiel.

'My God,' said Thiel, in a stricken voice, 'now
we'll get it! Good Jesus God!'

They looked down where the stampeded beasts
were running eastward. Among the cottonwoods by
the river, Jed thought he could see the disemboweled
mule.

'What'll we do now?' asked Thiel.

'Nothun,' declared Jed calmly.

'The old man'll beat us to death, I tell you! How'n
we pay for that mule?'

'We won't.'

'We just as well run away!' cried Thiel, in a shrill
hopeless voice. 'We'll be beat to death!'

'Oh, shut up.'

'I won't go back. You'n go, but I won't.'

'Well, I won't run away. If he beats me, he'n look
out.'

'That's big talk! You'll just grin and bear it. Jesus
God, that's all you'n do!'

'I'll kill him.'

'You'll just take it like you always done.'

'Don't fret yourself. The old son-of-a-bitch can't
beat me no more.'

They sat down and remained speechless for a long
while. Jed saw the camp-mover come out of the house
and catch his frightened beasts. He saw his father
help him, and then he saw the two men go westward

and look at the slain mule. Ham brought his horse with him, and upon it they loaded what they could find of the scattered cargo. They returned to the house, and a few minutes later the caravan left the front yard and went eastward into Burns.

'We just as well run àway,' said Thiel at last.

'I won't run away. Not till I get damn good and ready.'

'No, you'll just stick around and get beat to death. Anyway, why'd you want a-roll them rocks down?'

'Oh, go to hell!'

'You're always up to things, just to get a beatun.'

'I'll take care of that. I'll tell him you didn't do nothun.'

'No, you won't. I ain't a-sneakun out.'

Again they sat in silence. Jed looked far away into the west, feeling that his path of life lay through that blue valley and beyond. He had never been there. He had never been west of the Tompkins place. All his years of memory had been spent here in this great bowl, mountain-walled, sky-roofed. Of the enormous earth, of its tenants and its ways, he knew only what sheepherders and Henry Bord and his mother had told him. It was a wicked world, Henry declared; his mother said it was dark with lust and greed. But as he looked at the blue valley, feeling its immense depth, all its strange highways and retreats, he could not believe that it was very wicked or very dark. He felt that it was an enchantment of hungry trails, leading to the glory of cities and far shores; it called to him, it drew his soul out of him, and left him sitting like a husk of himself. The painted maps of it, in his geography book, were unexplored empires in his mind. Their designs, like his mother's patchwork quilts, were soaked with colors, and they allured and called and waited. He would go some day. He would throw away the short path of his life lying between the Tompkins home and his own, and he would lift a great journey into the world. He would scatter the miles behind him, and this starved loneliness of bitter things. He would voyage across the colored States, over the sheepwool brown of Nebraska, over the aspen green of Iowa, eastward into the sun; across the inky domain of the Atlantic, over the dull red kingdom of France — beyond and forever going! And he would never come back. He would go soon, in some morning full of bird talk, and he would never come home again....

'Well,' he said, shaken by his dreams, trembling with the hot blood of his longing, 'let's go and get it over with.'

He started down the mountain, and, after hesitating, after staring westward where his own thoughts had been richly grazing, Thiel rose and followed.

Jed went boldly to the house and entered. His father rose to meet him, and Jed saw in the man's face the clear language of his intent. He turned a little pale, but not from fear; it was from the desperate resolve which he had shaped. Within the next few minutes he was to face the supremest crisis of his life, the moment in which he must not falter, the crossroads of victory and defeat.

'I guess you know what you done,' said Charley, staring at him.

'Yes,' Jed declared, 'I know.'

'All right,' said Charley, 'come along. And you, too,' he added, addressing Thiel.

'He didn't do nothun,' Jed declared. 'I done it myself. He wasn't anywheres around.'

'Never mind your lip. Come along.'

Lela rose from a bench, where she was sewing rags into shirts, and moved forward in protest, but Jed went quickly to her and said everything would be all right. His father was joking, he said. Lela then looked at Thiel and saw that his face was very white. From somewhere outside, Charley called to them.

'Buck up,' Jed whispered to his brother. 'Everything will be jim dandy.' They went outside and toward the river.

'We should a-run away,' Thiel muttered.

'Only cowards run away.'

Thiel's eyes, thrust deep with terror, looked around him, searching vainly for a way out. He tried to swallow, but he made only a queer sound. In the brush by the river they found Charley waiting. As in former whiles of this kind, he went into woods and returned with a thick cudgel.

'Take off your shirts,' he said.

Thiel began to fumble with his shirt, but Jed did not move. He stared at his father and his gaze was unwavering. His hour had come. He wet his lips and spoke.

'Before you beat me,' he said, and his vibrant tone annoyed him, 'I want a-say something.'

'Oh, you do!' said Charley, and with yellowish green eyes he looked at his son. 'Never mind your say. Get your shirt off.'

Jed advanced and looked up at the man's face. He wet his lips again before he spoke.

'I want a-say something,' he declared, speaking as quietly as he could.

'Get that shirt off!' Charley roared.

'What I want a-say,' Jed went on, 'is this. If you beat me, I'll kill you.'

Charley was amazed. He looked down into Jed's eyes, and he saw in them the courage of a trapped wolf. He started to howl with astonishment, but the cry stuck in his throat. And then they stood there, father and son, looking into the eyes of each. Wetting his lips a third time, Jed spoke again.

'You beat me too many times,' he declared, his dark eyes filled with the inexorable purpose of his mind. 'I know you hate me. Well, I've always hated you. As far back as I'n remember, we've hated each other. But you can't just go on beatun me.' He paused for a moment and added: 'You'n beat me now if you want to. You're strongern me. But if you do, I'll kill you the first chance I get. I cross my heart and hope to die that's the truth.'

For almost ten seconds the man and the boy, father and son, read the meaning of the other's stare. Then Charley's gaze broke, and for the second time in his life he faltered. The club fell, as if from a dead hand, and he turned away.

VII

In Texas, Charley had known a man called Golddust Adams. People called him Golddust because he had spent twenty years, vainly hunting for gold, ranging in his lean pilgrimage from the Gulf to Canada, from San Francisco to Cheyenne. He had married, after Charley left Texas, and his wife had died in giving birth to a girl. During his next dozen years, Golddust had roamed hungrily, taking his daughter with him from place to place. The child's only tutoring had been found in the vulgarity of coarse men and the hardships of her father's journeys. Profanity and obscene words had entered her speech from infancy, and both had become so common to her that she had no power to distinguish between them and the language of politer folk. In sound and in meaning, 'whore' and 'God damn' were as commonplace to her, and as irreproachable, as 'lady' and 'gosh darn.' This daughter's name was Bonnie.

When Bonnie was ten, she had been lured into Oregon woods and raped by a miner. She had resisted only feebly, she had kept the matter to herself; and at the end of a month she looked back upon it with pleasure, and wished that she might have the same experience again. In her eleventh year she was intimate with a boy of sixteen; and thereafter she had many lovers, including her father's brother, whom she met among the copper mines of northern Idaho.

In 1908, Golddust's wanderings led him to Idaho Falls, and while there he learned that Charley lived up Snake River. He was told, too, that fields of gold lay buried at the head of Burns, and that coal stuck out of the ledges. Lured by this promise, he bought an old worn-out nag, and upon this beast both he and his daughter, now a girl of fourteen, rode up the river to the Bridwell place. In dusk one evening, in the summer of Jed's fourteenth year, they drew up at the door and made the mountains ring with their greeting. Their arrival marked the turning-point in Jed's life.

'Why, my God, if it ain't Golddust!' Charley cried, and came in his rolling gait to grasp the wanderer's hand.

'Yep,' said Golddust, 'it's me. And this is my gal.'

'Come in, come in,' said Charley. He turned to his sons. 'Here, stand the old nag to a pile of hay.'

Jed gave Bonnie one searching look and picked up the halter-rope. He hurried to the haystack, eager to return and feast his eyes upon this girl. In her father, too, of whom he had heard Charley speak, he had a hungry interest, because the man had come out of the great world, with his mind full of its distances and secrets.

Entering the house, he sat on the floor in a dim corner, his arms clasping his knees, and looked at Bonnie. She wore overalls and a blue denim shirt. Her hair was soft and brown like his mother's; her eyes were hazel and direct; her mouth was richly youthful and sweet. He could see the curve of her breasts, and her plump thighs filling the overalls. When she looked at him, he held her gaze until she turned away. He stared greedily and felt the quick leaping of his heart.

Then he looked at her father. Golddust was a tall gaunt fellow from whose bones the years had taken the flesh. His cheeks were sunken, and most of his front teeth were gone; his eyes were weary, as if they had seen too much, and they were far back in his skull. But out of his wide dead mouth came life, flowing in vivid jargon, each word stemming from the man's imperishable dream. He looked old and worn-out, but somewhere within him was a lively emotional fountain, and out of it gushed the vital waters of hope. In the present moment he was asking Charley why, in the name of the jumping Jesus, he was living here.

'When I seen you hit the breeze, I says myself, thet man'll be wealthy before nowhile. Thet man'll split the wind right. But here you be.' He looked around him, and his stare for a moment stood against Lela. 'Well, here you be. You ain't starvun, I reck, but you ain't a-rollun in the yeller dust, neither. You got a good grubstake, mebbe, and thet's about all.'

'That's about all,' said Charley, 'and sometimes I ain't got that. I'm leavun the wealth to damn fools like you.'

'Thet's right,' said Golddust, grinning. 'But they ain't no wealth for me, Charley. It steers clear my trail. I ain't never got in a ace the real thing. But they told me, down in Iderho Falls, they said, why, Jesus Christ, there's gold a mile deep up Burns way. Found nuggets, they says, big as a fool hen. And coal, acres and miles, only it's hard to get to. Needs a railroad built, I guess.' His eyes awoke and gleamed. 'Gold, they tell me. A vein runs plumb across here somewheres. And slick as a button to find. Slick as a greased belly, they said. Ain't you never seen no signs it?'

'Yes, plenty signs. There's plenty deer signs, too, but there ain't no deer meat in my house.'

'Charley, you're lazy, by God. Been right next door a gold mine and ain't found it yet. Lazy as a lizard. Man, see all thet fat you got. Thet's enough to find a dozen mines with. But me, I just got a backbone left.'

'And what'd you do if you found gold? You crazy damn fool.'

'Well, I'm nigh finished, thet's the demn truth. But my little gal could use it.' He looked with fondness at Bonnie. 'She could get some learnun. Travel, and like thet. I could give you a big wad. Mebbe my old mother's alive. I don't know. I ain't heared in twenty year.... Well, I'm about the end the trail, thet's right. A few more years and my old bones will sleep like a log. Been drunk too many times, Charley. Drunk as a fiddler's bitch. And my little gal a-tryun to sober me up. Hum-hum.' He was silent for a little while, staring at the floor, thinking of those times when he lay soaked with whiskey. Then he laughed in a queer mirthless way. 'But if I'n find thet gold,' he went on, his eyes hungry for the quest, 'I'll be sittun purty as a robin. And dog my cats, Charley, if I don't think I will. By God, I'n almost smell it now. I'n feel it in my old bones. I felt all the way up here, there's gold in them hills. I kep thinkun all the way here, I

looked at thet river, it's full a gold. In a week I'll have
my hands on it...'

Jed was looking at Bonnie. She divided her atten-
tion between him and Thiel, and now and then Jed
scowled darkly at his brother, regarding him as a rival.
He wanted to speak to her, but he had been taught
never to open his mouth before adults. If he left the
house, she might follow, but he doubted it; he wished
she would come over and sit on the floor by him. He
saw Thiel smile at her and he hated him.

How, he wondered, should a girl be wooed. A sheepherder had told him to throw girls down and lie on
them; to tickle their knees and their armpits; to hit
their stomach and knock their breath out. But he distrusted the love-lore of these lewd men. Jed had never
seen any girls, save the Tompkins daughters, little
Diana Hunter, and his own sister. And of these, his
sister was the only one to whom he had made love.

He had never been sexually intimate with Beth, but
he had seen her young body, he knew what a girl was
like. He had kissed her often. Under fragrant apple
trees, he had lain with her in his arms. Together with
Thiel he had gone swimming with her, the three of
them running naked on the river sands.

For Bonnie now he felt passionate love. It was a
broad and deep emotion, a converging of many hungers, a river of many channels that all came together in
one profound whirlpool. It fed upon his loneliness,
drank his bitter starved years, and washed into the unknown ways of life. In his loins it was a desperate ache,
but it also filled his heart, his throat, with something

holy and good. It was warm in his breath, infinitely tender in his hands.

And while he watched her, with an unobtrusive but intent stare, Bonnie went to the water pail for a drink. Then she spoke to Beth, but Jed could not overhear; and the two girls went out....

'What,' Charley was saying, 'ever became old Bill Berry? Did he marry that woman he got in trouble?'

'Old Bill,' said Golddust. 'My God, old Bill, thet's a demn funny story. He hit the blizzard right. Did you know thet woman he was bellyun around with? Ollie... Ollie... leastwise her name was Ollie. Thet woman was a rip-snorter. She had more airs than a bull. And when old Bill got his dose a trouble.... Did you know thet Mary Olson woman? Well, thet's the pettyskirt he married in the end. And how she done him in a reglar hurrycane, thet's the funny part.' Golddust brooded over his memories. Then he sniffed the air, smelling the richness of frying fish. 'By God,' he said, 'my belly's empty as a old panyerd. It's something, Charley, to have a place set down and eat a meal. I never had no such place yet.'

Charley laughed, his jolly fat quivering, and rose to help his wife. On the table he set tin plates and cups, knives and forks. He opened a jar of apples and dumped the fruit into a large earthen bowl.

'Skin out,' he said to his sons, 'and get some vegetables.'

Jed rose from the floor and left the house. He went to the garden and pulled carrots and radishes and onions, wiping on his trousers the earth that clung to the roots. Thiel had followed and now watched his brother.

'She's a good-looker, ain't she?'

'Who?' asked Jed, glancing searchingly at Thiel.

'That girl. Don't you think she's a good-looker?'

Jed whipped onions against his leg.

'Listen,' he said, 'she's mine. So don't snoop around.'

'Oh, the hell she is!'

'Yes, the hell she is.'

'Who said she is?'

'I did. You heard me say it.'

'She ain't yours no moren she's mine.'

'She's mine,' Jed declared, meeting Thiel's angry eyes. 'So don't get to spoonun around her.'

'Oh, sow-belly! And what if I do?'

'Then look out.'

'But she ain't yours!' cried Thiel desperately. He had always taken orders from his wolfish young brother. 'What right do you have moren I have?'

'She's mine. You'n have the next one.'

'Oh, yes, like God! There won't be no next one.'

'You'n have Jenny Tompkins.'

'Cats and balls on Jenny Tompkins! Why don't you take her?'

Jed shrewdly deliberated.

'She don't like me,' he said at last. 'She told me she likes you.'

'You're a liar!'

'Don't call me a liar.' Jed put his vegetables down. 'You'd better take that back.'

'All right, I take it back. But it ain't the truth.'

'Anyway, that's what she said. You're just so dumb you don't see.'

'But I like this girl bettern Jenny Tompkins. We'll draw sticks for her, then.'

'No, we won't draw no sticks. I said she's mine.'

'But, my God, why should she be yours?'

'You'n have the next one. Now shut up your jib.'

'But there won't be no next one,' Thiel persisted miserably.

'Then take Jenny. She's horny about you.'

Jed gathered the vegetables and set off for the house. Thiel followed, still protesting. On the way they met the girls. They both stopped and looked at Bonnie.

'What's your name?' asked Thiel, pushing the question past a lump in his throat.

'My name?' she said. She shrugged and looked at Jed, with something unfathomable in her hazel eyes. Then she looked with less interest at Thiel. 'My name's Bonnie.'

'Bonnie,' said Thiel, tasting the word.

'What's yours?' she asked.

'Mine's Thiel Bridwell.'

'Oh, I knowed it was Bridwell. I meant your first name.' Her voice was impatient. 'What's yours?'

'Jed.'

'I like Jed better,' she declared. 'It's a nice name.' To Thiel she said, 'Your name sounds like a girl.'

'Like a girl! Oh, the hell it does.'

'Jed's better-lookun.'

'I don't think so,' Thiel said.

'Don't you think so?' asked Bonnie, turning to Beth. Beth was silent. 'I think so,' said Bonnie, settling the matter. 'You got freckles,' she added. 'And I like dark hair.'

Thiel looked at his brother's hair and then at Bonnie's.

'Well,' he said, 'yours ain't so dark.'

'Don't you think I know it, you simple Simon!'

'Who's a simple Simon?' demanded Thiel angrily. 'You're a simple Simon yourself.'

Bonnie shrugged impatiently.

'Lord!' she said. 'Can't you think any names besides what I use? You're dumb as a dough god.'

Thiel stared at her with hateful eyes. He felt himself slipping, being made a fool of, but he hardly knew what to do about it.

'You're just horny,' he said. 'That's all your trouble.'

'Oh, am I! Well, sure I am. But not for nobody like you.'

'No, you want a sheepherder or something.'

Jed scowled at him.

'Shut up your jib,' he said.

'Listen, don't tell me to shut up my jib!'

'You're a wind-jammer,' said Bonnie. 'I'll bet Jed could knock all the tar out of you.'

'Oh, you think so?'

'Stop talkun to her,' said Jed.

'Go to hell!'

Jed put his vegetables down.

'Now,' said Bonnie, addressing Thiel, 'your bro-ther's ready to shut your gap up.'

'Stop your silliness,' said Beth, grasping Jed's arm.

'Let him fight,' said Bonnie. 'He'll learn him to keep his gap shut.'

'No,' said Beth. 'Pick them up and come on.'

Jed flung her hand off and squared himself.

'I ain't afraid him,' said Thiel. He clenched his fists and waited; and in another moment the brothers would have been fighting, fighting for the favor of this girl, but Charley appeared around the house and yelled at them.

'Come on with them vegetables!' he roared.

'Come on,' said Beth. 'You're silly as fool hens.'

'You walk with your sister,' Bonnie said to Thiel. 'I'll walk with Jed.'

'Come on,' said Beth, taking Thiel's arm. The arm trembled in her grasp.

Beth and Thiel walked ahead. Bonnie looked at Jed and smiled, and Jed was drunk with the nearness of her. 'I'll help you carry them,' she said gently. She took from his arms some of the green things, and then she chose a carrot and bit into its meat. 'Now you have a bite,' she said, and offered the carrot to him. He bit into the yellow wound left by her mouth. 'When we eat supper,' she said, 'I want a-set by you.' She looked at him as they walked. Then she added, 'I like you,' and rubbed her cheek against him.

In the house they all sat around the long low table spiked to the wall. Charley brought an empty barrel

into the house and Golddust's saddle. Golddust sat on
the barrel and Charley sat on the saddle, with his chin
barely above the table's edge. Jed and Bonnie sat side
by side on two of the box-chairs. Before them was a
great tin platter of fried trout, a bowl brimming with
apples, a tin basin of wild uncooked service berries; and
scattered over the bare table were the vegetables, now
washed clean, now filling the room with their earthy
smell. They all ate without knives and forks, using
their fingers to feed the warm dripping fish into their
mouths, spooning the apples into their tin plates, grasping the carrots and onions and devouring them root
and hide. They piled the trout bones on the table;
they reached into the berry basin and fed hungrily,
washing them down with rich milk.

'It tastes demn good,' said Golddust, stuffing his
mouth with trout and turnip, his sunken eyes winking
with quiet joy. 'It's the best meal I've et in a coon's
age.'

'Have some more apples,' said Charley. 'We got a
million bottles around somewheres.'

Golddust looked around him, with food-enamoured
eyes, as if wondering where so many bottles could be.

'Dough gods and hard tack,' he said, 'them's been
my fodder. And them's demn bad chuck for a man's
belly, year in and year out. I guess I ain't et a green
onion since the Almighty God knows how long.'

Charley rose and brought another jar of fruit.

'Have some more them apples,' he said.

'I wouldn't mind,' said Golddust. 'I got a big
mouth for apples.' He spooned fruit and juice into his

plate. From a pail of service berries, Charley filled the basin. He was always happy when feeding hungry men.

'Have some more them fish,' he said.

Golddust reached for a yellow slab of trout.

'If I had some salt-risun bread,' he declared to Lela, 'then I'd be plumb in heaven. But,' he added quickly, 'I ain't so demn long ways from heaven now.' He bit off a chunk of carrot and tongued it about his mouth, spending it with difficulty between his two molars.

'Mebbe you'd like some chokecherry jelly,' said Charley. 'Or some plum perserves.'

'No, I'm gettun along fine. It's the best meal I et in forty year. By gum, you know I used could chew with the next one, but I've spit my old teeth out one and another.' He struggled with a slippery piece of carrot. 'Now,' he said, 'I chew her if I can, and if I can't, I swaller her hull without chewun.'

Under the table, Bonnie drew Jed's bare feet between her legs. Thiel sat across from her, choking his food down, scowling at his brother.

When the meal was done, and nothing but dishes and a pile of fish-bones remained on the table, they all sat in the feeble yellow light of an oil lamp. Charley sat by the door and spit his tobacco juice into the front yard; and Golddust sat near him, smoking a huge cigarette of his own making. Bonnie sat with Beth in a dim corner, both leaning against the wall with their legs stretched out on the floor; and near them Jed also sat on the floor, looking searchingly into the gloom, now and then, to reaffirm his vision of hazel eyes and ripe mouth. Thiel had gone outside, with food like lead in his stomach, with a heavy emotion beating through him. When not staring at Bonnie, reading the speech of her gestures, or remembering the pressure of her legs, Jed listened to the romance which spilled out of Golddust's memory.

'In Nervada,' Golddust was saying, 'thet's where I seen him. He lived in a shack, the worst torn-downdest shack you ever see. But it was in a saloon I see him first. No, by God, I ain't a-tellun thet right. It was Brig Tibbets I knowed in Nervada. How'd I get it mixed up, I wonder.... Well, Brig, it was him. But I met this-year Jim in Market Street, San Francisco. Demned if I know, Charley, if I did or not. You remember old Buck Hooper?'

'Buck Hooper,' said Charley, and strove so hard to remember that he stopped chewing. 'Oh, Buck Hooper, hell, yes. He had one eye shot out.'

'Thet's him. Shot in his eye with a twenty-two short. But he was a jim-dandy guy. He could get a stope wrench with the best a them. I see old Buck when he died. And thet man suttenly died hard. I think he must a-had more life than a badger. He got a-holt a life, and by gum, he hung on bold as brass. Even when he was cold as clabber, his old eye, you'd see his old eye move, just like old Buck was a-takun his last look. Thet man looked around after he was dead. To hell and gone plumb out of life, and he still looked around. A vetenery, thet's all the doctor Buck had, and he thought Buck would never let loose.

Stubborn as a bobtail mule, thet man. Just hung on like grim death. Demn good feller, though. Buck, he was ugly enough to stop a nigger funeral. But I liked him.'

Golddust looked thoughtfully at his cigarette. Perceiving at last that it was out, he went to the stove. He knelt on the floor, made a long shaving from a block of wood, and thrust it into the grate. He put its glowing end against his cigarette, smacking his lips as he puffed, and then poked the shaving into the stove. When he sat again by Charley, his joints sounded like snapping twigs.

'Well, about Jim. Jim, he's dead, too. Dad-burn it, Charley, I'm gettun to be a old man. Been a desert rat all my days. Draggun my little girl hell-bent for wonder, and never findun no gold worth a Indian's beard. But I'll find this dust up Burns. I got a feelun it's there.... Well, this Jim.'

He made another cigarette and went to the stove for a light. In the gloom, Jed could see his mother, sitting on a box-chair with her face full of silence. Golddust sat again, with his joints creaking, and resumed his tales. He talked on and on, telling of gold-hunters who had died in the search, of one who found a fortune, of another who went mad and was sent East; of murder in an Arizona saloon, of a bitter feud between two men who staked the same claim; of a pack outfit that lost its way in Death Valley, and of their bones when found; and of his younger brother, Sam, who fell down a shaft in a Montana mine and broke his neck. Again and again he would think of his own quests and speak of these, or he would break off to swear by his dogs and cats that there must be gold up Burns. His mind was a reservoir of tales: of wanderings and disappointments and fights.

Jed listened eagerly, thinking of maps as Golddust talked. When Montana was named, he saw his geography map of the State, colored a fish-yellow; and he peopled it with the words that fell from Golddust's lips. He saw the long curve of California, the wedge of Nevada, the square of Wyoming; and across each of these, he took his imaginary way, following their haunted trails. Death Valley he saw as a black sunken place, full of ageless silence and bleached bones; Jackson Hole was a great open cave in the earth....

Charley stood up at last and said they would make their beds. The girls could sleep with Lela in the house; the others would seek the haystack. After spreading the roll of blankets upon pine boughs and the bear skin, he took four quilts and went outside. When Jed stood in the doorway, looking out, waiting, Bonnie came to him.

'Good-night,' she whispered, and pressed his arm.

Then Jed went to the haystack. He spread a pile of fragrant hay and laid two quilts upon the pile. Without removing his clothes — he wore only shirt and trousers — he crawled in between the quilts and looked at the stars, remembering Bonnie's warm mouth. A little later, Thiel came and lay by him.

'Give me some cover!' he howled, pulling at the top quilt.

'Shut up. You got your share.'

'Stop your racket,' said Charley, from beyond the stack.

Jed stood up and looked at his brother.

'We'll each take one,' he said. 'I'm sick of sleepun with you.'

'You ain't no more sick than me,' said Thiel.

'Shut up,' said Charley.

Jed strode away. After rolling himself in the quilt, he looked again at the sky. But he did not sleep for a long while. He was thinking of Bonnie's good-night, of the way she held his bare feet, of her pressure on his arm. Tomorrow he would ask her to marry him. He was almost fourteen, he was almost a man. They would build a raft. They would ride forth into blue distance; hand in hand they would enter the world.

'I love her,' he thought, and looked at the stars.

VIII

ON the next morning, Charley offered a grubstake, but Golddust said he would live at a sheep-camp. 'You take care my little gal,' he said, 'and I'll be all right.' He took Charley's six-shooter, mounted his nag, and rode up the canyon. He had hardly disappeared when Bonnie came to Jed and whispered:

'Let's run off somewheres.'

'I don't know if we can,' he said. He saw Thiel watching him. 'Mebbe we'll have to go fishun or something.'

'All right,' said Bonnie. She went to the house where two birch poles, with lines and hooks attached, lay upon spikes under the eaves. She brought these poles to him, and then turned to Beth. 'Jed and me, I guess we'll go fish a while.'

Beth's eyes were cunning with knowledge of this girl's ways.

'All right, sure.' She looked at Thiel, who was digging his naked toes in earth and scowling. 'Me and Thiel, mebbe we'll go, too.'

Bonnie considered.

'Well, you and Thiel go down the river, and me and Jed, we'll go up. In that way,' she explained, 'we'll get more fish.'

But Beth was not deceived by this sly ruse. She did not want Jed to go off alone with this girl.

'Or you go up the river,' said Bonnie charitably, 'and we'll go down.'

'What do you think?' asked Beth of Thiel. Thiel was too furiously jealous to think. He dug his toes into earth and trembled with rage. Bonnie looked at Jed, and then at Beth and Thiel. When she spoke again, her voice was sharp with impatience.

'Well, why can't we do like I said? You go up or down, take your choice.'

Beth was annoyed. She hated this girl.

'If you have your pick,' said Bonnie, 'what more do you want?'

'You don't intend to fish,' said Beth, looking at her.

'No? Then what you think I got these poles for? Just to trip and fall over, I guess!'

'You just want a-get off alone with Jed.'

'Oh, Christ Jesus!' cried Bonnie. She shrugged. 'You think I'll kill him, or what? You think I'll hurt your little brother?'

'You ain't a-foolun me,' said Beth. 'I'n see what's in your eyes.'

'Oh, my eyes!' cried Bonnie derisively. She turned to Jed. 'Look in my eyes and see what's there. Have I got something in my eyes?'

Jed was a little enraged. This jealous bickering was withering the romance of his forenoon.

'If they want a-come,' he said, 'why, let them come.' He looked at Thiel. 'Come on, you big lubber.'

'Go to hell!' said Thiel.

'He don't want a-go,' said Bonnie. 'He's just a big babe who wants his ma.'

'You're a fool!' yelled Thiel, looking at her with baffled eyes.

'Come on,' said Bonnie, and she turned toward the river, carrying the poles. Jed followed her. When he looked back, he saw Beth and Thiel staring after them. Bonnie went into brush by the river, dragging the poles after her. She stopped in a small clearing.

'You think they'll come sneakun along?' She listened.

'No, I guess not.'

Bonnie dropped the poles and looked around her.

'Your sister,' she said, 'is jealous for you. That's all's the miss with her.'

'I don't know,' Jed answered.

Bonnie stared at him.

'Are you jealous for your sister?' she asked.

'No,' he said.

'Well, she is for you. She's just so crazy for you her jaw aches.'

Jed stared helplessly at the poles. He knew what Bonnie meant.

'I know a good eddy near,' he said. 'I guess I'll set the poles.' He broke off a green bough of sage and walked back and forth, starting grasshoppers and then creeping upon them with the bough. He baited the hooks with the quivering red-winged creatures and then set the poles in the sod of the river's bank. When he returned to Bonnie, she was lying against a grassy mound. He sat down, a little way off, and she said to him:

'What you set over there for? Do I make you afraid?'

'Nothun makes me afraid.'

'Then come over here.'

Jed crawled over and sat by her.

'I like you,' she said. 'But you're awful silly.'

'Oh, am I! How?' He scowled at her.

'You're just silly.' She looked at him with eyes that had seen many things. 'Have you lived here all your life?'

'Yes.'

'Ain't you never even been to the valley?'

'No.'

'Good God!' said Bonnie. 'All your life in this hole?'

'Yes, I said yes,' he declared, angered by her astonishment.

'And you ain't never even seen a railroad?'

'No.'

'Or a store or a saloon?'

'No.'

'Or a city or a mine or a ocean?'

'No, I ain't never seen them.'

'Well, for the Jesus sake!' Her laugh stung him. She looked at him with renewed interest.

'Tell me,' he said, 'what the world's like.'

'No. Sometime, mebbe, but not now. Ain't you never seen any girls but your sister?'

'Yes, some. I seen the Tompkins girls.'

'Oh. Who are they?'

'They live down the river a long ways.'

'A long ways! The lickety Job, do you call that a long ways?'

'I guess it's quite a ways.' He began to break twigs; he was annoyed and humiliated by her scorn.

'And is them girls all you've seen?' asked Bonnie, watching his strong hands.

'Yes, them's about all.'

'Well, no wonder you're silly.'

'How'd you mean?' he demanded, meeting her eyes. Bonnie dismissed his question with a low laugh and a shrug. 'You got to tell me!' he cried.

'Let's talk about the weather.'

'No! I want you should tell me how.'

'Oh, well, you're just plain silly.'

'Oh, am I! Well, how?'

She looked at him for several moments.

'Ain't you never even been kissed yet?'

'Kissed! Yes, sure, I been kissed.'

'Who? Your mother?'

'Well, I kissed Beth.'

'Oh!' she cried, and her laugh was mocking. 'You mean you kissed your sister.'

'Yes, I've kissed her.'

'But you never done nothun but kiss her?'

'N-no.'

They were silent. Jed waited; and when she did not speak, he asked again: 'Well, how am I silly?'

Bonnie sighed wearily and looked around her. She pointed to a ragged creature sitting in a cottonwood.

'See that vulture,' she said.

'Oh, yes, I see.'

'And I'n see a hawk's nest over there.'

'Well, I guess you seen hawks' nests before this.' His tone was sullen, ironic.

'Mebbe,' Bonnie said, 'we'd better go to the house.'

'No. I won't let you go to the house.'

'Oh, you won't! Well, what you want a-do?'

'I want you to tell how I'm silly.'

She looked at him so intently that he flushed. Then she asked: 'Why don't you kiss me? But mebbe you're afraid.'

Jed felt sudden violent life in his heart. He stared at the vulture and broke twigs with his hands.

'I told you I ain't afraid of nothun.'

'I guess, then,' she said coldly, 'you don't want to.'

Again he met her eyes.

'Yes,' he said, in a low choked voice, 'I want to.'

Her laugh was scornful.

'Well, my God! You want to and you ain't afraid, and still you don't!'

For several moments Jed deliberated her challenge. He looked around and saw nobody in sight, though he imagined that Thiel was watching from a bush. Then he got on his knees and moved toward her; he put hands on her shoulders and stopped, confused. He felt her warm flesh tremble at his touch. Something in her eyes shook him, made him drunk, blind. He wet his lips and stared at her face, his sturdy hands still grasping her shoulders. Bonnie shut her eyes then, and Jed leaned forward to lay a brief kiss on her mouth. Her lips were warm, soft, parted. He took his hands away and sat back, looking at her, wondering if he should kiss her again.

Bonnie opened her eyes.

'Do you call that a kiss?' she asked.

'Sure,' he said. 'Why ain't it?'

'Oh, the squint-eyed Moses! What a fool you are!'

'What do you mean?' he asked angrily.

'Look,' said Bonnie, and taking his hand she kissed it lightly, imitating his shy and timid fervor. 'Do you call that a kiss?' she demanded, giving him a mocking hazel stare.

'Well, ain't it!' cried Jed.

'Oh, yes, oh, yes! Mebbe birds kiss that way. A little peck.' And again her derisive laugh stung him.

'Well,' he asked hotly, 'how do you kiss?'

'You want me to show you? But you'd get afraid and run.'

'I ain't never run from nothun yet.'

Bonnie looked at him thoughtfully. His eyes were dark with courage, his face was passionate and intent.

'All right,' she said, 'you come here.'

Upon hands and knees he moved toward her. Drawing his head down, she pressed her young lips into his mouth, and she held her lips there until he kicked out and jerked his head away.

'What's the matter?' she asked.

'My God,' he said, looking at her, turning scarlet, 'I had to breathe! You shut my wind off.'

'Oh, I shut your wind off! Love and mud, can't you breathe through your nose?'

'Through my nose,' he said, beginning to think that

kissing was a difficult matter. He had conquered
skunks and rattlesnakes and the river, he had dared
his father's wrath, but now he was helpless. All bold-
ness went out of him, and left his heart alone with this
new emotion, as strange and blinding as sudden light.
He was in love, he felt sure. He was in love head over
heels, abandoned to this girl, utterly lost. And he
made a queer throaty sound.

After a little while, Bonnie said to him: 'Come over
here,' and he went, having no power save to go. 'I
want you to kiss me.'

'Sure,' he said, beginning to feel drunk.

'Look at me,' said Bonnie. He looked at her, feeling
more bold now; he looked at her as he had looked at
all the enemies which he had slain. Bonnie gave a cry
of joy. He was not silly now, she said. She loved him
now.

'And I love you,' Jed declared, speaking out of the
hypnotic hour.

'Now you kiss me,' said Bonnie.

He moved forward, eager to please, hungry for her
warm mouth. But when he grasped her shoulders, she
said no: that was not the way to do. She leaned back
against the mound. She reached for his hands and laid
them on her breast, gently closing his fingers.

'Don't squeeze too hard,' she said. 'There, now,
kiss me.'

Jed sought her mouth. He pressed his mouth against
hers, remembering, though shaken like a reed, to
breathe through his nose. He saw that her eyes were
shut, he felt her bosom rise under his hands. After

holding the kiss for what seemed to him an incredible while, he turned away and caught his breath. Bonnie opened her eyes, now full of warm languor, and smiled.

'That was nice,' she said. 'Now put your arms around me and kiss me again.'

Jed slipped his arms under her waist and drew her to him. She was supple, limp, breathless. As he hugged her, he saw that her eyes closed, as if under the pressure of his arms. He kissed her again. He drew back to look at her hushed face, her sensuous mouth. Without opening her eyes she whispered, 'Kiss me!' and her hands trembled on his back. Jed lay at her side and pressed her slender body against him. He kissed her lips and her cheeks and her hair; he smelled the fragrance of her and of the heavy grass in which they were bedded; and he gave himself utterly to the full beating emotion that had riven them. Never before had he known such glory as this, such sorcery, such intolerable sweet rapture and pain. From a tree near by came the bell-like flutings of a meadowlark, and the song fell in such liquid syllables of light and joy that Jed felt as if the whole earth had burst into music. He heard, too, the rich woody cry of a flicker, the cool trilling of a warbler, and the clear tinkling lute-notes of a canyon wren. All the birds were gathering around him, singing into the old empty room of his heart; and the trees were taking the wind from the sky, drenching their boughs with it, and whispering out over him in a great wide breath; and flowing under their leafy sound, under the spilling bird-cries, was the wet wave-wash of river waters, lifting into the sky a gray cloud of music, beating their hunger into mountain walls. He closed his eyes and put his cheek against Bonnie's cheek. Her body against him seemed to be his own, a wandering and unfamiliar part of him, lost in darkness until now.

'I love you!' he said fiercely.

'Don't talk,' said Bonnie. 'Just lay quiet a while.'

And so he lay quietly, with passion and haughty pride making holiness of his heart. He looked at the sky, blue, sincere; at the rugged honesty of an old pine. He looked at the sun, like a yellow pool in the sky, like a hole in the golden depth of space; at the pale blue around it, at the acres of deep blue far away; and he felt as if both the blue and the gold were in his breath and mind. He was part of this vast enchantment, this blue and green wilderness, this unravished hush whose language was song. The silver body of the river was part of it, too; and this tangled garden of light and the bosom of this earth. Above the sound of river and wind and birds, above the trees soaked with daytime, lay a great field of wonder, fenced round with blue depth and curve; and above this field lay darkness and the stars.... It was more than his mind could grasp, more than his blood could hold; and it spilled out of him in a sigh, as if he flowed in rivers of emotion from an inexhaustible source. But it was also intense, as if he had drawn into himself all life, all ecstasy and meaning, and would henceforth burn like a thing of flame. In one moment it was a knot, a handgrip half of rage and half of joy; but in the next moment it was a softness spreading forth, a hungry vale of light that opened and drew the world in.

'I love you!' he cried again, and his hot words came out of the core of old trees, down from the sun and the sky.

'Hold me a little longer,' said Bonnie, and her arms drew him closer.

He held her with renewed strength. When his arms tightened, he felt vividness in his blood, the savage breath from his heart; but when, after a few moments, his arms relaxed a little, he felt only a vague and nebulous glory, an outrush of passion, as if he were quilted in clouds, as if the sensuous sky were filling his flesh. He closed his eyes, shutting out everything but the flavor of this mood, wild and intense and deep. When he opened his eyes again, he was astonished to find them wet. Bonnie looked at him.

'Why, you big silly!' she said.

He hurled her from him and sat up. He scowled at her.

'It's all right,' she said, and kissed his angry cheek. 'You love me, Jed?'

'Sure I do,' he declared.

'All right. Now lay down again.'

He lay down and looked into her eyes. He read their meaning, and the meaning of her cheeks and mouth. She put arms around him and again drew him close. He hugged her to him, and then was quiet. He could feel her heart against him, he could feel the deep passionate throbbing of his own. One of her hands explored upward and played in his dark hair.

'Now kiss me,' she said.

IX

FOR two weeks Golddust explored the upmost reaches
of Burns, Thousand Springs Valley, and the rocky
flanks of Hell's Hole. Jed hoped he would never come
back. These two weeks were a furious idyll of love and
dream. In a later time he looked back upon these days,
bounded by July sixth and July twenty-first, and realized that they had led him more certainly to joy than
any hours before or after; that he had discovered in
them more of the poetry of life, had lain nearer its
meaning and core. He loved again, in later years; he
found a sweeter mouth than Bonnie's; but he never re-
captured the cloudless blue ecstasy of this July inter-
lude. In later years his love spawned words, fell in
hate upon his emotions and tongued them into speech;
he became a wiser huntsman, he wrought a more enduring peace upon the geography of time; but in this
July while, his savage being found its fullest delivery
and its deepest hours. He lived a proud and intense
dream, in a garden of alfalfa land and pines, in a bowl
rimmed out of earth and loud with river-sound. Each
night was a time of fragrant memory, each day a shimmering vision of green and blue. His lust to conquer
and to humiliate lay dead within him, but only for a
little while.

He would sit up in night-time and stare at an in-
verted ocean of stars; he would listen, trying to hear
the breath of Bonnie, who slept on the other side of the

stack; and then he would lie down, wondering at the
beat of his heart. He exulted in his possession, in his
triumph over Thiel, and in his secret plans. He looked
back over his life, with its strange miscellany of deeds,
floored with old bones and the caricatures of death. It
was a record of ferocious achievement, and he was
proud of it. And Bonnie was proud, too.

He lay down under the remote ceiling of earth, looking at the brighter stars, or at the handful of gems
called the Pleiades. He thought of the morning, of another day in secret places, and turned again to sleep.
His dreams went back into his dark years.

In every day of these two weeks, he and Bonnie
went off alone. If Charley looked knowingly at his
son, Jed was unaware; if Thiel became more sullen and
vengeful, Jed did not see. He had eyes only for Bonnie
and for this bewildering new triumph that was his.

He always set his fishpole, and he often brought back
a panful of trout; but fishing was no part of his dream.
His dream was to go with her into a fragrant retreat, to
lie with her in his arms, and to listen to the wonder of
her talk. He asked many questions; he stored his mind
with knowledge of many things.

'How far is it to this-here place San Francisco?'

'Oh, mebbe a thousand miles. It's a far place.'

'I'll go there some day. I'll go all over the whole
damn earth. And how far is it to Cheyenne?'

'Oh, that's a thousand miles, too.'

'I'll go there. Some day soon I'll hit the grit.' He
looked into the blue sky and was silent. Then he
asked: 'How wide is a city street?'

'Oh, not so wide. About here to that-there tree.'

'And the buildings, they ain't as big as mountains. The biggest ones, I mean.'

'Good God, no. As big as hills.'

He thought of the Antelope Hills.

'But they ain't made out of logs, I guess. Pine logs?'

'No, you silly. The buildings, they're made out of stone. Bricks and rocks and such things.'

He scowled at her.

'You got a-stop callun me silly!' he declared.

'Well, you are. You don't know much.'

'Never you mind. Just don't call me silly no more. ... And the ocean, how big is it? What's it like?'

'Oh, the ocean, it's just a big bunch a water. Miles wide and deep.'

'What's it colored like?'

'Like, well, like grass and clouds.'

'I guess it's a grand sight to see.'

'No, the Grand Canyon the Colorado, it's the best.'

'How much biggern Burns is it?'

'Oh, Judas priest! You could throw a million like Burns in it and never see them. It's miles deep.'

'Miles!' he cried. 'You know how far a mile is?'

'Of course I do, you silly.'

Jed seized her and shook her. His eyes darkened.

'I said don't call me silly any more!'

Bonnie stared at him. There was fear in her eyes.

On another time she asked: 'How'd you get that scar?'

'Oh, a mule kicked me.'

'A mule! What was you tryun to do? Nip its heels?'

'Never mind.'

'Mebbe you thought you was a dog or something. A silly pooch, huh? Did you say bark-bark and snap your teeth?' With a finger she traced the scar's furrow. 'I like it, though,' she said. 'It makes you look more fierce.'

'Oh, you like me to look fierce?'

'Yes. I like men drink whiskey and kill things.'

Jed considered this.

'I've killed lots a things,' he said.

'But you ain't never killed a man.'

'No. But I will.'

'I know lots a men has. I know one's killed twenty Indians and Mexicans.'

'What's a Mexican?'

'I don't know. He's just a man comes from Mexico.'

'Well, I'll kill some Mexicans. I'll kill my old man some day.'

'No, you shouldn't kill your old man. Kill Mexicans. They ain't no earthly use.'

'I will. I'll kill my old man, too.'

'I know one man with lots a Indian skelps. Just about a hull house full.'

'What's a skelp?'

'Oh, the Jesus God!' She grasped his dark hair and jerked it. 'That's your skelp,' she said. 'If a Indian got you, he'd cut it off like this.' With a finger she circled his head. 'I knowed a man in Nervada. He was a sight now. His head was like a big billiard ball.'

'Well,' Jed declared, 'I'll skelp all the Indians I see.'

He stretched out on the earth, cradled his head in her lap, and looked up at her face. He liked the hazel light of her eyes. Drawing her head down, he kissed her lips, hungrily, in the way she had taught him.

'We'll be married,' he said.

'Oh, married! What'd you keep a wife on?'

'I'n work. I could trap and sell hides. I could take up a farm somewheres.'

'You're just a boy,' she said, searching him with a worldly stare. 'I could marry men if I wanted to.'

'Oh, am I!' he cried. 'I'n do anything a man can.'

'A man asked me to marry him. A man in Oregon, he asked me.'

'I'll kill him,' Jed declared, scowling at her.

'He was a big man, big as all outdoors.'

'I don't care. He wouldn't make me afraid. Did you ever let him ——?' He sat up, staring at her.

'No.'

'I don't care, then,' he said. 'We'll be married when your old man comes back.'

'Don't talk crazy. I couldn't marry a boy like you.'

Jed sprang to his feet and stalked away. He stopped and looked back, angry, dark, his eyes full of hate and threat.

'Come back here and don't try and be so funny.'

'Go to hell!' he cried. He disappeared into bushes and hid. He sulked there, hating her, loathing the world, until she went in and found him. She struggled with him, and at last she kissed his savage face; but it was a long while before he would talk again.

Sometimes in these days they went up the river and ran almost naked upon the warm white sand. At her slender body, coming into womanhood, he looked with bold eyes, storing his mind with the wonder of it, its beauty and grace. There was no shame in him, nothing but pagan delight, the clean unmoral rapture of wings and waving boughs. His vague notions of sin, harvested from the lewd talk of sheepherders, were stripped off with his trousers and shirt and piled with them upon the sand. He stepped forth into life, feeling its winds and sunlight on his skin, drinking its warmth out of the sky.

Nor was there any shame in Bonnie. From her first years she had been accustomed to nakedness; she had heard the language of sex, and, while gathering its meanings, she had not been overtaken by its implications of sin. And when she looked at Jed's body now, it was with critical interest, an appraisal of his rugged health, and not because she was virginly curious. When she embraced him, it was with no more embarrassment than she would have felt if she had been clothed.

She would lie face downward on the sand, and he would cover her, save only her head and one arm; and then he would lie by her, and with her free arm she would help to cover him; and bedded thus, they would giggle happily, feeling the sand like moving life on their flesh, looking across the afternoon at a lazy sun. Or, again, he would swim for her, taking great pride in his strength and skill, daring the most treacherous whirlpools, and returning to read the love in her eyes. It was his reckless deeds, he learned, rather than his

mouth and hands, which excited in her the most tenderness; and after he had dived into the pool by a
great stone; after he had pitched headlong from a
bluff, and then fought his way across swift waters; and
after he had grasped two heavy water-soaked chunks
of wood, and with the aid of these had walked head
downward through a channel, with only his feet visible, he returned to find her eyes bright and her lips
hungry for his kiss. She drew his wet body to her and
led him to a sheltered cove.

'I love you,' she said, hugging him. 'You're the best
swimmer I ever seen.' And he glowed with pride, wondering what else he could do to prove his manhood.

'I guess you'll marry me now,' he said.

'No, not now. But in a year mebbe I will. Then
we'll be fifteen. That's about the right age.'

'My mamma,' he said, 'she was only fifteen.'

'Well, I knowed a girl married when she was twelve.
Her name was Tessie.'

'Then why can't we be married now?'

'No, when we're fifteen. That won't be long.'

'But how? You won't be nowheres around here
then.'

'Well, you'n go with us.'

'Oh,' he said. And he lay on the sands, building his
dream into the hour of her going away.

Sometimes they went up Burns and ate wild fruit
until their mouths were dark and sweet with juice. Or
they would lie on the bank and watch the trout in a
bush-shadowed pool. The water, except where the

shadow fell in darkness, was as transparent as air, and they could see the spotted beauty of the fish, the small black pools of their eyes, the red breathing of their gills. Deep down lay large trout with golden bellies and with eyes as black as wells. Above them were the smaller fish, darting like sudden gray light or floating in quivering rest.

'They breathe water,' Jed declared. 'Ain't it funny? I tried it once and about choked to death.'

'You ain't a fish,' said Bonnie. 'See that big one watchun us. He's lookun for a hook.'

'No, he's asleep.'

'Like Jesus he is! You see now.' With a stick Bonnie thrust into the water. The trout smote once with the rudder of its tail and vanished. The smaller fish were a network of movement, swift, frantic. A fish attempted to escape, but upon the wide shallow outlet of the pool, it became stranded on a flat stone, its back emerging, its tail lashing desperately; and then it fell back and disappeared.

'I don't see any suckers,' said Bonnie, peering into the pool's depth. 'Suckers, they're like lots a men. They ain't up to much.'

'All the suckers is in the river. The bottom the river, it's covered alive with them.'

'Then where you think these little fish comes from?'

'I don't know. I never thought.'

'I bet there's a big old sucker down there. He has all these-here wives.' She looked at Jed. 'Would you like dozens a wives?'

'No,' he said, 'just you.'

'The Mormons, they have lots a wives.'

'What's a Mormon?'

'Oh, he's just a man with lots a wives.'

'I wouldn't never be a Mormon,' Jed declared.

'I wouldn't, neither. I wouldn't live in a houseful of women. I'd murder the bitches.'

They rose from the bank and went up the canyon. Bonnie led the way and her lover came after, dwarfed against a background of enormous mountains and sky, following an old elk trail through his dream. He looked at the fine hair on her neck, pale brown hair which he loved and owned; at the great wooded peaks standing around him; at the water talking under its roof of bushes and trees; and he trembled in the glory of this afternoon.

'Bonnie,' he said, and his voice was strange.

'What?' asked Bonnie, turning to look at him.

'I want a-kiss you,' he said.

'Oh, you silly!' cried Bonnie, but her voice was pleased. He put his arms around her and kissed her mouth; he stared at her with such strange dark eyes that she shrank from his touch. Then she followed the trail again. After she had gone a mile, turning with the stream, going under sunless shelters or over areas of stone, she stopped suddenly and cried, 'Look!' She pointed to a huge shaggy bear, standing ahead of them in the trail. It was staring at them out of its small ridiculous face.

'It's only a bear,' he said. He looked around him and gathered stones.

'Don't you throw!' cried Bonnie, grasping his arm.

She was frightened by the bear; but she was frightened, too, by something in Jed's face. What she saw was a deep intensity, of fearlessness and of cunning, in his eyes and around his mouth.

He said he would hit the bear lick-spit in its eye. He stepped forth and hurled a stone. It smote the earth near, but the beast did not move. With small pig-eyes it stared, curious, unafraid.

'Don't you hit him!' Bonnie gasped, choking with fright. He pointed to a cedar and told her to climb to its crotch. Then he would knock the beast spinning on its rump. She ran to the tree and climbed.

Jed cursed, his words vibrant with the ring of combat, and the mountains picked up his words and filled the canyon with challenging sound.

'Stop it!' Bonnie wailed. 'Jed, my God, stop it!'

But Jed shrugged and advanced. He threw again and again, aiming at the bear's head; but he missed, and having satisfied its curiosity, the beast moved slowly into brush and disappeared. Jed plunged in after him. Bonnie ran screaming up the trail, crying to him that she was afraid. Jed plowed his way out of tangled growth, his hands still clutching stones, and looked at her. She shrank again, more terrified of him than of the bear. It was something in his eyes and the implacable will of his mouth.

'I want to go home!' she cried, putting a hand to her sobbing mouth. She was white and shaken.

'You coward!' he said, looking steadily at her.

'Don't look at me that way! Take me home!'

Jed dropped his stones. He shrugged.

'What a coward you are!'

'Don't talk to me! I tell you I want to go home!'

'All right,' he said, disappointed, sullen. 'Hit the hike.'

One morning Charley boated across the river and Bonnie went with him. She was afraid of Jed now. He followed her to the river, and while his father bailed the boat out, Jed drew her aside. He was suspicious. He demanded to know why she was going.

'Oh, just for a boat ride.'

'I'n give you a boat ride.'

'Oh, well. I want to go, anyway.'

'You want a-see them Hunter kids.'

'Them who?'

'Vridar Hunter. You want to see him.'

'No, I don't.'

'You're a liar. That's all you want a-go for.' He grasped her wrist and drew her toward him, but she would not meet his eyes.

'Let me go!' she whispered hoarsely.

'Promise you won't,' he said.

'Let me go!'

'Promise you won't. If you do, I'll kill you both.'

'Oh, promise you I won't what!'

'You know what. Promise.'

'All right, I won't. Now let me go!'

Jed released her. His face was sullen with rage and doubt.

'Don't you forget. If you do it with him, I'll kill you.' She did not answer. She looked across the river at timbered acres.

'All right,' said Charley. 'Come on.'

'I mean it!' Jed whispered. He watched the boat put out and ride the waves. Bonnie sat in the rear end, with her head turned from him, her eyes looking south. He saw her leave the boat on the far shore and follow Charley into brush. Then he sat on a stone, wondering how he would know, how he could tell whether she had given her love to Vridar. He shook with jealousy and rage. He rose and stumbled through brush, again possessed by hatred; he sat down again and again, and strove to think the matter out, remembering the resentment of her voice, the bright look of her hazel eyes. His agony became unbearable. All the softness and pride, reaped from twelve golden days, went out of his life, and he was the savage youth of a month ago. And at last, unable to slay his doubt and pain, he went up the river and swam to the other side. He went quietly like a wild animal through the brush, climbed the high north bank of the Hunter farm, and looked at the house. At first he saw nobody at all. But while he watched, two people came around the house and toward him. One was Bonnie and the other was Vridar, with a white cane pole on his shoulder. Jed ducked out of sight and waited. He heard them pass along the upper bank; he heard Bonnie's talk and laughter, and his heart was beating fury within him. They went up the bank, found a trail leading down, and followed it to the river; and after them went Jed, slinking without sound. A hundred yards from the river, he stood behind a large pine and watched them. He saw Vridar bait his hook and cast his line into the stream; he saw

Bonnie standing by him, talking, no doubt, of the pleasure which her body could give. If he touched her, Jed resolved to go down and kill him. He would kill both of them and throw them into the stream. But Vridar did not touch her; and Jed little dreamed that this youth was bewildered and horrified, that his face was as red as fresh beef, because of what Bonnie was saying. He saw only that Vridar cast his line again and again, that he fished for an hour and caught nothing, and that he turned away. Jed followed them until he saw them enter the house. Then he ran to the river and swam home.

He did not meet her at the river. He dried his clothes first and then went to the haystack, hoping that she would come; and she came.

'Well, what you look so mad about?' she asked.

'I ain't mad,' he said, but he felt murderous.

'I kep my promise,' said Bonnie.

'All right. Mebbe you did, mebbe you didn't.' He looked stubbornly at his feet. He could not forget that she had walked with another.

Bonnie stared searchingly at his dark wretched face.

'He's a fool,' she said.

'Who?'

'That Vridar kid. He don't know a hill of beans.' She watched him shrewdly and saw him draw his breath.

'What'd you do over there?' he asked.

Before answering, Bonnie looked at him again, wondering how much he knew. She suspected that he had played the spy. His clothes were still a little damp.

'Oh, he wanted me to go fishun with him. So I went. But he couldn't catch a fish in a washtub.... Well, that's all. I went with him and then I went to the house.'

Jed looked up and met her eyes. He thought he saw in them cunning and dislike. But he could not be sure. And then, unable to resist, drawn by the whole power of earth, he went to her, trembling through and through. He took her in his arms, he kissed her soft mouth, and Bonnie's face was vivid with triumph. But she did not let him see.

'You love me?' he asked, in a hoarse voice that she thought ridiculous.

'Yes, of course.'

He stared at her with hungry blind love. For a moment all his hatred, all his rage, went out of him, and he was choked by an infinite bright rapture.

'And you'll marry me? And you won't go over there again?' He kissed her mouth and throat. She looked at him, swiftly, and again was frightened by the intensity in his face, in his dark eyes. 'When I'm fifteen,' he said.

'Yes,' said Bonnie, 'when you're fifteen.'

'You promise that?'

'Oh, of course I promise!'

His mouth was wolfish on her neck. He drew her close, and everything vanished, save the unspeakable reunion of lips and hands.

X

WITH empty eyes and an empty heart, Golddust rode down out of Burns. There was coal, he said, but a railroad would have to be laid to it. As for gold, there was no sign of it. There was more gold in an elk's tooth than there was in Burns, or in Hell's Hole, or in all the valleys of the Thousand Springs. He would have to hit the high lonesome for Alaska. There was gold there, he said, and his eyes shone again with hope. He would go to Alaska, and he would return in a year or two with his saddle-bags full. And he grinned, the feeble silly grin of a man chasing phantoms around his grave.

'I'll find it,' he said; but as soon as he spoke, the hope went out of his eyes and his face was old and pathetic.

He got his nag, said good-bye to Charley and Lela, and rode into the west. Behind him Jed and Bonnie walked to Rattlesnake Point.

'I'll come soon as I'n make a raft,' Jed promised. 'You'll wait for me?'

'Where?'

'Well, I don't know. In the valley somewheres.'

'If I can,' said Bonnie, 'I'll wait.'

'You got to!' Jed cried. 'I'll come right down. Soon as I'n build a raft I'll come.'

'All right. But come where?'

'Down in the valley.'

'Oh, you fool! The valley's big as all outdoors.'

'Well, you say where you'll be.'

'How do I know?'

'Ask your old man. He'll know.'

'He don't know. He don't know nothun but hit the trail.'

Jed was desperate.

'You don't want me to come!' he cried.

'Sure I do. But I don't know where.'

'Anywheres you say. Idaho Falls. I'll riae the raft plumb down to there.'

'All right. I'll wait in Idaho Falls.'

'By the river,' he said.

'Yes, by the river.'

'I'll be down soon. I'll make me paddles and row fast.'

'Why don't you take the boat?' asked Bonnie.

'I don't like to take the boat. But I'll be there. And you'll be by the river in Idaho Falls.'

'Yes.'

'You'll see your old man goes there?'

'Yes, I'll get him to go that way.'

'And you'll wait by the river?'

'Silly, didn't I say I would!'

Jed took her hand and kissed it. At the Point he stopped and drew her to him.

'You still love me?'

'Yes,' she said, looking at him curiously.

He kissed her mouth and strove to take himself away. The distance between them and Golddust was steadily lengthening.

'Mebbe I could walk!' he said excitedly.

'No. It's a long ways. Well, I got a-go now.' Again he kissed her mouth and both her hands.

'You'll wait?'

'Yes.'

'By the river. By the river in Idaho Falls.'

'Yes, that's where.'

'I'll come right away,' he said. 'Mebbe I'll be there first.'

'All right. I got a-go now.'

'Good-bye,' he said, clinging to her hands.

'Good-bye.'

He watched her run around the Point and disappear, and a horrible doubt and loneliness sucked at his breath. He ran after her, hoping to see her for another moment, but she had dropped under a hill and out of sight.

Jed never saw Bonnie Adams again.

He went back up the river, striding rapidly, wondering if he should take the boat. He thought of his mother and decided to leave it here. He would ride down on a couple of logs, as Charley and Henry Bord and many others had done.

He wanted to say farewell to Lela and Beth, and perhaps to Thiel also, but he did not want them to know he was going away. Looking into the house, he saw only his father there. He was sitting on the floor, sewing with buckskin a tear in one of his shoes.

'Where's mamma?' asked Jed.

'Don't know,' said Charley, without looking up. 'In the orchard, I think.'

Jed went quickly to the orchard. He found his mother gathering berries, and for a few moments he watched her. Her thin hands were stained with juice; her face was strangely white and calm; her lovely hair hung in a rope down her back. He went over to her, hardly knowing what to say. She looked at him. In her blue eyes for many years now, he had seen something that baffled him, an awful quietness, the shadows of things dead. Beyond the shadows and the quiet lay a dark pain. He had often seen her eyes darken until nearly all the blue went out of them; but the meaning of her stare he could only guess at. His mother was a strange secret, and his father, too, and life.

As she looked at him now, he saw her eyes fill with darkness until they were almost black. But he did not understand. He loved her, he would have died for her, but he did not understand.

'What is it?' asked Lela, speaking in that quiet voice which she had taken from the loneliness of her home.

'Nothun,' Jed declared, wondering what he should do. Again her thin slender hands gathered the berries. Again her eyes looked at him, full of something deeply haunting, unforgettable, lost. He hesitated, thinking it best to remain here; but when he thought of Bonnie, when he remembered his own bitter years and the waiting world, he felt an emotion leap and grow within him. He stepped close to her and kissed her hair, and then he sat at her side.

Lela put an arm around him.

'You're troubled,' she said. 'Something is on your mind.'

'It ain't nothun,' he declared, putting berries into the pail. 'No more than always has.'

'You're sorry Bonnie is gone,' she said, patting his dark hair. 'She'll come back some day.'

'No,' he said, 'she won't never come back.'

He rose to his feet and stared into the west. For a moment he was about to confess, to tell her he was running away, to tell her he would never come back; to speak his hatred of Charley and of this walled-in solitude that had been his home. But the words filled his throat and died there. He would have to go without saying good-bye. Even if his going killed her, even if she hated him afterward, he would have to go. He knelt by her, he put arms around her and kissed her cheeks, her forehead, her blue eyes. Then he was enraged, humiliated, because his eyes were wet. He turned away, so that Lela would not see, and stood with his back toward her. He stared through a haze at the west, despising himself, fighting his grief. And then, without looking again at his mother, he walked slowly away, down through the aisles of the orchard, across alfalfa which was now in full bloom, and into the river brush. He would go now, while he had strength.

Along the brush and out of sight, he went westward past Rattlesnake Point, and waded across a channel to a large island. Never looking back, pushing all thought of family and home out of his mind, he set to work. From a pile of driftwood he dragged two logs to the water's edge. He bound them together with long tough vines. Hatless, with nothing on him but a ragged shirt and ragged trousers, and without a cent in his pockets, he pushed his raft into the stream and leapt upon it. And with a great sadness fighting within him, Jed Bridwell began that daring pilgrimage that was to lead him into many strange lands of earth. Only once did he look back. Before rounding the first curve, he looked long and earnestly at the home he was leaving; and his thoughts were of Lela, sitting in the orchard, her face very calm and white. He believed in this hour that his own people would never see him again. He believed he would never come back.

He came only once. Eight years later, he stepped suddenly out of a bitter white winter and stood upon the threshold.

Book III
LELA

Book III

LELA

I

AMONG the people who knew the Bridwells, or who heard of them from afar, and built rumors into great tales, Lela became the darkest riddle of all. They summarized Charley as a lazy stinker, a brute, and the biggest-hearted fellow in Idaho; Jed as an inhuman wretch who played his devilish pranks without ever cracking a smile; but they found no words for Lela. It was less what she did than what she did not do, less her speech than her silence, that baffled those who talked about her; and even Prudence Hunter, a close friend, knew almost nothing of what lay in Lela's mind and heart.

'I love her,' Prudence would declare, 'but I don't understand her very well. She's a funny woman. Sometimes I think she loves old Charley deep as life, and then again, I think she hates him like poison. But I don't know.'

In this surmise Mrs. Hunter was right.

When Lela married Charley, in 1891, she did not love the man. She was only fifteen. At that time she loved no one, for she had no people of her own and no friends. Her mother had died of heart failure when Lela was a small child; her father had been slain by

Indians. Her uncles and aunts and cousins were all
scattered from ocean to ocean, and after her eighth
year she saw none of them. Her father died when she
was nine. She then traveled from place to place with a
man named Job Bush, a restless vagabond, and with
Job's wife, a lean and bitter shrew. Five years later,
she was deserted in Pocatello, and she had been a
chambermaid for a year in a dirty rooming-house
when Charley met her. He wooed her for three weeks.
When he offered marriage, she took it, believing that
any kind of life would be better than what she had.
She liked him, but she did not love him.

With infinite tenderness and with canny skill, he
drew the sunken part of her into light and air. He
awakened her emotions, he taught her how to weep,
until all the bitterness of her childhood was forgotten,
and she lived gently in his arms. When her children
came, three of them before she was nineteen, he was
midwife and nurse, and his great hands were tender
and wise. He scrubbed their small shabby room, he
washed the few baby clothes that they had, and he
often cooked their meals. After a birth, he made her
lie in bed, quietly resting, for two weeks; and he did all
the work, flooding the room meanwhile with talk and
song, until his child-wife smiled, until the pain went
out of her blue eyes. They were poor, they often had
little to eat but bread, and sometimes not even that;
but Charley was happy, and she was happy with him.

And she was happy, too, after they went up the
river and laid their home in Bane's cottonwood shack.
The ugliness of Pocatello, with its flat smoky houses

and coal-yards, had borne down on her spirit. She found, in the extravagant beauty of her new home, and even in the white winters, a magnificent peace. The architecture of life here, its prodigal richness, the lofty curves of its great reach and depth, suggested that God had lingered here a long while. And deeply religious as she was, though she had never been inside a church, though she had never seen a prayer-book or a hymn, she opened her heart to this vast retirement, this exiled beauty companioned by wild things, and discovered within herself emotions which she had never used. The meaning of these mountains, the eternal language of this river, were related, it seemed to her, to the sky and stars and the gray desert of the sea. The quiet of the former, and the frantic haste of the latter, were but a larger vision of something that had lived, unrealized until now, in her own soul. An enormous coppered sky at twilight, or a golden fragrant dawn; a wilderness of falling snow, or the dark tent of midnight: all these went down into her, reaching into her with waves of beauty, until she felt a deep emotion, like that in her womb when she carried her first child. Often it was so intense, so like the mystic rapture of Charley's first embrace, that she felt as if some incredible thing would be born from her throat. It was this emotion, too, though mixed with a kind of blissful terror, which she felt upon hearing the wintry sound of coyotes, the lean sky-haunted baying of wolves, the high and lonely challenge of a mountain lion. She felt it in spring-time, when acres of snow fell downward and paralyzed the trees; when hawks came down from sky valleys and sent their desolate scream out over the silence; and when rainstorms marched up the river, rolling thunder like madness from stone ledge to mountain wall. And when the sky was clear and summer grew on the earth, she felt it in the endless flow of the river, forever going and never gone.

So it was during her first years on the Bridwell place. She felt no estrangement in things. She looked across this bowl of life, and its sudden vehemence, as well as its tranquil blue, seemed to be part of what she had power to understand. And there grew within her a great love for Charley. Though an indolent husband, he was a tireless lover. In gossip about them, it was said that he waited on her hand and foot. He scrubbed their house, laundered their clothes, and often did the cooking. And he was always thoughtful, tender, kind. Not once in their twenty-five years together did he speak sharply to her, or coarsely of women, or waver in his devotion.

He wanted her to remain lovely and sweet and young, to keep the soft smoothness of her hands, the dark blue of her eyes. He did not permit her to labor in the garden, to carry water from the creek, or to gather wood for the fire. She was to be a kind of idle princess, a fair jewel of silence. And it was in this wish, born out of his tenderness, that he made his greatest mistake.

Because Lela was as ambitious as her husband was lazy. She did not like a quiet life, though he almost convinced her, for a long while, that she did. In consequence, she became more and more unhappy, more

dissatisfied with the chloroformed seasons of her life.
Nothing changed but the weather. Events stood in a
sober frame, becalmed, drugged. Across this picture,
fixed in her mind, the sun moved and disappeared and
moved again, and the river plunged across, from corner
to corner, forever going and never gone. And there
was no change in these. The sky was a yellow monot-
ony, now high or now low, and the river was a muddy
or silver haste, drunk with its own senselessness: two
weird calendars of the changeless, two circumferences
around birth and death.

But it was the river that haunted her most. If it had
been a deep quiet lake, full of shadows and sleep, a
mirror of the awful calm of mountains and sky, she
might have forgotten her desire to create, to build her
life into a thing of meaning. She might have killed the
restless part of her, as Charley wished her to do, and
become soaked in that lazy dreaming, or that dreamless mellow hush, which he loved. But the river was
not a lake. It was a tireless hunger, ancient but forever
young, baffled but forever seeking, as if under the
earth's calm surface there was a great unrest, out of
which it came eternally, speaking the eager language of
life. Night and day, day and night, she heard the
sound of its travel, its wet call to the sea; year after
year, she saw it eat banks away, melt islands until they
vanished, and hurl its unconquerable body against
walls of stone; until its image lay across her mind, until
its hunger washed upon the shores of her being, until
its sound made a reservoir of her heart. Upon the
walls of her house, against the mountains and the sky,

she saw a picture of moving waters; in the talk of her husband and children, of wind and storm, she heard the sound of moving waters; until life spun within her, like an eddy of feeling, isolated from all meaning, condemned to a timeless fever of striving, but exiled from all change.

To this mood in which she lived, each year made its unhappy contributions. Each year brought to a sharper focus her struggle between hatred and love. When she saw Adolph Buck take to his heels, white and terrified, when she saw Charley choke his son or flog his sons in later years until their backs were red, a violent anguish wrung her heart. She hated him, but she loved him, too. She tried to understand, to reconcile his tenderness, his hospitality, with the devilish and sardonic part of him. But she could not. He seemed to be two men, wrapped up in the same skin. She had two visions of him, and they were as far apart as the two Poles. And if she was bewildered by what the devil in him did, she understood even less the strange being that he became after he had sated his spite.

Because, after he had beaten his sons, he became wholly incredible. He would disappear for two or three days, to debauch himself with whiskey, or to hide somewhere in the mountains, only to return unshaven and haggard and silenced. And he seemed so saddened by the experience, so humbled and shamed, that her love went out to him even while her hatred remembered. By flogging his sons, or by delivering his cruelty in another manner, he seemed to purge himself, to chase the demons out of his soul, to get a new grasp on tenderness and peace.

About the dark part of him the years taught her little. She knew he was jealous of his sons, and of Jed especially, who was her favorite. She felt that he had once been ambitious, that his laziness was a retreat from life, and that he wanted his sons to achieve what life had denied him. But these were vague recognitions, feeble and uncertain, and of small use. She knew, too, that he was proud of his sons in many ways: of their skill as swimmers, of their courage, of Jed's cunning warfare against his enemies. He was proud of their knowledge of geography and of their ability to spell great words. When they astounded simple minds, she saw in his eyes an intent joy. And he was pleased also when they humiliated sheepherders with their pranks. But between the two, their knowledge gained from books and their impish doings, he seemed to make no distinction, and the whole matter became dark in her thoughts.

And so she lived through the years, alternating between hatred and love; now melting in his arms, yielding to his tender words and hands, now staring with contempt at his lazy back. In one hour he sickened her with some new jest, some wizardry of his diabolic mind; and in the next hour he amazed her with some generous deed or some magnificent gift out of his poverty-ridden life. In one summer, for instance, he offered to carry a valley fisherman across Burns; but in the deepest and ugliest part of the stream, he pretended to slip and fall, and the man bashed his face on a stone, breaking his nose. In the following winter, Charley braved the river ice, and for three weeks was an apostle of hope and charity to the Hunter family, stricken with smallpox. In one summer he helped his sons fill boards with shingle nails and strap these boards upon the faces of the rams; and with his sons he bent over, permitting the rams to plunge against his rump, until their faces were a mass of blood and dripping wool. But in this summer, too, he fed every wanderer who came to his door, warming each heart with his talk. And he not only gave of his scant store of food, but of his tobacco also, and of everything else that he owned, if strangers asked for it.

Though not stingy, Lela resented his lavish giving of the little they had. He fed good-for-nothing sheepherders, cowpunchers, and river fishermen, when there was less than enough for two full meals in the house. He killed an elk and gladly gave half, and often the better half, to greedy valley folk. In one autumn, when he had no meat in his own home, he killed two deer and gave both of them away, brightly assuring Lela that he would go out and get two more. His elk teeth, which he might have sold for ten dollars a pair, he gave to ranchers for watch-charms. His only source of income was his hay, perhaps twenty tons of it, which he sold to sheepmen when they brought their herds down in the fall; but even so, he turned into his haystack every hungry beast ridden to his door; or if the lucerne was still unharvested, he tethered the horse in a choice spot of his field.

Against his giving, or against anything else that he

did, Lela never protested, knowing that protest would be useless. She watched this wild place turn her sons into savages, but she felt that no power of her own could save them, or divert her life from its inevitable course. She retired into bitter apathy; she passed into legend as the silent woman. Those who came to her door seldom heard her speak. They looked at her sad face, at something in her blue eyes, and went away to marvel and to talk.

'When she looked at me I felt kind of queer. It's her eyes.'

'Yes, I know. I don't think she's just in her right mind. Locoed, that-there woman is. Old Charley has drove her bughouse.'

'Yes, that's it. She's crazy as all get-out.'

But Lela was not insane, though many declared that she was. Time and again, in an attempt to see the outlines of her defeat, she approached the border of madness, but Charley always drew her back. If she did not speak to men who came here, it was because she had nothing to say, because she hated their lewd faces and tongues. To Prudence Hunter she talked long and earnestly, at least twice in every summer, and she wept in a quiet way, as if never daring to touch the emotional reservoir within her. And the bright fixed stare of her blue eyes, their desperate coldness, was only the look of one baffled and shut in, of a prisoner who saw no escape, who saw nothing in the future but imperturbable peaks and a frantic river and a barren home.

Charley's keen eyes had seen this stare. He saw it

come to birth when he choked his son; he watched the bluish glitter of it become fixed. He had tried to soften and destroy it. But his tenderness and banter had no power to strip it away. He served her like a slave; he loved her with undiminished ardor; he often worked when he wished to sit and dream, digging weeds from the garden, watering the orchard, reaping his hay. But the look remained. Lela retired into a strange and unapproachable silence; and he did not understand. Her unhappiness made him suffer, but she never knew it. He would go off for hours, sitting out of sight somewhere, chewing his tobacco and thinking. And when, betrayed by the dark side of him, he beat his sons or debased a fisherman, he would vanish for a long while, and he would return looking haggard, as if he had kept a rendezvous with age. He tried to change his ways, but his ways were beyond change.

And so Lela might have lived here, until completely frozen within, with all the ambitious part of her drugged or dead, if four events, all happening between a July and a June, had not shaken the earth from under her and brought her life to its first crisis. The first of these events was the disappearance of Jed.

II

WHEN she sat by the berry bush, on that July after-noon, and saw Jed walk slowly away, she felt as if the sky had darkened. She did not see his tears, but she heard something in his voice, and she read the desper-ate meaning of his kiss. She wanted to rise and follow. But she did not. She sat by the bush, thinking of him, remembering years that were still vivid with his ways, colored by his passionate courage and pride; and re-membering, too, his long secret whiles with Bonnie, and his love for this girl. She supposed that he was only infatuated and that he had spent his time in harmless talk on river-banks.

And even now, after he had vanished, after he had walked out of her life, to be gone for eight interminable years, she hadn't the faintest notion of the grim pur-pose in his heart. She thought he was grief-stricken because Bonnie had left. He was lonely, as he had al-ways been in this vast bowl, under this great blue tent. He had gone down to the river, to sit and brood as was his custom, or perhaps to swim.

With her thoughts full of his hair and eyes, and the earnestness of his face, she filled her pail and stood up. Going to the south border of the orchard, she looked at the river and into the west, but she saw no sign of him. Then she sighed and went to the house.

She sat on a chair by the window, picking stems from the berries, looking up from time to time to see if

Jed was coming. Then she prepared supper, going often to the window to look out. When supper was laid, she went to the door. Thiel and Beth were coming up from Burns Creek.

'Where's Jed?' she asked, speaking out of a nameless fear.

'Don't know,' said Thiel. 'Don't give a hoot, neither.'

'Thiel, for shame. Where's your father?'

'Down at the crick fishun.'

'He's just caught a big one,' said Beth. 'Such a lollaper, you should see.'

'Tell him supper's ready.' She looked at Beth. 'You go find Jed, will you?'

'How should I know where he is! I guess he's follered that Bonnie bitch.'

'No, he's around somewheres.'

'I ain't seen him,' said Thiel. 'He's hit the grit.'

Lela stared at her children. She saw that both of them, in the present moment at least, were hateful toward her. And she wondered why. She did not know that Thiel was jealous of his handsomer brother, and that Beth, who loved Jed more than anybody save her father, had suffered madness and outrage after Bonnie came.

'Well,' she said, looking strangely at her children, 'supper's ready. Tell them to come.' And she entered the house, feeling sick and beaten.

Charley came, bearing an armful of trout.

'How's them suit you?' he asked, but Lela did not speak. She had eaten fish until she hated their sight

and smell. He watched her shrewdly while washing
slime from his hands. Then they all sat at the table
and began to eat. All but Lela. The food choked her.
She was sickened by the odor of wild duck, which was
their meat to-night. Charley ate ravenously, but his
alert eyes were on his wife.

'Ain't you feelun well?' he asked.

'No.' She pushed her tin plate back. Through the
gloom she looked at him, and his appetite became a
dead lump in his throat.

'What's the matter?' he asked.

Thiel and Beth stopped eating. They stared at
Lela. And Lela looked at Charley until he stood up.

'Where's Jed?' she asked, and her voice was strange.

Charley looked down at his plate, heaped with duck
and potatoes and green things from the garden. For
several moments no one spoke.

'Why,' said Charley, 'ain't no one seen him? Thiel,
where's Jed?'

'How should I know? I ain't seen him.'

'Beth, ain't you seen him?'

'Not since Golddust went. Last I saw him he was
walkun down the trail with Bonnie.'

'Well,' said Charley, with returning appetite, 'I
guess he's down at Tompkins'.' And grasping a fork he
again fed his hungry mouth. Thiel and Beth also resumed their eating.

Lela rose and went outside, and Charley followed
her at once. She turned and faced him; and across the
dusk, across this vanishing of their child, they stared at
each other for almost a full minute.

'That's where he is,' Charley said at last. He drew forth a plug, looked at it, and returned it to his pocket without biting off a quid.

'No, he ain't,' said Lela. 'I think he's dead.'

'Dead!'

'Yes, dead.'

She entered the house, filled the lantern with kerosene, and lit the wick. Carrying the light, she went to the river and Charley went with her. He thought this search was feeble nonsense, but he never let her go out into the night alone.

'I seen him come down about here,' she said, speaking in a gray voice.

Charley searched at the water's edge, but only stones lay there, and he could see no sign of bare feet. Then they went down the trail, lying in alfalfa crotch-deep, and to Rattlesnake Point. In the dust they saw the imprint of Bonnie's shoes and of Jed's naked feet; they saw where the naked feet stopped and turned back. For a little while they stood here, looking out over the river's swift darkness, into piles of shadow. Then they went back to the house.

Charley said his son was hiding somewhere and would appear soon. The four of them sat in firelight, silent, waiting. The fire died, a bat entered the room and smote the walls, and outside was the harsh going of nighthawk wings. Charley took the lantern, hours later, and went into the night, calling his son; but nothing answered him save his own voice. Lela saw the yellow light by the stable, then gleaming in river brush, and then up Burns. Nobody spoke when he returned.

They went to bed and took the mystery with them. Charley thought his son was hiding out somewhere, but Lela was convinced that he was dead. And as days passed into weeks, this conviction became a dull part of her, stored away among the other unhappy things of memory. Upon her there fell an awful quiet, and the look in her eyes made Charley afraid.

This winter was one of the severest in the history of Antelope. Blockaded by ice and snow, covered over with the gray estrangement of the sky, the Bridwell house stood like a brown stain against a great white solitude. The only trail anywhere was that leading to the stable. The river roofed itself with ice until its dark waters were hidden and silent. Each birch retired into a gleaming sheath; the brush seemed to be loaded with glass foliage; and against the south lay the blinding acres of the Hunter farm.

When Charley was inside, his shoes stood by the door. He took them off when he entered. And when Lela or Beth or Thiel left the house, they wore these shoes, because they had no others, except Lela's ragged and laceless ones. Thiel spent much of his time outside. He would sit on the floor and put the shoes on, and then he would wrap his feet and legs with gunny-sacking or old horse blanket; whereupon he would stalk forth, spending long hours in the stable, or going upon the river to fish. His thoughts were often of Jed. He believed Jed had run away, and little by little there grew within him a desire to leave this place. He laid his plans and waited for the snow to melt.

In a gray bitter morning of late January, Charley spoke to Beth and Thiel. He told them to bundle up warmly and to hit the grit. Beth put on the shoes and wrapped her feet and legs. Having no shoes, Thiel had to content himself with rags, and these he bound to his feet until he looked as if he were walking in two great pillows. They put on threadbare coats and caps and mittens. Then they looked at their mother, lying white and still on the bed, and went outside. They could take some matches, Charley declared, and if they got cold they could build a fire. Anyway, they would keep out of sight until he called them.

They went to the stable. The cow stood inside with frost growing in her hair. Brother and sister looked at each other for several moments.

'We'll soon have another member the family,' said Beth, and she shrugged.

'Yep, my God,' said Thiel.

'Or mebbe two. It's just like her to have twins.'

'Just like we ain't got enough to feed now.'

'Or to dress, either. Holy Jesus, look at these rags.' And Beth stared at her coat and mittens.

'Well, look at me,' said Thiel, eyeing the pillows on his feet. 'I ain't never had a pair a shoes.'

'Nor me, either.'

'Yes, you did. I remember a pair, long time ago.'

'When I was a baby, mebbe.'

'Well, that's more'n I ever had. I ain't had no nothun.'

'Just think,' said Beth. 'What'll it wear? She's been makun clothes out a flour sacks.'

'And sugar sacks. And salt sacks. I tell you we should both run away like Jed.'

'I know. I been thinkun that, too.'

'Or mebbe he was drownded,' said Thiel.

'No, he hit the hike. He's livun now somewheres with that Bonnie bitch.'

Thiel beat his breast and jumped around in his pillow-shoes. He went to the door and looked toward the house.

'How long'll it take her to have a kid?'

'Holy God, don't ask me. I ain't never had none yet.'

Thiel looked at her with approving eyes.

'You will, though,' he said. 'I guess all women do.'

'No, I never won't. I can't stand no kids.'

He looked at her warm mouth.

'Well, how about runnun away? I mean it, my Christ. I'll hit the breeze any day now.'

'Me, too.'

Thiel threshed about, trying to keep warm. He reached for the cow's udder and squirted a stream of milk against the wall.

'Don't do that!' Beth cried. 'You want us all to starve?' They laughed.

'I guess,' said Thiel, 'it's lots a pain to have a kid. A sheepherder told me they just about died. Yelled their lights out, he said.'

'Who told you that?'

'Adolph Buck.'

'Oh, him.'

'You're sweet on him,' declared Thiel, looking at her with eyes cunning and greenish like his father's.

'Oh, yes, like the holy hell!'

'If you wasn't my sister,' he went on, giving her a lewd grin, 'you could keep me warm.'

Beth shrugged. 'If I wasn't your sister I'd knock your brains out. It's just to be your sister makes me good to you.'

'If you was a Tompkins girl I'd drag you anunder a pile of hay.'

'Don't talk like a fool.'

'Just the same, I wish you wasn't my sister right now. I feel spoony, I do.'

'You're just like Bonnie Adams, that's it.'

'Sure I am. So are you.'

'I'm not. I hate men.'

'Oh, yes. Like you hate Adolph, I guess.'

Again Thiel jumped around in his pillows and flailed himself with his arms. He went to the door and looked out, and then he came over to Beth who was shivering by the manger. He blew a cloud of breath in her face and grinned.

'If you wasn't my sister, I'd kiss you good and hard.'

'Oh, shut up. Nobody wants to kiss you.'

'I know a song,' he said. 'It's a good song. I snuck up in the brush and heard Bonnie sing it to Jed.'

'Oh, you sneakun broomtail! I guess you seen things, too.'

'I sure did.'

'Well, what's the song?'

Thiel hopped about and chanted:

Ladies, left hand to your sonnies,
Here we go, grand right and left;
Balance all and swing your honeys,
Pick them up and feel their heft....

'That ain't so grand,' said Beth scornfully. 'Adolph, he knows better ones.'

'Oh, he's a wise old spooner, that-there Buck. Wait till you marry him. He'll take you through a course of sprouts.'

'Don't fret yourself. I wouldn't marry him if his heart was made of gold.'

'It ain't. It's made of flint rock and slate.' Thiel went again to the door and stared at the house. 'I can't hear a thing,' he said, listening. 'Mebbe you got a spankun new brother now.'

'A sister, more like it.'

'Both, mebbe. What's a new baby like?'

'God knows.'

'I hope it don't look like baby mice,' said Thiel.

'Or baby rats, neither. I bet the little bugger is homely as a wart.'

'Homely as a donkey, I guess. Homely as a manure pile.'

'Oh, Jesus! Homely as a skinned rabbit.'

Thiel went outside and to a pine tree. Breaking off some lower dead branches, he brought them into the stable; and upon its floor of frozen dung he made a fire. The smoke and reaching heat filled the stable, and the cow looked around, astonished by the warmth. Frost melted on her hide and her cold body sent off steam. A little later, she began to chew her cud.

'She's been a long time,' said Thiel, warming his hands. 'I never knowed it took so long.'

'Me, neither,' said Beth.

'You'n see what you're in for. Wait till you're married.'

'Yes, wait till I am!'

'Wait till Adolph gets his old arms around you. You'll be a plumb goner.'

'Him! I'd bust his head open.'

'You'll be meek as Moses. Just like butter in his arms, that's it. Just melt all over him, that's how you'll do.'

'Like the holy angels I will.'

'Sure. You'll split the wind when he says come here. Just pack up and go like a hurrycane.'

'You make me tired. Shut up your chin music.'

Thiel gave her another lewd grin. He looked at her tall slender body, wrapped around with old coats and a piece of quilt.

'I know you girls,' he said. 'You're all like Bonnie.'

'Oh, I said shut up!'

'Just all alike,' he persisted, his face loose and help-less in an amorous grin. He brought dry hay from the manger and threw it on the fire. He turned his back to the sudden flame and said: 'Well, me, I won't be much longer in this-here place. When spring comes, I'll hit the lonesome good and high.'

'Yes, I amagine you will.'

'I sure will. I'll lean out like hell kicked me in the end.'

'I'n amagine that.'

'I'm a liar, then, and you're a pretty boy. For why you think I won't?'

'You'll stay here till your old eyes drop out.'

'Well, just watch me lean out when the snow melts.'

They stood by the fire, Thiel thinking of his going away, Beth thinking of Adolph Buck. The cow moved out of her frozen silence and tongued leafy alfalfa into her mouth. Her gaunt sides heaved with content. Then Thiel saw a large pack-rat, crouching on the top log of the wall, staring at him with two dark cunning beads. He grasped a pitchfork. He attacked swiftly and impaled the creature on a tine, and then threw it out upon the gleaming snow. It turned around there, for a few moments, as if its back were broken, and then crawled away, leaving behind it a thin red line. Thiel stood again by the fire, which he fed with old hay and broken pieces of manger. From time to time he glanced at Beth's face, soft with warm memories of Adolph, and he guessed of what she was thinking. He grinned knowingly and filled his own mind with thoughts of the Tompkins girls. They stood by the fire in silence, thinking of love and waiting for birth.

An hour later, Charley shouted to them and they entered the house. Their mother lay on the bed with an infant in her arms. They could see only its tiny face and its blinking womb-dark eyes. Lela was very white and still.

'Is it a boy or a girl?' Beth asked, but neither parent answered her. A great fire sang in the stove and the room was very warm. Charley took the shoes from Beth, quietly put them on his own feet, and went out-

side. Beth and Thiel sat by the stove. They looked at
each other, and then at the mother and child. When
darkness fell, Charley and Beth prepared supper,
neither speaking a word. The three ate in silence, and
then Charley took to the bedside a dish of fruit, some
tender morsels of mutton, and a glass of milk. He
helped Lela sit up, and against her back he placed
bedding and pillows. She drank the milk and ate a
little of the fruit. She was very pale, and her hands
trembled. She lay down again, and the babe whim-
pered at her breast. There was no sound outside save
the howling of coyotes, and no sound inside save the
greedy speech of the fire. The room was full of shadows
and stovelight. Then Beth and Thiel made their
separate beds on the floor, the one in the southeast
corner, the other in the southwest. Thiel crawled between ragged blankets, pulled his trousers off, and then
dragged them forth to make a pillow for his head.
Beth also covered herself with a blanket before removing her clothes. Time and again during this night, and
during nights that followed, Thiel was awakened, and
he would look up to see his father laying wood on the
fire or moving barefooted about the room. He saw him
taking things to Lela, or he saw him cradling the babe
in his arms, and he wondered at this new vision of the
man, his tenderness and patience.

In this manner of hushed movements and low voices
they lived until the mother rose from her bed. And
even after she walked about, slowly regaining her
strength, very little was spoken in this house. Charley
devoted most of his time to her; and when he was not

busy with her needs, he would go out and chop wood, or he would sit by the fire, chewing tobacco and looking thoughtfully at the stove. Neither Beth nor Thiel knew quite what to make of him now. His banter was gone, his nonsense, his huge warm vitality and zest. And Lela for them was equally strange. She sat for long hours by the window, looking out, as if searching the white landscape for her lost son; and in her eyes was something that baffled them.

Often they would go out together, to feed and milk the cow, and they would talk of the matter. But they talked in low voices. They talked like people with minds full of inexplicable things.

'Soon as the snow melts,' Thiel would declare, time and again, 'I'll hit the grit. I can't stand this life no more.'

'And me, I don't know what I'll do.'

'It's funny,' he said. 'I never seen the old man like this.'

'It's funny,' said Beth, and shrugged. 'It beats all get-out.'

'It's a girl,' said Thiel. 'I know that much.'

'I know.'

'God all-hemlock. I'll go batty this way. I'll hit the trail soon.'

'And I'll have to stick around. You'n thank God you ain't a girl!'

'You'n marry some man. Then you'n hit the grit soon as you like.'

'Oh, yes, marry some man! Marry a tree, I guess.'

'Marry Adolph. I seen you up the canyon with him. Last summer, I mean.'

'Well, never mind. He'n go shoot himself for all I care.'

'Well, I don't know. I'll hit the hike soon. I should a-went with Jed, that's what. I should a-went years ago.' He stared at her and then added: 'I should a-went years ago...'

And three weeks later, when Rattlesnake Trail lay bare between melting fields of snow, Thiel followed his brother into the west. Lela sank under this blow without a word. And while she sat in deeper silence, half-crazed by the vanishing of her sons, the fourth event struck into her life.

III

ON that day when Adolph Buck, then a youth of eighteen, was frightened nearly out of his wits by Charley's jest, he did not stop running until he was completely exhausted. The story of his terror and flight became a common one. 'You seen any more bears lately?' men would ask him. 'Any more bears throwed a lasso around your legs?' Writhing under these taunts, burning with shame and rage, Adolph said nothing, but he planned to avenge himself against Charley Bridwell. He would even the score in some way.

And though many years passed, and found him still unavenged, he did not forget. As a sheepherder, he often passed the Bridwell house, on his way up Burns or on his way down, and he thought of many things to do. But he did none of them. He was afraid of this fat cunning man who grinned at him, as if remembering those terrified yelps. Nevertheless, a lust for vengeance grew rather than diminished, and in one summer, while sitting on his horse and looking at Beth, a thought entered his mind. Beth was then only twelve, but Adolph was patient. He would wait until she grew into womanhood, and then he would act.

Four years later, in the first August after Jed's disappearance, he was riding up Burns when he saw her gathering berries. He stopped and called, and Beth came over to him. She was sixteen, and Adolph was twenty-eight.

'How's the berries this summer?' he asked.

'Oh, not so many,' she said, looking up at him. He was a large and powerful man, with black mustaches, black wavy hair, and deep-set eyes that looked under an overhanging thatch. His lips were full and sensual, and drew away when he smiled from almost perfect teeth. He was smiling now.

'There's lots a good ones up the canyon,' he said. 'Currants and gooseberries, and huckleberries and thimbleberries away up.'

'I know,' she said, looking at the dark flanks of the canyon, and then at his vivid mouth.

'You come on up and I'll help you pick. I got lots a time.' Beth hesitated. 'Come on,' he urged. 'I know a swell patch half a mile up. You'n be back in a jiffy. You'n ride.'

He sprang down and helped her to the saddle. Beth rode up the canyon, with Adolph walking by the horse, grasping a saddle-string. Her skirt was pulled above her knee; from time to time he looked at her leg.

'I ain't seen you much,' he declared.

'Oh!' cried Beth scornfully. 'I don't hole up or anything. Mebbe you ain't looked much.'

'Ain't I, though! I ain't looked for nothun else.'

With shrewd eyes Beth stared down at his dark hair. It was full of wave and sunlight.

'I'n amagine that,' she said. He looked up, and their eyes met.

'When you was only knee-high to a cricket, I looked for you.'

'Sow-belly!' she cried.

'It's the plain truth. I've waited for years.'

'I'n just amagine.'

'It's the God's truth. For years and years.'

'Oh, well, what you been waitun for?'

'For you to be a woman. I had my eyes on you all the time.'

'All right, I'm a woman. Now what you waitun for?'

He stopped the horse. Again their eyes met, but Beth looked away quickly. The ardor of his stare thrilled her, but she distrusted it. She felt insincerity in his manner and words.

'What am I waitun for now?'

'Yes, what?'

'Well, right this minute I'm waitun for a kiss.'

'Oh, you don't mean it! Well, just go right on waitun.' He laid a hand on her thigh, and she trembled.

'Beth,' he said earnestly, 'just lean down here and give me a kiss.... Just a little kiss.'

'No, I come up to pick berries.'

'You'n do both,' he assured her. 'Kiss me first, and then I'll help you pick the berries.'

'Where is the berries?' she asked, looking around her.

'Up the crick just a short ways.'

'All right, let's go.' She rode again until she saw bushes overhanging the creek, loaded with yellow or black fruit. She sprang down and Adolph faced her.

'Now for the kiss,' he said.

'Never mind the kiss. I got to work.' He tried to take her in his arms, but she slipped away.

'Sometime,' he said, scowling at her, 'you'll want a kiss and won't get it. I ain't a man to fool with.'

Beth's laugh was derisive.

'In that case,' she said, 'give your kiss to some other woman.'

His face darkened. If he had become angry, Beth would perhaps have dismissed him from her life, and her future would have been quite different. But Adolph smothered his rage and became sly. He would make her pay for this. He turned with her to the bushes.

'If you won't kiss me, I guess you won't,' he said, stripping yellow currants from limbs. He looked at her shrewdly and added: 'Mebbe I won't never want to again. I'm funny that way.'

Beth said nothing, but her hands trembled among the berries. She wanted to believe in his honesty, but something in his eyes, something around his handsome mouth, filled her with misgiving.

'A dozen times in my life,' he went on, watching her face, 'I seen women I thought I loved. But I don't know. They always acted funny. Just when I was ready to love them like a man should, why, they up and done something queer. And love,' he added philosophically, 'can't stand a lot a crazy nonsense. Just when you think you got it, why, off it goes and you ain't got it a-tall.... That's how it's been with me.' He gathered berries for a few moments and then went on with his monologue. 'I remember now, this was years ago, a girl, a burnette I was in love with. Minnie, her name was. Minnie Orcutt. And this Minnie, I was plumb studhorse about her. But when I wanted to kiss her, what did she do? Up and got mad. Buzzed like a hornet. And a kiss ain't so damn much for a girl to give a man. If she loves him, it ain't.... Well, I kissed dozens a women, far as that goes. But it's one thing to kiss a girl you love, but to kiss just any woman, that ain't the same. Not a bit.... Women, they're a riddle for a man.'

Beth drank his words, still distrusting, still wanting to believe. Her hands trembled among the berries; she gathered more leaves than fruit. And Adolph saw her hands.

'It's enough,' he went on, 'to make a man give up. Women's so queer, that's a fact, I ain't sure I'll ever marry. Well, if I could find a girl loved me, one who didn't act like a kiss would kill her or something, why, then mebbe I would. But they just about all act alike. They fuddle a man till it's like he stood on his head. They just lead him on and on. And when he wants a kiss, even just a little kiss, they get all mad and buzz like a hornet.... Well, there's another girl I might a-married. Helen Olson her name was. She was sweet as a pitcher. And I remember one time we went — well, it was a place like this,' he declared, looking around him. 'A big canyon. We set under a pine and I played the mouth-organ to her. I played old tunes and I sung, too. I ain't got a bad voice, far as that goes. But when I play the mouth-organ, it makes me — well, it shows me if I love a woman or not. It makes me feel I could love a woman to death. That's how music does to me. But this girl ——' He broke off and shrugged. 'They're all alike,' he said, studying the emotion in Beth's face. 'Not even music means anything to them. The old love-tunes, for a woman, I mean, is just like water on a duck. Just like grease on a slick sole.... And I guess you don't like music, neither.'

'I do,' she said. 'But I ain't never heard much.'

'Well, I ain't got my mouth-organ with me or I'd play a little. Just to see how it makes you feel. If it didn't make you feel in love, then you don't like music. That's what I've learnt...'

On and on he talked, building the foundation of conquest. His voice was a little sad and hopeless in the stream's murmuring. His face now, she thought, seemed to be earnest and sincere, and little by little her distrust fell away, and she would have yielded to his mouth. But he was not a lover now. He was a humble and disillusioned man, baffled by women; searching for love and doubting that he would ever find it; telling his tales of bitterness and defeat. Her heart went out to him, but he pretended not to see. When her pail was full, he said good-bye, looking at her with sad and disappointed eyes.

'You'n be my sister,' he said. 'I like you, that's it. And if you don't want a-kiss me, why, it's all right, you'n be a friend.'

Beth went slowly down the canyon, feeling that she had blundered, afraid that she would never see him again. Nor did she see him again in this year. He avoided her, waiting for her to become more lonely, more hungry for men; waiting for her conviction of blunder to grow and possess her mind. And when Thiel, who had seen them go up the canyon, spoke of Adolph Buck, taunting her about him, her manner was derisive and bitter. She waited through a long winter and prayed that he would come again.

After Thiel vanished, Beth spent much time alone. She went often to Rattlesnake Point, the gateway of her world, and sat there on a stone, wondering where her brothers had gone to, hoping that Adolph would come back. Or sometimes she would wander up Burns, her eyes making romance of the barren bushes, of the tangled roof of the stream, where she and Adolph had gathered berries, where he had talked of women and love.

Beth Bridwell was a lovely girl. Her skin was soft and fair, her mouth was sweet. She was tall and slender, and she had beautiful arms and hands.

She was approaching her seventeenth birthday, and the time was late April, when she saw Adolph again. She had gone up the canyon, in a glorious afternoon, and was sitting on a fragrant bedded log, watching a purple finch, listening to the scolding tantrum of a woodhouse jay, when Adolph rode casually into her life. He was on a sleek horse, and he led a mule that looked absurdly small under bulging panniers. Her heart leapt, and she half-rose from the log. The great mountain-side became a blur of golden green.

Adolph stopped in the trail and looked at her.

'Hello, there,' he said, but in an offhand way, as if she were a woman he had once seen and almost forgotten.

'Hello,' she said, distressed by the fierce beating of her heart.

'It's a nice day. You pickun berries again?'

'Oh, yes! You see my bucket, it's almost full.'

From the left pocket of his gray shirt hung the yellow string and round tag of a Bull Durham sack. He drew the sack forth and rolled a cigarette. He lit the cigarette and watched her across the flame of a match.

'What kind berries you pickun?' he asked.

'Oh, all kinds. Strawberries and raspberries. Peaches and pears and apples and plums.' He grinned faintly.

'Well,' he said, 'I got a-be movun on.' But he did not move. He smoked quietly and stared at her. 'How's the world treatun you these-here days? You married yet?'

'Married!' she cried. 'What you think I'd marry, livun in a hole like this!'

'Well, I didn't know. Seems I heard you was to marry some one.'

'Oh, did you! Well, mebbe I am.'

'That's what I heard. Just thought I'd wish you luck and all.'

'Thanks!'

'I about got married last winter, too,' he declared, looking with calm speculation at her flushed cheeks. 'But I changed my mind. When I find a woman who loves me real, then mebbe I will.' He smoked for a few moments and added: 'But I guess I won't find that kind a woman.'

'Oh, mebbe you will,' said Beth.

'Nope. I looked for one now about ten years. I guess I won't never find one.' She moved suddenly, and he read the language of her movement. His deep eyes narrowed to slits of dark light. 'I brought my mouth-organ,' he said, now talking ahead of him up the trail. 'I'll go up in them mountains and play my old tunes. It ain't a bad life.... Well, I got a-be on the go.' He straightened in his saddle and looked around him, as if to see whether his cargo was all right. He looked at the peaks standing at his journey's end. When he struck his beast with a rawhide quirt, Beth rose and came toward him. He stopped, as if surprised by her coming; his eyes interrogated. Grasping the animal's mane, she looked up at him, trying to guess his intent, to read his inscrutable face. Her own face was flushed, her eyes were bright, and her breath came and went in a long deep movement.

'You want something?' he asked, pretending to be a little astonished.

For several moments she searched his face.

'Let's hear you play your mouth-organ,' she said. He shrugged.

'For why should I? I make my music only for them as like it.'

'Well, I'll like it.'

'No,' he said, and lifted the quirt again. 'I got a-be on the go.'

Beth grasped the bridle reins. In her eyes, as she stared at him now, was that sly cunning which looked out of her father's soul; but beyond it, there lay a dark hunger, loneliness and pain.

'Take your hands off them reins,' he said. 'I got a-be on the move.'

'No, I want a-hear you play.'

He looked at the sweet youth of her mouth.

'Give me a kiss, then, and I'll play one tune.'

Beth looked away, and color filled her cheeks. She heard a woodhouse jay scolding its mate.

'No,' she said, in a low voice, 'you play.'

'Not on your tin pan. A kiss or no tune.'

She hesitated.

'Well, you play and then we'll see.'

'Nope. You kiss me first, and then I'll make the music.'

For a little while she deliberated, gazing at her bare feet in the trail. When she looked up, all the cunning was gone from her eyes, and nothing remained but a pure luminous wish.

'Well,' she whispered, 'all right.' But if she thought Adolph would kiss her at once, if she thought he would dismount and take her in his arms, it was because she did not know his ways. He calmly made another cigarette; and when, after waiting a few moments, Beth looked at him he was faintly grinning.

'I don't like to kiss girls what don't want to kiss me,' he declared. 'By Jesus, it ain't no fun. I don't kiss no woman without I love her. And I don't want no woman kissun me just to hear me blow a tune.'

These words, she realized, urged her to a declaration of love. They said she was bartering a kiss for a tune, that she was making of love a mean and common thing. But she did not want to declare her love, or to say she would kiss him because she wanted to. The cunning returned to her eyes.

'And me,' she said, 'I don't want no man to kiss me and then just ride off and forget. That ain't no fun, neither.'

'Who said I'd forget?' he asked, frowning at her.

'Well, you will. You forgot all winter.'

'Oh, like hell. What you think I'm up here so early for? The sheep don't come for a month yet.... Well, why should I be here?'

'I don't know. I guess you have to be.'

'Like a pig's snout. I'n turn around and go back if I want to.'

Beth raised her eyes again and searched his face.

'You mean you come up just to see me?'

'Well, figger it out like you want to. Mebbe I want to be in them mountains alone. Mebbe that's all.'

She moved a little nearer, so near that she touched his leg. After a struggle, she said:

'Well, then, you'n kiss me. And you'n play or not play, just suit yourself.'

But Adolph had other cards up his sleeve.

'Why should I?' he asked. 'I don't kiss girls without they want me to.'

Beth looked at her feet and considered.

'And me, I don't kiss men, neither, without they want me to.'

Adolph leaned down until his face was against her brown hair.

'Do you want me to?' he whispered. She did not speak. 'Yes or no.' Very slowly she bowed her head.

'Say it in words,' he persisted, driving the blade of his triumph into her life. 'Say yes or say no.'

She hesitated again.

'Yes,' she said at last, in a voice so low he barely heard.

He sat up. She did not see the gleam in his eyes. Throwing one leg over, he jumped to the ground and faced her. He looked around, to see if Charley were anywhere in sight. He grasped her arms and drew her to him, and Beth came with sudden swift abandon, and stood trembling against him. He put a hand under her chin and raised her mouth to his, and he pressed his lips into the sweet youth of it. He kissed her again and again, until she was limp and white in his arms; but when his hands moved to her breasts, closing over them, she pushed him away. The drunken world steadied. He watched her shrewdly, and her color returned under his stare.

She looked down, and with her naked toe she wrote his name in the dust of the trail.

'Now you'n play,' she said.

'Not now,' said Adolph, still studying her face. 'I got a-be on the go. I got a-get my camp set up before dark.'

Under his name in the dust she wrote her own. Then she asked:

'How far up is your camp to be?'

'Oh, two or three miles,' he said casually. He put foot to stirrup and swung up into the saddle.

'When'll I see you again?' she asked, and drew her breath sharply.

'Whenever you like,' he said, looking down with triumphant eyes. 'You know where we picked them berries last year. I'll come down there.' He grasped a rope and jerked at the mule which had been sleeping under its burden. 'Come on, you bugger,' he said, and, without speaking again to Beth, without looking at her, he rode up the canyon and out of sight.

Beth went slowly down the trail, feeling the warm earth under her feet, hearing the rapturous arias of larks, the clear piccolo song of a wren, the powerful bravura of a blackheaded grosbeak. All the trees and bushes were singing, and the sky was full of sunlight and wings. It was a blue bowl, with the sun like a great orange in its depth, with a horizon of purple mountains and mist. She stopped and looked up the wide canyon, flanked deeply with evergreens, and with the tender undulating acres of aspen and maple; and her eyes made romance of these, made glory of the trail under her feet, and her breath drank love from the sky. A cloud of warmth was around her, blue haze and golden light, the vast fields of beauty and peace. She stood tiptoe, stretching her arms to the incredible wonder of the world, closing her eyes as she reached upward, drawing an armful of blue sky to her breast. She began to sing, not in words but in the ecstasy of bird-melody, her voice trilling out over the earth, mounting into that illimitable blue hush where the sun stood. She sat on the creek's bank, in a small garden of wild flowers, and sang into the stream's murmuring. The music of her voice waltzed among the cloudy wet sounds or rode away upon purling echoes. Then she

lay face downward and was silent, taking into her soul
this cool gurgling speech of melted snows, the calls and
whistles of a long-tailed chat, the painless rapture of
larks. She closed her eyes, remembering Adolph's
kiss, feeling his strong arms around her. She turned on
her back in the sensuous sunlight, and for a long while
she lay here, letting the witchery of earth fill her heart,
pushing her emotions into every curve and chamber of
her dream.

On the next afternoon, she bathed her face in cold
water and washed her hair, making it spread fluffily
down her back. And she was a lovely thing as she went
up the canyon, in a simple gingham dress, with her
hair flowing from her shoulders, her girlish body eager
to the touch of life. At mid-afternoon she reached the
berry patch, but Adolph was not there. He was there,
but he was hiding in the brush, waiting to see if she
would come. Peering out of a covert, he saw her sitting on a green bank. He saw her look up quickly when
she heard a sound. Then he withdrew, went quietly up
the canyon, and came down the trail whistling a gay
tune.

'Oh,' he said, 'so you're here.' His tone was casual.

Beth rose, trembling, and looked at him, her eyes
full of love and distrust.

'Yes,' she said, and the word was hardly more than a
whisper.

He dropped upon the green bank at her feet and
looked up.

'Set down,' he said.

Her eyes darkened as she stared at him.

'You didn't want a-see me,' she said.

Adolph changed his manner. He sprang to his feet and looked at her reproachfully.

'It's you, I guess, didn't want a-see me.'

'Oh, didn't I! Then what you think I come for?'

He reached for her hands, but she stepped back.

'I come hours ago,' he said, speaking as if she had jested with him. 'I waited hours, then I went away. Then I come again.'

'Oh,' she said, wondering if he lied.

'And now,' he added, 'if you don't want a-see me, I'll go.' He turned as if to go, and Beth seized his arm.

'Who said I didn't want to?' she asked.

'Well, then why say I don't? Good Jesus, I come and wait and you ain't here. I was a fool to come.'

'I'm sorry,' she said, trembling before him. 'I didn't mean to be late.'

'And now you ain't glad to see me,' he declared, scowling up the trail.

'That's a lie. You know it is.'

Their eyes met, and in Beth's earnest gaze he saw such confession that he turned away, momentarily ashamed.

'If you loved me much,' he said, 'you'd want a-kiss me. But you don't.'

'That's another lie,' said Beth bravely. And in spite of her will she began to tremble, until she could hardly stand.

'You sure?' he asked, remembering that hour when he fled in terror, with blood on his face.

'Yes.'

He took her shaken body in his arms and found her lips. She cried, as if choking, and shuddered against him. He then sat down and she sat by him, looking at him with misty eyes.

'Now I'll play a love-tune,' he said. He drew a small harmonica from a pocket and beat it against his thigh. Then he played for her old melodies, now blowing his organ, now pausing to sing the words. When he sang, he chose only the verses that would sink deepest into her heart, and sometimes he would deliberate, and then change a verse to fit the circumstance of their meeting.

> Oh, I met her in the mornun
> And I'll have you all to know
> That I met her in the canyon
> Where the pine trees grow...

'I like that-there one,' he said, and knocked the harmonica against his leg. 'When I play it I think of you. Last night I played it clear to hell and gone after bedtime. And I like this one, too.'

He played again, covering the instrument with his hands, moving his fingers until the notes quivered with sadness, with haunting memories of long-ago things. Then he sang these verses:

Her form was like the dove, so slender and so sweet;
Her long and chestnut curls hung clear down to her feet.
Her voice it was like music or the murmurs of the breeze,
And she told me that she loved me as we walked among the trees.

He said he called that one his Canyon Girl. Did she like it?

'Yes,' she whispered, and moved toward him.

Here's one,' he said, 'is a jim-dandy. I heard it from a feller used to run around with me.' After playing the melody he sang the words.

How much I dream of childhood days, of tricks we used to play
Upon each other when in school to pass the time away.
They often wished me with them, but they always wished in vain,
I'd rather be with Beth Bridwell, a-swingun in the lane.
     Oh, a-swingun in the lane,
     Oh, a-swingun in the lane,
I'd rather be with Beth Bridwell, a-swingun in the lane!

He played again and again, watching her furtively meanwhile, noting her parted lips and her deep breathing. 'Juanita,' he said, was a nice one; and in a strong voice he sang a part of it. He then knocked spittle from the organ and looked at her.

'That's what you should ought to do. Lean on my heart.'

Beth bowed her head and moved nearer. He lay against the grassy bank and she lay against him, with her mass of hair flowing over his breast. Putting the organ aside, he clasped her with powerful arms, his fingers interlocked over her stomach.

'Here's one I learnt in a railroad gang. But I changed it a little. Well, this is it:

She'll be comun up the canyon when she comes;
She'll be comun up the canyon when she comes;
She'll be comun up the canyon, she'll be comun up the canyon,
She'll be comun up the canyon when she comes!

Oh, who'll be there to meet her when she comes?
Oh, who'll be there to meet her when she comes?

Oh, I'll be there to meet her, oh, I'll be there to meet her,
Yes, I'll sure be there to meet her when she comes!'

While singing, he moved his hands slowly upward, very gently, little by little, until they cupped her breasts. His possession had been so sly, and she had been so oblivious to all save the meaning of his words, that she realized with a sudden start where his hands were. She pulled them downward, and he did not resist. He bewitched her again with soft crooning, with verses of love and passion, and inch by inch he moved his hands upward, letting them at first lie on her breasts, and then gently clasping each. And when she discovered them there, he anticipated her move and took them away; but a few moments later, her breasts again rested within the power of his fingers. A dozen times he moved his hands downward, and then upward, until she no longer resisted, but lay against him with her eyes closed, with her breath drinking the music of his voice....

She'll be mighty glad to see me when she comes;
She'll be mighty glad to see me when she comes;
And I'll kiss her twice or twenty, I'll kiss my love a-plenty,
Oh, I'll kiss her twice or twenty when she comes....

His melody died away, went off among the trees, or fell into the creek's murmuring. She lay breathing deeply, full of inexplicable sweet pain, trembling within the strength of his arms and hands. 'Do you love me?' he asked, and her head made assent in the loosed sheaf of her hair. When his hands tightened, she shuddered a little and closed her eyes. She was held by almost intolerable rapture, like a terribly sweet knife in her heart. Twilight filled the canyon, flowing in acres of gloom down the great walls; and before either of them moved again, the world was quite dark. Beth saw it shrouding itself with black air, saw the witchery of darkening leaves, heard the murmuring sorcery of a darkened stream; but she had no power to move. She caught her breath in a sigh and wished she might remain here forever, never asking the reason of her pain, permitting no words to reach out and shatter the glory. Adolph sat up, holding her on his lap, and kissed a hushed mouth, stared at quivering eyelids.

'I love you,' he whispered.

'I love you, too,' she said.

She opened her eyes, and their lustrous hunger shook him. He pulled her gown from one white shoulder and kissed her breast. She gave a low cry and stiffened. When he put a hand on her thigh, she choked for breath and blinded him with a cascade of hair.

'Don't!' she said, trying to draw his hand away.

'Why?' he asked. 'Honey, don't you love me?'

'Yes!' she cried, and turning in his lap she threw arms around him. He explored gently with his hand and she trembled with anguish.

'Please don't!' she implored, melting into the hour, fighting for escape. She shook her head against him, throwing the shower of her hair in his face; and for a moment her mouth was hot and frantic on his neck. 'Oh, please, please!'

'But you love me,' he said, speaking in his tenderest voice. 'And I love you. Beth, honey!'

'Oh, I know, I know!' She writhed in his lap, struggling to resist, but caught and held in the hour's long embrace. A great emotion was within her, desperate and mad, and it closed over her, swept through and through her, with implacable power. Her arms were limp against it, and her breath drew out of it, hot and choking. She shook under his hands, and then lay against him, white and still.

'Honey,' he said, 'look at me. Please.' She opened her eyes and looked through the gloom. When she saw his face, its remorseless and vivid hunger, she sprang away as if he had struck her, and stood trembling by his side. He jumped up and grasped her arms.

'Don't!' she said, drawing back from him, reading the meaning of his eyes.

'Then you don't love me!' he cried. 'Do you?' She bowed her head in mute assent. 'Then why do you act this way?'

'Oh, I must go now!' she said, trying to draw away from him.

'Oh, you want a-go now!' His voice was bitter, his words snarled. 'You just been a-foolun with me! You just play around!'

'I don't,' she said, wondering what he meant.

He dropped his hands and shrugged. He turned away, enraged, but still playing his part.

'All right,' he said. 'You're just like all women. You lead a man on just to fool him. You don't know what love means.' He came back and stared at her through the darkness. 'You just been foolun me!' he roared. 'You don't love music! You don't love me! You don't love anything but yourself!'

'I do,' she said, moving timidly toward him. 'I do love you.'

'It's a damn lie!' he cried bitterly. 'I just been made a fool out of.... Well, you won't see me no more, so don't fret. It'll be rainun cats and dogs before you see me again. I'll go up to camp and get drunk as a fiddler's bitch.' He turned away and took the trail.

'Adolph!' she cried, following him. He went up the trail and soon vanished into brush. 'Oh, Adolph!' she called, and her voice rang with despair. She ran after him, gouging her naked feet in the trail. 'Adolph, please!' She listened, and then ran again. 'Adolph, I'll do what you want! Adolph, come back and I'll be like you want!... I do love you, oh, I do love you!' She stumbled through darkness, sobbing, crying his name. 'Please, Adolph, please! I'll do what you want! I promise to do what you want!... Adolph!' The last word was a scream.

'What's the matter?' he asked, from somewhere in brush ahead.

'Please don't leave me! I'll be like you want!'

'You just want to fool me some more,' said a voice out of darkness. 'You don't love me.'

'I do love you! Oh, I do love you! Please come back!'

'I should go,' said the voice. 'When I love a woman, I don't want to be fooled with.'

'Oh, I won't fool you no more!' She groped toward him, sobbing, reaching for the path with her bare feet. 'Please come back!'

'But you don't love me,' he persisted.

'Oh, I do, I do! And I'll be like you want.'

He emerged from darkness and came up to her. She went to him, shaking with the anguish in her soul, feeling terrified and sick. She looked up at him, humbled, conquered, her lips trembling.

'I do love you,' she said. She waited, cowering under his fierce stare, wondering what awful thing she had done. Love was so dark now, its ways so unlike those of an hour ago!

'Are you sure?' he asked.

'Yes,' she whispered, still waiting for his arms.

'How much?'

'Oh, all I can. All the love I can.'

'Well, how much is that?'

'Just all,' she said simply, not knowing how to put into words the meaning of her heart. 'Just more than everything. Just deep and deep.'

He grasped her shoulders and said: 'Look at me.' She looked at him, and though her gaze faltered a little, because of the fright in her soul, he read more in her eyes than he had hoped for. He took her in his arms, and she clung to him, weeping out of her joy and grief, remembering that dark and awful moment when he disappeared.

'Sure you love me a lot?' he asked.

'Yes,' she said, pushing the whisper up her suffering throat.

'And you'll be like I want you to?'

'Yes.'

He drew her shaking body to him and led her to the green bank.

IV

He walked part-way down the canyon with her, and Beth came on under a full moon. The time was midnight. Upon entering the yard, she saw Charley sitting on the doorstep. He asked where she had been, and his eyes searched the change in her.

'Oh, just out and around.' He looked up the canyon, flooded with moonlight.

'Out and around where?'

'Just down by the crick. I been there a long while.' She moved to enter the house, but he stopped her.

'You been with Adolph Buck,' he said.

'No.'

'That's a lie.'

'All right, then, I been with him. But what if I have?'

'I'll tell you,' he said, laying great hands on her shoulders. 'That Buck is no good.'

'Oh, ain't he!' cried Beth hotly. 'You be careful what you say.'

'Listen to me,' said Charley, shaking her. 'He's no good. I don't want you to see him any more.'

'Oh, don't you! Well, if I want to, I will.'

'No, you won't, little lady. After this you stay in sight the house.'

'Yes, like hell! I'll see him if I want to.'

'And I say you won't. Now, get to bed.'

Beth tossed her long mane of hair and looked at him with bright angry eyes.

'We'll see about that,' she said, and entered the house.

On the next afternoon she tried to slip away quietly, but Charley had been watching her. She was going up the Burns trail when she came upon him, sitting by a log across her path.

'Now where you off to?' he asked.

Beth looked at him with baffled desperate eyes.

'Whose business is it, I'd like to know!'

'Listen to me,' said Charley quietly. 'I said you wasn't to see him any more. And I meant it.'

'Oh, you did! Well, I meant it, too, when I said I'd see him if I like. I will, and you can't stop me.'

'Go on back to the house.'

'I won't!'

He rose and came toward her, his eyes looking into her heart.

'I said go back to the house.'

'And I said I won't!' For several moments he stared at her, measuring her will, wondering what he could do.

'You're just out a your head,' he declared. 'That Buck is a damn good-for-nothun.'

'You lie!' cried Beth, stepping close to him, trembling with fury. 'You stop a-callun him names!'

'If he was a decent man,' said Charley, 'I wouldn't care. But he's just foolun with you.'

'He ain't. He loves me. And I love him.'

'If you'll come back and forget him, we'll move out next year. Then you'n meet some decent men.'

'Oh, yes, go back and forget! Just live in this damn lonesome hole, year in and year out, like I always done! Day in and day out and never see nobody! That's all you want.'

'I said we'd move out next year.'

'Yes, and that's a lie. You promised that last year and the year before and the year before that. And now, now I found some one I love, now you tell me to forget. I won't, I won't! I love Adolph and I won't give him up. Not if you kill me I won't!'

Charley shrugged helplessly. He looked at her flushed face, at the steady will of her eyes.

'How far,' he asked, 'has he went with you? Has he kissed you yet?'

'That's my business,' said Beth proudly. 'He loves me, and that's all I care.'

'Yes,' said Charley, 'that's all you care. But when you get in trouble, who'll care then? When you have a baby comun, and this man pulls up and leaves you, then what?'

'He won't leave me. And I won't have no baby comun.'

Charley's heavy shoulders drooped. He studied her face, the face of this girl whom, of all things on earth, he loved next to Lela.

'If you'll promise that,' he said, 'I'll let you go. Promise there won't be no baby and you'n go, if you'll be back by dark.'

'There won't be,' said Beth, but her stare wavered and broke.

Charley turned away, unable to cope with this

strong-willed girl. He went slowly down the trail, feeling very unhappy and old, thinking of the hellbent children he had sired. One son had threatened to murder him, both sons had fled; and now his daughter took her headstrong way to ruin. He had been ambitious for them, in his own way; he had hoped to see them grow up, with powerful bodies and clean minds. He had come here, away from the wretched sin of the world, believing they would grow up like trees, like flowers and winds.... But he had failed somehow. Floggings had been useless, isolation had driven them to the dogs. But his darkest blunder, for some incredible reason, was that quiet woman in the house, with the silence of death looking out of her eyes.

He sat by a tree, leaning his back to its fragrant life, and thought of his weird fumblings toward a philosophic plan. He turned the pages of his history, but they were meaningless and dark, meaningless and dark. The grammar of his doings, even in those first years after he came here, was a tangle of high motives leading to desperate hours, of sound premises spawning violent illogic. He could not tell why, or in what he had been at fault. But it seemed to him, after a while of thinking, that his life had been split open, his world had been pitched on the rocks, by whatever it was in human beings that drove them to seek that which they would never find. Deep at life's roots lay the poison of ambition, the greed of achievement, the blind lusting after unattainable ends. They were driven to acquire, to get their clutching hands on more than they had need of, and to conquer much that was meant to lie in

peace. The loveliest fields of life, its broad and pas-
toral acres, were to be grazed by emotions quietly, and
not with the ravening appetite of a starved dog. People should pasture their feelings as cows did, instead of
being money-grubbers, instead of desolating the earth
like herds of wolves. Of this, if of nothing else, Charley
was convinced.

His children had inherited, not his own big whole-
some laziness, not his wedlock of joy and peace, but
their mother's restlessness and the covetous hunger of
her heart. He chewed his tobacco and deliberated the
perils of ambition. He retired into his thoughts and
fell asleep. And he did not know, in this hour, that
forces were already at work that would turn his philosophy into bitter memory, that would send him old
and beaten into the wintry wasteland of Burns.

May passed, in leisurely golden days, and June
came, and with it the crisis that was to be the turning-
point in Lela's life. In almost every afternoon, Beth
kept her tryst up Burns. She always returned before
dark. Charley sat helplessly by, studying her with
shrewd eyes, hoping she would keep her promise. But
he knew too much of the world and its ways to believe
that she would.

One evening at dusk he was sitting by the house,
spitting tobacco juice between his legs, when he saw
Beth coming down the trail. And by the way she
walked, by the lifeless droop of her shoulders, he knew
that the hour had come. When she drew near, he saw
tear-stains on her cheeks and an awful bitterness

around her mouth. He went forth to meet her, but she pushed him away and entered the house. With her bedding in her arms, she went to the haystack, and spread blankets upon a mattress of lucerne. Then she threw herself face downward and was still.

He looked into the house first, to see if Lela were watching; but she sat by the window, with Hetty on her lap, staring at the eternal march of river waters. He went to his daughter and knelt at her side. Beth was weeping, in a deep way, without tears and without sound. Hair lay over her face, but he could see her trembling hands, clenched and desperate.

'Tell me the trouble,' he said gently. She did not speak; and when he urged her to confess, she made a swift convulsive movement and a bitter sound. 'Tell me,' he said. 'Has Buck ditched you? Tell your old dad.'

She cried aloud and shook from head to feet.

'Oh, go away!' she moaned. 'Please leave me be!'

'But I want to know,' he said. He moved nearer, and against her will he took her in his arms, a little appalled by the anguish that racked her. Her eyes were closed, her lips quivering, and her face was white. 'Tell me,' he said. When she did not speak, he asked: 'Have you got a baby comun?' He searched her face for signs of denial or assent, but her face spoke only of despair and pain. 'Have you?' he persisted. She fell back over his arm and stiffened. Knowing then that she was pregnant, that her promise had not been kept, Charley stared at her for several moments. 'And won't he marry you?' he said at last. In answer she

turned her head slowly from side to side. He laid her
on the bed and stood up. Into his eyes had come that
green cunning rage which paralyzed those who looked
at him. He turned away, intending to seek Buck at
once, but she sprang to her feet and stopped him. He
was amazed by the change in her.

'What you intend to do?' she asked.

'I'll make him marry you,' he said. 'I'll get a-holt of
him damn quick.'

'No, you won't!' she cried. 'I won't marry no son-
of-a-bitch who don't want a-marry me!' She stood before him, proud and invincible, her eyes gleaming with
anger and hate.

'But we got to do something,' he protested. 'I won't
have no bastards in my family.'

'Well, don't think it! I won't marry no Adolph
Buck. I'd as live die as marry him!'

'Don't you love him?' Charley asked.

She started to speak but faltered. She turned away.

'He don't love me,' she said.

Charley looked up Burns and deliberated.

'Mebbe he does,' he said, but he knew his words
were false. 'You can't tell about a man. He acts
mighty queer sometimes when he's head over ears in
love.'

'He don't,' said Beth.

'I amagine he does,' said Charley. 'You're just a
girl. You don't know much about men.'

'I tell you he don't,' she said, but her voice was full
of doubt and hope. 'He never did. He just fooled
around. He says you played a trick on him when he

was young. He just done all this to get even. And now ——'

'Oh,' said Charley, 'so that's it.' He was thoughtful again, and his eyes, still looking up Burns, became hard and cold. 'But like as not that was just a excuse. You done something, mebbe, that made him think you didn't love him. Then he got jealous and made up this yarn.' Charley knew again that his words were false, but he had to overcome her pride, to get a name for an unborn child. He turned to Beth and patted her shoulder. 'It'll be all right,' he said. 'He just lied because he was mad. I'll see him to-morrow and fix things up. So cheer yourself and grin.... It'll be all right.' Beth looked at him with wide eyes in which he saw tremendous love and hope. 'For shame, for shame,' he said, smiling at her. 'What mountains you young people make out a molehills.' He took her in his arms and kissed her cheeks. 'Now you lay down and dream your dreams. After I see him, it'll be all jim-dandy.' And he went whistling gayly to the house.

In the next morning, when both Lela and Beth were outside, he strapped his six-shooter around him under his shirt. Then he went out to the stack where Beth was sitting. She ought to keep cheerful, he said, and bent down to kiss her hair. She looked up with a great question in her eyes.

'I'll have a nice talk,' he declared, answering the question. 'I won't be long.'

He found the trail and went afoot up Burns, walking

slowly because of his fat. If Beth had seen his eyes now, she would have run after him, imploring him to turn back. They were mirthless, and they looked straight ahead. When he was out of sight, he drew the gun forth and buckled it around his waist.

He covered the three miles to Adolph's camp and stood looking across a small clearing. Adolph, on a saddle in front of his wickiup, was threading buckskin laces in a pair of tall boots. As Charley crossed the clearing, Adolph looked around him; then he went ahead with his lacing. Charley came close to him and stood looking down, but for several moments the man pretended to be unaware. Then Charley spoke.

'You seem to be fixun up for a weddun,' he said.

Affecting a start, Adolph looked up quickly.

'Oh, hello!' he cried. 'Where the hell'd you come from?'

Charley grinned.

'I guess you'll be off to the valley pretty soon,' he said.

'The valley! Why the Jesus should I go to the valley? I'm up here for the summer.'

Charley sat in front of him, with his legs crossed, and continued to grin. Adolph looked at a rifle standing by a tree.

'When was you plannun to go?' Charley asked.

For a few moments Adolph was busy with the laces.

'I don't know what you mean,' he said.

'That's funny. Beth was tellun me you plan to get married soon. This week, she said, near as I remember.'

'Me!' cried Adolph. 'Say, when I get married, you just tell me about it. And don't forget.'

'I won't,' said Charley. 'I might as well tell you about it now. The way I got it figgered out, you'll be married tomorrow.'

'Oh, yes?' said Adolph, glancing toward his rifle. 'Well, all I'n say is your figgers ain't worth a hoot in hell.'

Charley's grin slowly disappeared.

'Tomorrow,' he said. 'I come up to tell you. Beth'll be ready about eight o'clock.'

Adolph snorted with contempt.

'So that's your idea! You think I aim to marry your girl! Well, as I just said, your figgers ain't worth a God damn.'

'That's how I figger it out,' said Charley quietly. 'I got it sized up like this. Two days from now you'll be a married man or a dead one. You'n take your choice.'

'A dead man,' said Adolph, looking at him. 'You think you'll bluff me into marriage, is that it?'

'One or the two,' said Charley, grinning again. 'And here's another thing, while I remember it. After you marry Beth, you'll be good to her.'

'You talk damn big,' said Adolph, looking at Charley's gun.

Charley unbuckled the belt and tossed the gun aside.

'Stand up,' he said.

But Adolph did not stand up.

'When I fight,' he said, 'it'll be about something more important than a woman. And listen here! Why should I marry your girl? Didn't she chase me plumb to hell and gone? It was her fault. She wouldn't leave me alone.'

'I don't care nothun about that. Just remember three things. First, be down there at eight o'clock. Second, act good to her or she won't go. And, third, be good to her after you're married. Is them all clear?' He picked up his gun and strapped it again to his waist. He turned down the trail, and before he vanished from sight, Adolph heard him whistling.

An hour later, Charley said to Beth: 'It was just like I thought. He'll be here at eight o'clock to-morrow.'

Beth threw her arms around his neck.

Promptly at eight, Adolph rode out of the canyon and up to the door.

'Where's Beth?' he asked.

'Out in the orchard. She's waitun for you there.'

Adolph strode off to the orchard. In a few minutes he returned with Beth. She was radiant and smiling. Lela stood in the doorway with the babe in her arms.

'We're to be married today,' said Beth.

'The hell you are!' cried Charley. 'Well, this is some surprise.' He went over to Adolph and shook his hand. 'I wish you happiness and a long life. I know you'll be good to our girl.'

'Oh, sure,' said Adolph ironically. 'I'm marryun her, ain't I?'

'And I know you'll be good to her,' said Charley, with a threat in his stare. He lowered his voice and added: 'I'm wishun you a long life, a *long* life.'

Lela laid the babe in Charley's arms and went into

brush by the stable. Shoeless and stockingless, Beth was astride the saddle, smiling and ready to go, when her mother returned. Lela came up to her, patted her hand, and pressed thirty dollars into it.

'For some clothes,' she said, and entered the house.

Adolph mounted a donkey which he had brought with him.

'Come and see us,' Charley said. 'We'll want a-know how you get along.'

'Don't fret about us,' said Adolph. 'We'll get along all right.'

Charley kissed his daughter. Then Beth looked around her.

'Mamma,' she called, 'good-bye!'

But no answer came from the house. Lela was sitting by the window, rigid with emotion, unable to speak or weep. Charley had told her nothing, but she guessed the truth. She had no power to act; she knew of nothing to be done. Her sons had fled, and now, with hopeless eyes, she watched her daughter ride away. They were gone, the three of them, past any recall; and she remained here, desolate, beaten.

She sat by the window for a long while, seeing the empty trail over which Beth had gone; seeing the great southern wall of her home; looking at the flowing hunger of river waters. And behind her on the doorstep, Charley sat in silence, chewing tobacco and thinking of God alone knew what. Their house was a dreary thing now. The world outside was hushed, as if remembering those who had gone, voices that were once here, and running feet. It was all a great basin of memories, a phantom land. Life had walked out of it, and in its abandoned quiet, river-haunted and mountain-walled, she would sit in the vast shadow of what might have been — deserted and exiled and lost.

V

BUT Lela was not beaten and she was not lost. For
many days, after Beth's going away, she saw little and
heard nothing. Of Charley's whistling and song, of his
attempts to give her new life and hope, she was almost
wholly unaware. And she might have gone mad, she
might have yielded to the fixed and deadly isolation of
her mood, if there had been no child at her breast. It
was Hetty who saved her, who reached down into her,
with baby cries and eager mouth, and shook an emotional depth that was becoming estranged from life
and breeding its own death. When she sat by the window, as indifferent to Charley as an eddy to the main
stream, it was the babe's sudden cry that stirred her,
that plunged into her sunken stillness, and drew a part
of her again into meaning. When she lay in bed at
night, drugged but not asleep, with her thoughts like a
stagnant pond, it was the child's lusty yell that made
her move, until something alive and clean, like morning wind or flowing water, felt its way into her and
drew her back to mid-channel. And she came to realize, at last, that the life of her fourth child lay in her
hands. She looked around for a way out. She was still
searching when Mrs. Hunter came over to bring garden
seed.

'Where's your children?' she asked.

'Gone,' said Lela, 'all gone.'

'I don't know what you mean. Gone where?'

'Run away. Married.'

'Married!' cried Prudence, amazed.

'Beth, she is. The boys run away.'

There was a long silence.

'It's too bad,' said Prudence. 'What does Charley say about it?'

'Him, what would he say!'

'Well, it just goes to show you can't bring children up and beat them to death. You lose out in the end.' Lela gave no answer. She was remembering that Joe and his wife had planned, through slavery and self-denial, to send their children to college. That was their dream. On the river's one side, the sons and daughter would go to far places, to harvest wisdom and power; and on the river's other side, the sons would be wild vagabonds, and the daughter would give birth at seventeen.

'Well,' said this stern woman from across the way, 'you have one left. That don't help what's gone by, but it's something to live and work for. I don't like to advise people. They ought to know best what they want to do. But if I was in your place, I'd say to Charley, "Just listen to me now. You've had your chance. You let your children run like wild hoodlums. It's my say now. I intend to educate the one's left, and if you don't like it, you'n jump in the river." That's the way I'd talk.'

'But how,' asked Lela, turning blue eyes upon her visitor, 'could I do all that? I ain't got no money. We just live from hand to mouth, year in and year out.

What we borrow we don't never pay back. We owe you folks now, God knows how much.'

'Well, don't worry none about that. You could make money. You got a dandy place here, just the place you need to raise turkeys. They fetch a good price. They ain't easy to raise, but this is just a dandy place...'

Prudence Hunter talked for a long while, telling how she fed and clothed her own family, with money from chickens and cows, from the cheese she made and peddled in the valley, riding for sixty miles in a lumber-wagon; telling how her husband was building up the farm, buying machinery and cattle, and laying by a small sum in each year with which to send their children to school. She talked, too, of that inescapable duty which parents owed to offspring; of that stern voice of conscience which demanded, no matter at what cost, that sons and daughters should be given a fuller chance at happiness, and a more reasonable way of life, than any their parents had.

'If my daughter ever has to work like I've worked, then I'll consider myself a failure. If my sons has to work like their father, just plain dirt farmers, cleanun stables and milkun cows, and wearun stinkun clothes all their days, then I'll say we shouldn't a-had any children. If we can't do better by our children than our parents done by us, then we should hide our faces in shame. We should blush to call ourselves Christians. That's the way I see life. We'll educate our children, even if it takes our last cent. Even if we have to work our flesh to our bones. That's our big ambition. That's all we work for, and we work with all the strength we got...'

Lela stared at this woman, at her large aggressive chin, her straight indomitable mouth, her toil-worn and broken hands; and she rose to this challenge, this duty, which her neighbor laid across her path. The ambition which had slept in her, the desire to shape the world to her wish, to wreak upon life an enduring achievement, now awoke and shone in her blue eyes. A door opened on the future and she looked through; and she saw deeds shaping under her hands, saw one child standing within this new vision, gowned in lovely things, taking her place among the bright events of earth. And when she thought of Charley, his fat and indolent way of life, she resolved to push him aside and follow her path to freedom. No longer a house-fixture to be adored, sitting with useless lovely hands, she would go boldly into life, even as the river went; she would get her hands on tasks waiting to be done, she would feed her hungry heart into ceaseless activity, and gather from work a deeper meaning for her days. Then she remembered that the time now was July, and that another long winter lay before her, curved with loneliness, calcimined with gleaming snows.

'But it's too late now,' she said. 'It's too late.'

The time was late, Prudence admitted, but there were many things which Lela could do. The hay and fruit were to be harvested; and now that Charley's sons were gone, he would probably do nothing at all. To farmers on the Antelope benchland she could sell a part of her fruit. She could sell chokeberries to valley folk. 'When I take a load of cheese out, I'll be glad to haul them down for you.' She could gather a sackful of vegetables, boat them across, and upon one of Joe's horses she could peddle them over the bench.... Opportunities lay all around her; she had only to reach forth her hand and grasp.

'And work'll help you forget,' Prudence declared. 'There ain't anything like work for unhappy minds. I go on the jump all day long. If I was to stop, if I was to set around like you, I'd go mad. I'd be in a sylum before long.'

'Well, that's what I'll do,' said Lela, staring ahead at all these things to be done. 'I'll work and work, till I'm all dog-tired out. Mebbe I can forget a little.' And she saw clearly that in labor, in days filled from dawn until midnight, lay her only road to peace.

When Charley came in from the river, bearing a string of trout, his wife sat and looked at him. He felt ill at ease under her intent stare. He went to the door and spit his quid out. He came to the stove and made shavings for a fire.

'You look tired,' he said, kneeling with a chunk of wood between his legs. 'You'd better lay down and I'll cook up some chuck.'

'No, I won't lay down,' said Lela, and her words fell sharply on his ears. 'When I lay down again, it'll be when I can't stand up.'

He placed shavings on the grate, piled wood upon them, and struck a match. Why, he wondered, had the ambition-crazed Mrs. Hunter been over here, and what had she talked about.

'I got something,' Lela declared, 'I want a-say to you.'

Charley did not speak at once. He blew at a lazy flame until his face was red. 'All right.' His voice was gentle. 'What is it?'

Now Lela was silent. She began to tremble, in spite of herself, because she was afraid of this man, of the volcanoes asleep under his gentleness, of the power in which he had held her for years and years.

'What you want a-say?' he asked.

'It's this,' said Lela, drawing forth all her courage. 'I been married to you now for eighteen years. In all that time you've had your way. In everything you have. You drove our boys from home. You beat them ——' She looked through the window. She looked at the river, symbol of the upreaching life, and its going gave her strength. 'Well, eighteen years, and we got less than we had then. If we go on this way, we won't never have any more. The one child we got left will just run wild.' She paused and considered. Charley was cutting the trout open and rolling the yellow flesh in a plate of flour. 'You've had your way,' she went on, her voice ringing. 'From now on, I intend to have my way. I intend to bring Hetty up like she should be. I'll work for her and make money and educate her. I won't set around no more and be just something to look at. I won't!' she cried, becoming hysterical. She stood up, shaken by her desperate will. 'I tell you I won't! I'll have my way, I tell you! Do you hear, do you hear? I'm sick and tired the kind a life you make me live! I won't set around and just go mad, go mad…. Oh, I tell you I won't! And if you try and stop me ——' Her voice died away in a low sobbing cry.

Charley came quickly to her and forced her upon a chair.

'All right,' he said, wishing that Prudence would stay on her own side of the river.

'I want to work!' she cried, pushing him away.

'All right, honey, all right. But don't get all upset. It's silly to work when you don't have to. But if you want to ——'

'I tell you I will!'

'All right, sure. I didn't say you can't.'

She rose and went to the door. She stood in the doorway, shaking with desperation. All her dead and empty years, years buried under idleness, seemed to rise within her and cry for another life. Through twelve bitter winters, through twelve golden summers, she had lived on this place, and she had done nothing worth remembering. She had seen Joe Hunter and his wife, like two beings driven, turning a wilderness of brush into acres of hay and grain; adding year by year to their equipment; laying money aside with which to send their children away. And while they had pioneered, taking into their faces and hands the stern beauty of labor, building stone by stone the foundation of their dream, she had been a princess of laziness. She had eaten stolen meat until the memory of it choked her. She had eaten borrowed food, worn borrowed clothes, as if out of the sweat and toil of others she had been privileged to steal. And what she and Charley

might have reaped, with a little labor, had been
scorned and left to rot. Sometimes their hay had been
mowed, and then left in wind and sun; and in three
summers it had never been gathered at all, save two or
three loads for the cow. The fruit which they did not
need had rotted upon the ground. The furs here had
been trapped and sold by others. They had done
nothing. Against old age they had built no fortress.
And if Charley had his way, they would go on in thiev-
ing indolence, and at their journey's end they would
sit in this shack, deserted by their children and eating
plundered food...

She turned and looked at Charley, who stood by the
stove, breathing heavily and frying fish.

'And there's something else,' she said. 'I won't eat
anything ain't my own. Nor anything that's borrowed,
neither. We just been plain thieves ever since we come
here. If I can't earn my own livun from now on, I'll
starve to death.'

'All right,' said Charley quietly, his face red from
stove heat. 'Just as you say, honey, it's all right with
me.'

'Oh, it is! Then why ain't we earned our own keep
in the past? Why we been a plain common thief?'

'I don't figger I been a thief. Anyway, there's more
ways than one to steal things.'

Lela made no answer to this. She did not understand his strange philosophy of life. He had declared,
time and again, that every man exploited his neighbors; that some forms of exploitation were approved
by law, and some were not; and that the thief was

merely one whose methods were visible. With such statements as these, Lela had sympathized in former times; she had thought him very wise and clever; but now he seemed to be a lazy parasite, a cunning thief, who looted and pillaged in the name of wisdom. Behind the mask of his jolly talk, his jests and laughter, he filched what he could, and thumbed his nose at all honest ways of life.

But even so, as she watched him now, carefully frying fish to suit her taste, browning flour in a hot skillet to make gravy, or twisting with his mighty hands the cap from a jar of plums, she knew that she loved him, that nearly all people loved him, jester and brigand that he was. And she struggled between love and hate, her emotional bondage and her wish to be free. When she remembered his laziness and his pilfering and his beating of his sons, she hated him; but when she remembered his tender hands, his waiting upon her hand and foot, she loved him. Against his thievery, her mind set his kindness to people in distress, and his hospitality; against his cruelty to his sons, she measured his devotion to her. And she shuddered at the enigma, the dark tangle of the good and the bad. She went out to the barn, and while sitting there on a pile of hay she recruited her courage and laid her plans.

'I love him,' she thought, 'and I hate him. I hate him, but I love him. My God, I don't know, I don't know!'

She resolved to go on, to fight and build and conquer. She was still young, though she would be a grandmother at thirty-four. When Prudence Hunter came here, she was twenty-nine. She was now thirty-eight.

'I'm only thirty-three,' Lela thought. 'In five years I'n do many things. I'n have as many chickens and cows as she has now. I'n have money put by.'

Not five years but seven she fought to make this dream come true. She would have fought more wisely and with richer gains, if she had understood that baffling person who, at this moment, was removing slabs of trout to a tin plate. If she had understood how implacable was his laziness, how uncompromising his scorn of ambition and greed, she might have wrung from slavery an eventual happiness and peace. But he was a riddle, and she pushed him aside. She saw him as a fat and worthless nobody. Intent on her dream, she retired into the stern holiness of work, and became known as the silent woman. And in that hour of mid-winter, seven years later, when she went forth into freedom, she forgot that deeper than ambition, as deep almost as motherhood itself, was her love for Charley Bridwell; and she did not remember until it was too late.

In this summer there were things to be learned, work to be done. She would have to build coops. She would have to acquaint herself with turkeys and chickens, with their feeding and diseases, because she knew nothing about them. And so she learned, first of all, to row the boat, and then went often to the Hunter place. She walked with Prudence among flocks, saw her manner of feeding and nesting, heard the need of sanitary coops and yards, of gravel and eggshells and green food in diet; and learned the cause and cure of dropsy and roup. She was an apt and eager student. For future use, she stored away a rich and various knowledge, the husbandry of almost twenty years.

'Mites,' said Prudence, 'is the worst trouble I have. The pesky little things!' And she pointed to a shaggy hen sitting dolefully on her rump. Lela had never seen a mite. She wanted to know the pest and how to kill it. She entered a coop and thrust her hand into the straw of a nest. When she drew her hand forth, it was covered with a swarm of tiny black things.

'They get in your hair,' said Prudence. 'Sometimes I lay awake all night, scratchun my head.' But if coops were whitewashed with lime and cleaned twice a week, mites would not be a serious bother. She was too busy making cheese and milking cows, and with lumber-wagon journeys to the valley, to give to poultry

the care they needed. And her coops, too, were the
worst sort, being nothing but dugouts in the earth.

'There's big money in poultry,' she said, 'if a person
has time to do it right. But you can't do nothun in life
halfways and expect to get anywheres. You got to
have big clean coops, full of light. Keep them away
from hogpens, too. It's lots of work,' she said, and
drew a deep sigh. 'But work, that's what God made
us for.'

In late July, Lela saw that the hay was turning white
from drouth. She decided to harvest it at once.

'You borrow a team somewhere,' she said to
Charley, 'and I'll cut and rake it. Then I'll help haul
it in.'

But Charley protested, as he had been protesting
now for two weeks. This earnest and tireless woman
was playing havoc with his peace. In former whiles,
he had often lain abed until noon; but now Lela rose
before the sun, and with groans and jesting he pulled
his trousers on. He sat sleepily on the doorstep, hearing the industry of breakfast behind him, wondering
what his life was coming to.

'I won't have you ridun a mowun-machine,' he said.

'If you don't get the team,' said Lela, 'take care a
Hetty and I will. One or the two.'

For an hour he gently exhorted her to sanity and
quiet, but at last he had to yield. He wabbled down to
the river and put forth, puffing above the oars and
cursing all ambitious people. Lela waited impatiently
for his return. Quite as she surmised, he took his noon
meal with the Hunters, and then sat with Joe in shade,

chewing tobacco and talking of life. It was almost dark when he came home, with a mowing-machine nearly sinking the rear end of his boat. On the next day he went again, and again it was dusk when he returned, bringing with him this time a set of harness and a team. He led the dripping beasts from the river, and at once Lela began to harness them.

'It's too late now,' he protested, looking at the evening sky.

'I don't care if it's midnight. You didn't have to stay over there all this while.'

With groans and protests he harnessed the beasts and hitched them to the machine. Lela gathered the reins, but he took them from her hands.

'If it's got a-be done to-night,' he said, 'I guess I'n do it.'

He bit off a fresh quid, and then, without bothering to oil the machine, set off in a noisy clatter for the hay. He was now so large and fat that the seat sank under him, and the neck-yoke was raised against the horses' throats. With Hetty in her arms, Lela followed him to the hay and watched its rich green wilderness shudder under the knife and fall. Charley circled the field and stopped.

'It's time to quit,' he announced cheerfully. 'See how them horses sweat.'

'That's river water,' she said. 'Mow another round.'

'No, it's time to quit. Honey, I'm starved. I could eat the tail out of a skunk.'

'You take Hetty and let me mow a round.'

'No, it's time to quit.'

A little after daylight, she went out and watered the team, squirted oil into every part of the mower that seemed to need it, and prepared a simple breakfast of green vegetables, milk, and fruit. She ate alone, for Charley was still snoring; and leaving the child with him, she harnessed and hitched the team, and mowed round and round the field. The sun was three hours high when he came out. He watched for a little while and said nothing. Against such aggressiveness as this, he felt helpless and old.

Lela ignored him. But when he chuckled, upon seeing her pump oil where none was needed, she looked at him.

'Well, it's funny, is it?'

'You don't put oil on the outside a that pitman. Put it inside.'

'Oh, I do!' she cried, staring at a smoking wheel which she had drenched.

'First thing you know,' he said happily, 'the whole damn thing will fall apart.' He took the oil-can from her hands. 'Well, I'll mow a while and you run to the house.'

While he oiled the machine, she gave a breast to the child. Then she laid the babe in his arms.

'I'll mow,' she said. 'I want to.'

'No, it ain't work for a woman. You just set by the orchard and watch.'

'I tell you I want to. So please don't argue with me.'

She mounted the seat and rode down the field. Charley stared after her, baffled, distressed. He did not know that this simple task of reaping, of laying swath against swath, gave her profound joy, lifted her thoughts away from dark memories, and made her feel that she was proving her right to happiness and life. Had he known that her heart sang with the mower, that her being trembled in the glad rhythms of labor, he would have been amazed. He read something of all this in her eyes, when he approached, an hour later, and offered to take her place.

And after the hay was all down and he had boated a rake across, he marveled again as he watched her piling the windrows. Bareheaded in the sun, with lovely hair streaming down her back, she was an unforgettable picture. In her eagerness to harvest this field, in the simple pride which she took from work, she was like a child. And he saw, too, that she seemed to grow younger, almost girlish, as if ten years had been lifted away.

'It beats the band,' he reflected, sitting by an apple tree. It was a queer world. For eighteen years, and in every possible way, he had saved her from labor; and now she thrust him aside, made a nurse of him, and slaved at haymaking like a man. He thought he perceived, nevertheless, that people who loved toil were strange folk who had never learned how to use idle time. Silence filled them with dread. In a full afternoon, with no work in sight, they seemed to feel a terrifying insanity. Prudence Hunter did. He had heard her declare that Sunday, of all days, was the one she feared. Upon this day her religion bade her rest, and she sat in a great loneliness, with her gnarled hands hungering for the next dawn.

'It's a fine fix,' he thought, watching Lela windrow the hay. 'I don't know what the hell I'll do with her.'

When the hay was all mowed and raked, she begged him to take the machinery across and to bring the wagon to her. Failing in beseeching and threat, she took the mower to the river's edge, and was trying to put it upon the boat when he went to her aid. He boated it across and returned with two wheels of a wagon; whereupon, declaring that he had done as much in one day as any man ought to do, he took his pole and went fishing. On the third day he went again, and on the fourth he completed the task. On the fifth he assembled the wagon, and on the sixth, after being importuned for an hour, he placed the rack upon it. And when Lela declared that they would haul hay at once, he said there was no hurry about it. Alfalfa needed a long time in which to cure.

'It's been a week now!' she cried. 'I guess you want it to get rained on and rot.'

'I amagine it's still green as a leek,' said Charley, sitting in the house's shade. 'Rain won't hurt it. Rain'll settle it down and make it easier to pitch.'

But Lela hitched the team to the wagon, tossed a pitchfork on the rack, and drove out to the field. She was straining under the weight of haycocks, or climbing up to tramp them, when Charley stood up with a groan and went out to help. While she loaded, he pitched the mounds up to her, tossing them with effortless ease. At the stackyard he removed one horse from the wagon and hitched it to the derrick cable; and then he stacked while Lela handled the huge Jackson-fork. It was a heavy thing for one so slender, and the strain of lifting it and then thrusting its long curved tines into hay made her tremble with weakness. Even more exhausting was the task of dropping each great forkful. 'Let her go!' Charley would roar, and Lela would jerk frantically at the trip-rope, scalding her hands, drawing from her quivering body every ounce of strength. Charley watched her intently, distressed by her drawn face, yet hoping she would get enough of it and take a woman's place in the house. When the load was off, she sat on the rack, breathing deeply and shaking from head to feet; but in a few moments she grasped the reins and started for another load.

'That's enough for to-day,' he declared, halting the team. 'One load a day, that's about our size.'

'It ain't. We'n haul five loads a day. Or six or seven.'

'No,' he said, and began to drop the tugs.

'Stop it!' Her voice was shrill, desperate. 'I won't be all summer haulin this hay. There's other things to be done.'

'All right, then. You go to the house and I'll get a jag.'

'No, I won't go to the house.'

'Now, listen, honey, we got all summer to haul this dab a hay.'

'We ain't, I tell you. I got a-build chicken-coops and — my God! So just hook them tugs up.'

Charley hitched the tugs and went with her for another load. When it was off, she lay on the rack for several minutes, very white and shaken. And in spite of his entreaties, she went out for a third.

But in this night she did not sleep. She tossed from side to side, moaning, quivering, exhausted. Between whiles of snoring, Charley lay on his back and deliberated the tremendous ruin that ambition was making of his life. They would sell the hay for a hundred dollars; but how could money, or anything that money had power to buy, compensate them for nights of agony or for days of slavery under a burning sun? It was all so unnecessary, so ridiculous, so futile! He decided to be firm on the morrow. The hay could shrivel and rot before he would have his wife, his darling of blue eyes and long curls, making a drudge of herself. Let the fools of earth, the clodhoppers and brush-grubbers, wade in labor to their ears, trying to wrest triumph from inexorable ground. Let them sweat, let them turn dry furrows and curse an improvident sky; let them spade and hoe, cry at the ravages of misfortune, and become as twisted as naked roots. Such a life was not for him. He would not petition Destiny with greedy hands. He would not lust after the unattainable, or race hellbent ahead of the hours....

But Lela overrode his will with one imperious gesture. She had tasted of work, had found in it a mighty healing power, and nothing could stop her now. She had been swept into the searching stream of life; she had tapped that source out of which hunger springs; and she would go on, laying her pathway to the valley and freedom.

'Set on your lazy rump!' she cried. 'But I won't!

I'll work and work and work!' Her words came out with such ringing vehemence that he was appalled. Like a man undone he harnessed the team; he rode out to the field with his shoulders drooping, with his eyes fixed upon Joe Hunter's widening acres of hay and grain.

When the hay was gathered, Lela turned eagerly to other work. From her hiding-place in the brush she got the remainder of her money and entrusted it to Prudence. She asked her to buy sugar, a few groceries for the winter, a few clothes; and to keep the rest of the money until next year when she would buy turkeys and ducks. Then she gathered fruit; and after the sugar came, she made preserves and jellies, bottled apples and service berries and plums. Charley did nothing, during this time, save to pick a bushel of chokeberries for wine. These he put into a barrel, poured water over them, and stole several pounds of Lela's sugar. Two or three times in each day, he would stir the fruit and sip the foaming juice. After the fruit-making was done, Lela borrowed glass jars from Prudence, and then canned green peas and beans. With a shovel next she dug the small patch of potatoes and stored them in the house. She tended the cow, too, milking and feeding her, and she made a little butter from cream; and one afternoon she drove the cow up Burns to find a bull. Later in the year, she sold most of the hay to sheepmen; and after writing a list of things to be bought, she gave the money to Charley and he made his annual pilgrimage to the Lorenzo store.

'And this time,' she said, 'you ain't to buy no whiskey. Just what tobacco you need and that's all.' He thought of his wine-barrel.

'All right, honey,' he said. Nevertheless, he brought with him a half-dozen quarts, but he stopped at the Point and buried them there.

From morning until night Lela was busy, always finding many things waiting to be done. Sometimes, in three or four days together, she said nothing, and her periods of silence grew in depth and length. She had only one plan, one dream: to earn and save money, to flee with Hetty, to find her sons. She thought of these sons most of her time. Jed was somewhere waiting for her, humiliated by the past, too proud to come home. She would find him, she would find Thiel; and she would put Hetty in a great and noble school. This ambition lived and grew within her; it shut all else away. It retired her into silence and work. In two years, in three or four or five, she would be ready to go.

'In just a few years,' she thought, again and again. 'In two years... or four... or six. Then I'll leave this place. Then I'll be free...'

But time and again, too, she faltered and wept. In spite of her will, of one desire that had become an obsession, she would think of Charley, she would become aware of his tenderness and pain. She would turn away, shuddering with doubt.

VII

FOR seven years something stood against her dream, the shadow of a man whom she both hated and loved. If he had abused her, if he had taunted her, now and then, her way would have been easier; but he never said a sharp word, he never mocked her toil. His gentle melancholy, the quiet sadness that sometimes lay in his eyes, often sapped her strength, made her question and falter, pervaded all her work with a vast and futile insanity of purpose; until she recoiled upon herself and wondered if she was shaping a fool's dream. After hours of labor, she would come in to find him, fat and indolent by the door, spitting his juice and looking at life with calm eyes; and she felt, in such moments, even though obscurely, that he was more in harmony with earth and sky. His way was timeless, somehow, like that of mountains, of the soil which she spaded, of the smell of water and trees; and her way, like the river's, was a rather weird frenzy, a blind reaching into darkness, an aimless craze of working and saving and growing old. She did not understand, but she felt this difference between them. She disliked the house, because it was old and silent; she shrank from the great calm of mountains and sky; and often, when weak from toil, she sat by the river, staring at its broad liquid pilgrimage, hearing its eternal and haunting sound. It was constantly going but never gone — never gone! Year in and year out, it poured its journey into the valley and the sea; but it would always be here, always in a hurry, always blind. After she was dead, after her sons were dead, this impetuous darkness would be here, cutting its way into new land, drawing banks and trees into its flowing will. And she felt in it something silly and mad, the same force that was driving her until she shook and wanted nothing but sleep. Time and again, after staring at its senselessness, feeling in it more of death than of life, letting its sound meet and murmur in her soul with the restless cry of her own being, she would go in quest of Charley, to be reassured and quieted by the ageless peace of his way. And seeing in her something stricken, he would take her in his arms, and she would rest against him, feeling within him the deep and untroubled power of growing life, the holy quiet of forests, darkly beautiful and still. And what she felt in him, she dimly suspected, was not laziness at all; it was a tranquil wisdom which her morbid soul had no power to make its own....

But on the next day she would scorn him. She would go forth with renewed zest, laying her eager hands on labor until it was transformed, and dollars stood in its place. In spring and summer and fall she was never idle, save when doubt struck; and in winter-time, too, she busied herself with little things. She sat by the window, making sketches of the deep white beauty outside; and these she hung on the walls. Among them was a river scene, with the river buried under ice, its waters lost in a black and cold and flowing graveyard. Charley did not like this one. It made him think, he said, of something that had slaved all its life and then got lost, that had entombed itself with labor. He preferred summer scenes, warm sunlight, silent alfalfa acres and trees. Of the river sketch he said: 'Hang it in the corner by the stove. Mebbe it'll thaw out.' And so she hung it above the stove. She also painted Hetty, and even Charley's round florid face, deftly catching its patience and calm. But it was not for her drawings that she became known, though people did talk of these. Her only phenomenal success was with turkeys. Another word was added to her title, and she was called the silent turkey-woman.

Prudence Hunter's fowls made a silly clicking sound when half-grown, and shook their pale heads; became shaggy-feathered and sick, and at last sank upon their heels to die; but Lela's were sleek bronzed creatures, brightly alive and vivid. Prudence was forever doctoring hers, buying for them expensive foods, herding them away from marsh lands. Lela's birds, on the other hand, ate nothing but wheat and grasshoppers, foraging for the latter upon the mountain-side.

'She's a whizard,' Prudence would say, marveling at her neighbor's success. 'I can't see what she does but just let them run wild. I think she has some secret.'

But Lela had no secret, save that of keeping her flock away from water and damp ground. Prudence was constantly looking for sickness, for small signs of disease that might ravage and annihilate. When she saw a fowl a little drooping and apathetic, she took it to the house and stuffed it with medicines; and under her

watchful care, under her compounds of physics and
tonics and grits, it sank irresistibly into death. Lela
did not look for sickness. When she saw a turkey that
seemed to be dull and feeble-eyed, she ignored the
creature, or asked Charley to cut its head off. But
among her flocks the torpid ones were few.

In the third summer after Beth's marriage, she had
an enormous drove of four hundred. At night they
roosted upon the stable, under the manger within, and
upon trees roundabout. The aspens, the cottonwoods,
the huge pine, were full of them, sitting like rows of
shadows along branches. Sometimes too many would
sit on a limb, and the limb would splinter and spill its
load, whereupon they would walk slowly around in
darkness, making their queer sound of distress, looking up into the trees. Staring at a perch, they would
squat and spread their wings, time and again, before
attempting flight. Then they would spring into air
and knock other birds from limbs, and these, too,
would pace around and cluck, and eye those perched
and asleep.

In the daytime they roamed over the farm and
mountain-side, a great moving sea of brown, full of
alert heads or sudden beating wings. Grasshoppers
fled, crackling and hopping before them. Red-wings
and yellow-wings cruised in the air above, and then
come down to be instantly devoured. Large wingless
and green-bodied crickets jumped from spot to spot,
but were overtaken and stored into bulging craws. As
days passed and food became scarcer, the drove moved
farther up the mountain; and toward evening they

took to their wings and came down. Sometimes they came down over the house, and the sky was full of them, the air darkened. They were like a landslide of shadow. The stronger ones sailed far out, even to the river's edge; and now and then one, carried away by its momentum, struck the bright water and disappeared downstream....

The task of marketing them was long and difficult. Night after night she and Charley dragged turkeys from their perch and thrust them into gunnysacks. Often Charley had to climb far into trees, to recover a bold one that had flown upward, from limb to limb, to make its sleep alone. On the next day they boated them across, and Mrs. Hunter hauled them to the valley below. When the labor was all done, and only twenty hens and three gobblers remained, Lela had a clear profit of four hundred dollars. She buried half of this in a glass jar. With the rest she bought food and clothes for the winter, and a second-hand mowing-machine and hayrake and wagon, all of which Joe purchased and delivered to the opposite bank. When Lela wanted to pay for his service, he frowned and said nothing.

'It's all right,' declared Prudence. 'We want you to get a start first. Later, mebbe, we'll see.'

'I'm ashamed myself,' said Lela. 'We've lived off a you folks for years. I don't feel right.'

'Don't bother about it. Wait till you get a start in life. Then we'll see.'

In the next summer, Lela gave birth to her third

son, Beth visited her for a few days, and Thiel came home. Beth was thin and quiet.

'Are you happy?' Lela asked her, and Beth shrugged.

'I manage to get along,' she said. 'I ain't noticed life is so chuckful a happiness. I guess I could a-done worse.'

When Charley found her alone, he said casually: 'Well, girlie, did things turn out all right?'

'Nothun in life turns out very all right, I amagine. I ain't complainun.'

Charley stared at her, wondering how much she was hiding. He never knew. To every question she gave a shrug or an indifferent answer. She was too proud to tell. She visited for a week, and then smiled and rode away, carrying a babe in her arms.

A few days later, Thiel rode down over Hunter Bottom, swam the river, and came in drenched clothes to the house. Charley was inside.

'Where's mamma?' asked Thiel, dripping in the doorway.

'Why, hello!' cried Charley, staring at his son, a tall rugged youth of nineteen. He came forward, with outstretched hand, but Thiel turned away. He went up Burns, where he saw Lela driving a horde of turkeys. Approaching her softly, he clapped hands over her eyes.

Lela cried and stiffened. She thought it was Jed.

'Jed, is it you?'

'No,' Thiel declared, dropping his hands, 'it's only me.'

She turned swiftly and threw her arms around him,

pressing her cheek to his wet breast, crying his name. From the doorway Charley watched them. Thiel held her for several moments. He patted her trembling arms and kissed her hair. She stepped back to look at him. Her eyes were drowned in tears.

'Oh, you're a man now!' she said. 'And you was just a boy when you went away!'

'I'm a little bigger. I been a long time gone.'

'Oh, Thiel, dear Thiel!' she cried brokenly, and drew him to her, with her lovely hair in his face. She stood for many moments, trying to realize fully that one of her sons had come home.

'Did you find Jed?' she whispered.

'No,' he said.

'Oh, didn't you never hear a word about him? Thiel, not a word?'

'Not a word.'

'You'll not go away again, will you?' she asked, holding him close. 'Never, never!'

'Yes, I guess so. I couldn't stay here very long.'

'Oh, Thiel, dear!'

'Well, I'll stay a little while. But I couldn't never stand a winter here again.'

'And you never heard a thing about Jed?'

'Not a thing.'

Charley left the doorway and went down by the river. He did not come in for supper. He did not come in until long after dark.

Thiel remained here for two weeks. Almost single-handed he gathered the hay, rising early and working late, and sternly rejecting his mother's offer of aid. He ignored his father. No longer a boy to be flogged, he was unafraid, and he did not conceal his contempt. For the most part he was very quiet, as if the last three years had chastened him. He never spoke of what he had seen, of the places to which he had gone. He never hinted of his plans. His eyes were dark with memories and his ways were full of silence.

One morning he went out to Lela and declared simply that he was going away. When she urged him to remain with her, he looked into the west and shook his head.

'No, I got a-go now. I'll come next summer to put up the hay.... Well, good-bye,' he said, and kissed her white cheeks. Freeing her clinging arms he strode to the river, plunged in with his clothes on, and swam to the other side. She saw him enter brush and disappear without looking back. With her heart breaking, she dropped upon river sands and did not move for a long while.

Soon after Thiel's going, she gave birth to her third son. Charley was again patient midwife and nurse. The contempt and hatred which Thiel had shown toward him had made him older, and they now haunted his eyes and voice. But Lela saw no change in him. Shut away with memories, and with her dream for a daughter and son, she knew only that he was tender and lazy and quiet. He washed baby-clothes and warmed them at the stove. He sat on the floor by her and caressed her thin white hands.

At the end of two weeks she left her bed, and gave herself again to labor. She had two children to educate, instead of one; and more than ever, Charley was thrust aside, forgotten. Thiel came in the next summers; he reaped the hay, swam the river, and vanished. He was more silent in each visit, more thoughtful and strange.

'Have you seen Jed?' Lela would ask, running to him and searching his face.

'No.'

'And ain't you heard from him? Oh, Thiel, not a word?'

'Not a word.'

Once or twice Charley strove to draw his son into talk; but his son ignored him. He did not even look at him. He came to this place as if driven by one wish: to reap the hay and haul it in. He was tender with Lela, but he had little to say. She was working too hard, he declared; she would have a nervous breakdown.

'I got to work,' she said, looking at him with darkening eyes, thinking of Jed. 'I'd go crazy if I didn't work.'

'You should leave this place,' said Thiel, and he looked at many things which he both hated and loved.

'I will. I will soon. Oh, Thiel, please find Jed!'

'You should leave now,' said Thiel.

'Not now. Next year, mebbe. When I've saved a little more money, then I'll go...'

And she toiled with all her strength. She became very thin, almost emaciated; her cheeks were white and sunken; her eyes were a strange bright blue. Little by little she added to her savings in the buried jar, until she had a thousand dollars put away. No longer did she live on another's beef. She was independent now, and some day she would be free. In an hour, not far ahead now, she would leave this awful loneliness and never return. For seventeen years she had lived here, and in all this while she had never been farther than the Antelope benchland on the south or the Tompkins place on the west. For seventeen years she had been a prisoner, walled in by mountains, roofed by an ageless sky. But a door stood ahead now, a door to a new life, and she was slowly opening that door....

Little did she realize what lay beyond.

VIII

SCORNED by one son, held in contempt by his wife, and made to realize that flogging had achieved nothing but hatred, Charley employed another method with his youngest child. He had earnestly desired to rear clean-minded and obedient sons, and he had striven, in what seemed to him the best way, to shape them with a club. Recognizing his failure, he now went to the other extreme; and instead of using a cudgel, he taught his young son Hamlin, named for a great-uncle, to chew tobacco and curse his Lord. When Ham was barely three, his tutoring began. He went often with Charley to fish, and together they would sit on a stone and throw their lines. Ham, like his brother Jed, was bold and self-reliant, even when so very young; and he was an eager student of his father's words and ways. He learned a great deal of profane language; and though it was meaningless, though God meant no more to him than gosh, he swore with gusto when his mother was beyond hearing, and felt that he was almost a grown man. When he jerked at a fish and tangled his line in brush behind him, he would stand up and curse with such deadly earnestness that his father would nearly fall off his rock with laughter.

'The God-damn trees!' Ham would shout, in his small enraged voice. 'Who put them there, I'd like to know! Christ and Jesus on them, the sons-of-bitches!'

And little by little, by taking at first only a tiny

quid, and spitting it out before it sickened him, he
learned to chew tobacco. Both his cursing and his
chewing became known to many people long before
Lela discovered them; and people still talk of that
summer, in 1916, when this four-year-old lad spit his
juice and swore like a trooper. Ham never cursed or
chewed in his mother's presence until a certain mid-
winter day. These mighty words, Charley told him,
were not to be used around women; and before going
to the house he would wipe the tobacco stains from
Ham's mouth.

And so, during their last summer here, father and
son often sat side by side, catching trout and chewing
tobacco and profaning.

'Don't swaller the spit,' Charley admonished, one
afternoon.

'Jesus, no,' said Ham, squirting as far as he could
into the stream. 'It might make me sick.' He looked
at Charley and asked: 'Don't women never chew the
cock-eyed stuff?'

'No, it'd make a woman sick.'

Ham shrugged his arrogant shoulders. 'It don't
make me sick,' he declared, and drew his hook in to
put upon it another writhing worm. He threw his line
out with an imperious gesture; and he slyly watched
his father to see how he did things. If Charley jerked at
his line, Ham jerked, too, even though nothing had
struck his bait. If Charley swore at the fish, Ham
swore also, or at anything else which stirred his father's
wrath. And from time to time he would look up at
Charley's face, to see if he was moving his jaws or

letting his tobacco soak; to see if he was looking dream-
ily at a far bank or intently at his line; to see if he was
angry or pleased. And in all these matters, Ham imi-
tated closely, taking his cue from a look or a word. If
he spit out a great oath and Charley roared with joy,
Ham would also laugh, nearly falling off the stone, and
wondering what there was to laugh at.

'The bastard!' Charley yelled. 'I nearly hooked one
that time a yard long!'

Ham waited for a few moments and then gave a
prodigious jerk. 'The bastard!' he cried. 'I nearly
hooked one six feet long!'

Charley rocked with laughter and Ham rocked with
him, bending forward if his father bent forward, or
pausing to spit if his father did so. And while the lad
sat here, day after day, listening to diabolic tutoring,
Lela slaved with her turkeys or gathered and preserved
her fruit; hoed weeds in the garden or taught Hetty to
read and write. Charley made his annual journey to
the valley, taking Ham with him, and returned with
the winter's supplies. Summer passed and autumn
came, with its flaming maples and its loneliness. The
turkeys were sold. And still Lela never suspected that
her son was not as he should be. She was too occupied
with work and with thoughts of Jed, too obsessed by
her dream, to observe that Ham often looked at her
with knowing eyes, as if his knowledge far exceeded his
years. He became bolder, day by day, now swearing
at his sister with whom he slept, or now importuning
Charley for a quid. After cold weather set in, he did
not often leave the house, and his opportunities both

to chew and to profane became more and more infrequent. As a consequence he took matters in his own hands; and when his parents were outside, he sought and found Charley's tobacco and cut for himself a tiny plug. Thereafter, hiding his doings from Charley's watchful eyes, he would chew discreetly while sitting by the woodpile. When nobody was looking his way, he would spit upon chunks of wood or into the stove. Tiring at last of this, he became increasingly bolder, and sometimes he would open the door and spit outside. He would also curse in his breath, testing the loudness of his speech, profaning as openly as he could without being overheard. And he became steadily more daring until he precipitated a crisis.

In a day of January, when the snow lay impassably deep and the world was frozen to its heart, Charley went up Burns after an elk. Ham moved restlessly about the room, with a quid in one cheek, wishing that he, too, could take a gun and go forth. Lela sat by the stove, teaching Hetty from an old and ragged second reader. Ham would draw near and listen. Deciding that they were both engrossed in utter nonsense, he would pinch Hetty's arm, and when she looked at him, he would stare at her with sober scornful eyes; until at last, after he had pinched her severely, she turned and slapped his cheek. This was too much for him. Forgetting his father's warnings, he burst into loud and headlong cursing. Profanity roared out of him, every oath which he had learned. His savage little face darkened; his eyes gleamed with derision and spite. When his outburst was over, he boldly raised a lid and squirted brown juice into the stove.

'A stink on you!' he cried, and thumbed his nose at Hetty.

Lela rose from her chair and stared aghast. In this furious little monster she had seen a vision of Jed.

'What's in your mouth?' she demanded.

'Nothun,' he said, now remembering his father's warnings.

She seized and shook him; she set him on her lap.

'Open your mouth!'

'Nope,' said Ham, and shut his lips tight.

Lela shook him again, and then thrust a thumb and finger into his mouth. She drew forth a small mushy quid; and still unable to believe the truth, she smelled of it. She sat dazed, staring at the tobacco, smelling of it again and again.

She made a strange sound as if she had been struck. Hetty began to weep. Lela put Ham on the floor and looked around her. She grasped him again and shook him, hardly realizing what she did.

'The holy Christ Judas!' Ham roared. 'Stop it!'

His oath reminded her of what until this moment she had forgotten, of the crazy meaning that had been beating in her brain. She shook him again, and so violently that he began to whimper with fear and rage. She sat again on the chair, her white bloodless hands in her lap. She looked so crazed, staring ahead of her at nothing, that Hetty wept aloud, and Ham retreated to the wall, hoping that his father would come soon. In Lela's darkened mind, but very slowly, there opened a full revelation of the truth. She tried to stand up, but her legs broke under her, and she sank to the chair, and fell from the chair to the floor. She lay on the floor as if dead. Her eyes were closed and her face was very white. Hetty knelt by her, sobbing with fright, and strove to open her mother's eyes. Whimpering by the wall, Ham looked from his mother to the door. He stepped softly to the window and looked out: the world was flooded with moonlight. He went back to the wall, his grief and rage now running into gurgles and moans.

'Help me lift her up!' Hetty cried.

Ham went over, and together they clutched Lela and strove to make her sit up. But she fell back, her head striking the floor. She was dead, Hetty declared, and the children began to wail.

At this moment Charley entered the house.

He also thought, at first, that Lela was dead, and his florid face went white. He sprang forward, gathered her in his arms, and turned toward the window.

'Lela!' he said. 'Lela, speak to me!' His words rang in the house. Hetty shrank into a corner, wailing with terror. Ham began to sob as if he had been slapped. Putting her on the bed, Charley leapt outside and returned with a handful of snow. He held this snow against her white forehead; he told Hetty to bring him an old rag. He told her to soak it in cold water and bring it quick. Shivering and moaning, Hetty thrust a towel into the water pail and carried it dripping to him. She went back to Ham, and the wailing of the two filled the room....

'Lela, look at me!' But for many minutes, Lela did

not open her eyes. Her breathing was slow and deep, as if life were going out of her. 'Lela,' he whispered, 'Lela!'

He looked around him. He swung like a bear. 'What happened?' he asked of Hetty. 'Stop your cryun and come over here!'

Shaking with fear, Hetty crossed the room and stood by him, her horrified eyes searching her mother's face.

'What happened? Speak!'

'I don't k-know!' Hetty sobbed. 'She just — she just — f-fell down!'

'Here, wet this towel again! Take it outside and rub it in snow!'

With the icy towel Charley laved her face, his great hands moving gently; and at last she opened her eyes. They were such crazed eyes that he recoiled.

'Lela, what happened?' he asked.

She closed her eyes and lay quietly for several moments. Then she began to moan and tremble in his arms. She looked at him, and her eyes were bright with unutterable loathing and dread.

'Get away!' she cried, and her voice was shrill with hatred. 'Great God, get away! Get away!'

But Charley held her firmly. She beat against him with feeble hands, she beat at his face, she turned her head from him. He strove to quiet her, to learn what terrible thing had brought her to this; but when he questioned her, she fought at him, blindly, and implored him to get away. Hetty and Ham were weeping aloud.

'Shut up!' Charley roared. And then: 'Lela, what is it? What have I done now?'

He kissed her hands and her hair. She struggled, smote his face, shrank shudderingly from his mouth. She begged him not to touch her, but he held her close, murmuring her name, kissing the loathing out of her desperate hands. With both arms she fought him, freed herself, and stumbled to her feet, shaking through and through. He drooped, helpless, and stared at her. When he moved toward her, she stopped him with a trembling gesture.

'Don't touch me!' she cried, tormented beyond endurance. 'If you do I'll kill you!'

These words were almost a scream. They appalled him. Twice in his life now, he had been threatened with death by one of his own family. He turned for a moment to the window. He stepped back, drooping, baffled, and looked at her.

For a few moments she did nothing except to tremble, as if her legs would again snap under her. She swept an arm blindly across her face; she heard the children wailing by the wall; she took a step forward, faltered, and was rigid. Charley swung around, thinking he had heard some one outside. He listened.

Lela shut her eyes, swayed, and went tottering to the chair. But when he moved toward her, a threat stopped him like the lash of a whip. For a little while she sat there, trembling, fighting for strength.

'Lela!' he said.

'Don't speak to me!' she shrieked. 'I can't stand to see you or hear you! Oh, great God!' The last words

came out of her in a shudder of anguish, dark as hatred,
bitter as gall. Hetty's wailing now was almost a
screech. Ham moaned and clawed at his eyes.

Then Lela moved again. With an imperious gesture
she stood up. She turned to her clothes, hanging on
the wall; she stripped them from nails, ripping them,
jerking with desperate hands.

'Do you intend to leave me?' he asked.

She swung and faced him. She looked at him with
steady bright eyes, and he saw in them only fear and
hate. She looked at her cowering children by the wall.
And Charley thought, in this moment, of his dark and
fumbling methods, of his futile attempts to chasten
with the rod, and of the demon within him that had
made a jest of all his worthiest desires, a clown of himself. But he would have to make a stand now. He
would have to save the integrity of his own home.
Again he asked: 'Do you intend to leave me?'

'Yes!' Lela said, and the word hissed.

'I won't let you,' Charley declared. He felt futile
and old. He looked around him and added: 'Do you
mean you don't love me any more?'

'Love you! I hate you! I hate you deep as death!'

'You don't mean that,' he said gently.

She now stepped close to him, her body shaken
again, her eyes a blue blaze of memory.

'And why shouldn't I hate you! I've worked like a
slave here! I've worked myself right down to the bone!
Look at me!' she cried. He looked at her trembling
wasted body; he looked at her thin white face. 'And
you, oh, you know what you've done! You know all

right! While I worked like a dog, you took Ham behind my back, you learnt him to chew and swear, and
God only knows! I hate you, I say! I hate you! —
hate you! — hate you!' She was crying the words in
his face, her eyes alight as he had never seen them
before.

'I guess I done all that,' he said, drooping before her,
his own face drawn and pale.

'Yes, you done all that!' she went on, her voice
ringing, her voice leaping out of her in bitter words.
'Tell me, now! What have you ever done to make me
love you? What! You beat Jed and Thiel, you made
them leave home! Yes, and for years and years you
told me the world would despise me, the world would
just think I was something low as dirt! And, my God,
I believed you once! Oh, I was a fool, and I believed
you then!' She stopped, sobbing with hatred, with all
the welling bitterness of twenty years. She looked at
him again, her blazing eyes narrowing, her lips quivering with grief and scorn. 'But I see through you now.'
Her voice was low, bitter, hoarse with pain. 'I see
what your scheme was!... Oh, you couldn't fool me
forever with your lies and lies! I see now what you
are! You're just a big lazy thief, you're just a big fat
brute! A drunkard and a thief and a coward, that's all
you are!'

'A coward?' he said gently, his shrewd eyes looking
through her.

'Yes, a coward!' she cried, but she faltered on the
words. 'And you ask now do I love you! No, and I
never loved you! You've spoiled my life, and I'll hate

you till I die! I'll hate you when I'm dead!' She leaned against a wall and put a hand to her beating forehead. She stood there, white and shaken, her strength spent, her heart filling with awful and bitter doubt.

'I been good to you,' he said quietly. 'I always tried to, anyway.' He moved to take her, but she waved him off.

'Don't touch me!'

'But you can't leave me now. Lela, after all these years together?... You can't leave me now.'

She turned upon him again with renewed strength and fury.

'Oh, I can't, can I! Just wait and see! I been plannun to leave you for years and years! Oh, you knowed that! What you think I slaved like a dog for? Just to give you money for whiskey, I guess! Just to give you —— Yes, I'm leavun you, and I'm leavun you tonight.'

Charley watched her again gather wraps. He thought he would bolt the door against her going. He would break her will with tenderness and kind words.

'You can't leave me now,' he said firmly. He turned to lock the door.

'Don't you do that!' Lela screamed. She ran to him, she beat at his face with implacable hands. He seized her and she struggled like a wildcat. Ham began to bawl with madness and terror. Hetty clapped hands to her ears and shrieked.

'You can't go!' Charley cried. 'I won't let you go.'

'Leave me alone!' she wailed, fighting blindly,

desperately. 'I'll kill you, I say! Oh, my God, my God!'

Charley pushed her back, forced her down upon the bed, and turned again to the lock. But at this moment the door was hurled open, and Jed Bridwell stood upon the threshold.

IX

He stood there, for a few moments, filling the doorway and looking in. Lela did not see him; she heard no sound; and Charley saw only a tall powerful stranger, black-bearded, deep-shouldered, ominously intent. Jed stepped inside then and closed the door. A river of moonlight vanished, and the room was lighted only by a small oil lamp, the white window, and the glow from the stove.

'What do you want?' Charley asked.

The stranger did not speak. He looked around him, at the children by the wall, and at the things of this room which he had once known. He saw that the bed was still a bed on the floor, that the chairs were still box-chairs, and that the table was four slabs spiked to aspen legs. He crossed the room and looked down at Lela, who was shaking, with her face in her arms. There was a dark threat in the way he moved, in his mouth and eyes. He swung around and stared at Charley. Then he bolted the door.

Lela now rose on one arm and looked through the gloom. Jed looked over at her and their eyes met. But he did not move. They stared across at each other; the room was very still. Little by little she rose, first to a sitting posture, then to her feet; she swayed, struck an arm to her brow, and then fell as if under a blow. Jed still looked at her for several moments. He crossed the room and knelt by the bed.

Charley went to the window and stared out. He saw a world of bitter winds and gleaming snows. The children still cowered by the wall, tears on their cheeks, their eyes bright and strange. They seemed to be carved out of wood, with only their eyes alive. Charley looked at his two big hands, looked at the two guns lying above the door. He knew now that his other son had come home. And he knew why.

He looked again from the window; but he saw only gray winds, an acre of brush bowered with snow and moonlight, and the gleaming blindness of a frozen world. Jed had been outside, he now realized, standing by the door and listening to the frenzy of Lela's hatred. ... He heard a low choked laugh, a mad laugh ringing on its hard dry sobs. He heard the sound of a stranger's feet on the boards. Then he felt the dark power of the man behind him, waiting for him to turn. But he did not turn at once. He was not afraid. He felt sad and old and lost.... He stared at the bitter wind, whipping its fury and greed over a depth that it had already paralyzed. Life, it came to him now, was like that: it conquered, and then, still unsated, it drove the blade of its will through age and into death. He saw the wind driving at a naked tree.... Yes, that was life. He turned and faced his son.

He looked at the man, the big fearless darkness of him, with mouth tight, with eyes full of the mind's thought: his own son, and yet never his son. He met Jed's stare and held it. And Jed was remembering his savage youth, those beatings with cudgels, and that night alone on the river's bank when his back was blood

and welts: memory of these and of one vengeance not
yet fulfilled was written plain in his eyes. Charley
looked at this remorseless giant, his kin and yet a
stranger, and for the third time in his life he faltered,
his will was stripped like flesh to the bone. He felt that
sick emotion which filled him, long years ago, when the
club dropped from his hand. Time had not chastened
this savage heart.

This was the Jed who had annihilated hornets and
snakes, who had taken vultures from the air, who had
threatened his father with death; the superb artist in
cruelty, who never forgot vengeance or permitted an
enemy to escape. The same, unchanged: but more
powerful now, and more implacable. And Charley
knew, as clearly as if words had spoken it, why the
man had come. He held the stare and waited.

'I guess you know why I come.' The voice was deep
and strong, like the man's frame, but the words were
spoken so low that Lela did not hear. It was a voice
speaking out of an old and unalterable purpose.

'Yes,' Charley said, 'I know.'

Jed turned and looked at his mother: she was lying
again with her face buried. He went to the door, un-
bolted it softly, and passed outside. Understanding
this move and Jed's swift backward glance, Charley
followed tiptoe, and in the dooryard they stood face to
face. The house and world were as quiet as moonlight,
save only for the blind winds. Jed advanced, and his
right fingers curled, tightened into a knot. Charley
saw the move. He spoke again.

'Well, get it over with. Do what you come to do.'

Jed stepped forward again, his face as grim as a wolf's mouth. The clenched hand was sudden, swift. Charley spun backward under the crushing blow on his teeth; fell over the woodpile, and pitched headlong into his iron-toothed harrow, half-buried in snow. He staggered to his feet, ran a moist tongue over his cut lips. He felt a stab of pain in his skull: it made him dizzy for a moment, and the moonlight trembled like black mist.

Jed came up to him, both fists clenched now. The look on his face was one Charley had seen there before. He had seen it when Jed brought home his first live snake; when he emerged from the river after being thrown in; when the club dropped from Charley's hand.

'You intend to fight?' he asked.

Charley eyed him steadily. He could feel blood running down his chin; he could feel the pulsing stab in his skull.

'No,' he said.

'You're yellow!' Jed cried, and his voice fed on scorn. 'You're a coward! You was a coward when you beat me, and you ain't changed a God-damn bit!' He looked around him, as if wondering how to wreak upon this man a satisfying vengeance. 'So you intend to just be knocked down like a dog!' He advanced, his great hands ready. 'Is that it?'

'Yes,' Charley said.

'You yellow son-of-a-bitch!'

He struck again, with the full power of his shoulder behind the blow. Charley was knocked around, under the horrible impact, and pitched again upon the harrow-teeth. He did not rise at once. He remained there, on hands and knees, an awful darkness swallowing his mind. He did not see the door open or Ham appear. He spit out a tooth, and licked with his tongue into the warm hole. Then the old lust rose within him; the old unconquerable rage shook his heart.

He got to his feet, with all meaning and intent converging to one point, with all his mighty strength beating in his shoulders and arms. Blood slobbered from his mouth and spilled in red foam over his breast. His eyes were green implacable fury. Advancing softly, swiftly, with his big easy cat-movements, he threw himself upon Jed and got unpitying hands on the man's throat. His strength rose in a blind surge, flowed into the death-grip, and became rigid as iron. With one wrench he brought Jed under him, rammed a violent knee into his stomach, and broke him to earth. Jed's tongue fell out of him. And in another minute Charley would have been kneeling upon death if Ham had not shaken his mother and brought her to the door.

She screamed and ran to the two men. Her insane hands beat on Charley's skull, rained hard little blows on his eyes; but he was emotionally mute and rigid. All his power had run into one grip and frozen. Turning then and crying with hysteria. Lela seized a club; and without hesitating, she laid it with all her might across Charley's back. The blow relaxed him. It shook his fingers loose, broke the single fixed purpose in his mind; and when Lela smote again, he became aware for the first time of screams and of the grim work to which he had put his hands. He shuddered and rose to his feet. He wiped his mouth, having forgotten that its warmth was blood; he stepped back, hearing now the bitterness of her words, understanding a little of what she said.... In a fog of nightmare he heard himself called brute and coward; heard it declared that he had chased his son away and had tried to kill him when he came home. He felt her hands still beating against him.

He saw Jed shaking on his feet, got one swift vivid glimpse of the rage and hatred in his face; saw Lela clinging to him, heard her begging him to be quiet.... Dazed, trying to understand, Charley fumbled toward the house and entered. He went to the stove and sat on the floor, his big shoulders drooping, his face haggard with grief and shame.... A few moments later, he heard some one come in, heard the sound of feet, the gathering of wraps. His mind was clear now; he understood, but he had no power to move. He had no wish now....

The door opened again. Ham spoke.

'Ain't you comun?' he asked. 'We're all ready to go.'

Charley did not look up. He did not speak.

'Good God, I say!' Ham roared. 'They intend to leave you, I tell you now, and you'd better hurry!... Ain't you comun along?'

'I guess not. I guess I'll stay here.'

Ham was baffled. He stared at the cottonwood

acres where Jed and Lela were digging for the money-jar. He looked at his father, humped over his legs, his face in his huge palms.

'Well, I got to go…. Good-bye.'

'Good-bye,' Charley said. He heard the door close, heard Ham's running feet; and then silence moved in, full of the wind's greed and the night.

He sat for a long while without moving. Then he rose, feeling again the stab in his skull, and drew forth several bottles of chokeberry wine. He sat on the floor by the stove, with the wine by him, and began to drink. The fire died, and the room became gray with cold. And still he drank, emptying one bottle and then another, striving to shut out all memories and all sense of loss. He poured it down like water, his hands rising, now and then, to wipe his mouth, or to fumble with his skull. From time to time he would look at the six-shooter on the wall-spike. And at last he began to weep, in a big silent way, with great tears running down his cheeks. The lamp burned its last drop of oil, the flame sputtered and went out, and for a little while the wick was a red coal. The red faded and died, and the room was a room of darkness, save for moonlight that lay in a cold pool. And still he sat there, drinking the dark wine, weeping without movement or sound….

Two empty bottles stood by him, then three, then four. He uncorked the fifth and began to laugh. His laughter, at first, was like that of a child in pain: it choked up out of sobs. But it grew steadily into sardonic chuckling, and then fell into a demoniacal roar.

He lay back, shaken by bitter mirth, and bellowed until tin plates rattled in the cupboard, until the house rang. He sat up and bent over his knees, pouring his woe into great agonized shouts; and tears so blinded him that when he turned for wine, he had to feel rather than see. For a little while then he would be very still, his fogged mind trying to summarize his past.... He was drunk, drunk with wine and desolation. He swayed from side to side, one hand clutching the bottle, the other cupping his chin. One thought rose, drunk and leering: he had been deserted, he had been left sitting here like a clown. He would break again into violent laughter, devilish, insane; but the sound always broke, rumbled in his chest, and died. He would drink again, and again he would be still....

And so he spent the long cold night, trying to drink his grief under, trying to laugh it away. Morning came, the room filled with gray light, and he was a little afraid of being here. He staggered to his feet, reeling under the pain in his skull, and looked around him. Some of Lela's clothes hung on the wall. He went over to them, felt of them, rubbed them against his cheeks. He tried to laugh again, but nothing came out of him save a bitter dead sound. He stumbled outside and to the barn; saw the frozen hole which Jed had dug; stared through gray gloom at the long dugway up which Lela had gone. Reeling back to the house, he put on a ragged overcoat and wondered what he should do here before leaving this place.

He went again to the barn and saw the cow: then he knew what it was. He untied her and turned her into the haystack. His big hand slapped her cold hide. Going to the house again, he buckled the six-shooter around his waist, stared for a few moments at Lela's clothes, and went outside. He went eastward into the gray dawn, eastward into the white wasteland of Burns. Drooping and swaying, and looking to neither right nor left, he moved steadily into the empire of solitude. By none who knew him was he ever seen again.

EPILOGUE

EPILOGUE

THE Bridwell place is abandoned and desolate now. It is so overgrown with hoarhound and cactus and Russian thistle that its acres are impassable; and over its one dusty trail, lying from end to end, cattle take their way in single file between hedgerows of needles and barbs. Its orchard is a few dwarfed trees, which put forth in each summer a sackful of bitter apples and plums. Its stable is four rotting walls. The house, with window knocked out and door torn away, is a refuge for beasts in hot months. The floor is bedded with cattle dung; the nails are tufted with hair. The stove is brown with rust. Lying behind and under the stove are six empty wine-bottles, deep with silence and age. And above hangs one of Lela's paintings, netted in spider-webs. It shows a mighty river, caught in the power of its own unresting greed, smothering itself with bitter white death.

THE END

1931

VARDIS FISHER
WAS NOT A MORMON

In a book, **The Mormon Experience**, published in March, 1979 (Alfred A. Knopf, Inc., released by Random House), Davis Bitton and his collaborator, Leonard J. Arrington, have a paragraph on page 330, that says:

"In the field of fiction perhaps the most important writer of Mormon background has been Vardis Fisher, whose series **Tetralogy** (1932-23) and **Testament of Man** (1947-1960) are recognized as major achievements. There are differences of opinion on Fisher's importance, perhaps, and it may be that the next generation will be in a better position to evaluate him. In any case, his Mormon upbringing had a powerful influence not only on Children of God (1939), a novelistic, basically sympathetic retelling of the Mormon epic, but also on his other novels."

THIS IS A LIE. Arrington knew that it was a lie; but it is possible that Bitton did not. Arrington knew that although Fisher's parents had been baptized into the Mormon Church as children, they did not practice the faith; and cared so little about Mormonism, that they never bothered to have their own children baptized. Mormon influence was negligible during Fisher's formative years, almost non-existant. The strong religious influence in his life — strong to the brink of disaster — was the **Old Testament**, as Leonard Arrington well knows.

But at the age of twenty (1915), Vardis was voluntarily baptized into the Mormon Church, because, like so many young people today, he needed an anchor for his life, and hoped to find it in this religious cult. However, when he read the Mormon literature after his baptism, he was appalled to learn what the Mormons really believe, and left the Church immediately — within the year — an apostate, without ever having experienced a religious conversion. There was no Mormon bias in his thinking, except in a negative way — his life-long hatred of the "tyranical hierarchy which exerts such rigid control over the minds and lives of the Mormons."

An even more monstrous lie than the paragraph quoted above, appears as a footnote to that paragraph, footnote 71, which cites as source material an incredibly crass piece of sophistry, by Leonard J. Arrington and Jon Haupt, which was published in a Brigham Young University Studies journal in 1977. The footnote describes this outrageous fakery, **The Mormon Heritage of Vardis Fisher**, as a "revisionist article that corrects earlier assumptions." The only "earlier assumption" this "revisionist article" "corrects" is any assumption anybody might ever have entertained that a Church Historian for the Church of Jesus Christ of Latter Day Saints must be a man who has a high regard for the Ten Commandments, and a thorough grounding in proper procedures for scholarly research.

In a book to be published early next winter, entitled: **...False Witness**, I shall offer a fully documented exposé of this ghoulish attempt by the Mormons to claim as their own — now that he is dead and defenseless — a man whom they alternately vilified and courted for years, *but never dared to claim while he lived*. Fisher never made any secret of the fact that he had nothing but contempt for the Mormon hierarchy, the Mormon "religion" (which in his opinion was not *religion* at all), and for the Mormon way of life, which he considered stultifying in the extreme.

Nobody needs to take my word for anything: Vardis will speak for himself in my book, beginning with sonnets from his first published work, **Sonnets to an Imaginary Madonna** (1927), to his scholarly **Testament of Man Series.** There will be quotations from interviews and articles; from personal letters; and statements or letters from persons who knew Vardis all those years.

VARDIS FISHER
WAS NOT A MORMON

In a book, **The Mormon Experience**, published in March, 1979 (Alfred A. Knopf, Inc., released by Random House), Davis Bitton and his collaborator, Leonard J. Arrington, have a paragraph on page 330, that says:

"In the field of fiction perhaps the most important writer of Mormon background has been Vardis Fisher, whose series **Tetralogy** (1932-23) and **Testament of Man** (1947-1960) are recognized as major achievements. There are differences of opinion on Fisher's importance, perhaps, and it may be that the next generation will be in a better position to evaluate him. In any case, his Mormon upbringing had a powerful influence not only on Children of God (1939), a novelistic, basically sympathetic retelling of the Mormon epic, but also on his other novels."

THIS IS A LIE. Arrington knew that it was a lie; but it is possible that Bitton did not. Arrington knew that although Fisher's parents had been baptized into the Mormon Church as children, they did not practice the faith; and cared so little about Mormonism, that they never bothered to have their own children baptized. Mormon influence was negligible during Fisher's formative years, almost non-existant. The strong religious influence in his life — strong to the brink of disaster — was the **Old Testament**, as Leonard Arrington well knows.

But at the age of twenty (1915), Vardis was voluntarily baptized into the Mormon Church, because, like so many young people today, he needed an anchor for his life, and hoped to find it in this religious cult. However, when he read the Mormon literature after his baptism, he was appalled to learn what the Mormons really believe, and left the Church immediately — within the year — an apostate, without ever having experienced a religious conversion. There was no Mormon bias in his thinking, except in a negative way — his life-long hatred of the "tyranical hierarchy which exerts such rigid control over the minds and lives of the Mormons."

An even more monstrous lie than the paragraph quoted above, appears as a footnote to that paragraph, footnote 71, which cites as source material an incredibly crass piece of sophistry, by Leonard J. Arrington and Jon Haupt, which was published in a Brigham Young University Studies journal in 1977. The footnote describes this outrageous fakery, **The Mormon Heritage of Vardis Fisher**, as a "revisionist article that corrects earlier assumptions." The only "earlier assumption" this "revisionist article" "corrects" is any assumption anybody might ever have entertained that a Church Historian for the Church of Jesus Christ of Latter Day Saints must be a man who has a high regard for the Ten Commandments, and a thorough grounding in proper procedures for scholarly research.

In a book to be published early next winter, entitled: **...False Witness**, I shall offer a fully documented exposé of this ghoulish attempt by the Mormons to claim as their own — now that he is dead and defenseless — a man whom they alternately vilified and courted for years, *but never dared to claim while he lived*. Fisher never made any secret of the fact that he had nothing but contempt for the Mormon hierarchy, the Mormon "religion" (which in his opinion was not *religion* at all), and for the Mormon way of life, which he considered stultifying in the extreme.

Nobody needs to take my word for anything: Vardis will speak for himself in my book, beginning with sonnets from his first published work, **Sonnets to an Imaginary Madonna** (1927), to his scholarly **Testament of Man Series.** There will be quotations from interviews and articles; from personal letters; and statements or letters from persons who knew Vardis all those years.

Here is an example of what I'm talking about: In 1942, on page 459 of **Twentieth Century Authors**, edited by Stanley J. Kunitz and Howard Haycroft (New York: H.W. Wilson), Fisher was quoted: "I have one brother, Dr. V.E. Fisher, a psychologist, and an atheist like myself; and a sister, Irene, who is pious enough for a whole tribe." In their dishonest article, Arrington and Haupt have perverted Fisher's contemptuous dismissal of his sister to their own ends as follows: Leaving out the first part of the quotation altogether, they say: "There is a touch of pleasure and need in Vardis' characterization of his sister as 'pious enough for a whole tribe,'[5] as though he were counting on her to arrange that his temple work be done for him after he died (which of course she did)." (Footnote 5 cites **Twentieth Century Authors** as the inspiration for this pious, hypocritical drivel!)

In the paragraph following the above quotation (page 28, B.Y.U. Studies, Fall issue, 1977), the authors say: "Fisher was not an apostate; he never renounced his religion..." If it's true that these men actually read Fisher's tetralogy, as Arrington assured me they had, they knew this was a lie when they wrote it. In the third volume (**We Are Betrayed**, 1935), page 34, Fisher, as Vridar, says unequivocally: "I am not a Christian." On page 255 in this book (he is still a student at the University of Chicago) he says: "Vridar now definitely renounced all orthodox religions; because they all sprang, it seemed to him, from guilt and vanity and fear." On pages 247-248, Vridar not only renounces Mormonism, but denounces it, when two young Mormon missionaries appear at his door and declare that they have been sent to reclaim him for the Church. He amuses himself by baiting them for an hour or so, until one of them finally says: "Then you don't want a-be a Mormon any more?" And Vridar answers coldly, "Of course not. It's the silliest of all the Protestant religions."

Fisher's last important interview was videotaped at the University of South Dakota, in 1967. In it, he said flatly that he was not a Mormon. Dr. John Milton then asked: "Are there problems in your family? Do they resent the fact that you have left the Mormon Church?" Fisher's mocking, ironic reply: "Oh, yes. I suppose. Those closest to me have resented it." (Milton chuckles.) "And there's my sister! My dear, devout, devoted sister (said derisively) — is *still* doing her best to save my soul." (Milton is amused.) "But, uh . . . Some persons who read **My Holy Satan** in my **Testament of Man** series of novels, are now trying to save my soul also, because *they* are devout Catholics. So, now I have both Catholics and Mormons trying to save me, and I think my chances must be pretty good!"

Open Letter to:
Spencer W. Kimball, President
Church of Jesus Christ of Latter-Day Saints

Dear Sir:

Having read the press release, you know that I am going to expose the fraudulent, hypocritical article published in a Brigham Young University Studies Journal in 1977, by Leonard J. Arrington, Mormon Church Historian.

In addition to the book I am compiling to set the record straight, I shall also see to it that there is a page of biographical data in every Fisher book that comes off the press from now on. Yes, even after I'm dead; even after the copyrights have expired. And I've set up a fund to be sure that the books will be in print in perpetuity. These biographical data sheets will make it clear, for the guidance of future researchers, that the Arrington/Haupt article is a lie.

That's what *I'm* going to do about it.

Now. The question is: What are *you* going to do about it?

What are you, as President, Prophet, Seer and Revelator of the Church of Jesus Christ of Latter-day Saints, going to do about it?

Are you going to do the only honorable thing possible? — admit to the world at large, and to those trusting students at B.Y.U., who were deliberately deceived, that VARDIS FISHER WAS NOT A MORMON; did not have a Mormon indoctrination during his formative years in the home of his father; that he had apostatized from the Mormon Church within a year after his baptism, without ever having followed through on anything that would have qualified him as a Mormon? Are you going to remove this crass and stupid forgery from the Mormon archives? Are you going to instruct B.Y.U. Press to destroy any copies it has on hand, and make sure that this Church-owned school never again publishes such a lie about Vardis Fisher?

Or are you, by remaining silent, by doing nothing, going to put your God in the position of supporting the pious, hypocritical lie published by your official Church Historian?

Over four millions (it is said) of Latter-day Saints look to you as God's representative on earth, and believe that God speaks to them through you. There are, then, over four millions of naïve, credulous faces of the faithful turned towards you always; and, on occasion, beyond them, there are millions of faces of the skeptics looking at you with tolerant amusement, with smirks of contempt, with leers and jeers, or with purely clinical interest, to see what you will do when your Church is called to account.

Judging from your past performance, I haven't the slightest notion of what you will do this time; but I take my position among those who will watch with clinical interest, curious to observe the psychological reaction of a cult leader, when he is faced with the fact that there are still persons around who are not to be intimidated, either by superstitious dread, or by the wrath of an extremely wealthy and powerful and ruthless and well-established church.

I am one of them,
Opal Laurel Holmes
(Mrs. Vardis Fisher)

A Word to the Reader

I very much regret having to put this unpleasant material into all of Fisher's books, but when one lone citizen is fighting (at Fisher's expressed wish) an organization as rich and powerful, as ruthless and relentlessly vindictive, as determined to prevail, as the Mormon leaders, one must use any means at hand that may prove effective.

His sonnets said it, as clearly as any man ever said it, that Fisher was an "unbeliever" (see sonnets forty-three through forty-nine and the one on page fifty-eight)—an atheist.

He had, in 1916, after one incredulous reading of the Mormon "holy books," following an impulsive baptism, cast the "stupid, primitive stuff" out of his life, in the spirit in which one tosses a piece of worthless paper into a wastebasket; and never again gave it serious consideration except as a motivating factor in a fascinating episode of American history. That was eleven years before **Sonnets to an Imaginary Madonna** was published, and twenty-three years before **Children of God**, an American historical novel, was published.

I read a paper on this subject (Arrington's lies about Vardis Fisher) to a small group, and after it was over, a Mormon woman introduced herself and said, with heavy sarcasm: "You say Dr. Arrington didn't properly research the article in the B.Y.U. journal — I'd like to point out to you, that *Doctor* Arrington earned a Ph.D. — *that* ought to prove something!"

It certainly does! It proves that you can lead a donkey to logic, but you can't make him think.

To the EDITORS:

BIOGRAPHICAL DATA: Vardis Fisher was born March 31, 1895; died July 9, 1968; B.A. University of Utah, 1920; M.A. University of Chicago, 1922; Ph.D. (magna cum laude) from the University of Chicago. He was a Phi Beta Kappa. Married three times: Leona Mc-Murtrey (two sons: Grant and Wayne), 1917; suicide 1924; married Margaret Trusler, 1928 (one son: Thornton Roberts); divorce 1939; married Opal Laurel Holmes, 1940 (no children).

"...Fisher had three reputations — as a writer of regional and naturalistic novels in the late twenties and early thirties [**Dark Bridwell, In Tragic Life**]...as a writer of historical novels with a western setting]**Tale of Valor** (Lewis and Clark), **The Mothers** (Donner party), **City of Illusion** (Comstock Lode)]...as a writer of historical novels with a powerful and controversial evolutionary thesis (his **Testament of Man Series**)." This is taken from an introduction to a bibliography by George Kellogg, Ph.D., Humanities Librarian, University of Idaho.

"The methodology which Fisher employed in writing the historical novel lends itself to being criticized with the same techniques as those used in history...can be criticized with the same strictures because it is constructed by methods similar to those used by historians... [Fisher insisted] that a broad social science approach to gathering historical evidence is necessary... he created a new concept of fiction and a new task for the historical novelist..." Ronald W. Taber, Ph.D., Literary Historian.